a return from the grave

He was supposed to be dead.
Yet here he was,
swearing Laura to secrecy . . .

It took her a while to really
believe he was alive. And by
that time, he wasn't . . .

Now she could be sure of only two things:

The police suspected she was the
murderer . . .

And the murderer knew she

"Mrs. Eberhart is o
thorough and inger   n
the trade, and th   ce
example of

—N

Books by
MIGNON G. EBERHART

Another Man's Murder
Postmark Murder

Available from
WARNER BOOKS

ATTENTION: SCHOOLS AND CORPORATIONS

WARNER books are available at quantity discounts with bulk purchase for educational, business, or sales promotional use. For information, please write to: SPECIAL SALES DEPARTMENT, WARNER BOOKS, 666 FIFTH AVENUE, NEW YORK, N.Y. 10103.

**ARE THERE WARNER BOOKS
YOU WANT BUT CANNOT FIND IN YOUR LOCAL STORES?**

You can get any WARNER BOOKS title in print. Simply send title and retail price, plus 50¢ per order and 20¢ per copy to cover mailing and handling costs for each book desired. New York State and California residents add applicable sales tax. Enclose check or money order only, no cash please, to: WARNER BOOKS, P.O. BOX 690, NEW YORK, N.Y. 10019.

POSTMARK MURDER

MIGNON G. EBERHART

WARNER BOOKS

A Warner Communications Company

WARNER BOOKS EDITION

Copyright © 1955, 1956 by Mignon G. Eberhart
Copyright © Renewed 1983 by Mignon G. Eberhart
All rights reserved.

Published by CBS Inc. by arrangement with
Random House, Inc.,
201 East 50th Street,
New York, N.Y. 10022
Distributed by Warner Books.

Warner Books, Inc.,
666 Fifth Avenue,
New York, N.Y. 10103

Ⓦ A Warner Communications Company

Printed in the United States of America

First Warner Books Printing: July, 1983

10 9 8 7 6 5 4 3 2 1

ONE

Matt stood at the window, looked out at the gray lake, the gray December sky and talked of fear. "Fear is a virus," he said. "It's a creeping paralysis. It stops thinking. It stops action. In the end it destroys the heart and soul." His rangy figure, his black head were outlined sharply against the gray light beyond him. There was a bitter anger in his voice, anger at the injustice of a world which can make a child its victim.

Laura glanced uneasily at Jonny. The child was listening too. She sat very still in an armchair which was too big for her, so that her feet dangled above the rug. She looked, now, very American in her short white socks and black-strapped pumps, her simple, blue wool dress with its pleated skirt and white round collar. Her smooth brown hair was parted in the middle and two fat braids ended in neatly tied red ribbons. Only her Slav blue eyes and the generous breadth of the cheekbones in her round little face suggested her Polish blood. Her eyes were suddenly very grave, watching Matt. Her lap was full of a tangle of new hair ribbons, yellow and blue and green and red, which Matt had brought her, and her square little hands were quiet, too, holding the ribbons.

The kitten sat beside her, a watchful regard on the ribbons. His eyes were as blue as Jonny's.

Laura said, "Careful. She's beginning to understand more English than we think."

"I know." Matt swung away from the window and came back to them. The slatey look left his eyes when he looked down at Jonny. He gave her a gay, reassuring twinkle. "Everything is all right now, Jonny. Good. Understand? *Dobre.*"

Jonny's grave gaze searched his face for a moment. Then some inner secret alarm, which his voice when he spoke of fear (rather than the words of which she understood so little) had seemed to rouse, quieted. It was as if she had asked a question and he had answered it promptly and comfortingly. Gaiety came back into her face like sunshine. "*Dobre,*" she said. "Good." The kitten made a dab at a ribbon, and Jonny laughed.

Matt said, "Well, I've got to be on my way. What do you want for Christmas, Jonny?"

"We mustn't spoil her," Laura said, but knew that she was smiling at the child as fondly as Matt.

"No fear of that," Matt said, rather shortly. And, of course, he was right. They knew very little really of Jonny Stanislowski's short past but they knew that in all probability it had not included gaiety and fun, walks along the lake and visits to the zoo, hair ribbons and Siamese kittens and all the little treats and surprises Matt arranged for her. Matt brought her some sort of present almost every day, and now Jonny seized upon the gaily wrapped box with confidence. It had been that which had brought forth his outburst of anger that afternoon. Jonny had run to the door to meet him. She had flung herself upon him; she had chattered in her own rapid, excited mixture of Polish and English, which was as a matter of fact mainly Polish, only studded by the few English words she knew but lighted by her gay, expressive face and gestures. Then she had gone through his overcoat pockets confidently in search of her present. She had found there the package of ribbons. She had opened it laughing and triumphant; it was a game she and Matt understood.

As Matt watched her his mobile Irish face had sobered. "Can you imagine that, Laura, a month ago! She's a different child." And then unexpectedly he had talked of fear, fear which can infect even an eight-year-old child.

Jonny understood about Christmas; she and Laura and Matt had all talked of it, Laura and Matt searching for words in the Polish dictionary with which Laura had supplied herself when Jonny was placed in her care, but baffled as usual by the pronunciation of the mysteriously placed consonants, resorting to English and to what Matt called sign language. Matt had told Jonny Christmas stories, with the child listening as intently as if she understood every word of them. He had recited "The Night before Christmas," prompted, when memory failed, by Laura. Jonny had painstakingly recited it after him, a phrase at a time, pronouncing the strange English words with great care. She was delighted with the names of the reindeer and repeated them over and over, slowly and tentatively at first, then more confidently, "Up Donner, up Blitzen—"

She laughed at Matt now. "Saint Nich—o—las—" she said, carefully dividing the syllables.

"Right," said Matt. "Old St. Nicholas is coming down the chimney with a bag full of presents. You wait and see." He touched the child's brown head, tweaked the square little chin, then went into the hall, got his hat and coat. Laura and Jonny followed. Matt said, "If it is a nice day tomorrow we might go to the zoo again. How about it?"

Jonny said clearly, her high childish voice vibrant with confidence and delight, "Bears."

"Okay, honey, the bears it will be. And hot chocolate in the

6

little restaurant in the trees." Matt opened the door of the outside corridor and looked down at Laura. His eyes were suddenly very blue and dancing. He said unexpectedly, "You are a honey, too. Did that ever occur to you? See you tomorrow."

He was off down the corridor toward the bank of elevators. Laura closed the door slowly—and something very gay and yet rather mysterious went out of the day.

She stood for a moment in the small entrance hall watching Jonny who now was making a game with the kitten, dangling a red ribbon and laughing as Suki darted at it with swift, sepia-colored paws.

Matt loved Jonny and Jonny loved Matt. And the moment little Jonny Stanislowski had walked down the gangway of the plane from Vienna, clinging hard to Matt's hand, but with something sturdy and self-reliant about the small figure, too, she had walked also into Laura's heart.

Perhaps she reminded Laura of her own childhood, not too far away, when Conrad Stanley—born Stanislowski—had been her only friend. So it was of course Laura's duty to offer to see to Jonny temporarily, until something could be settled, for Laura, young as she was, had been named by Conrad Stanley as one of the trustees for the perplexing Stanislowski provision in his will. It was also her duty to take the child into her small apartment, if only to discharge in some small measure the deep debt of gratitude she owed Conrad Stanley and consequently to his little great-niece.

The circumstances in which little Jonny Stanislowski had come so unexpectedly to live with Laura were simple. Conrad Stanley, dying, had left a very large fund to his nephew, Conrad Stanislowski, living in Poland. All efforts to communicate with Conrad Stanislowski had failed, but his child, little Jonny, had been found and brought to America.

Doris Stanley was the obvious person to see to Jonny; she was Conrad's young and lovely widow. Doris quite frankly had not wanted her. Charlie Stedman, who was Laura's co-trustee and an old friend of Conrad Stanley's, lived a comfortable bachelor existence at his club; clearly it was impossible for him to undertake Jonny's care. Matt would have liked to take Jonny, but again it was not practicable.

Matt was not married; he was a lawyer, his office in the Loop; he was young, he had a small but growing practice; he lived in a hotel apartment. If he had taken Jonny it would have involved a troublesome business of finding a housekeeper and, indeed, a different and larger apartment. The practical problems of undertaking a child's care were difficult to solve. But it had been Matt

7

who found Jonny and brought her to America, for he was Doris Stanley's lawyer.

He had once been engaged to Doris, before her marriage to Conrad; he had known Doris for many years, but he was her lawyer, too. When Conrad Stanley died, three years before, Doris had instantly turned all her affairs over to Matt. And that of course had involved Matt in the chore of carrying out the provisions of Conrad Stanley's will. It had proved to be, in fact, a rather onerous chore for all of them, Laura and Charlie Stedman and Matt, that is. Doris, quite comprehensibly, had not been much interested in finding Jonny's father, Conrad's nephew, and certainly not much interested in Jonny.

But they had all met the plane, Laura, Charlie and Doris, riding to the airport in Doris' luxurious, chauffeur-driven car. There had been a little discussion as to what to do with the child. Doris had said flatly that Jonny should be put straight into a boarding school; she had indeed made some preliminary arrangements. Charlie had debated it, as he always debated anything, and then said that that might be the best solution. Laura had thought of her own small apartment and the tiny extra bedroom across the hall from her own; it would be easy to transform that room into a child's room with gay chintz on the bed and at the windows, a small chair, a little table, shelves for toys—her thoughts swept irresistibly on. However, she told herself firmly, it wasn't possible for her to take Jonny.

Laura was a secretary for a law firm; she had got the job immediately after Conrad Stanley's death. She worked for no particular member of the firm or staff; her services and those of several other trained secretaries were called upon as and when needed. It was consequently a busy and exacting sort of job, interesting in its variations and rewarding as a challenge. But the hours were long. She was away from home all day, leaving shortly after eight in the morning, coming home in the crowded bus which stopped eventually at the corner of Lake Shore Drive, a half-block from the towering apartment house. She reached her own apartment if she were lucky at about five-thirty. She was proud of her little apartment; it was small and inexpensive but it had light and air and sunshine and a wide view of Lake Michigan, and more than anything it was home, the only real home Laura had had since she was a child, almost as young as this strange little girl they were going to meet. But there was no place in it for a housekeeper as well as Jonny; besides, it would be almost impossible to find exactly the right kind of housekeeper, a motherly, sensible woman they could trust with the child. No, she couldn't take Jonny.

8

The three of them stood in a little group, watching the plane land. It was a bright, windy day. Doris' exquisite profile was almost buried in her furs; her smart black hat hugged her blond hair. Even there, in the windy, chill space at the gate, the scent of a perfume like carnations in a summer garden drifted like a fragrant little cloud from the handkerchief in Doris' handbag as she took out a compact and scrutinized her lovely face in the tiny mirror. She moistened her pink lips and smiled, closed her handbag and watched the incoming plane.

Charlie stood beside her, watching the plane, too, as it came in to a landing. His head was bent against the wind; he held on his dignified gray homburg with one neatly gloved hand; the other was at Doris' elbow. And then the plane moved slowly toward the gate and stopped. At last figures began to descend the gangway, hats and coats and skirts swirled by the wind, and Matt's tall figure was among them. He saw them and waved and pointed them out to Jonny, who gave them a grave look and clung to Matt's hand.

Doris flashed into vivacity when she saw Matt; her pansy-brown eyes and her pink lips smiled. She ran to meet the two figures; she kissed Matt; she greeted the lonely little figure beside Matt, briefly and it seemed to Laura perfunctorily. Jonny eyed Doris soberly and clung to Matt's hand.

Doris was not at all pleased with the fact that there was a Jonny Stanislowski. And she liked a child to be attractive, well mannered and well dressed; Jonny was neither. Her little face was set, almost stolid in its immobility. She wore a faded, purplish coat which was too small for her, a round sailor hat which was too old for her, long black stockings and awkward, ugly shoes. Only her blue eyes, meeting Laura's, betrayed the fact that she was frightened. Laura, unexpectedly, had bent and kissed Jonny. Matt then had kissed Laura, too, lightly, on the cheek, before he spoke to Charlie.

Afterwards in the car they talked of Jonny while the child sat, still and rather frightened, yet trying not to show it, close beside Matt. "I'll take her to my apartment tonight," Doris said. "But the place for her is Harthing. You know, the Harthing School for girls. I've already talked to Miss Harthing on the telephone. I am sure she will take Jonny."

Charlie agreed. "It seems a good plan, at least until the estate is settled. Then we'll have to make some permanent arrangement for her."

But Laura looked at Matt and he was looking at her; then she said quite suddenly, "No, I'll take her—I'll give up my job. I can get another one later, when we decide what to do about her. I'd like to take her now."

9

Doris bit her lip, but looked relieved. Charlie said after a moment, thoughtfully, that was very kind of Laura. Matt said, his eyes flashing blue, that it was splendid. "—It's the perfect solution. I don't want her to be put in school among strangers."

"Laura is a stranger," Doris said quickly. "We are all strangers, even you, Matt."

He had Jonny's hand close in his own big one. "Not I. We got acquainted. She's a good little traveler."

Charlie said sensibly that there was a matter of expense to consider; if Laura were serious in her offer to give up her job to look after Jonny, she must be reimbursed from the estate. "Don't you agree, Matt? Doris?"

In the end it was settled without much discussion. Doris' big car deposited Laura and Jonny and one of Matt's big leather suitcases at the apartment house. The suitcase held an odd assortment of clothing—two dark woolen dresses which had obviously been passed on to Jonny as they were outgrown by other children, a woman's sweater, darned, a heavy flannel petticoat, more long black stockings neatly rolled together, and a Paris doll, which Matt had given Jonny, wrapped tenderly in paper. The next day Laura and Jonny had gone shopping. That night Matt came to tell Laura the whole amazing story of finding her, of cutting through red tape, and of bringing her home. He had come nearly every day since then—to see Jonny of course, but Laura had seen him, too. But the daily visits would end in January; by then, three years after Conrad Stanley's death, the estate would be settled. The permanent arrangement for Jonny would be made. And Matt's daily visits would end, for almost certainly he and Doris Stanley would then be married.

So then, too, this curiously happy interlude for Laura would come to an end. Jonny would no longer provide a gay and warm focus; Laura would go back to work; the routine of her life would reëstablish itself. It had been a pleasant routine, well flavored by her sense of independence. But it wouldn't be so pleasant now and Laura knew why. She would miss Jonny—but she would also, too much, too constantly, too deeply and too hopelessly, miss Matt.

Jonny drew the red ribbon teasingly across the rug and the kitten sprang upon it furiously, its little black tail lashing in pretended anger. Just then someone knocked softly on the door. It was so unexpected that it startled her. It wasn't Matt returning; he wouldn't knock like that. The soft, almost furtive knock came again. She opened the door.

A man stood outside. He was rather small and thin, too small somehow for his clothes, which looked bulky and clumsy—foreign, Laura thought. He had a slender, pale face, a high, narrow

10

forehead and sharp features, an intellectual face but a rather weak one. His eyes were pale blue, and looked washed out yet very intent. He said, "I am Conrad Stanislowski."

TWO

"*Conrad*—" Laura stared at him incredulously. "But we tried to find you! For nearly three years we've tried to find you!"

"I was in Poland. May I come in?"

"Oh—oh, yes! Please come in."

He slid instantly into the hall and closed the door behind him. There was something furtive, too, in his quick movements and in the way he closed the door. Suddenly Laura thought, he's frightened. He said, however, quickly, "I've come to see my child. She's here, isn't she?"

Laura's impulse was to say, certainly; she is in the next room. But in the very instant of speaking she remembered her responsibility as trustee. From his position directly before the door he could not see the living room, but she moved a few steps down the hall and closed the door into the living room. His eyes flickered; she was sure that he knew why she closed the door but he did not move. She said, "We didn't expect you. We had given up trying to find you. We wrote you—so many times, but we didn't hear from you. Two of our letters came back. They had been opened. They were marked 'address unknown.'"

"Naturally. Probably your letters only made it harder for me to escape."

"You speak English very well," she said unexpectedly.

He shrugged. "Of course. That's my job. Languages. Didn't you know that?"

"As a matter of fact we could discover very little about you, only that you were born in Poland and were living there for a time after the war. Conrad—your uncle, Conrad Stanley, knew that although he did not know exactly where you were. We assumed that you were still in Poland up to the time when Jonny arrived at the orphanage two years ago."

"And I suppose you also assumed that I was dead. Well, I'm not. Now may I see my child?"

Again Laura's impulse was to let him see Jonny at once. Instead she put her hand apologetically but firmly on Conrad Stanislowski's bony wrist. "I'm sorry. But as you know I am one of the trustees for the Stanley will. I must tell the others that you are here."

"Before you let me see my child?"

"You must understand. It's only a matter of identification. Formalities. Routine. I believe you but—"

"But there's all that money," he said, with a tinge of bitterness.

"I'm sorry," she said again. "But Jonny is in my care. The others gave me that responsibility and I—"

He interrupted. "The others?"

"Yes—you must know. It was all in the letter which was left at the orphanage in Vienna?"

"Oh, the letter. Yes. Yes, I have it."

"Then you know all about Conrad Stanley's will."

"Oh, yes. My uncle."

"Matt told you about it in the letter. That's Matt Cosden. He brought Jonny here. He is—he explained it all in the letter. He is Mrs. Stanley's lawyer. And then, of course, there is another trustee, Charlie Stedman. All of them will be very interested to know that you have arrived. I will telephone to Matt and—"

"Wait, please!" he said, suddenly and peremptorily. "I would like to see my child first. Can't all this—this formality wait?"

Laura hesitated. "I think I should let them know that you are here as soon as possible. And then, you see—well, they will expect you to give some proof of your identity."

"I understand. There's all that money!"

"Well, yes. They told me, Matt and Charlie Stedman, that when you came, if you came, we would have to be sure—"

"You want my dossier. Very well. I was born in Cracow."

"Yes, we knew that." Cracow: the cradle of culture, the begetter of scholars for one-time sturdy and self-reliant Poland. A Poland which for much of its life had suffered invasion, division and redivision, but somehow always had retained a stubborn flame of life, so it gathered itself together again, piece by piece, and limb by limb. Who can say, Laura thought, that this country is now dead, lost, forever surrendered? Poland had always somehow, sometime, asserted its own stubborn independence. Battered and bleeding after the German invasion in World War II, and then again made captive, still, somewhere, a secret flame of liberty might smolder. The man standing before her was a symbol of that.

He had not followed the swift course of her thoughts. He said

12

slowly, as if merely reciting facts that were completely objective and impersonal, "I studied languages. I was going to teach. I went to England to study, and just before the war, when I knew the war was inevitable, I came to Poland again. I was there that September."

His voice took on an even more impersonal and chilly quality, as if those terrible September days had killed feelings as they had destroyed cities and people. "Eventually I joined a Polish brigade. We were sent to Russia and then to Africa. After the war was over I returned. There were some difficult times; I need not go into that. However, I managed to live. I was married. Jonny was born. My wife—" He checked himself almost imperceptibly; his eyes seemed suddenly very bleak and guarded, his face more closed in on itself. He went on rather quickly. "I was left to see to Jonny who was then two years old. I did my best but—that was not good enough. I wished to leave Poland, escape, but meantime I had to live and support Jonny. I became—that is, I joined the government party. I was a language expert." He shrugged. "I was useful. Eventually I became a member of a minor commission. Two years ago I had a chance to send Jonny to Vienna. I intended to follow her as soon as possible and escape to England or America. However, it took a long time, two years in fact, before I contrived an errand to Vienna and had an opportunity to do so. When I went to the home where I expected to find Jonny, I found instead your letter." He paused and looked at her steadily. "Now may I see my child?"

It was a reasonable and a factual account of himself. Laura forced herself to question it. She said, "You will have your passport, of course. Or the letter from Matt. Perhaps some means of identification."

Again his face seemed to withdraw warily into itself. "I do have these things," he said. His thin shoulders seemed to brace themselves under the awkwardly tailored coat. His rather weak chin lifted. There was a thin edge of defiance in his voice. "I have everything which you will need or any of the others will need to convince you that I am really the man I say I am. I do not have them with me. I do not intend to show them to you at this time."

The defiance was as surprising as his flat statement. Laura said, "But—but I don't understand. You must see that—"

He interrupted, "I only know that I want to see my child now. Only let me look at her, Miss March. I will not talk to her. I will not touch her. I will not speak to her. But I must see her—only for a moment." He put a thin and shaking hand on the door.

And Laura thought, but Jonny will recognize him! That will be proof of his identity. She opened the door to the living room.

He took a quick step or two inside. Laura began "Jonny—"

13

and stopped, for then she saw that Jonny had retreated swiftly as a bird into a thicket, to the cautious stillness and silence which had characterized her first few days with Laura, in a strange home, in a strange country.

She must have heard their voices in the hall, for she was standing now behind an armchair as if it were a bulwark. The kitten stood on the arm of the chair, humped up and gazing with serious blue eyes at this intruder. But Jonny's face was completely still. She made no movement, she made no cry of recognition, she simply stood there, her eyes blue and fixed and perfectly blank.

The stillness and silence lasted for perhaps a few seconds. Then Conrad Stanislowski said to Laura, "Thank you," and turned abruptly back into the hall.

"But you—please wait—where are you going?"

"I told you I would only look at her and be sure she was here." He was already at the door to the corridor.

She cried, "But you can't leave now. Let me phone the others—"

"No," he said sharply. "Don't do that." He took a long breath and said, "Miss March, I must ask you to do something—it is extremely important, otherwise I would not ask you to do it. You won't understand—only believe me. I must ask you not to tell the others of my arrival. Not yet."

"But I must tell them!" she cried. "I have to tell them. They will want to see you. Besides, Jonny—"

"That will wait," he said. "Please promise me now, to keep my arrival a secret? I realize this is an extraordinary request. I must make it."

Suddenly there was something desperate and beseeching in his face and his thin body. He opened the door.

"But—but I can't let you go like this! Where are you going?"

He turned back. "I'll tell you that. I got to a rooming house— 3936 Koska Street. I trust you, Miss March. I believe you will keep a promise. In a few days—only a few days, I'll come back. I'll do everything that's required of me. I'll show you all my credentials, all my cards of identification, everything. But until—" He stopped, gave her one long intent look and unexpectedly, as if she had yielded to his appeal, said, "Thank you." His thin figure with its bulky overcoat turned into the corridor and disappeared.

For a moment Laura did not move. Then she went to the door; he had already reached the bank of elevators. He did not look back; the door closed after him. Somehow she knew that it would have been useless to pursue him, useless to question him. But she stood for a moment staring at the blank, closed doors of the elevators, halfway down the corridor. They were as blank and in a way as baffling as that unexpected and extraordinary encounter.

Why had she let him leave, like that?

How could she have stopped him!

And when after some time she turned back into the hall again, Jonny also had disappeared and with her the kitten.

Jonny had not gone far. There was nowhere to go in Laura's small apartment. She found the child back in her own small bedroom, bending over a book of drawings to be filled in with colored crayons. The kitten sat on the low play table beside the book, watching with deep concentration, for sometimes a crayon could be transformed into a moving object; Suki greatly interfered with the accuracy of Jonny's drawing. But the child was apparently in engrossed study over the book of pictures. So that was all right, Laura thought, and returned to the living room.

For a long time she walked up and down the room, pausing to stare at nothing out the window, thinking of the curious affair of Conrad Stanislowski's appearance. She had entirely mismanaged the interview.

Intending to do what she thought was right, she had only wounded him—and perhaps Jonny—by interfering with their reunion. And then she had let him go, not only with very few facts in her possession but with a tacit promise on her part to keep his arrival a secret.

Yes, she had mismanaged that curious but important interview. She had failed in her duty as trustee. Certainly she should not have allowed him to leave believing that she would keep his arrival a secret. Her obvious duty was to go straight to the telephone—tell Matt, tell Charlie, tell Doris of Conrad Stanislowski's amazing appearance and of his still more amazing request to keep his arrival a secret.

Yet there was the pleading in his eyes, in his voice. There was something intangible, indescribable that touched her heart, and made her believe at least for the moment in him and in the validity of his request. Whatever the reasons for it were, just there and just then she had believed that there were reasons.

She thought unexpectedly, he doesn't look like Conrad Stanley; there ought to be some family resemblance.

There was none. Conrad Stanley had been a stocky, strongly built man with a fresh color, wide cheekbones and a broad forehead, a firm and determined nose and chin, massive and blunt. He had had light, Slav blue eyes, but they were intelligent and determined, clear and sparkling—never a bleak and faded blue.

15

And Conrad had never been nervous, uncertain, desperate; he had always known exactly where he was going, and why, and how he was going to get there.

Laura had known Conrad Stanley and loved him since she was a very small child. She could not remember when Conrad Stanley had not been a part of her life.

THREE

Conrad Stanley's story had been the success story of many Americans. He, too, was born in Cracow. Laura had often heard the details of his early life, for Conrad as he grew older, like many self-made men, liked to talk. He did not boast; there was only a kind of candid surprise and pleasure about him when he talked of his life, which was almost naïve except that Conrad was in no sense naïve; he was instead remarkably worldly-wise, understanding of human frailties as well as human strength, and deeply compassionate about the whole.

"Rags to riches," he would say and chuckle. "I came up the hard way. I was younger than you are now, Laura, when my mother brought me to America."

There had been then a brother, Paul, older than Conrad. A still older brother, Stefan, remained in Poland. Conrad, his mother and Paul had landed in America with only a few dollars. Laura had felt dimly that their reason for emigrating to America was not only poverty and a desire to better themselves—but that there might have been some distant but then operative political reason for their departure. In any event, they had landed in New York among its teeming emigrants from other shores and had tried to make for themselves a new life. When Conrad was twelve he got a job in a machine shop.

He had native ingenuity and, as became increasingly evident, great intelligence. He also had the drive of a pressing need for money. Nothing was too hard for him to do; no hours were too long. His brother Paul, working in a steel mill in Pittsburgh where so many Polish laborers drifted about that time, was killed in an accident. Conrad worked harder, in order to care for his mother.

Somehow he found time to go to a trade school at night. But necessity was the forcing house for the quality of genius he possessed. After his mother's rather early death, when he was relieved of the pressing need for money, he turned that quality of genius toward invention. In the end he went to Chicago in the hope of buying a small manufacturing plant with the small savings he had by then accumulated. At the same time he was working nights with various ideas for inventions. It was about that time that he became acquainted with Laura's father. He also, by then, had legally changed his name from Stanislowski to Stanley; long ago he had become an American citizen.

Laura's father was an assistant vice-president in a small suburban bank near Chicago. Conrad, needing more money to buy his factory and money to promote the invention he was then working on, had gone to the bank in the hope of negotiating a loan. Laura's father had believed in him. He had advised the loan.

The factory Conrad bought prospered; he both manufactured and sold the invention which then engrossed his attention. This first project was a kind of slide fastener with a mechanical clip and bolt. It was a gadget in the beginning; it blossomed into a sizable business. Conrad then extended his patents to cover all sorts of by-products and variations; in the end he developed a very big business and accumulated a very large fortune.

It was from the beginning a one-man business; it remained so to the end, with Conrad not only keeping his own hands on the helm but a close and minute observation upon every detail.

It was like Conrad to look upon Peter March's belief in him not as an impersonal matter of sheer business intelligence but as a personal favor. So Conrad himself pursued and made a friendship of the business relationship. Laura as a child became accustomed to the regular appearance of this dynamic, sturdy, strong-featured man with his Polish accent, his keen mind and his never-failing kindness to her. Perhaps Conrad's warm heart rejoiced in the taste of family life his friendship with Peter March gave him. In those days Conrad was too busy and too engrossed to think of marriage—that or he did not meet the kind of woman he wished to marry. But he liked Peter March and showed it, and he was always devoted to Laura's mother, a quiet, slim, lovely young woman whom Laura only dimly remembered.

Peter March was a hard-working, imaginative and contradictory man. He liked books, he liked music; he had no gift for money-making and very little interest in it as such, yet he was efficient in his work at the bank. He looked upon Conrad Stanley, this rock of a man who had so determinedly and resolutely become his close and intimate friend, with a kind of amused awe. But Peter was idealistic, too.

When World War II began and the Germans marched into Poland, Peter had already seen the handwriting on the wall and had quietly made his plans. Probably to the surprise of everyone except Laura's mother and Conrad, Peter March gave up his job at the bank, said good-bye to his wife and small daughter and Conrad Stanley and went to England to enlist.

He knew, or at least believed, that America would sooner or later get into the war but he would not wait for that. He was overage; he would never have been drafted. He had only a strong feeling of individual duty and he was idealistic. Somewhere he had learned the rudiments of flying; probably it was one of his unexpectedly adventurous, out-of-the-ordinary diversions. In any event, fliers or men who knew anything at all about flying were then desperately needed. And in a bombing run over Germany during the first days of spring, when the Germans made their seemingly irresistible sweep down through Belgium and into France, Peter March was in a plane which never returned.

Laura, even now that she was older, still had very little idea of how her mother felt about Peter's enlistment. She did remember that after the cable came to the effect that Peter had not returned, all her mother's interest in life seemed to fade; she died scarcely a year later and Laura, at very nearly Jonny's age, was alone in the world.

There were of course distant relatives, none of whom showed any particular interest in taking care of Peter March's orphaned child; probably they felt that Peter March would have done better to stay at home and see to his own family. There were a few rather cold and tentative offers but they were not needed for Conrad Stanley stepped firmly and promptly into the situation.

There was very little money; an assistant vice-president of a suburban bank does not have a salary which permits of much saving or investment. Laura's mother's small annuity died with her. Conrad Stanley saw to all the small business affairs resulting from Peter March's and then Margaret March's death. What money could be saved he put in a savings account in Laura's name. He then found a school for Laura.

He did not touch any of the modest savings account. Laura knew later that it would not have been adequate in any event to see to her education, but mainly Conrad wished to keep the small fund intact. He paid, himself, for all her school expenses. And even more important, in a definite way, it was Conrad who arranged little treats for Laura; it was Conrad who came to see her; it was Conrad who took her with him on carefully planned trips during her vacations. It was Conrad in fact who tried and in many ways succeeded in taking the place of a father and mother whose images gradually retreated into the past. Conrad had been

18

more than a father to her; he had been a guardian, a teacher and a bulwark against the world.

As she grew older, she began to realize the great debt of her gratitude to Conrad. She could not pay him back in any way for the generosity and affection his great warm heart had so willingly given her, but she could, sometime, pay him for her school expenses; when she was seventeen she made a stand: she wished to go to a school which would teach her a profession. Then when she could work, she would pay back to Conrad, at least in money, some of the debt she owed him.

It was like Conrad to agree to this. He didn't want the money, that was clear, but it was equally clear that he liked and wished to encourage her sense of independence. He agreed; when Laura could work she could pay him; he had kept an account of all the money he had spent on her.

So she went to a secretarial school. She worked hard, driven by her deep affection and her sense of gratitude for Conrad and also by that growing independence which perhaps Conrad himself had taught her. When she emerged from the secretarial school, Conrad had taken her into his own office; she was to be his secretary.

Spurred by her deep affection for Conrad, she learned at least some of the ins-and-outs of his business, and Conrad not only helped her in her new task, he taught her many general but sensible and forceful business precepts.

When Conrad died he made her a trustee for the Stanislowski fund for his will.

There were reasons for this. He trusted Laura, perhaps that was the first reason, another reason was the training he had given her. He knew that he had taught her the fundamentals of business; he knew that he had inculcated in her certain character traits. He also knew that she loved him and would be loyal to his wishes no matter how unusual they seemed to be.

And, of course, the Stanislowski fund was unusual, yet it was exactly like Conrad.

Laura had finished school, and was at work in Conrad's office, when he met Doris and married her.

He was old to marry by then and Doris was young; she was, in fact, only a few years older than Laura.

It was a shipboard romance; Conrad was making one of his more and more frequent trips to Europe in connection with his increasing European markets. Doris, then Doris Fitz-Green and engaged to marry Matt Cosden, and her mother were on their way to Paris.

Doris, in a frank yet perhaps purposeful moment, had been candid about that. "We couldn't afford the trip. We didn't have a bean. But my mother wanted to get me away from Matt. He didn't have a bean either." That was after Conrad's death, when Doris had begun to see Matt often. She had given Laura a thoughtful look, and then smiled sweetly. "Of course, Matt was in Chicago then, starting a practice. We were going to be married as soon as he made enough money. But I met Conrad—"

Conrad was by then a very important man and obviously a very rich man. Perhaps Mrs. Fitz-Green, Doris' mother, had encouraged their acquaintance. In any event by the time the short voyage was over the three of them were close friends. They saw each other in Paris, in Rome, and then in Madrid. Six weeks later when they returned to New York Doris and Conrad were married. They came to live in Chicago, in the vast apartment Doris wanted. What Matt's feelings were when his one-time fiancée turned up in the same city where he had chosen to live, married to another and a very rich man, no one, certainly not Laura, knew. She saw him once or twice at dinner; he was friendly and polite with Doris; he was also friendly and polite with Conrad—and, Laura thought, began to like and respect the older man.

Laura had been prepared to find in Conrad's wife a close and intimate friend; she had been certainly prepared to welcome her. Doris astonished her. She was too young, too beautiful, too glamorous; she was not at all the sensible, settled and matured kind of woman whom Laura would automatically have expected Conrad to marry. Conrad, however, was obviously and indulgently in love with her.

He had spent all his life in business amassing a fortune; he knew, he must have known, that he had not many years yet to live. He took what the gods gave him and was very happy with his young wife. Whether or not Doris was happy was not certain. But certainly she enjoyed her life as the rich, young Mrs. Stanley.

By unspoken but probably mutual agreement, Doris and Laura achieved a cordial relation; they were never intimate friends. Perhaps the closeness of their ages in contrast to their very different relationships to Conrad forbade an intimate friendship. Laura was like a daughter, a dearly loved ward of Conrad's. Doris was his wife, a lovely and cherished gift life had brought him for which, indulgently yet philosophically, he paid generously; Doris was from the beginning recklessly extravagant.

Laura began to know Matt Cosden only after Conrad's death. That had occurred suddenly, three years before, yet Conrad had had intimations of its occurrence; his will was found to be completely thought out in every detail, although, typically, he had drawn it up himself with only the most cursory legal aid. It was a simple enough will in its main provisions. He canceled Laura's debt in money to him; he could never have canceled her debt in gratitude. He divided his very large fortune among his young wife, Doris, and his Polish nephew, Conrad Stanislowski, whom Conrad Stanley had never seen. The Stanislowski provision was the problem.

It was a gesture of family loyalty. It may have been due to a wish to preserve and carry on his name; it came also from Conrad's deep and intense patriotism. He felt that everything he had done, everything he owned, every happy day in his life which certainly included his relationship to Laura, to her father and mother and his late, but on Conrad's part, very happy marriage to Doris—all of it was due directly to his emigration to America, his becoming an American citizen and his taking advantage of the rich opportunities America had offered him. He wished to pass on this gift to one of his own blood and name. And there lay the perplexities of the Stanislowski fund.

Conrad Stanislowski, his nephew who lived in Poland, was to receive half of Conrad's fortune only if he also came to America, became an American citizen and made his life in America. And they could not even find Conrad Stanislowski, let alone inform him of the fund set aside for him.

They had made every effort to do so. Their letters vanished into space, except for the two which were returned and had been opened and were marked "address unknown." Matt, by the way Doris' lawyer, had said that there was a spot censorship and perhaps it was sheer accident that the letters to Conrad Stanislowski had undergone that. There was, however, an alternative—which was that Conrad Stanislowski had either died or disappeared in the confusion after the war.

Many Poles had been placed in camps; there was a terrific shifting of population. Eventually they began to feel that looking for Conrad Stanislowski over the face of the earth was not only like looking for a needle in a haystack, it was like looking for a needle which had disappeared long before it had been lost in the haystack.

Time went on. Gradually they were beginning to admit failure. Then in August, by way of combing the relief organizations again, Matt had discovered that there was a child, named Jonny Stanislowski, living in a home for children in Vienna. She had been there for two years. After much correspondence he was convinced that she was in fact the child of Conrad Stanislowski, Conrad Stanley's nephew.

In October Matt flew to Vienna. There was red tape to cut but the American Army Headquarters and the relief organizations helped him; in November he came back from Vienna with little Jonny.

There was still no news of Conrad Stanislowski. It was not even certain that he had been alive at the time when Jonny arrived at the orphange; indeed, the more than probable explanation was that he was not alive and that Jonny, somehow, like so many hundreds of other little waifs, had drifted into the orphange. The circumstances of her arrival were mysterious and so far as Matt could discover Conrad Stanislowski himself had had nothing to do with it. However, there was no doubt about Jonny's identity; there was her own birth certificate; there was also, in the thin little file labeled Stanislowski, Jonny, a photostatic copy of Conrad Stanislowski's birth certificate. It was not at all unusual, the head of the orphanage assured Matt—rather wearily, as if nothing that developed in that post-war melee of displaced persons, of homeless children, was really unusual; people took the greatest care to establish their own and their children's identity with whatever means they could employ. It was tragically, terribly important. Jonny was the child of Conrad Stanislowski, who was the child of Stefan Stanislowski, Conrad Stanley's older brother; there was no doubt about that.

Matt had taken time in Vienna to explore every possibility of getting in touch with Conrad Stanislowski; his attempt at communication came to nothing.

There were, of course, several reasons to account for Jonny's presence in the orphanage. The logical conclusion was that her father was dead. Yet there were alternatives; perhaps he was sick, perhaps he was unable to care for her and in some way had contrived a way to get Jonny to Vienna. There was even, Matt had suggested, the possibility that Conrad himself intended to escape Poland and had sent Jonny ahead of him. And then for some reason Conrad had failed to get to Vienna.

That, according to Conrad Stanislowski himself, was the truth.

It had grown later as she stood at the window, staring out at the lake and the sky, thinking of Conrad Stanislowski, of all the circumstances surrounding him and surrounding her long association with Conrad Stanley; trying to discover exactly what Conrad Stanley would have told her to do. Suddenly and reassuringly it occurred to her that Conrad Stanley was a man who believed the best of his fellow beings and acted on that faith. He would have granted Conrad Stanislowski's request for secrecy; he would have followed his own instinct, as she had done. Yet what did Stanislowski intend to do during those few days?

And why had Laura felt that he was frightened?

It was only then that it struck Laura that Jonny's reaction was not all right; it was all wrong.

FOUR

The child had shown no recognition at all of the man who stood in the doorway looking at her. There had not been a smile, a cry of greeting; she had not flung herself joyfully upon him as she flung herself upon Matt, when he arrived. In two years' time, even though two years is a long time in the life of a child, Jonny could not have forgotten her father. Yet there had not been so much as a flicker of recognition in the still little face, the rigid, sturdy body; her Slav blue eyes had been completely blank and without expression. So then if Jonny had not recognized the man, he was not her father!

He was an impostor! Charlie and Doris and Matt had talked of that possibility; they had warned Laura. There was so much money involved that there might be impostors claiming it. The man of the afternoon with his mysterious request, with his refusal to show any kind of identification, asking her only to see Jonny (which in itself had a certain curious and questionable implication as if perhaps he only wanted to make sure that Jonny was there), calling himself Conrad Stanislowski, was an impostor! She would telephone to Matt at once.

The room had grown darker. Away below, along Lake Shore Drive, the homeward traffic rush had long ago begun; lights from cars swept by in constant four-lane streams. The long two-noted whistle of the traffic policeman came clearly to her ears. She turned on lamps in the room and went into the hall. But with her hand on the telephone she saw the little red Polish dictionary which she had supplied herself with when Jonny came to live with her. Why not question Jonny?

The child understood some English, and Laura had trained herself to find Polish words and painstakingly labored over their pronunciation until there was some current of understanding between her and Jonny. They made, in fact, a game of it, she and Jonny. She snatched up the Polish dictionary and went to Jonny's room.

It, too, was dark. She turned on the light. Jonny was huddled at the low table, her head in her arms, sobbing convulsively. It was the more touching because Jonny was crying with such desperate silence, as if she must control even the sound of her sobs. Laura ran to her. She took her in her arms. Jonny pressed her hot face against Laura's shoulder and allowed herself the luxury of sobbing aloud, great, strangling gulps.

So Conrad Stanislowski was really Conrad Stanislowski and Jonny's father.

A wave of compunction swept Laura. She had been overconscientious, overanxious about her responsibility as trustee, overcautious. She ought to have let father and daughter meet, freely and happily, without question. Even the kitten seemed to eye Laura with disapproval.

She held Jonny in her arms and talked to her. "We'll see your father, we'll telephone to him, we'll have him here right away. We'll see him, Jonny, he's not gone, he'll come back." She didn't know how much Jonny understood of the words, but perhaps her tone was comforting, for gradually Jonny quieted. But her sobs had been the heartbroken sobs of a child perplexed by the ways of a world in which a father could appear and then disappear in a matter of moments.

The telephone rang.

It rang and rang again, jabbing insistently, before Laura at last disengaged Jonny's arm from around her neck and went to answer it.

If it was Matt she was going to make an exception to her resolution and tell him the truth about Conrad Stanislowski. She owed it to Jonny, and no matter what Conrad Stanislowski had said, nor what the reasons for his request for secrecy were, it was more important to restore the confidence in Jonny's heart which she and Matt had been at such loving pains to build.

She took down the telephone. A woman's voice said, "Is this Miss Laura March?"

It was a strange voice, flat and toneless, with a heavy foreign accent. Laura said in surprise, "Why, yes. I am Laura March."

"Come at once. It is Conrad Stanislowski. Come to 3936 Koska Street. Bring a doctor."

"But who—*what do you mean? What has happened?*" Laura stopped. There was an unmistakable click of the telephone and then nothing but silence.

"Come at once," the woman had said—what woman, who was she, what did she know of Conrad Stanislowski? But the address was right, 3936 Koska Street. "Come at once. Bring a doctor."

Conrad Stanislowski had been in an accident! He had had a heart attack—something! Hurriedly she telephoned for her own doctor, Doctor Stevens; he was out on a call, his nurse said; she didn't know when he would return; however, she took the Koska Street address and the message. Laura then telephoned to Matt.

24

She had already decided to tell Matt of Conrad Stanislowski and, certainly, in an emergency an implied promise to Conrad Stanislowski meant nothing. Matt was not in his office; she tried his apartment, he was not there. In desperation she tried Charlie Stedman's office; there was no answer. She tried his club and he was out. There was no use phoning to Doris. "Come at once. Bring a doctor."

She could not leave Jonny alone. Besides, if Conrad Stanislowski were seriously sick, circumstances might be such that she ought to let him see the child, she thought swiftly. If not—well, if not, she could protect Jonny. Certainly she could not leave the child alone in the apartment. She hurried back to Jonny and washed the tear stains from the child's little face. Jonny was tired now and weary; when Laura got out Jonny's little red coat and red hat, Jonny put them on and asked no questions. Laura caught up her own gray coat, full and swinging free from the shoulders, light and soft as fur; she snatched up a white silk scarf with her initials embroidered in red upon it, a scarf Matt had given her, and her big red handbag. Five minutes later Laura hailed a taxi at the entrance of the big apartment house.

It was then around five o'clock and foggy. The streets were jammed with cars and taxis and heavily laden buses. Already, with the early December dusk, it was growing dark. She gave the taxi driver the address and saw his faint look of surprise. "That's in the Polish section," he said.

It would be in the Polish section, of course. Laura had not thought of that. She said, yes, and settled back in the taxicab with Jonny beside her. The taxi drew away from the curb and plunged into the streams of traffic. They went along Lake Shore Drive with all its lights and its crowded buses, along Michigan Boulevard with its gay glimpses of shop windows already decorated for Christmas. The Wrigley Tower loomed up white and clear at their right and across from it the massive, lighted bulk of the Tribune Tower where brilliant ranks of windows glimmered through the fog; there were always lights in the Tribune Tower, night and day. The bridge luckily was down, although as they crept across it amid the slow traffic Laura could hear the dismal hooting of a barge somewhere in the river below. Away off now at the right a rosy radiance in the fog marked the great bulk of the Merchandise Mart. Immediately after they had crossed the bridge, they turned right again and onto Wacker Drive which slanted crosswise, following the path of the river which was lower and hidden by dusk and fog.

Again, at the bridge westward, they crept slowly along, wedged in with other homeward-bound traffic. The fog here was heavier. Eventually they turned into one of the great business

25

streets which go directly westward. This, too, was lined with stores. The street lights, red and green, were haloed in the fog. They went west and still west, slowly because of the heavy traffic. All at once the names and signs in the stores changed, became bristling and indecipherable consonants. They were in the Polish section. Laura's heart quickened. It seemed to Laura a long time; the December twilight had turned almost to night when they turned off the business street on to a quieter residential street. She saw a sign suddenly: Koska Street.

There was a drug store on the corner, and a lighted grocery store with a Christmas wreath in one window. Immediately, then, it became a street of houses, and two- or three-flat apartment houses. There were few pedestrians here. It was perhaps at the deserted hour of the night when workers had not yet returned home. Lights glimmered only dimly from windows here and there. They drew up suddenly and the taxi driver peered through the gloom. "I think this is it," he said.

It was a narrow, two-storied house, painted brown. There was about it a look of neatness and cleanliness yet it was sparse, too, and a little forbidding. There was only a dim light in the hall, behind the high, old-fashioned transom on which were painted very clearly, in large letters, 3936. The house and the street before it seemed singularly deserted. There were no pedestrians, no cars parked at the curb. The doctor, then, had not yet arrived.

For an instant Laura was tempted to stay in the taxi and wait for the doctor's arrival. The memory of the urgency in the strange woman's voice over the telephone forbade it. She got out of the taxi and Jonny followed her. Jonny was puzzled; she looked at the house and then at Laura, questioningly. Laura paid the taxi driver, who was curious, too, and lingered a moment, watching them. She led Jonny across the damp sidewalk and up a narrow flight of white stone steps, scrubbed to a state of pristine cleanliness, but which somehow were grim and uninviting. At the top of the steps Laura looked in perplexity at the brown-painted door. There was no bell. What was she to do? And where was Conrad Stanislowski?

Obviously the thing to do was to open the door and walk in. As she was about to do so, however, the door was flung suddenly open.

A woman stood in the doorway. She was outlined dimly against the light from behind. Laura had only a swift and hazy impression of a loose brown coat, a dark beret pulled anyhow over dark hair, and a rather broad and very pale face which looked haggard in that eerie light, and deeply lined. The woman came with a rush out on the step, tugging a battered, canvas carryall after her, and then stopped and stared at Jonny.

26

Laura cried, "I am Laura March. Did you phone to me? Where is he?"

For a second or two the woman only stared at Jonny, and did not reply. She wore no lipstick; her mouth looked strangely colorless and stiff.

Laura said, "Please answer me. Did you phone to me? I'm Laura March."

"Go away," the woman said at last, flatly, scarcely moving her pale lips. "I should not have done it." Her eyes shifted then from Jonny in a curious, swift, yet controlled glance along the street. She saw the yellow taxicab, and clutching her canvas carryall, ran suddenly down the white steps, across the sidewalk, and scrambled into the taxi.

"Wait," Laura cried and started after her, but she was already in the taxicab. It started up with a roar and went down the street. Its yellow gleam passed under the street light, turned the corner, and vanished.

Laura stood for a moment transfixed, clasping Jonny's hand. She was bewildered and indeed rather frightened by the odd encounter. She was sure that it was the woman who had phoned her, for she had the same flat and toneless voice, the same heavy foreign accent. Now, she said, "Go away."

Laura couldn't go away. Conrad was somewhere in that house, awaiting the doctor, needing help.

The door was still open, revealing a narrow hall, painted brown, and a narrow flight of stairs going upward. Laura took Jonny's hand and entered the house.

There was a rank of doors along the hall, all of them closed. The only light came from a small, unshaded bulb above the transom. Again she looked for a bell and found none. But there must be a landlady somewhere. There must be lodgers.

She knocked on one door, and then another. No one answered, no one came to inquire. There was the heavy, rather ominous silence of complete emptiness in the house. The sound of her hand on the door only emphasized it.

But Conrad Stanislowski must be there, somewhere. Laura and Jonny went upstairs—slowly and, on Laura's part, and perhaps Jonny's, too, uncertainly and cautiously. The treads creaked under their footsteps, yet no one came to inquire. They emerged in the second-story hall which was almost an exact replica of the narrow brown hall, lined with doors, on the first floor. But here Laura saw, halfway along the hall, one door that was thinly outlined with light.

It must be Conrad Stanislowski's room. She went to the door and knocked on it. Perhaps she knocked on it quickly and nervously and thus harder than she intended; the door was not latched and it swung slowly open.

Laura's first act was sheerly instinctive. She thrust the child behind her and away from the door.

Then she looked at Conrad Stanislowski.

FIVE

He was lying on the floor near a small writing table. His head was turned at a preposterous angle. A light from a lamp on the writing table fell strongly on his thin face with its high forehead and weak chin and open faded blue eyes which stared at nothing. There were dark red patches on the back of his gray shirt. He was dead. There was an instantaneous and terrible clarity about that. The doctor, nobody could do anything for him now.

She turned around and put her hand on Jonny's shoulder; the child looked up at her questioningly but with utter confidence.

"Stay here," Laura said, contriving a smile. "Stay here, Jonny dear. Don't move."

Jonny did not answer but she seemed to understand. She nodded and moved to lean against the newel post. Laura left the sturdy, red-clad little figure, Jonny's blue rather troubled eyes following her, and went into Conrad Stanislowski's room.

She closed the door behind her so Jonny could not see. She went across the room and looked down at the figure on the floor. He was lying so she could see his back, and the ugly, spreading red patches on his shabby gray shirt. His hand was flung outward on the floor. And with equal clarity another fact instantly established itself. His own hand could not have wielded the force that produced these dreadful red patches. By no manner of means could he have contrived to stab himself like that, in the back. *Murder*, Laura thought with cold incredulity. Murder.

But she must make sure that there was nothing she could do to help him. She took off her glove and forced herself to kneel beside him. She put her hand on his wrist. After a time she was sure that there was no pulse, but she remembered the tiny mirror in the powder compact in her handbag. At last she permitted her shrinking fingers to leave that inert wrist and opened her handbag. She took out the compact, and leaning forward held the mirror at the pale lips. After a time she could again permit herself to move back, for no faint misting had clouded the tiny mirror. So he was dead and there was nothing that she could do about it. Nothing the doctor could do, nothing anybody could do.

If there was murder, there must be a murderer!

The house was still, utterly, completely quiet. There was not a shuffle of foot on the stair, no rustle of garments, no sound of anyone at all. It was as if no one had ever lived in the house.

But there was the woman she had met on the steps! Where there is murder there must be a murderer. Could the woman on the steps, dragging her baggage after her, running for the taxi, disappearing into the fog-laden night—have murdered Conrad Stanislowski?

She had said, "Go away." She had said, "I should not have done it." Did she mean, I should not have killed a man?

But she had also telephoned to Laura, asking for help. She had told her to come at once, to bring a doctor. Would she have done that if she had in fact murdered a man?

But she had then escaped.

And she had said, "Go away." It was as if an imperative voice spoke from somewhere inside Laura, saying, too, *go away. Get Jonny out of here.*

She got to her feet but for a moment could not look away from Conrad Stanislowski. Whatever had been the reason for his mysterious appearance, whatever had been the reason for his begging her to keep that appearance a secret, she would now never know it. And he would now never again see the child, with whom she had prevented the reunion that was his right. She would not think of that then. She glanced swiftly, almost in spite of herself, around the room.

It was a bare little room; there was not much to see. There was a bed, a chest of drawers, an armchair covered in faded cretonne, a rug or two, a wash basin. On the bare writing table above him there were two glasses which looked shiny and clean. A suitcase, shabby and closed, stood at the foot of the bed. His overcoat, that bulky, dark overcoat which had looked too big for his thin body, lay on the bed. A shabby gray suit jacket was flung across a chair. Go away, she thought again. Get Jonny out of here.

She turned swiftly and in the moment of turning saw a crumpled-up piece of white, like a handkerchief, stained in red, on the floor. It did not matter. Nothing mattered. She had to get Jonny out of that terrible silent house which had apparently then only murder as its tenant. She opened the door.

Jonny was standing in the hall; her eyes met Laura's anxiously as if seeking reassurance. Laura said, "We'll go now. We'll go," and took Jonny's hand. Their footsteps along the hall and down the stairs seemed very loud in that strangely silent house. Surely someone would hear. Surely someone would come to inquire. Surely some lodger returning from work would open the door as they descended. No one did.

There must be a telephone somewhere; the woman who had fled into the night had telephoned to her. But Laura had to get out of the house, she had to get Jonny out of the house; she wouldn't stop to hunt for the telephone. She opened the door.

The street was still, dark and deserted. There were a few pedestrians at sparse intervals here and there, passing under the street lamps. The doctor had still not arrived; no car stood at the curb or approached the house. A taxi crossed at the intersection, going into a side street. There were a few lights in nearby houses. What should she do?

Suddenly she remembered the business street which they had left in order to turn into Koska Street. There had been the rosy neon radiance of a drug store at the corner. Wherever there was a drug store there would be telephone booths. The thing to do was telephone to Matt. He would know what to do. She led Jonny down the steps and along the street.

She forced herself to walk quietly, not to hurry, but some odd, old instinct nudged at her so she looked back swiftly at the silent brown house. Its white steps loomed up clearly in the dusk. The closeness of the yellow brick, three-flat building beside it cut off the light from the room where a man lay murdered. No one opened the door; no one started after them through the dusk.

No one stealthily followed them.

But no one had been in the house; no one except a dead man. There was no one to watch their leaving.

They passed a pedestrian, a woman with a market basket, who gave them a fleeting glance and went on. As they neared the brighter area of the business avenue, there were other pedestrians—none of whom gave them more than a glance. Nevertheless when they reached the cross street, it was with a sense of escape.

The lights here were bright. They paused to wait for the traffic signal and then crossed to the drug store, whose bright lights and neon signs seemed to beckon. The warm interior was laden with the mingled scents of coffee and hamburgers and powders and perfumes and cigarette smoke. A telephone booth stood against the back wall.

Laura went back to it. "I'm going to phone, Jonny. Phone— Stay here, dear." Jonny nodded, her eyes serious and blue, understanding as Laura opened the door to the little booth. Sign language, Matt had called it. Laura entered the booth and fumbled for a dime, then closed the door so Jonny could not hear. The light above flashed on. Then, her hand shaking, she dialed Matt's office number.

The telephone buzzed and buzzed. And all at once Doris Stanley seemed to stand beside her in the small telephone booth. The image of her lovely little face came so clearly to Laura's mind, that she almost turned to her before she realized that it was not Doris, it was Doris' perfume; there was a faint odor of carnations in the telephone booth, a delicate trace of the perfume which Doris habitually used. Laura thought in some remote level of her mind, someone wearing Doris' perfume has been here in the booth. Nobody answered the telephone in Matt's office.

It was late; she had not thought of that; his secretary had gone. She put down the receiver, and her dime fell with a disconsolate little clink into the receptacle. Matt should be at home by now. She knew his hotel apartment number, and dialed that, but again the phone buzzed and buzzed and did not answer. Probably it was exactly the time when he was fighting homeward-bound crowds and had not yet reached his apartment. Phone to Charlie, she thought, phone to Doris. And then she thought, why, the police of course!

When it was murder it had to be reported to the police.

If she reported it now and here, what would they do? Answers to that flashed sickeningly through her mind. They would tell her to wait, of course. They would arrive, squad cars hurtling through the night. They would take her and Jonny back to the silent, terrible rooming house. They would ask them questions. They would question her—but they would question Jonny, too.

Jonny would understand too much—too much to forget.

Get Jonny out of here, Laura thought, imperatively. There was nothing else to do. Telephone the police later—tell Matt, tell everybody later, but take Jonny to a safe place first. She left the hot telephone booth with its fugitive trace of the fragrance of carnations, and again taking Jonny by the hand, led her out of the lighted, pleasant, welcoming store, and onto the street. They stood at the curb, and after a moment a taxicab came around the corner.

It seemed a long drive back through crowded streets. Eastward and farther eastward, across the river again, with its misty dark expanse below and the great girders of the bridge looming ghostily up into the sky above them. It was dark by now, yet the lights of the Loop reflected themselves in the fog so a kind of golden cloud, tinged with orange, seemed to hover over the city. They turned again on Wacker Drive, slippery now from the fog. This time as they crept along Michigan Boulevard, the bridge was up and they waited five minutes or so along with other cars, their engines throbbing, hooting occasionally with impatience. Eventually the great twin bulks of the bridge lowered and traffic resumed. Lighted store windows shone out on either hand, gay and frivolous, filled with luxury goods, decorated in red and green and tinsel. They went on and into Lake Shore Drive and stopped at last at the lighted entrance of the apartment house where she lived.

It was in a curious way like a nightmare in which one tries and tries to run, and cannot escape; she hurried Jonny through the lighted foyer, back to the bank of elevators. Yet she felt as if she took the image of a bare little room, in a silent, brown, rooming house away out on the west side, and a man staring at the light with eyes that did not see it, along with her at every step.

The elevators were self-operated. One or two other residents entered the same elevator and Laura was queerly grateful for their presence. One got off on the sixth floor; the other, a woman carrying packages wrapped in Christmas paper, nodded at Laura and said she lived on the top floor. Her nod, her voice were pleasant and matter-of-fact. For a strange second it seemed remarkable that she did not also see the image that accompanied Laura so stubbornly. And at that, Laura caught back her own frightened, racing fancy. She must keep her head; she must see to Jonny. Laura stopped the elevator at her own floor, the ninth. She and Jonny walked along the carpeted corridor and she got out her key. Once inside the door, warmth and safety surrounded them.

She bolted the door; it was an instinctive act. No one had followed them all the way from the silent rooming house. She took a long, steadying breath.

Trying to keep her voice easy and calm she talked, as she always did with Jonny—a little running accompaniment to action. They would put away coats and hats; then Jonny would have some milk. Jonny with her customary and rather touching self-reliance put her bright red coat neatly on a hanger, standing on tiptoes, stretching the length of her sturdy little legs.

She seemed tired, Laura thought, watching her, as they went back to the kitchen and got out milk and cookies, tired and perhaps still a little puzzled, but that was all. Suki heard them from Jonny's bedroom and came in, meowing hoarsely in greeting, and eyed the milk with interest. She left Jonny pouring milk into a saucer for Suki, smiling at Suki who in the frantically voracious way of a Siamese kitten dove into the milk, sputtering it widely as he lapped. So that was all right, Laura thought; she was certain that Jonny was not aware of the real and terrible significance of those moments in the house at Koska Street. She left Jonny in the kitchen, closing the door so the child could not hear, and went to the telephone. This time when she dialed Matt's hotel apartment he answered.

32

"Matt! Oh Matt, he's dead!"

"Laura, for God's sake, who's dead?"

"He was murdered. I saw him—"

"Who?"

"Conrad Stanislowski."

"Conrad— What on earth are you talking about?"

"Matt, he came here. This afternoon. Just after you left. He came to see Jonny. And then a woman phoned—" The story poured out like a flood, short as words could make it, long enough to cover the span of a man's life. Halfway through, Matt cried, "Laura, take it easy! Say that again. *Where* did he go? *Who* phoned you?"

She told him again, and then couldn't stop herself repeating until Matt said suddenly and sharply, "Okay, I've got it. You are sure he was dead?"

"I saw him. I felt his pulse. He was murdered. He couldn't have killed himself—not like that—"

"What's the address again? All right, I've got it. I'll see to things. Wait till I come."

SIX

She put down the telephone. The terrible, invisible burden slipped for a moment from her own shoulders.

There was a mirror above the small table where the telephone stood, and she had a swift glimpse of herself in it—her short brown hair rumpled, her gray eyes brilliant, her mouth, lipsticked with crimson, looking very red and tense against the whiteness of her face. Her white silk blouse was wrinkled. The tiny string of pearls Conrad had given her on her eighteenth birthday gleamed softly in the light.

She gave Jonny supper; she fed the kitten. She read aloud from Jonny's favorite book—her favorite probably because it was profusely illustrated with pictures that perhaps made the story, in English, reasonably clear to Jonny. Still Matt did not telephone. It was Jonny's bedtime.

Jonny was efficient and self-reliant in all the little chores of tooth-brushing and nail-scrubbing and dressing; there was something oddly pathetic in the matter-of-fact way she set about the nightly routine, for obviously she had been trained to do all those things for herself at a very early age. She had her bath, she got herself into her pajamas, she brushed and braided her hair, she got herself briskly into bed. The kitten, worn out with chasing a crumpled piece of cellophane around the room, curled himself up on Jonny's shoulder, his eyes as blue as Jonny's and as sleepy. Jonny's black eyelashes were drooping when Laura turned out the light.

Tragedy, so far, had not touched her. Laura was sure of that.

Matt came only a few moments later. The buzzer sounded sharply and she ran to open the door. His coat was flung over his shoulders; his black hair was damp from the fog, his Irish blue eyes were blazing in a white face. "I came as soon as I could."

"What have they done?"

"You look— Wait." He dropped his coat over a chair and went back to the kitchen. She followed him and watched as he got ice from the refrigerator and glasses from the cupboard. He knew where she kept her small supply of whiskey and poured a generous amount into each glass, filling it up with water. "Here," he said, "take this. Drink it." He put the glass in her hand and led the way to the living room. "Sit down there."

She sank down into a deep lounge chair, with its sage-green upholstery which she had chosen so carefully so the room would be all grays and greens; gray rug, soft gray walls, green chairs, gay primrose-yellow curtains, and bright splashes of yellow and green and blue in the patterned cover for the sofa. It was a charming, a warm and pleasant room; a few old pieces of gleaming, dark wood gave it dignity and grace. It was not a room in which to talk of murder.

"What did you do?" Laura asked.

"I reported it to the police, of course. Then I drove out to Koska Street. They were already there, that is, a squad car was there when I got there, and then the rest of them turned up. Your Doctor Stevens arrived in the midst of it. He said you had called him to come there and he had been delayed on a previous call. There was nothing he could do, of course. The police will be here to get your statement, I told them why you had to come home before you called them or anybody. I explained about Jonny and I think they understood. Where is Jonny? Asleep?"

"Yes. I don't think she realized what happened, Matt. Seeing her father upset her; she cried afterward. But I don't think she knew anything about the—the rooming house. I mean, what had happened there. She stayed in the hall; she couldn't see. She was puzzled; she knew something was wrong. But she's all right now. I'm sure she didn't guess anything like the truth."

"That's all right then. Now," Matt sat down in the chair oppo-

34

site her, "tell me everything again, Laura. All the details. Don't hurry. Take your time about it."

He glanced at his watch, though, as he spoke. She thought, Matt is a lawyer, he wants to hear everything; he wants to go over it with me before the police arrive. Because I found a man, murdered.

She told the story in detail, slowly, taking her time. He watched her, his face a little in shadow above the shade of the lamp on the table beside him, his eyes intent, lifting his glass now and then and sipping from it. When she had finished he thought for a moment. Then he said, "All right. That woman who phoned you, are you sure it was the woman you met on the steps?"

"Yes. It was the same voice, the same accent. Besides, there was nobody else in the rooming house."

"Would you recognize her again if you saw her?"

"I think so. Yes. I recognized her voice. Matt, *could* she have killed him? She was running away. She had her bag with her. She ran across the sidewalk and jumped into the taxi and was gone before I could stop her. And then on the steps she said, 'Go away. I should not have done it.' That's all she said. Did she mean—" Laura caught her breath. "*Did* she mean, 'I should not have killed him'?"

"Yes, I've been thinking that, too— I don't know. I do know that she was one of the lodgers in the rooming house. Her name is Maria Brown. The landlady—the police questioned her—said that Maria Brown had been there for a month or so, she had her rent paid ahead of time for about three weeks, she had given the landlady no warning of leaving. That's all I heard. There was a good deal of commotion out there, of course, with fingerprint men and flashlights and everybody milling around, the whole mechanism of investigation. The police will find Maria Brown, all right. But about Conrad Stanislowski—I wish we knew more about how he happened to come here. I'd like to know why he begged you not to tell anyone he was here. He told you to wait for a few days before you told us. He said that he could identify himself. Why would he want to keep it a secret, even for a few days? What did he expect to do in that time? Rather," Matt said slowly, "why should it conceivably be necessary for him to do *anything* before he could come forward openly and identify himself to us?"

There was no answer to that. Laura said, "I think he was afraid. There was something about him— I am sure he was afraid of something."

Matt lighted a cigarette. "Of course, that suggests some quarrel that it was necessary for him to settle. And it suggests that that quarrel may have ended in murder. The woman you saw could have been the instrument. Did she look, well—foreign? Polish?"

"Her accent is foreign. I don't know whether it's Polish or not. She was dark, pale— I only got a glimpse of her."

Matt said thoughtfully, "Orders can come from behind the Iron Curtain. Things like that almost certainly have happened. Maria Brown could have been an instrument. If she were Polish —" He stopped. After a moment he shrugged. "But on the other hand, she may have been only an innocent bystander. She was a lodger in the house; perhaps she heard something of the murder, obviously Conrad told her your name and she may have phoned to you merely in the hope of helping him. But then he died and she simply got scared and ran away. There are people like that. Afraid of trouble. Afraid of the police. Another possibility is that she knows some evidence which she feels is dangerous to her and she is afraid to see the police. There are all sorts of possibilities, too many of them! Well, the police will certainly find Maria Brown. You said you started to question Jonny about her father. Did you?"

"No. I went back to her room and that's when she was crying so hard and trying not to. I was sure then that he was really her father, so I didn't question her. She was only beginning to stop crying when the phone rang and it was Maria Brown."

"Didn't she show any sign of knowing her father?"

"No, not a thing. She didn't speak. She didn't smile. She just froze. You know—whenever she is frightened or confused, she shrinks into herself and doesn't even move."

"I know. That's the habit of fear. Yet perhaps that very cautiousness shows that she did recognize him. Perhaps she was waiting for him to speak or make some move or— Oh, I don't know! How did you feel about it, Laura? Did you feel that he *was* her father?"

"Y-yes. At least at first. Then later I thought perhaps he was an impostor. But I went back to Jonny and she was crying, so I was sure he was her father."

"And while he was here you believed him?"

"Yes, I did. It puzzled me. It was an extraordinary kind of thing. He seemed frightened and hurried and I couldn't understand why he asked me to keep his arrival a secret, but somehow I—I did believe him."

Matt gave her a long look, rose and began to pace up and down, his tall figure and dark head outlining themselves against the gray walls and the primrose yellow curtains at the end of the room. He stopped to pick up an ash tray, look at it with unseeing eyes and put it down again; he came back to lean one elbow on the mantel and look, in deep thought, at nothing. He had a thin, rather bony Irish face with a hawky nose, a sharp jaw line, and deep-set eyes below eyebrows that were so black they were like slashes across his face. It was not a handsome face, but it was sensitive and intelligent, and lighted by his eyes which could turn as vividly blue and sunny as a summer sea. They were then, though, a slatey cold gray. He said, "This Brown woman *could* have known Conrad in Poland, or she could have known of him. He went to the rooming house at 3936 Koska Street, so it is perfectly possible that he knew her address and went to the rooming house because she was there. Now then—she could have had orders to kill him. Or she could have killed him because of some private quarrel between them. The third alternative is that she was merely an innocent bystander. But if she stabbed him, then she either regretted it and telephoned you for help, or she phoned to get you to come to the house and thus involve you in the murder."

"Me! But the police can't say I did it!"

"I'm only suggesting possibilities," Matt said quickly. "If she actually murdered him, perhaps she didn't expect either you or the doctor to get there so soon, before she could get away. But on the other hand, as I said, if she was only an innocent bystander trying to help him, that would explain what she said to you on the steps. 'Go away. I should not have done it,' could mean simply she shouldn't have phoned to you and got you into it. If, that is, somebody else killed him."

"Who?"

"Well, for one thing he as much as admitted that he was a renegade Communist. He said he was only a minor official but still—" Matt went to the sofa and sat down, stretching out his long legs. "You said she stared at Jonny. Did she seem to recognize her?"

"No! That is—I didn't think of that, Matt. I don't know. It all was so hurried. She did stare at Jonny. She looked as if she couldn't take her eyes from her. But then she saw the taxi—"

The buzzer in the hall sounded sharply. Matt sprang up. "There they are. Just tell them what you told me."

Somehow Laura had expected a whole body of policemen, big bulky figures in blue uniforms. Instead Matt ushered in a slight, rather elderly man in a wrinkled gray suit. He had hazy gray eyes and a long, tired-looking face.

"This is Lieutenant Peabody," Matt said. "Miss Laura March." The Lieutenant said, "How do you do?"

Laura, her voice unexpectedly husky, said, "Will you sit down, Lieutenant Peabody?" Suddenly and indeed absurdly the instinct of a hostess caught at her. Her home, her guest. Except he wasn't a guest; he was a policeman coming to question her about murder. She steadied her thought and her voice and said to Matt, "I expect Lieutenant Peabody might like a drink, too."

37

"Yes, of course." Matt started for the door. "What will it be, Lieutenant? Scotch, bourbon?"

"Thank you," Lieutenant Peabody said, "I am on duty. Not that it isn't the kind of night that calls for a drink. But not now." He sat down on the long sofa, at right angles to Laura, and suddenly and very wearily sighed. But in the same instant his hazy glance drifted around the room, noting details, seeing the tiny red Garnet roses on a side table, the picture which had belonged to Laura's father, a Normandy landscape, gay with its sunlight and blue sky and its purple-pink plum trees. He examined the Chippendale wall-desk which, too, had belonged to Peter March; he eyed a table with a piecrust edge. He seemed to approve the chairs, the sofa, the odd bits Laura had added, and to guess that she had done so, a piece at a time as she could pay for them, around the nucleus that Conrad Stanley had saved for her, from her home.

Yet in the same long and observing moment Laura felt that the police lieutenant had also noted and filed away every detail of her appearance. At last his glance lingered openly on the little gay heap of colored hair ribbons which still lay on the floor. And Matt said, "I've already told Lieutenant Peabody all that we knew of Conrad Stanislowski, Laura. Why he came here—Jonny—all that." He turned to Lieutenant Peabody. "Miss March has been telling me what she knows of the thing. The fact is Stanislowski was here for only a few moments. He talked very briefly to Miss March. Some time after he had gone, the Brown woman phoned for help, so Miss March went out to the rooming house and there she found him murdered. She had the little girl with her so—"

Lieutenant Peabody interrupted. "First, Miss March, I want to know about this Brown woman. Describe her, will you? Tell me exactly what she said to you over the telephone."

SEVEN

Laura told it briefly. When she had finished the short recital the Lieutenant nodded. "Maria Brown is probably an assumed name. The landlady didn't know much about her but said she was obviously a foreigner. The landlady doesn't know where she came from; she had a sort of part-time job in the Loop. She took the room about a month ago and has paid her rent for another few weeks. How old is she? Young? Middle-aged?"

"She looked middle-aged," Laura said unexpectedly, "but she moved like a young woman."

A flicker of satisfaction touched the Lieutenant's face. "You'd know her if you saw her again."

"Yes. I think so."

"What did she wear?"

"A brown coat—tailored, with pockets. A black beret. She had a sort of carryall with her."

"What kind of taxi was it? Yellow, checkered—"

"Yellow."

The Lieutenant rose. "The telephone?"

"In the hall," Matt said. "I'll show you."

At the doorway the Lieutenant turned back to Laura. "Did you see a knife in the dead man's room or anything that could have been used as a weapon?"

"No! No, nothing like that!"

"Ah," the Lieutenant said and went to the telephone. Matt came back into the room. Both of them heard the policeman's terse orders. The woman, Maria Brown, was wearing a brown coat and a black beret. She was a young woman. She had taken a yellow taxi.

The Lieutenant returned. "I think we can pick her up," he said, "although her description fits thousands of other women in a big city." He sat down again and paused for a moment as if to let himself dive into some invisible filing cabinet and select the exact record that he wanted. He crossed one knee over the other, linked his hands together and looked at them thoughtfully. "Now then," he said. "Mr. Cosden gave me the general background of the Stanislowski situation but I'll just go over it quickly and see if I've got it all right. Conrad Stanley, the button king—"

Matt said in a sort of aside, "It wasn't buttons really, it was a fastener, a slide and clip. He extended his patents to all sorts of things, surgical instruments, rubber tubing, mechanical bolts—that sort of thing. Then he developed, patented and manufactured a number of other devices—gadgets most of them but very successful—"

The Lieutenant nodded briskly. "The point is he made a lot of money. He was born in Poland, emigrated to America when very young, changed his name from Stanislowski to Stanley and made a fortune."

"He came up the hard way," Matt said. "He had nothing at all when he arrived here. He attributed everything he had made of

39

his life to American citizenship. He was deeply and sincerely patriotic. He loved America."

Lieutenant Peabody nodded shortly again. "Conrad Stanislowski, this murdered man, claimed to be his nephew. The little girl then is Stanley's great-niece."

"Yes," Matt said shortly. "We're sure of that. Stanislowski, however, refused to show Miss March any sort of identification."

Lieutenant Peabody glanced at Laura thoughtfully. "I see," he said. "Well, we'll get to his talk with you in a moment. About Conrad Stanley now—how old was Conrad Stanley when he died?"

Matt replied, "Up in his sixties."

"I understand he left a widow. Is she about Stanley's age?"

"Well," Matt said, "no." Laura thought she saw a flicker of indecision in Matt's face as if he considered preparing the Lieutenant for Doris' youth and beauty. If so he contented himself by saying only, "She's younger. In fact, they were married only a couple of years before Stanley died."

Matt, of course, had every reason to remember the exact date.

The Lieutenant said, "Second wife?"

"No, he'd never married before. I think he'd been too busy to consider marriage. He concentrated on his business, you see; he not only invented all these things, he manufactured them, too."

"Ah," said the Lieutenant politely, and continued. "As I understand it he died three years ago. He left his money divided, half to his wife and half to be held in trust and to be handed over to his nephew, this Conrad Stanislowski."

"As I told you," Matt said, "there was a provision to that. His nephew was to have this trust fund only in the event the nephew would leave Poland, come to America, take out citizenship papers and live in America. Conrad Stanley felt it was a sort of debt of gratitude that he wanted to pay. Also, since he had no children, I think he wanted to make it possible for his family to be continued here in America where he had always lived. As I told you he was a very patriotic man and a very happy man."

Lieutenant Peabody did not this time say, "Ah," politely, agreeably and merely, Laura thought, as a kind of punctuation, allowing him to continue his main line of questioning. He eyed Matt for a moment and said, "Any other relatives besides this Conrad Stanislowski?"

"None there's any record of. He had two brothers, one in Poland, father to the nephew; he died before the war. The other brother came to America with Conrad, went to work in a steel mill in Pittsburgh, was killed in an accident—oh, years ago."

"Unmarried?"

Matt looked startled. "Why—I don't know. Do you, Laura?"

She tried to think back to Conrad's tales of his early days. "He talked of his brother. I don't remember much of it. But I'm sure if the brother had married, Conrad would have helped his widow—"

"Or his children," Lieutenant Peabody said.

Matt said, "There almost certainly was no widow, Lieutenant, and no children. But we can make certain of it."

Lieutenant Peabody nodded dreamily. "I was only thinking of —persons who might have an interest in this murdered man's claims. As it stands, the only Stanley blood relative now is this child, Jonny Stanislowski?"

"Right," Matt said.

"Did Mr. Stanley know about her when he made his will?"

"No, he knew nothing of her. In fact, we knew nothing of her until this fall."

Again Lieutenant Peabody seemed to think for a moment. Then he said, "Well, we'll talk about that later, too. What about her mother, Conrad Stanislowski's wife?"

"We know nothing about her, but the way Stanislowski spoke of her to Miss March suggests that she died when Jonny was a baby."

Lieutenant Peabody looked at Laura. "What exactly did he say, Miss March? Tell me the whole story. You'd better begin at the beginning. Cosden says that you had no warning of Stanislowski's appearance. He says that all of you thought he was either still in Poland or, since his child turned up in an orphanage in Vienna, that he was dead."

"Yes," Laura said. "He just—came here this afternoon. He dropped out of the blue. I didn't expect him, I knew nothing about him. He—knocked on the door."

Lieutenant Peabody nodded. "Go on. Tell me please, Miss March, everything you can remember. Everything he said."

She told it all again as she had told Matt. Neither of the men seemed to move as she talked. Except for her voice the room was very quiet; she could hear like a remote accompaniment the deep murmur of traffic sounds from Lake Shore Drive. Again when she had finished, Lieutenant Peabody seemed to review all the record with which she had now provided him and had instantly stored it away in his filing cabinet, as she talked. He said finally to Matt, "How did you get hold of the child?"

"Well," Matt said, "it was a long process. In spite of all our efforts we were never successful in communicating with Stanislowski."

Peabody gave a little short nod which seemed to be one of his characteristics; it was very brief and effortless, as if he wished to conserve his energy. He said to Laura, "He told you that, in

41

fact, your letters may have made it only harder for him to escape?"

Laura nodded. "Ah," Peabody said and turned to Matt. "Go on, please."

Matt said, "We had, of course, got in touch with all the relief agencies. During the war, as you know, thousands of Polish people were shifted around from one camp to another, displaced persons. We thought it possible that Conrad Stanislowski had turned up in one of these camps or at some relief agency. In a last effort to comb the various agencies for him we discovered that there was a child by the name of Jonny Stanislowski in Vienna, and according to her birth certificate which was on file at the orphanage, she was the child of Conrad Stanislowski—our Conrad Stanislowsky, the son of Stefan, Conrad Stanley's brother—"

Laura listened while Matt explained it in detail. Lieutenant Peabody nodded. "No doubt of the child's identity," he said. "What did you do then?"

"I flew to Vienna. The American Army Headquarters and the relief organization helped me straighten things out. She was his child all right but her appearance at the orphanage was a little on the mysterious side. Certainly her father had not brought her there, she had arrived in the escort of a man named Schmidt. We assumed either that her father was alive and for some reason had no way to care for her, or that he was dead and some friend of his had managed to get her into the orphanage. This was the most reasonable theory. And, of course, as the will reads, Stanislowski could claim the fund only if he fulfilled the conditions. He didn't turn up in America; the reason didn't affect the interpretation of the will. On the other hand—Jonny was his child."

Lieutenant Peabody nodded. "So you felt obliged to bring her home?"

"Certainly," Matt said. "I—we couldn't leave the child in an orphanage! Obviously the thing to do was to bring her back to America. Besides, it was a question whether or not her father was dead; if he were dead, then she was her father's heir, and we felt that there was no question of Conrad Stanley's intention in establishing the fund."

"Ah," Lieutenant Peabody observed.

Matt hesitated for a second as if it had been a question. "It's a perfectly clear situation," he said. "If her father was dead—"

"But you don't seem to have been able to prove that he was either dead or alive," Peabody said mildly. "However—please go on. You brought the child here."

"Yes. The American Army Headquarters helped cut red tape. When I took her away I left the letter outlining the whole situation with the head of the orphanage. There was full information about the Conrad Stanley will in it, and the names of Doris Stanley, Mr. Stanley's widow, and, of course, the name of Miss March and the other trustee, Charlie Stedman. We really had nothing on which to base a hope that Conrad Stanislowski himself would turn up in America, ever. At the same time we had a moral and humane responsibility for the child. And there was also the consideration that if her father were dead, she was his heir. In any event we all knew what Conrad Stanley would have wished us to do."

The Lieutenant turned to Laura. "Now, as I understand it, Miss March, this man this afternoon told you that he had received that letter?"

Laura said, "Yes. And he must have had it, otherwise he wouldn't have known my name. He wouldn't have known that Jonny is here."

The Lieutenant neither agreed nor disagreed; he said thoughtfully to Matt, "There must have been, then, a sort of time limit to this will. That is, you were prepared to accept it as a fact, either that Conrad Stanislowski was dead or that he was not going to arrive here and take out American citizenship papers and claim this fund."

Matt said, "We had to come to some sort of conclusion. You are quite right, Lieutenant. There was a time limit to the will—three years. That is, if Stanislowski did not turn up in that time or couldn't get to America or we had no word from him, then the Stanislowski provision of the will was to be waived."

"Three years," Lieutenant Peabody said. "You say Conrad Stanley died three years ago. The time limit is about up."

"Yes. In January."

After a moment Lieutenant Peabody said thoughtfully, "So he got here just in time. What was to happen to this fund if nobody turned up to claim it?"

Matt replied again, "That's all in the will. After a three-year wait, if Conrad Stanislowski failed to turn up and claim the money, or if we could not discover him, then his portion of the estate was to be divided between other heirs."

"What other heirs?"

Matt said too easily and too matter-of-factly all at once, "It would have gone in equal shares to Mrs. Stanley, to Charlie Stedman and to"—he nodded at Laura—"Miss March."

"I see." The Lieutenant looked dreamily at Laura.

Matt said, "Miss March was a sort of ward of Stanley's, that is, not legally, but Conrad Stanley was a friend of her father's and helped Laura with her education. Laura then worked for him as his secretary. That is why he made her a co-trustee for the

43

Stanislowski fund. Charlie Stedman is the other trustee. I think I told you that. He is a manufacturer, and an old friend of Conrad Stanley's."

There was again a short silence in the room. Laura sensed rather than saw a kind of uneasiness in Matt; perhaps it lay in his stillness, or in the intent yet somehow guarded way he looked at a tiny silver box of matches he was turning in his hand.

Then Lieutenant Peabody said quietly, "It's odd that you should find the claimant to all this money murdered, isn't it, Miss March?"

EIGHT

There was a little clatter as Matt dropped the silver box on the table and rose. Laura said in a suddenly brittle voice that did not seem to belong to her, "Lieutenant Peabody, I did not kill Conrad Stanislowski in order to get a third of his money."

"My dear young lady!" Lieutenant Peabody managed to look rather shocked yet his dreamy gaze was very observant.

A curious cold kind of anger flicked Laura. She said directly, "I thought that's what you meant."

Matt glanced at her with a quick flash of approval.

The Lieutenant said very politely, "I'm sorry. I was only reasoning logically that now that the claimant to this fund is dead, a very large sum of money will be divided among you, the other trustee and, of course, the widow. So in a sense it is advantageous to you that Conrad Stanislowski died."

Matt said, "You've forgotten the child."

The Lieutenant eyed him. "I see. What exactly did you intend to do about her? I mean, if this man had not turned up this afternoon?"

"That's why we brought her from Vienna, Lieutenant. I thought I made that clear. We regarded her as her father's heir and we thought it logical to assume that he was dead. In any event, whether he was dead or alive—"

44

Peabody interrupted. "Let me get this straight. Did Conrad Stanley specifically mention any heirs of his nephew in his will?"

"No, he didn't. You can take a look at the will yourself."

"I'll do that, Cosden," Peabody said quietly.

Matt said, "Mr. Stanley drew it up for the most part without legal aid. He was like that. Of course, it's a perfectly legal document, all clear and properly witnessed. He referred to his nephew by name, he had never seen him and he had had no communication with him. In fact, he must have been himself a little uncertain as to whether the nephew was still alive. Nevertheless, he had a feeling about his name and his blood relatives and, as I told you, Conrad Stanley always felt that he owed so great a debt to America for the opportunities it had given him that he wished to pass on this opportunity to his nephew. The three-year provision was, I suppose, in his mind a reasonable provision, meant to cover the very likely contingency that his nephew would not be found. Naturally, since he did not know that his nephew had a daughter, he made no specific provision for the child. And, of course, he made no provision at all to cover the exact situation which had developed, that is, that we were able to find Conrad Stanislowski's child but were not able to find Stanislowski himself. But however the will might be interpreted, Conrad Stanley's intent was very clear. Our idea is that the trust fund should be continued until Jonny is of age and should then be turned over to her as her father's heir."

"Is that settled?"

"No. It isn't settled yet, legally. It will have to go through the courts. But I don't think there's much doubt of the interpretation of the intent of the will."

"But you have agreed to this among yourselves. I mean Mrs. Stanley, Stedman and Miss March—all of you have agreed to petition the court to continue the fund for the little girl?"

Matt hesitated for a barely perceptible second; then he said, "There is, I'm sure, no disagreement among us. We have postponed the exact and legal arrangement until the date when the estate is to be settled, which would be the normal time to do anything like that. That is, in January. The point is, Lieutenant Peabody, nobody stood to gain by the death of this man who came this afternoon. You're looking for motives, of course, but that one is out, believe me."

The Lieutenant said quietly, "Somebody killed him."

There was another rather long pause. The traffic roar along the Drive had dwindled as it grew late. A heavier fog must be coming in from the lake for the foghorn near the Navy pier gave a low hoarse warning through the night. Presently Lieutenant Peabody shifted his position slightly. He said, "Now let's go over this interview you had with this man, Miss March, again. First, did you have any doubt as to his claim?"

"No," Laura said. "At least not while he was here."

"What do you mean by that?"

"It's just as I told you, Lieutenant. When he saw Jonny he didn't speak to her and Jonny didn't speak to him. He then asked me to tell no one of his arrival, and went away. There was something about him that I believed. I wasn't sure I was right, though, not to tell Matt and the others of his arrival. In any event it suddenly struck me that if Jonny had recognized him she would have shown some sort of reaction. Even if at the very moment when she saw him she had been startled or perhaps frightened, still it seemed to me that later on she would have shown some sort of feeling. So then I thought that the man must be an impostor. But when I took the Polish dictionary and went to question her—"

The Lieutenant interrupted. "Did you question her?"

"No. It was then that I found her crying. So I knew that she must have recognized him and that he was her father."

"But you did, at least for a moment, waver in your conviction that he was Stanislowski?"

"Yes. But only for a moment."

"He gave you no hint as to what he intended to do during these few days when he wished his arrival to be kept a secret?"

"No."

"You explained to him the entire situation—that is, that he would have to see Mrs. Stanley, Cosden, the other trustee?"

"I intended to phone to Matt then. He asked me not to. He seemed—frightened."

"That's an odd thing, isn't it? Why should he be frightened? He merely came to see you, and to see that his child was safely here, in your care?"

"He seemed frightened," she said stubbornly.

"Well," the Lieutenant said, "that's a matter of opinion, isn't it? However, he did know all about this will."

"Yes, of course. He had the letter which Matt left at the orphanage."

"But he refused to show you the letter. In point of fact, he refused to show you any sort of identification."

"He said he would have everything in the way of identification we required in a few days."

"He didn't say that he was going to see anybody?"

"No. He only told me his address."

The Lieutenant said unexpectedly, "You are very young to be made a trustee for the Stanley will. You must have thought over your responsibilities very seriously. Cosden here"—he nodded at

46

Matt—"and the other trustee, Stedman, must have warned you that there was a possibility that someone would hear of this very unusual will and attempt to claim the money."

"Oh, yes," Laura said. "That's why I questioned him about his identification. I didn't want to; I wanted to take him to Jonny immediately."

The Lieutenant leaned forward slightly. "Miss March, are you sure that he was dead when you found him?"

"Yes! There was no question of it. I felt his pulse. And then I got a little mirror out of my compact and held it to his mouth—"

The Lieutenant interrupted. "Did you try to help him?"

"No. No. There was nothing I could do. He was dead."

"Describe the room, please."

"The room? Why, it—it is just a room, small, not much in it. A bed, a writing table. He was on the floor, near the table. There was a chest of drawers. His suitcase stood on the floor near the bed. The overcoat he had worn was across the bed. His jacket was on a chair." She remembered the gray shirt he wore and the red splotches on the back of it. She stopped.

"Any other details about the room?"

She could still see the brightly lighted little room in all its bareness and its tragedy. "No— Oh, yes, I think there were two glasses on the table."

She knew, of course, that Lieutenant Peabody had already examined the room and had seen everything that she had seen. He said, however, in a very quiet, almost a casual voice, "Did the glasses look clean?"

She hesitated. "Yes. Yes, I think so. I don't remember seeing anything in them."

The Lieutenant said, "What exactly did you do?"

"I told you—"

"Tell me again."

"I—felt for his pulse and tried to see with the mirror if he was still breathing. Then I glanced around the room but I really was thinking only of Jonny and that it was murder. It was—horrible. I only wanted to get away—"

"So you knew at once that it was murder?"

"How could it be anything else? The wounds were in his back."

"The Lieutenant said, "It seems to me that your mind was working very clearly if you reasoned at once that it was murder."

Matt said, "It was perfectly clear, Lieutenant. He couldn't have killed himself like that. It was a physical impossibility. Anybody would have known at once that it was murder."

"No doubt," Peabody said. "But it must have been a great shock to you, Miss March. People do not ordinarily encounter a murder. At least, people who are not in my profession. You must have been interested in the papers which he claimed to have, his passport and his papers of identification. Didn't you look for them?"

"No! I never thought of it. All I could think of was Jonny and —and that he was murdered."

"You are sure you didn't—say, open the suitcase, search his coat pockets—"

"No!" Laura cried. "I didn't!"

"What are you getting at, Lieutenant?" Matt said suddenly. "Didn't you find any papers of identification?"

"Not a thing," the Lieutenant said. "No passport. No letter from the orphanage. We found no letters at all, in fact. No cards of identity. He had a bill folder with about a hundred dollars in it, American money. There was nothing else. No initials on his clothing, nothing whatever to identify him except of course"—his dreamy gaze shifted to Laura—"his visit to you and his claim to be Stanislowski."

NINE

"But that suggests—" Matt began, but the Lieutenant interrupted. "That suggests that his murderer took such papers. It also suggests, however, that he had no such papers." He took a small envelope from his pocket. "Another question, Miss March. Did he speak to you when you went to his room at Koska Street?"

"He was dead—"

"He didn't die immediately after he was stabbed. You knew that. Didn't you?"

There was a tone in his voice which bewildered Laura. "I thought he must have been alive when the woman, Maria Brown, phoned to me. Otherwise she wouldn't have known my name. She wouldn't have asked me to bring the doctor to help him. But he was dead when I saw him."

"You have described the room exactly as you saw it? There's no detail you have omitted?"

Laura thought back to that brightly lighted little room which was like a clear photographic image in her mind. "No," she said slowly, "nothing."

"As a matter of fact," the Lieutenant said, "there were bloodstains on the armchair across the room—"

"I didn't see that. I—"

"And there were a few smears of blood along the floor. It looks as if he was stabbed when he was sitting in the chair. Then he was either helped by somebody else or dragged himself along the floor toward the writing table. In any event, he lived certainly for a few moments after he was stabbed."

Matt said, "He must have been conscious when he told Maria Brown to phone to Miss March; she had Miss March's name and telephone number. She told her to bring a doctor, and to come at once. She wouldn't have said to bring a doctor if Stanislowski had been dead then. And don't forget, Lieutenant, that she did run away from the house, and when she saw Miss March and Jonny on the steps she told them to go away, and she also said," Matt said with a peculiar, hard note in his voice, "that she shouldn't have done it."

"So Miss March says."

Matt's voice cracked like a whip. "There would be no point in her lying about it. That's why she went to the rooming house. That's why she telephoned to the doctor."

There was something like a whip in the Lieutenant's voice, too. He said, "So you are going to take the stand that the Brown woman murdered him? Then when he didn't die at once, she telephoned for help, and said to bring a doctor. And when he did die, she gathered her luggage together and ran away, after warning Miss March to go away, and after making what you interpret as being tantamount to a confession. Doesn't it all seem rather inconsistent?"

Matt said more calmly, "I don't say Maria Brown murdered him. I do say that he went to that address on Koska Street and the Brown woman obviously was already there. I do say that she telephoned for help. I do say that after his death, she ran away, leaving her room, giving the landlady no warning, with her rent paid ahead. And I do say that he had escaped from Poland. He told Miss March that he had been an official of some kind in the government and—"

The Lieutenant interrupted with a touch of impatience. "We'll explore all that. It will take a little time." He, too, went on more calmly. "Now as I understand it, the story this man told Miss March, as far as it went, squared with what you knew of—Stanislowski."

Matt answered, "We knew very little about him. We knew that

49

he had been born in Cracow. We knew Jonny was his child. And that's just about all."

"You must have tried to establish the circumstances of the child's arrival at the orphanage."

"Certainly. You will understand that during the years since the war relief organizations had been flooded with applications. It is very difficult, in spite of everything they can do, to keep exact and detailed records. However, a man brought Jonny to the orphanage; his name was Gustave Schmidt, not as you will realize an unusual name. He gave an address; when I was in Vienna I tried to find him but could not. In the two years since Jonny was at the orphanage, the apartment house which he gave as an address had been razed and a new and modern building erected there. I failed to discover even whether or not it was a bona fide address; it could have been and probably was but I could not discover the names of the previous tenants. In any event, I didn't find him. Apparently he said that he was a friend of the child's father and had brought her to the orphanage because there was no other way to care for her. He didn't make the statement that the father was dead or if so it did not appear on the record. There happened to be nobody on the staff of the orphanage who remembered any details of the interview with Gustave Schmidt; that is comprehensible, too. They're very busy; there is a terrific volume of such interviews. You have to undertake a thing of this kind, Lieutenant, before you get an idea of the confusion which has resulted from the great numbers of displaced persons, of families separated, moved from one place to another."

"But as to Stanislowski," the Lieutenant said, "your most hopeful theory was that he was alive and hoped to escape Poland and had sent his child ahead in the hope of eventually getting himself and Jonny out of Vienna."

Matt nodded. "It was only a possibility."

The Lieutenant said to Laura, "But it was in fact the exact story which this man this afternoon told you."

"Yes," Laura said.

"And which you had discussed in detail many times with"—he nodded toward Matt—"Cosden and the other two people who are directly interested in the Stanislowski provision."

Matt said, again too easily somehow, too quietly, "Certainly we had discussed it, Lieutenant. But we had discussed the other possibilities also, that is, that Stanislowski was either dead or for some reason could not care for Jonny. The point is, so far as settling the will is concerned, it didn't matter. If Stanislowski did not arrive here before January, the Stanislowski provision was out so far as he was concerned. That, it seemed to all of us, was

50

automatic. On the other hand, as I told you, we all felt that Conrad Stanley's intent was perfectly clear and that therefore we should turn the fund over to Jonny, to be held in trust for her until she was of age."

"But you've done nothing definite about that?"

Laura felt that Matt was keeping down a rising flare of temper. He said, "There is nothing we could do until January."

The Lieutenant was insistent. "But you have all agreed to this?"

Matt's mouth looked hard. He said in a level voice, "I've told you the exact situation, Lieutenant. You understand I have nothing to do with this directly. I'm only Mrs. Stanley's lawyer but it would devolve upon me to assist in carrying out the provision of Conrad Stanley's will."

"To the best of Mrs. Stanley's interests," the Lieutenant said in a mild way.

"Certainly. You must realize, Lieutenant, that all of us feel a strong affection and responsibility for Jonny."

"No doubt," the Lieutenant said politely, and added almost absently, "Of course, her arrival does take a large sum of money from the estate which would otherwise have been divided among Mr. Stedman, Mrs. Stanley and Miss March." He opened the envelope in his hands. He took from it a scrap of white, stained with blotches which were a kind of rusty, dry brown. It was a woman's handkerchief, a small square of linen neatly hemstitched. He held it toward Laura, "Does this belong to you, Miss March?"

The rusty, brownish blotches were dried blood. She shrank back from it. "No!"

"You said you didn't try to help Conrad. Are you sure you didn't take your handkerchief and hold it to the stab wounds?"

"Oh, no," Laura cried. "No!" Again the bright clear picture of the room returned to her and this time, with it, the recollection of a scrap of white, stained then with bright red. "That was on the floor! I remember now. I saw it as I was leaving. I looked around the room, and I saw that but—"

"Why didn't you tell me about it when you described the room?"

"I forgot. I simply forgot." It was the truth; it didn't sound like it.

"It obviously belonged to the Brown woman," Matt began, and the Lieutenant said rather wearily, "Oh, yes, yes, the Brown woman. I'd like to take a look at your handkerchiefs, if you please, Miss March. Not that that is likely to prove anything. I expect any woman has some odd handkerchiefs. They don't all match, now do they?"

Laura glanced at Matt and he gave a sort of shrug and nodded slightly. She rose and led the Lieutenant back to the hall into her own bedroom.

"Jonny is sleeping," she said softly to the Lieutenant and nodded toward the closed door of Jonny's room. The Lieutenant eyed the door for a moment. "I'd like to talk to the child."

"Not now," Matt said firmly. "You can talk to her later but not tonight."

The Lieutenant yielded. He crossed Laura's neat, small bedroom to the chest of drawers where Laura took out all her supply of handkerchiefs, in their little silken cases. It was with a feeling of something like nightmare that she put them on a table and watched the Lieutenant set them out one by one, his fingers unexpectedly deft and light. A faint scent of lilacs came from the sachet in the cases. Matt stood watching, his hands in his pockets, his face inscrutable as the Lieutenant went one by one through the handkerchiefs, glancing now and then at the stained, crumpled handkerchief he had put down on the table beside the others. There was no handkerchief which matched it exactly.

With incredulity and yet with a kind of queer, cold fear somewhere within her, Laura watched the process. But as the Lieutenant had said, of course, it didn't prove anything. The bloodstained handkerchief was simply a woman's handkerchief with a small hemstitched edge. Laura—Doris, anybody—could have had a handkerchief exactly like it.

Whatever the Lieutenant thought of the little display he said nothing. But then without a word he wandered around the bedroom, pausing to look down at the bedside table with its little assortment of engagement pad and ash tray, cigarette box and clock; he paused to examine a photograph of Laura's father, a snapshot of a youthful figure in a flyer's uniform, his eyes squinted against the sun.

It was a pleasant room, airy and light, with its white curtains and one or two pieces of furniture which had belonged in Laura's home—her own four-poster bed which she had had as a child, the little dressing table which had belonged to her mother, with its old-fashioned, curved drawers. Laura had taken pleasure in furnishing the bedroom, in buying the scattered green rugs, in selecting the wallpaper with its big red cabbage roses and the white and green cover for the lounge chair. It was not a luxurious room, but it was feminine and orderly. It increased her sense of nightmare incredulity to see a police officer strolling around that room—looking for evidence of murder. It wasn't true; it couldn't happen. But it was happening, because still without a word Lieutenant Peabody strolled out of the room and into the little kitchen.

If he were looking for a knife, he'd find it, Laura thought; there were small knives in the cutlery drawer. He did not open the drawer. He merely glanced in a long and leisurely fashion around him and turned away.

When they had got back to the living room and still the Lieutenant said nothing, and only looked into space in a thoughtful and preoccupied way as if he were still intently filing away records in that invisible filing cabinet, Matt dived directly into the implications of the oddly cursory yet terrifying search.

"Lieutenant Peabody, it's your job to investigate, we understand that, but let me ask you this. If Miss March killed that man and removed traces of his identity, would she have done anything at all that she later did? Wouldn't she have simply returned here and told nobody? Would she have telephoned to me and reported murder? Who would know that he had ever been here at all? And more than that, if she had intended to murder him, would she have taken the child with her? *Would* she have phoned for a doctor and asked him to go there?"

The Lieutenant said coolly, "On a hypothetical basis, Mr. Cosden, and in answer to your last question, I'll say, yes, she might have phoned for the doctor. It would have been a rather clever move, in fact. The doctor was out on a call; the chances were that he wouldn't arrive at Koska Street for some time and she'd get there first. Yes, to call a doctor who could almost certainly be counted on not to arrive until after a man is dead—murdered"—he nodded—"I'd call that a clever sort of move. Almost as good as an alibi."

TEN

"But I didn't!" Laura cried. Her throat felt oddly numb, her voice did not seem to belong to her or to carry any weight. "I phoned to the doctor but I did that because Maria Brown asked me to. I didn't kill him."

Matt said, "It would be a very dangerous move, too, Lieutenant, to phone for a doctor. He might have arrived before Miss March, he might have arrived at exactly the time of the murder."

"If he had arrived before the murder, that could have been postponed. Miss March says that the house was very quiet; it would be a logical assumption that a lodging house in that district would be quiet at that hour of the afternoon, when most of the roomers had not yet returned from work. She would have been able to hear the doctor's approach. Remember, it takes only a minute or two to kill a man. But if the doctor had arrived before the murder, then it could have been postponed. Wait—" The Lieutenant put up a hand to check Matt's protest. "I'm not saying that happened! I'm only saying that phoning to the doctor, which of course we can confirm, does not automatically clear Miss March. Remember this, Cosden, she found Stanislowski and she was the only one of you who knew he was here in Chicago. Or at least—admits it."

"Believe me," Matt said, "I didn't know it. Mrs. Stanley didn't know it. Charlie Stedman didn't know it. Miss March said that she told none of us and that's the truth. Every word that Miss March has told you is the truth."

"I'm not saying it isn't." Suddenly Peabody's voice became reasonable and rather friendly in a curiously disarming way. "See here, Cosden, I'm only doing my job. I'll have to talk to the other two people interested in this man's arrival. When I say that Miss March is the only one who admits knowing of him, I meant naturally that perhaps someone else, perhaps someone you don't know, perhaps none of these three people but certainly someone in Chicago, knew that Stanislowski was here and had some reason to murder him."

"I can't deny that." Matt's eyes were blazing but he still kept his voice quiet. "But consider this, Lieutenant. If Miss March had murdered him, as she didn't, all she'd have had to do was keep quiet about the whole affair. Tell nobody that he had come to see her, refuse to go to the rooming house when the Brown woman phoned—"

"The child saw him when he came here," Lieutenant Peabody said dryly.

"That's no good. Jonny is only learning to speak English. Even if she had mentioned her father, say, to me, would I have believed that he had in fact been here? Wouldn't I have believed rather that she was making some childish game or joke with me, or some reference in her mixture of English and Polish which I couldn't understand? Wouldn't I have believed Miss March if she denied it?"

Lieutenant Peabody folded the envelope holding the ugly stained little handkerchief and put it carefully in his pocket. He said in a faraway voice, "I'm sure you'd have believed Miss March."

For some obscure reason it seemed to take the wind out of Matt's sails. He hesitated, checked for a fraction of a second, and then went on too quickly. "The fact is there'd have been no credible witness to Stanislowski's arrival here in Chicago. Somebody would have found him murdered, the landlady or somebody would have reported it to the police. You yourself say there were no means of identification found. Eventually he'd have gone down on the police record as an unidentified man found murdered in a rooming house. Nobody would ever have known anything more than that about him. That's the fact, Lieutenant, and you can't deny it."

"Can't I?" The Lieutenant eyed Matt thoughtfully. Then he said with that disarming air of frankness, "Well, it's a fact I'd like to identify this man. We'll have to question the child, you know. An interpreter might help; I'll get hold of one. Surely the child knew whether or not he was her father, and if she makes an identification that will simplify our problem to a degree."

Matt said tersely, "You mean that if Jonny says he was her father, you will include all of us in your list of suspects?"

"That's my business, Cosden," the Lieutenant said. "But I don't mind saying that I'll include anybody on the list of suspects who had a motive for getting rid of Stanislowski."

Matt was still angry. "Miss March has given you an exact account of what happened. It would help your task of gathering evidence very much if you would take it as the truth."

"I tell you, I'm not accusing Miss March. And if I did arrest her," Peabody said softly, "I expect you'd turn up armed with the law and get her out. At least you'd try it." He turned to Laura and said abruptly, "Why exactly is the child here? You didn't tell me that. It seems to me Mrs. Stanley would have been the logical person to take care of her."

The Lieutenant merely looked at her but she had a curious feeling of invisible tentacles reaching out into the air for information.

Matt supplied it briefly. "Conrad Stanley was an old friend and a very close friend of Laura's father. His name was Peter March. He was killed in the war. Laura's mother died shortly after that. There was very little money; Conrad Stanley stepped in and gave Laura an education. When she had finished school, he employed her as his secretary. Does that answer your question, Lieutenant Peabody?"

Peabody nodded shortly. "So you gave up your job to see to the child?" he asked Laura.

"Yes," Laura said.

Again Matt explained. "Our intention is to reimburse her for

55

any expenses for the child from the estate when it is settled next month."

"And how about your job?" Lieutenant Peabody asked Laura, very politely and quietly and yet with a kind of skeptical undertone.

Laura said, "I'll get another one."

Matt said, "Our plan is to put Jonny in school somewhere. We'll see to it that Laura has a job."

"I see," the Lieutenant said. "Now, one other question, Miss March. As I understand it, when this man Stanislowski left, you didn't promise him in so many words to keep his presence a secret. That's what you told me, isn't it?"

"Yes. I—I implied a promise, at least he took it as such and went away."

"It seems to me that you'd have gone straight to the telephone, no matter what he said about keeping his presence a secret. It seems to me that you'd have thought it your duty to telephone to Cosden here, and to the other trustee and to Mrs. Stanley, all three of them, and tell them right away that the man you'd been looking for had turned up. Why didn't you?"

"Because," Laura said, "I—believed him. He said there were reasons; he said that he'd come forward in a few days. I believed him."

"I see," Peabody said in a way that suggested that he didn't see at all. He turned to Matt. "Cosden, will you give me Mrs. Stanley's address and Mr. Stedman's?"

He was going to question them, of course. He took out a little notebook and wrote the addresses as Matt gave them to him. Doris' address was that of a beautiful and luxurious apartment house not very far from Laura's. Charlie's address was his club. "Thank you," the Lieutenant said and gathered up his coat and hat. "I'm not sure when we'll set an inquest; there's the question of identification. I'll want your formal statement, Miss March. A man will be here in the morning." He walked out of the room.

It was so unexpected in a way that it took Matt and Laura both by surprise. Then Matt sprang after Peabody. After a word or two the door to the outside corridor closed. Matt came back.

"Matt," Laura cried, "he can't suspect me! That handkerchief wasn't mine. It must have belonged to Maria Brown. But he looked, he searched my apartment. He was—he was looking for evidence!"

"Take it easy. That's only his job. It's a preliminary investigation. The handkerchief only proves that someone was in Stanislowski's room and apparently tried to help him. Obviously it was the Brown woman." Matt picked up the telephone. "I'd better telephone to Doris and Charlie and tell them about it before Peabody turns up to question them. Doris isn't going to like it because I haven't told her about it before now! Or Charlie either for that matter."

She listened as he talked, first to Charlie and then to Doris. Charlie asked incredulous and stunned questions. Doris was incredulous, too; she wouldn't be convinced. Matt kept repeating, ". . . but it happened, Doris. . . . No, that's all Laura knows about it. She didn't telephone to tell you about him, she didn't phone to any of us because he begged her not to. . . . She doesn't know why but he told her it was very important and he said he'd come forward in a few days with all his credentials. . . . No, he only wanted to see Jonny. He didn't speak to her, he didn't do anything, they didn't talk. . . . Jonny didn't say a word. . . . Yes, it is queer but she might've been frightened. Then she began to cry and . . . well, I know that doesn't prove anything but that's what happened. . . . Then this Brown woman phoned. . . . I think it is perfectly clear. Laura *had* to go to the rooming house! She couldn't have refused to get a doctor and go out there. . . . Well, she had to take Jonny. She couldn't leave her alone. . . . Yes, the police are out there now and a Lieutenant Peabody is here. He's just gone. He asked for your address and Charlie's. . . . Of course, they want to talk to you. . . . Why? Because they've got to question everybody concerned with Stanislowski. . . . No, I can't come now, I'm with Laura." Here there was a long pause while Doris talked. At last Matt said, "All right, all right, I'll come."

He put down the telephone and turned to Laura. "Doris is upset. She wants me to be there when the police see her. I rather think Lieutenant Peabody is on his way there now. I suppose I'd better go."

"Of course," Laura said. But she didn't want him to go. He took his coat up over his arm and in the doorway paused to give her a searching and somehow dissatisfied look as if he wanted to say something but didn't know what. Finally he said, "You'd better eat something. Try to sleep. It's late. I'll let you know in the morning if there is any news."

She nodded and said good night.

But after he'd gone the small apartment seemed suddenly very big and empty. Yes of course, he'd go to Doris if she wanted him, whenever she wanted him. It had always been that way.

ELEVEN

There was, as it happened, only one small evidence of pursuit that night and at the time it did not strike Laura as pursuit. That happened shortly after Matt had left.

She was in the kitchen trying to make herself drink some hot soup when the telephone rang; she went to answer it. "Hello." There was silence at the other end of the telephone but it was, somehow, a listening silence. Laura cried, "Hello," again more clearly.

There was still silence, yet it seemed to Laura that she could hear the faintest sound of rather rapid breathing at the other end of the phone. Then the telephone clicked in her ear. The dial tone came on.

After a moment Laura put down the telephone. It was a wrong number. Her own telephone went through a small switchboard which was located in a little niche off the foyer of the apartment house. A girl sat there who took messages; if a tenant's telephone rang for some time without an answer from the tenant, she cut in and took a message. There could have been some mistake at the apartment switchboard. Laura went back to the kitchen, tried to eat and couldn't. She made hot chocolate for Jonny and put it in a thermos bottle. Jonny was an early riser and it was her custom to come into Laura's bedroom very quietly in the morning and help herself to chocolate, while the kitten romped about the room. In order to keep Jonny company during that pleasant morning hour, Laura also prepared hot milk for herself, very slightly flavored with coffee, and put it in another thermos bottle. This Jonny would open, too, and serve to Laura with a gay, housewifely little air. The two of them, with the kitten chasing madly around the room, stalking objects which did not exist as well as Jonny's bare toes or dangling braids, would sip their hot drinks and then go into the kitchen and have a real breakfast—usually urged on by Suki who had in the morning, or any time, a voracious appetite. That night, as every night, Laura heated milk, poured hot coffee into it, and poured the mixture into another thermos bottle. She set both bottles on the table.

58

She cleared up the few dishes, opened the door from the kitchen to a small service hall and put out empty milk bottles. There was at last nothing more to do, nothing to require even a fraction of her thought. She drifted back to the living room.

The tiny gilded hands of the French clock on the mantel pointed to nearly twelve-thirty. She wondered how Lieutenant Peabody was coming out with his questioning of Doris and of Charlie Stedman. She lighted a cigarette, went to the window and looked down at the now almost deserted boulevard below. The lake and the sky blended into blackness. There were street lamps along the boulevard and occasionally a car swept past, its lights spreading a wide bright fan ahead of it. The night was still foggy and the pavement far below was glittering and wet. She wished that Matt had not gone. But then, she thought again, he would always go when Doris wanted him.

Thinking of Matt and of Doris, Laura wondered as she had wondered before why they had chosen to wait to marry until Conrad's estate was settled, as they seemed to be waiting. Doris had been free and a lovely and desirable young widow for three years. Perhaps Matt was determined this time to make sure of Doris' love. She had jilted him once. But he was in love with Doris all the same. He'd always go when he wanted him.

And that was just Laura's bad luck. It wasn't as if she hadn't known it either. She had walked into love with Matt with her eyes open—except it happened unexpectedly, too, between one heartbeat and the next.

Yet there was nothing dramatic, nothing to mark it that one clear, sunny afternoon early in December, when Matt had strolled along the lake with Laura and Jonny. After a while he glanced at his watch with an exclamation of impatience and said he had a client waiting for him. He had got in a taxi to go back to the office. All at once, with the disappearance of that tall figure with its black head, the blue sky seemed less bright, the sunshine less warm. A strange and happy kind of significance about the day seemed to vanish, too.

Suddenly Laura thought, watching the winter-blue lake, why, I'm in love with Matt!

Then she thought, and there's nothing I can do about it.

Laura scooped up the hair ribbons and began to roll up the bright little bands of red and green and yellow. Almost certainly Jonny was not aware of the tragedy of the afternoon. The child's gaiety and confidence had been growing during the past weeks, like seedlings stunted by frost but with warmth and care leaping into bloom. Conrad Stanislowski's death, his murder must not be permitted to touch Jonny.

It was late. She went back to Jonny's room and opened the

59

door. There was no sound from inside; the child was asleep. She left the child's door open and her own, so she would hear if Jonny awakened during the night. As she drew the curtains in her room she glanced out into the fog-veiled night, and wondered where in that great city Maria Brown had gone, what refuge she had taken. Had she gone to some previously prepared hiding place because she had orders to murder Conrad Stanislowski and her escape was made ready? Or had she fled, frightened, leaving the taxicab somewhere, hunting for another quiet, remote rooming house?

She went to the kitchen and got the two thermos bottles and put them on her bedside table. She tried to read. Eventually she slept, for it was daylight when a soft paw touching her cheek awoke her. Suki gave a hoarse but enthusiastic yell of greeting. Jonny, in pajamas which were striped in red and white like peppermint candy, was helping herself to the hot chocolate. With a rush the whole ugly and frightening shape of murder returned to Laura.

But Jonny knew nothing of it. Laura scrutinized her gay, round face, her laughing blue eyes, as she talked in Polish to Suki and Suki replied with cries that sounded like the squawk of a rusty hinge. There was not a shadow in the child's candid gaze.

Morning launched itself as usual, except for the newspaper. Laura had expected headlines; there were none. She found on one of the back pages only a very brief account of the murder. Her own name and the Stanley name were omitted. She felt a wave of passionate gratitude for that.

There were only two or three paragraphs. A man, supposed to be Conrad Stanislowski, had been found murdered in a rooming house on Koska Street. A woman, going by the name of Maria Brown, had left the rooming house; her description was given; the police were searching for her. There was no apparent motive for the murder. The police were investigating. That was all.

Matt did not telephone. No one telephoned. But about ten-thirty Lieutenant Peabody and two policemen came. Peabody was brief and hurried; would she please repeat her statement concerning Conrad Stanislowki and her discovery of his body. One of the policemen was a stenographer.

She had told it now so many times that it fell into a familiar pattern. When she finished, Peabody told her that it would be typed up and he would then ask her to sign it. And after he'd gone—quickly as if he had urgent business somewhere else—the second policeman said politely that he was instructed to take Laura's fingerprints.

She performed the little operation with a rather unnerving sense of putting herself irrevocably on record, yet it was a reasonable and matter-of-fact request. She didn't like it, however,

60

when they took Jonny's fingerprints, too. Peabody had not attempted to question Jonny; he had not even asked to see her. Yet did he plan, somehow, to use Jonny in establishing a case? Jonny took a pleased interest in the proceeding. After the policemen had thanked her politely and gone away, Jonny retired to her own room, where with a box of watercolors Charlie had given her, she experimented at making her own fingerprints and paw prints of Suki's.

Shortly after the police had gone Charlie Stedman came.

Charlie Stedman was perhaps forty or forty-five, much younger than Conrad Stanley, but he had been a long-time friend and indeed had joined with Conrad in some of his manufacturing enterprises. To Laura, Charlie always looked like an ultra-cautious diplomat, or an extremely conservative and discreet banker; he now looked rather like a banker who has discovered an unexpected deficit. He was dressed that morning as usual in a conservative Oxford gray suit and dark tie; he was as usual immaculate, well shaven and very neat. His thick, curly hair was gray; his figure was rather slight but very erect; his cheeks were pink from the cold. His face was imperturbable and calm; only his usually cool but astute gray eyes betrayed a glimmer of excitement. "Laura, my dear! This is a dreadful thing! I want to talk to you about it. How is Jonny?"

Jonny heard his voice. She came running from her room, her hands still smeared with watercolors. Charlie stooped to kiss her lightly on the cheek. Laura put it to Charlie's credit that he did not wince when he perceived a long streak of vermilion watercolor left on his otherwise immaculate shirt. He was always friendly with Jonny, in his own cool remote and impersonal way. He had brought her, even that morning, a little present, an engaging toy, a bird with a yellow head and red wings, and he must have, Charlie told Laura, a glass of warm water. When it was brought, as precisely as if he were auditing a bank statement, Charlie took the little bird, held its yellow head in the glass of water for some time, then set the bird on the table. It began to nod up and down, up and down, with an absurd and sober animation. Jonny squealed and watched, her blue eyes intent. Charlie lifted an eyebrow suggestively at Laura and nodded toward Jonny's room.

It was plain that he didn't want Jonny to hear their conversation; even if she understood little of the words she might sense something of their meaning. Laura took the child back to her own room. When she returned, Charlie was sitting in a lounge chair lighting a cigarette.

"A dreadful thing!" he said again. "It must have been a frightful shock to you. Matt told me all about it and, of course, the

61

police Lieutenant, Peabody, came to talk to me. To question me, as a matter of fact. It's a very unfortunate thing. I'm sorry you went to the rooming house, Laura."

"I had to go, Charlie."

"Oh, of course, of course. What about this woman, Maria Brown? Do you think that she murdered him?"

"I don't know."

"Well, she did run away," Charlie said thoughtfully. "There's no getting around that. Laura, have you asked Jonny whether or not this man was her father?"

"No. Not yet."

Charlie looked surprised. "Why not?"

"I'd rather—wait. You see, Charlie, after her father left she cried so hard that I felt sure that he was her father. Seeing him had troubled and frightened her. I don't want to upset her again. Not now. Not until it's a little in the past."

"I understand Lieutenant Peabody intends to question her."

"He was here this morning. He didn't question her then."

"He will though," Charlie said. "He'll have to. This is a most unusual situation, Laura. I don't know what to say. In fact, I don't know what to think. But just now the point seems to be, *was* that man Stanislowski?"

TWELVE

"I think so, Charlie."

He considered that deliberately for a moment as he considered everything. Then he said, "According to Matt and Lieutenant Peabody, Jonny did not recognize him."

"She didn't speak to him. But I think she may have been—oh, frightened. Surprised. It was all so sudden. You know how Jonny shrinks into herself when she's confused, or uncertain. But then after he'd gone she began to cry."

"Is that your only reason for believing he was Stanislowski?"

"N-no. That is—" Laura thought for a moment. "I can only say that I believed him."

62

"Matt says that you asked him for his credentials and he put you off. The police say there were no credentials found in his room."

"I know. But that doesn't really prove anything, does it?"

Charlie sighed, rose with his usual neat deliberation, walked to the windows and looked out. It was an overcast day, threatening rain or snow. He said, "Laura, I don't like to say this; it was suggested by the police. Understand me, I believe every word you say; I've known you a long time. But the police believe that Stanislowski—if he was Stanislowski—lived for some time after he was stabbed—"

Laura interrupted. "He had to tell Maria Brown my name and my address. Matt thinks and I think that it was after he died that she became frightened and ran away."

"Maybe," Charlie said, "or maybe her telephone call to you was part of a plan. However, what I want to ask you, Laura"—he turned to face her—"*did* Stanislowski speak to you when you arrived at the rooming house?"

"No! I told the police that!"

He waited a moment, scrutinizing her face. Then he said, "The police feel that he might have talked to you."

"I told them exactly what happened." Anger touched her suddenly; she knew that her voice was impatient and sharp.

Charlie heard that sharpness. "Forgive me, Laura, for questioning you like this. But it is important, I mean the question of this man's identity. It does seem doubtful whether or not Jonny really recognized him. There might have been some other reason for her tears. Even when we question her we may not get anything like satisfactory or convincing answers. The fact is, the child's sobbing is no real proof of the man's identity. He had no papers of any kind. The police say they have searched the room; I'm sure they would have overlooked nothing. And it is important to prove whether or not he was Stanislowski."

"But the trust fund goes to Jonny, anyway," Laura began.

Charlie interrupted. "We can consider the fund later. The point is now that the police feel that money is the motive and that Stanislowski's death—well, I'll put it to you straight, the police believe that Doris, you and I had an interest in his death. We are, in short, their only suspects. So far, at least," Charlie said, "and until they find this Maria Brown. But the case, such as it is, is built on his claim to be Stanislowski. If there were any way to prove that he *wasn't* Stanislowski"—Charlie lifted one eyebrow and sighed rather wistfully—"then I must say we'd all be in a rather more comfortable position. Now, my dear, if you still insist that he was Stanislowski—"

"I don't insist. But I—I believed him," Laura repeated with a sense of her own inadequacy.

The door buzzer sounded. "I'll go," Charlie said.

It was Lieutenant Peabody again, still hurried, still preoccupied. "Good morning, Stedman. Miss March, I'd like you to go out to Koska Street with me. Only to take a look at the room, see if it is as you left it. I'd like you to come out there now."

Charlie said, "Is that necessary, Lieutenant Peabody? It was a very shocking experience for Miss March—"

"I'm afraid it is necessary. We've a car waiting, Miss March."

Charlie turned to Laura. "Well, it won't take long. I'll go with you."

"I don't want to take Jonny out there again."

"No," Charlie said. "No—well, then, I'll stay with Jonny."

The Lieutenant did not say, "Hurry up," but he looked it. Laura went to her room and changed quickly into her gray suit. She put on red lipstick with a kind of defiance, as if it were a banner. She put on her small gray hat and the white silk scarf Matt had given her. It folded softly and warmly under her chin; she took up her red handbag.

They went down in the elevator quietly, Laura and Lieutenant Peabody and a policeman who was with Peabody. No one was in the foyer. The girl at the switchboard did not turn as they passed. A police car was waiting.

It was a typical December day, cold, with an overcast sky which seemed to press close above them and a few sparse snowflakes drifting down. They turned on Wacker Drive and then again west.

Peabody sat beside Laura in the back seat. A policeman drove and the other policeman sat in front, beside the driver. As they went west and farther west, all at once they seemed to enter a city within a city; the signs on the shop windows were again in a strange and incomprehensible language. The Polish neighborhood, the taxi driver had called it. There was the drug store where she and Jonny had gone the night before. Peabody eyed it but said nothing. They turned into Koska Street.

The street looked different by daylight; there was nothing shadowy or ominous about it. It was instead a remarkably neat and clean street, lined with substantial, well-cared-for houses. Lieutenant Peabody said suddenly, eyeing the houses, "There is a large Polish settlement here. There is in any big city. I should say Polish-Americans. They've made good citizens, reliable, thrifty, honest. It's a sturdy blood."

They stopped at 3936 Koska Street. There were the white steps, there was the door with the transom above it. A passer-by,

64

a woman with a market basket, looked at them curiously as they went up the stairs. Lieutenant Peabody opened the door and this time a woman came out from the back of the hall.

Peabody introduced them briefly. "This is Mrs. Radinsky, the landlady. This is Miss March."

The landlady, neat in a blue print dress, her dark hair tight under a net, gave Laura a sharp glance, nodded and said, "Good morning." Her dark eyes shifted to Peabody. "You'll want to see that room again. I hope you will be through with it soon. I'll have to have it all cleaned and painted. This is a bad thing to happen in a rooming house."

"I want Miss March to take a look at it."

Mrs. Radinsky shrugged in a fatalistic way. "You have the key."

Again Laura went up the creaking stairs, this time with Lieutenant Peabody and the policeman following her. They emerged into the narrow brown-painted hall. Lieutenant Peabody took a key from his pocket and unlocked the door which Laura had opened in the silence and dusk to find Conrad Stanislowski.

It was dark in the room, shadowed as it was by the yellowish brick wall of the flat building next door. Snowflakes drifted in a desultory way beyond the window, looking large and white against the wall. Objects in the room, the bed, the shape of a chair, loomed up dimly. Then Lieutenant Peabody snapped a light switch and instantly the room sprang into being. There was the writing table. There was the armchair. Peabody said, "We've taken his suitcase and his coat and hat. We took the glasses which were on the writing table and, of course, the handkerchief we found. But will you look closely around the room—aside from his suitcase and his clothes, and the two glasses, is there anything at all different?"

Chalk marks made the irregular outline of a man's body on the floor. This time Laura saw, too, a brownish smear on the cretonne-covered armchair.

"I didn't see that."

Lieutenant Peabody understood her. "There's a couple of smears on the floor, too."

"I didn't see them. But otherwise I can't see that anything is different."

"And you're sure you didn't see a knife anywhere?"

"I'm sure of that. I'd have remembered that."

"All right. Sit down, Miss March."

She hesitated, feeling that nothing in the room, no small detail should be disturbed. He understood her hesitation. "Oh, it's all right. We've gone over everything. Fingerprints, photographs, everything. Found the fingerprints of your right hand on the door, as a matter of fact," he said and pulled a straight chair forward for her. He then went to lean against the writing table, and said, on an unexpected tangent, "After Conrad Stanley's death, what was done about his estate?"

"That was all settled in the will. He knew that his wife, Mrs. Stanley, could not run the business. He advised that it be sold immediately and his patent rights retained. It was a good business and Charlie and Matt, we all, agreed that that was the thing to do. It was essentially a one-man business. There was nobody in the company who could take over. It was sold, oh—perhaps four or five months after Conrad Stanley's death."

There was a short silence. Almost certainly Laura thought, he had asked Matt Cosden that question; he had asked Doris and Charles Stedman. But then perhaps he only wanted to know whether all four of them told exactly the same story. Yet how could there by any inconsistencies in the account of so open and frank a transaction! Presently the Lieutenant nodded and with what seemed to be habitual abruptness, rose. "All right," he said briskly. "We'll go."

As they went single file down the stairs, their footsteps echoing through a house which again seemed to be empty of tenants, the landlady came to wait for them in the hall below. Peabody said, "All right, Mrs. Radinsky, we can turn over the room to you now. I left the key in the door."

He added casually, as if merely as an afterthought, "You are sure, Mrs. Radinsky, that you did not see Miss March when she came yesterday afternoon?"

Mrs. Radinsky shook her head. "No, I told you, Lieutenant, that I was at the delicatessen and then at the butcher store, at exactly that time. I've talked to the butcher. He says your policeman questioned him, too. I was there!"

Peabody said pleasantly, "We had to check on your story, but it's only a matter of form."

A little flush rose in the woman's broad face. "I understand that, Lieutenant. But I am a good citizen, I have always been a good citizen. I hold my head up among my neighbors. They will tell you, all of them, anything you want to know. I've never had anything like this happen in my rooming house before. I keep a good rooming house."

"Yes, we know that, Mrs. Radinsky. This is only part of an investigation. Have you ever seen Miss March anywhere before?"

THIRTEEN

It was said again so casually and so quietly that for a second Laura did not quite take in its significance. But then she realized that Peabody wanted to find out whether or not Laura had known of the rooming house, had visited it at any time—whether, in short, she had come there in order to investigate it, to send Stanislowski there—to plan a murder. Mrs. Radinsky gave her a slow, painstaking look. "Many people come here. Many people inquire for rooms, I don't take everybody, you understand. But, no"—her bright dark eyes searched Laura's face—"no, I don't remember Miss March."

"Ah," the Lieutenant said. "All right, Mrs. Radinsky. Thanks. I'll have to ask you to attend the inquest—merely to answer a few questions. But that will not take place until—well, I'll let you know. And when we find Maria Brown we'll want you to identify her."

The landlady nodded. They went down the steps and got into the police car. The murder, of course, had attracted a certain amount of interest and observation on the part of the neighbors. A woman and a man were standing across the street, watching them with frank interest. The lace curtain of a window in a neighboring house moved surreptitiously. "We'll go back to Miss March's apartment," Peabody told the policeman who was driving the car.

It seemed a long way back. Snow was still falling but in a half-hearted, indecisive way, so the flakes slid from the shining black hood of the car and melted as soon as they touched the pavement. Lights were on everywhere, that dark day, making gleaming tiers of amber and gold high into the gray sky.

At the entrance of the apartment house, Peabody got out, opened the car door politely for her, said, "Thank you, Miss March," and got back into the car again.

Laura took a long breath of the crisp, cold air. The police car started out into the traffic again and she entered the foyer. Curiously, her knees were shaking as she entered the elevator and pressed the button for the ninth floor. The visit to Koska Street had not been difficult really; it was in no sense what could be called police grilling. Yet she felt obscurely frightened and she didn't like Peabody's attempt to discover from the landlady, Mrs. Radinsky, whether or not Laura had ever visited the rooming house before. The elevator stopped.

Charlie and Jonny were in the living room. He rose as she came in. "Well, how was it?"

"Not too bad. They only wanted to know whether anything about the room was different. I suppose they wanted to know whether anyone had entered the room after I left it last night."

"And was there any difference?"

"No, nothing that I could see."

"There were a couple of telephone calls while you were gone, Laura. One was a wrong number, I suppose. At least I answered it and nobody replied. It was—rather odd though because I felt sure somebody was on the line. But then later there was another telephone call. I think I'd better have Jonny stay with me for a while."

"Jonny! What do you mean?"

"The second time the phone rang somebody asked for you, very distinctly, Laura March, and then said something in Polish. I couldn't understand it. But I'm sure two words came out of it. Jonny's name. Jonny Stanislowski. I said, 'Who is it? Speak English,' but whoever it was hung up."

Laura's throat tightened. "But what did he mean?"

"I don't know," Charlie said slowly. "But I'm inclined to think it was either a threat or a warning."

"A threat—" The tightness in her throat made it difficult to speak. "To Jonny?"

"Or a warning," Charlie said. "I don't want to alarm you, Laura, but it did seem to me that there was something threatening about it. In any event, it occurred to me that perhaps it wasn't a good idea for you and Jonny to be here alone. Until this thing is settled, at any rate. You see, Jonny might be—another target."

Laura's thoughts raced. "Was it a woman's voice? Was it Maria Brown?"

"Yes, I thought of her, too. But unless she's got a very flat masculine voice—"

"It is flat! Toneless. Low—"

Charlie debated and shook his head. "No, I think it was a man. It wasn't a good connection. But Jonny—Doris could see to her. Or I can take her. I'll go to the Drake, take a suite and get somebody in to see to Jonny."

Another person, a stranger, an outsider. Charlie would be away

68

at his office; Jonny left alone with a complete stranger. "No," Laura said. "I'd rather have her here."

"As you like, Laura. But I didn't like that telephone call."

Laura didn't like it either. "What did you mean, Charlie, by saying that Jonny might be another target?"

Charlie rose. "I don't know what I meant exactly. Except if this man *was* her father and—oh, I suppose some thought of vengeance or a blood feud or something like that struck me. I'm an old maid. Don't pay any attention to me. I'll tell Peabody about it." He went to the door and picked up his hat and coat. "You're sure, Laura, that you really feel that this man was Stanislowski?"

"Yes."

"Do you want to tell me your reasons?"

"No, I—" There were no real and sound reasons.

Charlie said, "All right. I can see you don't want to talk. If you do decide to send Jonny to me, only let me know and we'll fix it up." He gave her an absent smile which she felt was meant to be cheering and went away. But, she thought, Jonny: another target. Why?

Only then she remembered that the night before the telephone had rung and when she answered there had been no reply. A wrong number, she had thought, as Charlie had thought. But it was curious that that should happen twice within so short a space of time.

Perhaps it was the same person who, at last grown bold, spoke to Charlie. A threat—or a warning.

Suddenly her small apartment, so gay, so warm and charming and up to then so safe, was like an island besieged by an invisible, ominous force.

Matt still did not telephone. The sparse snowflakes diminished and stopped. Heavy gray clouds, tinged with yellow, lowered inexorably down over the city. Again a fog began to come in from the lake.

In the end, when it was nearly time for Jonny to wake from her nap, Laura telephoned herself to Matt's office. His secretary answered. "Oh, Miss March. You're back. Mr. Cosden told me to tell you that he'd like to stop in and see you later this evening. Is that all right?"

"Yes," Laura said. "Thank you."

It was about three when Laura and Jonny went for their usual outing, a walk this time along the lake. They were followed probably from the moment they left the apartment house.

Laura was not aware of the pursuit for some time. They turned north along Lake Shore Drive, Jonny, a bright and happy figure in her little red coat and hat, trudging along beside Laura. It was

69

foggy and cold. Laura turned up the collar of her coat, and the scarf Matt had given her seemed to provide a particularly gentle warmth around her throat.

The sidewalk was damp from the fog. At that time in the afternoon traffic was slower but still cars swished constantly over the wet pavements. Off at the right, across the Drive, the lake was only a blank gray, almost hidden in fog. They passed various pedestrians, the women bundled in furs, walking briskly along. Jonny stopped to speak to a black French poodle scampering gaily at the end of a yellow leash, and his owner smiled and talked to Jonny as Jonny fondled the dog.

Frequently they took one of the several subway passages, long tunnels for pedestrians, which went under Lake Shore Drive and its thudding traffic, and came out at the short strip of park and Oak Street Beach. This time, however, the steps going down into the crossing at Division Street looked dark and rather forbidding. Somehow Laura did not wish to enter the long tunnel with its echoes, its damp concrete walls, its few lights. They went on toward North Avenue, and the entrance to the park. It was as they stopped for a traffic light at Scott Street that she first saw a man trudging along through the fog about two blocks behind them. She glanced idly at him and away as the traffic light changed and they crossed the street. Perhaps halfway down the next block Laura thought suddenly, why, he reminded me of Conrad Stanislowski!

That was odd. In spite of herself she glanced back. The figure was still there, strolling along behind them, still about two blocks away, apparently paying no attention to them. But she then knew why he had reminded her of Conrad Stanislowski for, even at that distance, there was something vaguely foreign in his appearance. Perhaps it was his bulky black overcoat, or his wide-brimmed hat that pulled in a straight line over his face. He was hunched up, his hands in his coat pockets. She couldn't see his face.

But of course, that was it; merely a chance resemblance of clothing had reminded her of the murdered man. They went on, crossed North Avenue and entered the park.

The benches were damp with fog and it was too cold to sit for long, anyway. They took a brisk pace along the winding pathways. Here, perhaps because of the foggy weather, there were not as many pedestrians as usual, fewer people exercising capering dogs, no neatly uniformed nursemaids pushing huge perambulators. Indeed the park itself began to seem oddly unpopulated. Unexpectedly, for no reason, Laura glanced back along the sloping, winding path. The man in the bulky overcoat had entered the park, too. She caught the barest glimpse of him through some bare, brown shrubbery.

And suddenly she thought, Jonny, another target!

They would go over to Lake Shore Drive. They would take a taxi home. She hastened her footsteps and Jonny's. They reached Lake Shore Drive again. A taxi was drifting along the street. Laura signaled it. As she got in she glanced back through the glass. There was no sight of the curiously persistent, curiously ubiquitous walker in the fog.

Had he in fact followed them? They had met other people along the streets, but they passed and went on; they turned and took different ways. The figure in the dark coat had trudged on through the fog, going where they went, pausing apparently when they paused, always just far enough away so she could not see his face. Yet he had not approached them. He had not spoken to them.

It was a short ride back to her apartment house. As they drew up at the entrance, another taxi went slowly past them. Its single passenger was only a dark blur in the shadow of the back seat.

FOURTEEN

Probably it was not the man in the park. Perhaps the man in the park was a policeman in plain clothes, set to watch her. Yet that, too, was rather frightening.

Suki came to greet them, complaining bitterly of their absence and consequent dire neglect of a small, long-legged Siamese kitten. But even with his reproachful welcome and with lights turned on all over the apartment, it did not seem as cheerful and safe as usual. Laura went back to the kitchen and made sure that the kitchen door was bolted. Then, to cheer herself more than anything, to rout a persistent chill little fear that was as vaguely threatening as a man's figure trudging stubbornly behind them, she lighted the wood fire already laid in the tiny fireplace. As the kindling crackled and sparkled, the door buzzer sounded. It was Doris Stanley.

"Laura!" she said. "What a dreadful thing! How could you have let it happen!"

"I don't see how I could have stopped it!" Laura said and heard the snap in her own voice. There was something between her and Doris which from the beginning would have made it fatally easy to quarrel.

Doris was already in the hall and sliding out of her long fur coat, a new coat and a new rosy beige shade of mink; my little Christmas present to myself, Doris had said that fall.

Doris was as always lovely. She was small and slender with a delicate face and pansy brown eyes. Her nose tilted upward delightfully; she had a charming, gentle smile. Her cheeks were now lightly pink from the cold. She wore a black dress so extravagantly simple in the lines and the way it clung to Doris' lovely figure that Laura knew it was a very expensive dress indeed; she wore a small, chic and very expensive black hat over her blond hair. Altogether, Laura thought with mingled admiration and an obscure irritation, Doris could have appeared then and there in any fashion show as a shining example of what the perfectly dressed city woman might wear.

She stripped off white gloves; the bracelets on her small wrists clanked. Doris always wore jewelry. Conrad had heaped jewels and furs upon her, and since his death and she had had control of so much money, she had dipped into it lavishly, herself. A triple string of pearls at her lovely throat was fastened by a large cabochon emerald; her hands with their rosy fingernails flashed with rings. A fragrance like carnations wafted out from her as she dropped her gloves on her coat, and said to Laura, "I don't suppose you could have stopped it, but I don't see why you had to go out to that house and I don't see why you had to take Jonny there. Laura, I want you to tell me all about it. They questioned me last night. Think of it, questioned me! What really happened?. Where is Jonny?"

"I'll give her some hot chocolate. Then we can talk. Go in the living room, Doris. There's a fire."

Ten minutes later, with Jonny contentedly sipping thick hot chocolate for which, perhaps, her stay in Vienna had given her an affection, Laura returned to the living room. Doris was sitting on the sofa; the primrose-yellow of the curtains behind her was scarcely more yellow than the lights the fire struck in her hair.

"Will you have tea, Doris? I can fix it in a moment."

"No, thanks. Matt is coming to dinner and I've only got a few minutes, but I want to talk to you. First, Laura, what about this man? *Was* he Stanislowski?"

All of them ask the same question, Laura thought wearily. She sat down opposite Doris and wished in an odd little feminine layer of her mind that she had changed to a different dress. Her gray suit and white blouse felt like a drab, working-girl's uniform in contrast to Doris' perfumed and jeweled smartness. She said. "Of course he was Stanislowski!"

Doris' gentle brown eyes became rather fixed. She watched Laura for a moment, then opened her suede handbag, got out a gold cigarette case and looked vaguely around for a light. Laura started to rise to get matches for her and again some curious feminine impulse asserted itself. "There are matches on the table, Doris, right beside you."

"Oh, I see. Thanks." Doris lighted the cigarette. "You seem very certain of this man's identity," she said as she maneuvered the cigarette between her pretty lips, softly touched with pink lipstick.

"I've told Matt and the police everything I know, Doris. There's no use in asking me anything else. Matt told you all about it, didn't he?"

"Oh, yes. But I wanted to talk to you myself. Jonny should know whether or not he was her father. Have you questioned her?"

"No. I want to be sure that nothing that happened yesterday has—hurt her."

"Oh, nonsense!" Doris said impatiently. "You and Matt and Charlie all act as if that child is so sensitive! The fact is she's as phlegmatic as a potato. Aren't the police going to question her?"

Jonny was always a little frightened of Doris. There was no real reason for it, unless she felt something of Doris' hidden resentment. Doris had not liked admitting the fact that Jonny was Conrad Stanislowski's child; she had not liked admitting the fact that Jonny had any sort of claim upon the Stanislowski fund. She had tried to conceal her resentment, Laura thought; perhaps Matt's affection for the child accounted for that. She made overtures of friendship—rather few and grudging, but overtures. In Doris' presence, however, Jonny always seemed to withdraw into the cautious stillness which was like a kind of protective coloration.

There was no use in trying to explain that to Doris. Laura said, "Lieutenant Peabody said he would bring an interpreter who would try to talk to Jonny in her own language."

Doris said sharply, "I should think that would be the very first thing they would do. It's so important—his identity, I mean."

There was again something rather fixed and hard in her brown eyes. It sent a tingle of warning through Laura. She said slowly, "Why, yes, it's important. But not so far as the money goes. I mean, all the Stanislowski fund eventually goes to Jonny anyway."

73

Doris started to speak, stopped, bit her pink lower lip and then rose, walked to the fireplace and looked down at the flames. The lovely curves of her figure were outlined sharply in black against the rosy light from the fire. Her hair looked like a shining gold cap. She said softly, over her shoulder, "Well, of course that's to be decided. However"—she turned to look at Laura—"that's not the point right now. It's this murdered man! I don't understand why you didn't phone to me yesterday? Why didn't you phone to anybody? Oh, Matt says that this whoever he was, the murdered man, begged you to keep his arrival a secret, but didn't that strike you as very odd?"

"I believed him," Laura said flatly. Again she had a sense of answering the same questions, except from different people; yet certainly Doris had every right to ask them. "I believed him and I didn't think a few days' silence on my part would do any harm."

"I think it was very wrong of you to take that attitude! No matter what he said I think you ought to have let us know! When was he here, about what time?"

"I don't know exactly. It must have been about four-thirty."

Doris leaned over the fire and carefully shook an ash from her cigarette. "That means you must have got out to the rooming house about—what time would you say?"

"I don't know that either. Not exactly. Something after five, I think."

"And there was nobody in this rooming house?"

"Nobody except, of course, Maria Brown. The woman I met on the steps."

"Matt said that you went to a drug store somewhere in the neighborhood, to phone to him. Where was that?"

"On the corner of Koska Street."

"And you didn't see anybody that you knew, anywhere?"

"No. I'd have told the police." It struck her that Doris was strangely persistent. "Do you mean anybody in particular?"

Doris' slender figure looked suddenly a little rigid. But she shook off more ashes with a casual gesture and turned to face Laura. "How silly! Of course not. I only want to know everything. Why not?" She went over to the chair again, sat down, discovered something that didn't satisfy her about one of her fingernails and examined it minutely. "It does seem to me that you might have seen something that would be, well, evidence against this woman Maria Brown, for instance. The point is"— Doris lifted her brown eyes to look directly at Laura—"the police suspect every one of us. You and me and Charlie. They think it's the Stanislowski money. Of course, it doesn't bother me because I have an alibi; it never occurred to me to be thankful that I was

74

at the dentist's but that's where I was all yesterday afternoon and nobody can say I wasn't. So I've got an alibi. But nevertheless it's not nice! None of us is going to be very comfortable until this thing is settled. If this man *was* Stanislowski, the police think that I and Charlie, and you, my dear, don't forget, had a motive in doing away with him."

"Well, I didn't kill him!"

Doris' slender eyebrows went up; her eyes opened wide like a child's. "I didn't say you did. And if the man was *not* Stanislowski, then of course it has nothing to do with any of us. That's the point. Why are you so sure that it was Stanislowski?"

"Because I think he was!"

"You must have some reason?"

"I believed him," Laura said again. "And Jonny cried."

Doris shrugged lightly. "That means nothing. She could have been crying about anything." Suddenly Doris' soft voice became decisive. "I don't think he was Stanislowski. And it does make a difference about the money."

"But it goes to Jonny—"

"Why are you so determined to give that money to Jonny?"

"Why, because that was Conrad's intention. The will is perfectly clear—"

"Oh, is it?" Doris said suddenly. "I'm not so sure about that."

"Do you mean, Doris, that you intend to oppose Jonny's inheritance?"

"I didn't say that. But I do say that Conrad's will is not at all clear. You assume that that money goes direct to the little girl. All that money! Conrad meant it to go to his nephew. He didn't mean it to go to a child. He didn't even know there was a child."

Laura leaned forward. "Doris, let's get this clear. Are you going to oppose our plan for keeping that money in trust for Jonny?"

Doris gave her a long, queerly thoughtful look. Then she rose and put out her cigarette. Her bracelets glittered. "All that has to go through the courts." She picked up her handbag, slid the gold cigarette case into it and closed it with a decisive little snap. "Oh, I know why you're so interested in Jonny, Laura. I know why you took Jonny in the first place! Obviously she ought to have been put in school but, no, you insisted on bringing her here. I didn't see through it at the time but I do now."

"I took Jonny because I wanted her—"

"I know exactly why you did it and I know exactly why you want Jonny to have that money. You intend to establish yourself as her friend, her guardian, her long-time associate. You intend to fasten upon her the way you fastened upon my husband, Conrad Stanley."

75

FIFTEEN

"That's not true!"

"It is true! Is there any other reason why you should care whether a child like that gets any money or not! I'd see to her all her life; there's no question of that. But why should she have such a large fortune? No, the reason you want her to have all that money is because you intend to profit by it. And that's not all. You've been making a play for Matt ever since you brought that child here."

"Doris, stop it!"

"And I'll tell you this! Matt and I were engaged once, you knew that. We were engaged when I met Conrad. And Matt is still in love with me and I'm in love with him and we're going to be married and there's nothng you can do about it."

She turned, walked into the hall, paused at the mirror to adjust her smart hat, and said, "I don't want you to be hurt, Laura. That's why I'm telling you about Matt and me—although, of course, you must have known. And you knew that Matt would come here to see the child and you'd see him, too! But perhaps I was hasty in saying what I did about the money. You are so set in your opinion about it that I—well, usually when anybody fights for money there's a reason for it."

"The reason is Jonny!"

Doris slid into her coat deliberately, looking at herself in the mirror, adjusting the collar. "You'd have to say that—wouldn't you, darling?"

After she had strolled down the corridor, her high heels clicking lightly, after Laura had closed the door and gone back to the living room and stared for a long time out the window into the gray, heavy sky—even after all that, the traces of Doris' perfume lingered in the room, recalling Doris' presence.

Recalling, too, a stuffy little telephone booth in a drug store away out on the west side, and a fragrance of carnations which had brought Doris' lovely image into Laura's mind.

But Doris herself had not been in the telephone booth. She

76

had been at the dentist's all that afternoon: she had an alibi and, Laura thought rather wryly, as good an alibi as anybody could possibly establish. One, certainly, which the police could easily check. And then she thought with horror: alibis! She had none. She had found the murdered man.

The low sky seemed almost to touch the windows, yet the visibility downward to the street was fairly clear. Pedestrians were trudging along homeward, foreshortened, so they looked like toys. She thought of the persistent walker in the fog. *Had* he followed them? There was nothing definite, nothing tangible about it.

The telephone call which Charlie had reported was definite and tangible; either a warning, he'd said, or a threat.

She wished Matt would come. It was curious, in a way a commentary upon the relationship between Doris and Laura, that she had not told Doris of the man in the Park.

But there had been from the beginning a kind of instinctive antipathy between the two young women—Doris, Conrad's wife, and Laura, who had been so much like a daughter to him. Perhaps Laura had suspected Doris' motive in marrying a man so much older than she; Doris had now made it abundantly clear that she doubted the sincerity of Laura's deep affection for Conrad. It was equally clear that Matt was still in love with Doris; that was not news to Laura. And in a way it was not news that Doris did not intend to give up a third of the Stanislowski fund. She intended to fight for it, not because she needed it, but simply because Doris liked and spent money.

The door buzzer sounded again, Matt's ring, and Jonny and Suki, as if both recognized it, too, came at a gallop along the hall.

Matt's coat and hat were damp from fog; he shook them and put them down. "It's a foul day out. Hi, Jonny! Ouch—" The kitten had swarmed with the aid of needlesharp claws up his trouser leg, and settled on his shoulder. Matt rubbed his leg. Jonny dived her hand into Matt's coat pocket. Matt said, "No presents today, Jonny. I didn't get time. Ah, a fire! Any chance for a drink?"

"I'll get it," Laura said and went to the kitchen. She brought back a tray with Scotch and soda, ice and a glass. Matt dislodged the kitten, poured himself a drink, sat down and stretched out his long legs with a sigh. "The only news there is, is no news. They haven't yet found Maria Brown. And until they find her I don't see what they can do."

"They took me out to Koska Street this morning."

"Why?"

"Lieutenant Peabody questioned me, asked if anything in the room was different. He asked the landlady if she had ever seen me before. She said no, of course. Matt, I think a man followed us in the park this afternoon. And then there were some telephone calls." She told him of the shadowy, persistent walker in the fog.

Matt's face grew hard as he listened. "Could you identify the man?"

"I couldn't see his face. He never approached us or tried to speak to us. Perhaps it was nothing. I'm in a state of mind to jump at a shadow."

"I don't think you'd jump at a shadow. What do you mean by telephone calls?"

She told him of that, too. A wrong number, or at least what she took to be a wrong number, the night before; another that morning while Charlie was there, and then the second telephone call and someone speaking this time, in Polish.

"That doesn't sound like Charlie to get the wind up over something like that. A threat or a warning," Matt said thoughtfully, quoting Charlie's words. "Whatever it was it means something. The point is, who phoned?"

"Matt, it's safe here, isn't it?"

"I think so, Laura," he said slowly. "As safe as it would be anywhere. I'm going to talk to Charlie."

SIXTEEN

She listened while he telephoned to Charlie. When he came back, he looked puzzled. "I don't know what to make of it. Of course, if there *is* some sort of family feud or vengeance back of this murder, it is perfectly possible that Jonny *is*—"

Laura whispered, "Another target."

"No," Matt said quickly. "But—perhaps a motive. The trouble is we don't know why this man was murdered. If he was not Stanislowski, then it has nothing to do with any of us. If he *was* Stanislowski— Well, I'll talk to Peabody about this. So will Charlie. I saw Peabody today but he wasn't very communicative. Laura, don't think too much of the man in the park this afternoon. If he had wanted to—" His eyes went to Jonny. Laura suddenly whispered again. "Do you mean he may have intended to take Jonny?"

"No! But if it happens again, or anything happens that seems odd, call me, call Peabody." He glanced at his watch briefly and sat down again. Laura thought, Doris is waiting.

He stayed, though, lingering over his drink and pouring another, talking mainly of Maria Brown. "The trouble is, she is so inconspicuous. In a city of this size a woman answering her description could disappear forever. And that seems to be what she intends to do. Well"—he looked at his watch again and rose— "I've got to be going. Look here, that girl downstairs at the switchboard—wouldn't she announce callers, if you asked her to?"

"Why, yes. But people as a rule don't stop at the desk."

"I wish there were some way to make sure you would know just who came up here. It seems to me anybody could walk in. I'll tell you, Laura, make sure who it is before you open the door. Not that I think anything is going to happen!"

But she must have given some evidence of the small, swift pulse of alarm that caught her, for unexpectedly he put his arm around her, kissed her cheek lightly and released her. And went to keep his dinner engagement with Doris.

The red glow of the wood fire lost its charm. Jonny and the kitten sat together, suddenly quiet and thoughtful, watching the dying embers. Jonny, who, Matt said, might be a motive for Conrad Stanislowski's murder. Laura went to Jonny and knelt down to put her arm around the sturdy little shoulders. "All right," she said, forcing a note of gaiety into her voice. "Now for supper."

There was another telephone call that night.

That was after Jonny was in bed and asleep. Laura had read the evening papers and the story of Conrad Stanislowski had leapt, not to prominence, but at least to more space; her own name was there, this time. Miss Laura March, who had been a secretary to Conrad Stanley, had found the murdered man—who had claimed to be Conrad Stanislowski, a nephew of Conrad Stanley. It set a kind of seal of authenticity upon what had been nightmarish and unreal, yet real and terrible, too; Laura March, in black and white, like that.

But still the police had not told all they knew. There was nothing said of the Stanley will, although Conrad Stanley's name alone was enough to insure the story a certain prominence. The murdered man had been supposed to have arrived very recently from Poland. The woman, Maria Brown, was still missing; there was again a description of her; the police were combing the city for her because, the account said cautiously, she might have some evidence.

Nothing was said of the telephone call to Laura. Nothing was said of Jonny, for which Laura was grateful. There was, however, in the very brevity of the account a kind of threat, as if Lieutenant Peabody were reserving his ammunition. Manifestly, he had withheld some of the facts.

She put down the papers and lighted a cigarette and the telephone rang and again no one answered.

"Who is this?" she said sharply. *"What do you want?"*

For answer the telephone clicked. She put it down. There were ways of dealing with such things; the police, the telephone company. Matt had told her to let him know, let Peabody know if it happened again.

She would tell him at once. What could he do then and there, that night? Besides, he was with Doris.

She debated for a moment and decided to tell him of it the next day. But her apartment seemed again exposed and lonely, high up in the cloud-laden city, like a target.

She turned on the radio and dance music swirled out into the room; she went back to the kitchen and went through the nightly routine of making hot chocolate for Jonny and hot milk flavored with coffee for herself. She put them as usual in the two thermos bottles, set the empty milk bottles outside the kitchen door in the service hall and went back to the living room. She was restless, as if the telephone call had touched off a deep uneasiness. She had left the radio turned on and the dance music threw its spell around her; it suggested gaiety, lights, voices, dancing; she listened, caught by the golden net of a dream.

The little French clock on the mantel chimed eleven. She turned off the radio and went to the black, glittering windows, seeing her reflection on them. A slender figure in gray skirt and white blouse.

She looked at her image with sudden disapproval; nothing glamorous, nothing chic and elegant about her, only Laura March, her face white, and her gray eyes deeply shadowed in that reflection. Her level dark eyebrows and the slender line of her cheek gave her a faint resemblance to the picture of Peter March in her bedroom.

She approached herself in the shifting reflection, leaned so near that it dissolved except for a shadowy outline, and looked down through the night to Lake Shore Drive. The traffic had dwindled to only an occasional sweep of headlights along it. Street lights glimmered in the long bright curve out toward the Navy pier. The pavement looked wet and slippery and desolate. The lake was black now, invisible in the blackness of the night. She wanted to shut out the night and its unspoken threat. She drew the draperies across the windows with a quick swish of yellow silk.

Someone was in the apartment.

The knowledge seeped out of nowhere. Her hand clutched a fold of yellow silk. Then she knew why she was listening with every nerve. There had been some sound.

The curtains had swished, rustling, across the window. And immediately there had been a sound from somewhere in the quiet apartment. It was as if a door had very softly closed.

Jonny, of course!

She went back quickly to Jonny's door and opened it cautiously. But Jonny hadn't awakened; she was still in bed, still asleep. Suki was sitting up on the pillow, his black ears alert, his eyes reflecting the streak of light from the hall. Laura closed the bedroom door again softly, and it was exactly that small click she had heard.

Doors don't open and close themselves. She ran into the kitchen.

No one was there. The kitchen door was closed; she had set out the milk bottles and closed the door. She hadn't bolted it, she thought suddenly. It wasn't her habit to bolt the door. Perhaps it hadn't quite locked.

Perhaps it had swung itself open. And then closed itself again?

There were always wandering currents of air seeping through the innumerable corridors of a big apartment house. Still it seemed an odd feat, even for a very whimsical draft.

But the kitchen was obviously bare of an intruder; so was the little niche called a dining room adjoining it, with its ruffled white curtains, its small table and chairs. There was no place for anyone to hide there. She went to her bedroom, she opened closet doors, her heart pounding as she forced herself to thrust clothes aside. She did not stop until there was scarcely a square inch of the rooms she had not searched.

Gradually her heart resumed a more normal pace. Nobody had entered the apartment. Nobody could enter it now.

She took the two thermos bottles to her room and put them on the bedside table. Again she left the door to Jonny's room and the door to her bedroom open so she would hear the child if she stirred during the night.

She would hear anything else, too.

There was in fact nothing to hear except the regular low moan of the foghorn, so accustomed a sound that to well-trained and faithful Chicago ears it is like a lullaby.

Morning was brighter, with the sun struggling in golden patches through gray clouds. It was colder, too, so Laura, waking at the same time that Jonny came sleepily into the room, sprang out of bed to close the window and turn on radiators. She and Jonny huddled themselves in bathrobes as they opened the thermos bottles. That morning though, hot milk flavored with coffee did not strike Laura as adequate for the day almost certainly to come; she wanted real coffee, hot and very strong. She gathered her white wool bathrobe around her and she and Jonny and the kitten all went to the kitchen. Again breakfast was a lively affair on the part of Jonny and the kitten, and when later, Laura started to pour out the contents of her thermos, the kitten leaped up on the table beside her and expressed his interest in the hot milk in no uncertain terms.

"You'll get your breakfast, Suki," Laura said. "You won't like this. It's got coffee in it." But the kitten said emphatically that he wanted to taste it, so she poured a little in a saucer. Suki dived upon it voraciously, and Laura washed out the thermos bottles while Jonny ate her oatmeal. Suki, however, lapped only a little; then apparently exhausted with his self-appointed morning chore of rousing Jonny and Laura, he ignored his breakfast, curled up on a chair and went to sleep. He slept through all the morning routine, the tiny tip of a pink tongue showing below his sooty nose.

That morning on an impulse Laura ordered the Christmas tree; it was early but its trimming would divert Jonny—and perhaps herself. The tree, she was told, could be delivered that day.

There was that morning a series of telephone calls, none of them threatening and anonymous. Matt telephoned first.

"Everything all right?" he said.

"Y—yes. There was another of those phone calls." She told him what there was to tell.

"It's a damn queer thing," he said slowly. "No point to it. At least, none that I can see. I'll tell Peabody about it. Everything else all right?"

She had fancied the night before that someone had entered the apartment; it was only fancy. She said, "Yes, all right."

"Look here, if you take Jonny out today, stay with other people, will you? Don't go to the park."

She wouldn't, she told him; and yes, she and Jonny would be at home by late afternoon when he said he'd like to come in to see them.

She had barely put down the telephone when it rang again. She was beginning to feel a prickling awareness of the telephone, like dread; she picked it up and answered quickly before fear could fasten its hold upon her. This time it was the doctor, Dr. Stevens, polite, kind, asking if he could be of any help. He'd meant to call her before; he'd been busy; her discovery of the murdered man must have been shocking. "I gather the inquest is to be held off

82

for a few days, pending identification of the man," he said "He told you he was the little girl's father, didn't he? Well, the police will clear it up. Anything I can do for you? No, don't apologize, my dear; you were quite right in calling me."

And then, as people read the morning papers and saw her name in connection with the account of the murder, there were other telephone calls—old Laura Slakely, her godmother, who lived in the country near Libertyville, and was shocked, sorry, and insisted that Laura come immediately to stay with her. "I'll send a car for you. Bring the little girl—what do you call her?—Jonny. But, my dear child, your mother wouldn't hear of you staying in that apartment alone! You must come out here at once!"

She was with difficulty persuaded that it was better for Laura to remain in town. "There's no danger at all," Laura said and hoped she was right. And then Ellen Stone, a friend from early school days telephoned, and Marie Field and Joan Cavert, all three of them shocked, kind, offering to help if there was any way to help—and, quite naturally, excited and intensely curious. One of her former employers, the senior partner in the firm, telephoned, too. "What's all this, Laura? What's all this? Now see here, if you need any of us—" He was hurried, brisk, but like Dr. Stevens, sensible and matter-of-fact, and all of it bolstered up her spirits. But then Lieutenant Peabody arrived and brought with him an interpreter, whom he introduced politely.

"I think we must question the child now, Miss March. I let a little time elapse; it seemed advisable. But we can't wait any longer."

There was nothing to do but agree. And at the end of a patient and long hour of questioning, they still knew nothing.

The interpreter, a stolid, sturdy little man in a shabby brown suit, was patient and gentle with Jonny; Peabody suggested questions and he put them into Polish, but Jonny only shrank against Laura, occasionally shook her head and steadfastly refused to reply. Her face was still and wary; her blue eyes perfectly—purposefully—blank. In the end, the interpreter turned to Peabody with a hopeless shrug. "I am sure she understands me."

Laura put her arm around Jonny; the child was trembling. She said, "Isn't that enough?"

"The question is why doesn't she answer?" Peabody said dreamily.

The interpreter looked at him and again shrugged. "I am sorry, Lieutenant. I've tried every way I know. I asked her if she had seen her father lately. I asked her what her father looked like. I've asked her everything and—you can see for yourself. I think it frightens her."

"Yes," the Lieutenant said, "I think you're right. And that's odd." He got to his feet. "Well, thank you." He paid the interpreter, who took the money in a businesslike way, then bowed to Jonny and said something in Polish at which Jonny permitted herself a faint, cautious smile. He said to Peabody, "I told her to be a good little girl, that Christmas was coming and St. Nicholas is nice to good little girls at Christmas."

Plainly, he felt sorry for the child. Laura said, "Thank you," and the interpreter bowed politely to her, too, and went away.

"Now then," the Lieutenant said, "these telephone calls you say you've had. Tell me all about them again."

There was, of course, not much to tell, and she was not at all sure that he believed her brief account.

He said thoughtfully, "Of course, we can have these calls traced but that involves practically a twenty-four-hour service at the switchboard. Even then it is difficult, particularly if the calls are made from a pay telephone. Stedman seems to feel that in the telephone call that came while he was here, I mean when somebody spoke to him, there was an element of threat. Did you feel that?"

"Nobody spoke to me. But that's what is frightening."

"Ah," Lieutenant Peabody said. "Whoever called spoke to him but refuses to speak to you. Of course that might suggest that that one call was made by a different person. Well, I'll see what I can do." He looked at Jonny and unexpectedly patted her head. "It's all right my dear. Don't be frightened, it's all right." He glanced at Laura. "I hope she understood that."

Jonny replied by suddenly and shyly smiling at Lieutenant Peabody.

SEVENTEEN

So that was that, Laura thought, after he'd gone; they had questioned Jonny and Jonny had told them nothing. Yet, as Peabody had said, that in itself was rather queer. If Stanislowski had been Jonny's father, why shouldn't she have said, "Yes, I saw my father"? Why had she refused to answer any questions put to her in Polish?

Perhaps Jonny *had* sensed something, something incomprehensible yet frightening. Perhaps her instinctive childish reaction was to take refuge in silence.

She must get Jonny outdoors; she must divert her somehow with some special little treat. Matt had said, go where there are people.

Laura searched the moving picture columns of the newspaper. The day cleared as it wore on, so the sun was out fully by noon, bright and sparkling on the winter lake. They had lunch. Jonny took her nap. The kitten still slept. Laura thought, but vaguely, how long the kitten is sleeping. Early in the afternoon Doris telephoned.

"Have they questioned Jonny yet?"

"Yes."

"What did she say?"

"Nothing."

"Nothing! *What do you mean?*"

"She wouldn't reply at all. She just stood close against me and shook her head."

There was a silence. "Well," Doris said at last, "there must be some way to get her to talk. What are you doing this afternoon?"

"I thought I'd take Jonny to the movies. There's a Disney film."

"I'm coming, too," Doris said flatly. "I'll pick you up in the car at two."

There was nothing to do but agree. Jonny awoke, and in the little rush of getting ready to go it did not strike Laura as unusual that the kitten did not, as was his custom, accompany them to the door with strongly disapproving comments. She and Jonny were standing at the entrance of the apartment house when Doris' big car swept elegantly up and stopped and the chauffeur sprang out to open the door for them.

Doris was wrapped in her pale beige mink, subtly perfumed, and as perfectly dressed as if she were going to a cocktail party. Jonny sat between Doris and Laura. The car purred powerfully out into the traffic. And the bright and sunny day lifted Laura's spirits. It was a typical Chicago winter day, charged with a contagious kind of sparkle and color.

They drew up at the movie. Immediately and magically they entered an enchanted land. But when the picture was over and they went out again into the street, Laura found herself suddenly searching through the crowds of people, searching for a man in a dark overcoat, bulky and awkward, with a hat pulled over his eyes, and an indistinguishable face. If there was such a man she did not see him. They went through the flooding crowds from the movie, past the laden shoppers along the streets, to the car which stood directly at the door waiting for them, loftily ignoring the protesting squawks of taxis behind it.

Inside the car it was safe, and quiet except for the powerful rush and roar of the Loop, the shrill two-noted whistles of the traffic policemen. It was already dusk, but a sparkling dusk with lights shining brightly from the great buildings along Michigan Boulevard. The traffic was heavy and slow. It was almost dark when the car deposited Jonny and Laura at the apartment house. Doris had had enough of the afternoon and she had had enough of Jonny and Laura's company. She said good night, quickly and impatiently, and the car moved away before Jonny and Laura had reached the door of the foyer. Laura stopped this time to pick up mail; there were no telephone messages. The girl at the switchboard eyed her curiously as she gave it to her; clearly she had read the papers.

Matt had not arrived; he had left no message; he was not waiting in the foyer or lounging in the window of the corridor outside Laura's apartment. She closed the door of her apartment and, an unpleasant and recent habit, bolted it. Jonny had taken off her red coat and hat, put them neatly away, and gone back to her bedroom, calling Suki, and Laura was absently looking at herself in the mirror, smoothing her hair, when the door buzzer sounded sharply.

Because she was expecting Matt she went to the door, and then, her hand on the latch, remembered his warning. She called through the door, "Who is it?"

A feminine voice replied. It's Doris, Laura thought, and opened the door, too quickly, for the woman, Maria Brown, stood outside.

She wore the same brown coat and black beret pulled over a short fluff of dark hair. Her face was pale; again she wore no lipstick. Without knowing it Laura made a swift move to close the door but Maria Brown was quicker. She slid purposefully into the hall. She closed the door firmly behind her. She said, "Is the child here?"

Her words were strongly accented; her voice flat and toneless; it was the voice of the woman on the telephone, there was no doubt of that. It was the way she had spoken to them, briefly, on the steps of the house in Koska Street. The light on the hall table cast a glow upward into her face. This time Laura scrutinized it, telling herself she must remember details, and this time it seemed to Laura there was something Slavic in her broad cheekbones and sallow skin. She took a step nearer Laura. "Answer me. Is the child here?"

Jonny. She ought not to have opened the door. It was too late to think of that.

She must keep the woman from seeing Jonny. She must also try to hold her, try to find out where she was staying, try to find out something about her. How? The telephone stood five feet away. Could she reach it?

The woman's hands, in shabby black gloves, clutched her handbag purposefully, and she stared at Laura. And suddenly Laura thought, suppose Maria Brown has a gun in that black handbag. She knew that Laura could identify her; she knew that Laura had seen her as she escaped the house on Koska Street, and murder.

For the first time a sense of personal danger caught at Laura. Maria Brown moistened her pale lips. "Why don't you answer me?"

"Where have you been?" Laura cried. "Where did you go? Why did you telephone to me?"

Maria Brown stared at Laura with fixed, unfathomable eyes and set her pale lips firmly. Her face had strongly marked features, deeply lined, yet nevertheless it was a young face. Talk to her, Laura thought, talk to her—and try to reach the telephone. She hoped that Jonny, attracted by voices, would not come running down the hall. She grasped for words. "You phoned to me, didn't you? Did he tell you to send for me? Where did you go? The police are looking for you." That was a mistake; she added hurriedly, "They think you may have evidence. Something you—you saw or—" Her stammering words fell flat, came to a full stop as Maria Brown's gaze did not waver, and certainly revealed nothing.

Finally the woman moistened her lips, and said tonelessly, "I know the police are looking for me. I read the newspapers. They will never find me. I have had experience. I know how to hide. The police—what are they doing? They search for me; I read that. But that is all. There is too little in the paper. It is too short. There are other lines of—of inquiry. That is kept secret. What do they believe? What do they suspect? Tell me—"

"I—I don't know."

Marie Brown did not believe her; her dark eyes searched Laura's with frank skepticism. Talk to her, Laura thought desperately; she wished that Matt would come; he would know what to do. Be diplomatic, she thought; be cautious. "If you *are* a witness, Miss Brown, if you have any evidence, why don't you tell the police? They won't hurt you. They won't do anything to you. Don't be afraid."

"Bah!" Maria Brown said. "The secret police! I know them. They'll never find me." Scorn flashed in her face. And then she saw Laura's slight instinct of movement toward the telephone.

"Do not touch the telephone! Do not try to call the police. I

87

tell you I will not—" Her stocky body moved swiftly. She clamped one hand down hard on the telephone.

She must not show fear; try to reason, Laura thought, swiftly. And keep that implacable strong figure in the hall, away from Jonny. Somehow she made her voice steady and quiet. "You can't hide forever. It's better to come forward now and tell them if there's anything you know. They think you may be a witness. He was alive when you telephoned to me, wasn't he? And then he died—"

Jonny's fluty high voice called suddenly and in distress from the kitchen. "Laura—Suki!"

The woman's head jerked toward the kitchen, and Laura seized her by the wrist. Maria Brown pulled away with one hard motion, swung around to the door, flung it open and was gone, her heels thudding hard down the corridor.

By the time Laura reached the door, Maria Brown had already got to the elevator. It still stood at that floor, the door open, and Maria Brown slid into it and out of sight. Laura could see only her gloved hand pushing the signal button. The door of the elevator shut irrevocably almost in Laura's face. And from the doorway of her own apartment Jonny wailed, *"Laura!"* A flood of Polish words followed, incomprehensible except in their tone of fright and distress. Laura ran back. Jonny held the kitten in her hands, and something was very wrong with the kitten. His little body was limp, his eyes blue slits, his mouth slack and half open.

Stop the woman, Maria Brown! How? Call the police! Call Matt—but first do something about the kitten.

She managed to look in the classified advertisements of the telephone book and find a nearby veterinarian. She dialed his number and told him about the kitten. She listened to his directions.

"Sounds as if the kitten has been accidentally drugged," he said. "Give him some very strong coffee. Pour it by the teaspoonful, into his cheek. He'll swallow some of it. If he doesn't start to come out of it in a few minutes, let me know. I'll come."

She telephoned to Matt while she was making coffee, and Jonny, holding the kitten anxiously, stood beside her.

"Maria Brown!" Matt shouted. "Hold everything. I'll be there as soon as I can make it!"

Somehow Laura contrived to reassure Jonny. Somehow she steadied her hands and drew the kitten's little lips away and got a few drops of coffee into his cheek. His heart was beating slowly, but beating. She tried another teaspoonful of coffee. She stroked his throat gently. At last there was a faint swallowing motion. It seemed hours; it was in fact twenty minutes before the kitten sputtered, shook his head and opened his eyes to give them a blue dazed look. By the time Matt arrived he was on his feet wobbly and uncertain.

It was like Matt to take time to lift the kitten in his hands, to examine him, to comfort Jonny, to tell her the kitten was all right. He was all right, or about to be; he achieved a weak and hoarse purr as Matt stroked his throat.

And then Matt questioned Laura swiftly and telephoned to Lieutenant Peabody Apparently Lieutenant Peabody was either angry or skeptical, or both. Matt said, "Well, that's the way it happened. She gave no warning of it. She just arrived. . . . Miss March tried to question her.   No, the woman wouldn't answer. The only thing she asked about was Jonny 'Is the child here?' . . . She asked what the police were doing. She said you'd never find her.   She said the secret police and she said she knew how to hide, so it looks as if she's had experience, in Poland perhaps or—well, that's what she said! . . . Well, then she heard Jonny's voice and Miss March caught her arm, she thought she might have a gun She got away. . . . There was no way to stop her, Lieutenant !   All right "

He hung up, his face hard and white.

"He doesn't believe it," Laura said.

Matt hesitated for a moment. Then he said, "There's a girl at the switchboard downstairs How do you ring her?"

There was a house number. Laura gave it to him.

"Hello," said Matt, "hello. I'm calling for Miss March. I wonder if you happened to notice a woman in the lobby, a short time ago. She was dark and short. She wore a brown coat and a black beret. I see, thank you." He put down the telephone.

"She didn't see her," Laura said.

Matt shook his head. "She said she was busy. And, of course, this is a busy time of day with lots of people coming and going and lots of telephone calls. I wish she had seen her."

"Lieutenant Peabody will not believe me?"

"He'll have to believe you," Matt said and looked at Jonny and the kitten. "Now then, what's the vet's number?"

Again Laura listened while he talked to the veterinarian He turned at last from the telephone.

"He says the kitten was drugged. Says it was a kind of sedative, very strong, sleeping capsules, for instance."

"But I have nothing of the kind, Matt ! There's nothing he could have got !"

"What did he have to drink that was different? Who gave it to him? Has anyone fed him except you?"

"No, of course not. Oh, sometimes Jonny gives him a little milk. This morning he had his usual breakfast, some cat food, fishy I threw out the can There s nothing in that, that could hurt him. He lapped a little of the milk and coffee from the thermos. You know, Jonny has chocolate from one thermos and I have a kind of cafe au lait from another early in the morning—"

"Yes 1 know," Matt said He hesitated. "Did you drink the rest of it

"No. I didn't want milk this morning. I wanted real coffee—"

"Was there anything else at all that the kitten could have eaten?" There was something odd in his voice. something icy and angry in his eyes.

Laura said slowly. "Jonny gave him some cream from her oatmeal."

"Jonny had the rest of the cream on her oatmeal, right? And there's nothing the matter with her. You didn't drink any of the milk and coffee from the thermos— Where's the thermos?"

"I washed it. That and the saucer the kitten drank from but I—" A strange and terrible speculation leaped from nowhere, stood clear and unavoidable.

EIGHTEEN

Matt was already aware of it; it was in his face, in his questions, but he didn't know of a door which had closed at a time when two thermos bottles stood on the kitchen table. He said quickly, "What is it. Laura? What—"

"Last night I thought someone was here—I heard something—

She told him of it. aware of the icy anger gathering in his face As if to conceal it, so as not to alarm her, he turned abruptly away, went into the living room, walked the length of it, stood at the window for a moment. and then came back. He paused to stroke Suki; he said, "He's all right now, Jonny." The kitten lifted blue eyes, and purred and snuggled against Jonny's shoulder.

"He's going to make it," Matt said. He sat down in one of the lounge chairs and stretched his long legs out in his habitual posture and stared at the rug. "Now, let me get this straight, Laura. That's all you heard? Just the sound of the door closing? What time was that?"

"I don't know. About eleven, I think. It seemed late I was just about to go to bed."

"You hadn't heard any other sound in the apartment?"

"No, nothing. It doesn't seem possible that anybody entered the apartment."

"Was anything disturbed? Anything—taken?"

"No, nothing. Not so far as I know."

He rose without a word and went out to the kitchen. Laura followed; he was experimenting with the kitchen door, opening and closing it, working the lock. "You'd better keep this bolted Night latches are very easy to open. A piece of celluloid, a thin knife. Keep it bolted. Keep the chain on." He put the chain across the door, and came back again to the telephone.

"What are you going to do?"

"Report this to Peabody."

This time Peabody seemed frankly skeptical, and impatient. "No," Matt said. "She didn't see anybody in the apartment last night. She heard a door close but the thermos was on the kitchen table then. You'd believe it if you'd seen the kitten! The vet says he was heavily drugged. Obviously that was intended for Miss March, not for Jonny. The other thermos held chocolate in it. Anybody would guess that milk flavored with coffee was meant for Miss March and the chocolate for the child. It would be a logical guess. . . . No, she washed the thermos and saucer. . . . No, there's no proof! But it happened and it shows that somebody wanted to—" Matt checked himself, with a glance at Laura, listened for a time and then said shortly, "All right," and hung up.

Laura said, "He didn't believe that either!"

"He's going to talk to you about it. Look here, Laura. I don't want to frighten you. But—"

"I know," Laura said. It was a nightmare; there was no reality about it; yet, as in a confused and yet terrifying dream, a fancied voice may speak words that seem clear and significant, those words emerged. "It was meant for me."

"If it was like that," Matt said, "then there's got to be a reason for it. It would be easy enough for anybody to get in that kitchen door and put stuff in the thermos bottle. It would be the logical guess that the thermos with coffee in it was for you, and the chocolate was for Jonny. Laura, is there anything that you haven't told the police that would give them an idea as to the murderer?"

Murder, Laura thought—and attempted murder. But murder

91

was for the newspapers, for other people. It had nothing to do with her! Yet murder had touched her when Conrad Stanislowski had come to her apartment. She had brushed its skirts when she entered the rooming house and found Conrad Stanislowski in that bare, brightly lighted little room.

"No," she said. "No. I've told the police everything that happened. There's no reason—there's *no* reason why anybody would—would—" murder me, she thought incredulously; murder *me!*

"You'll have to accept the fact that it happened, Laura. If the small amount that the kitten lapped was enough to put him asleep for the day, there must have been a pretty big amount of it in the thermos."

Even in the pleasant, orderly room, a kind of cold and terrible disorder seemed to make itself manifest, intangibly, seeping from somewhere outside like a chill little wind. That was fear.

She took a long breath. "There is nothing I know that threatens anybody, Matt! Nothing!"

He began to pace up and down the room, restlessly, hands thrust in his pockets. "Could there be then something you know and—and don't realize that you know? That's possible, isn't it? Something which, put with something else perhaps, would add up dangerously to the murderer."

Laura's thoughts traveled again an all too familiar path, familiar and in its way clearly outlined, yet it was like a path winding amid dark and treacherous undergrowth. "No," she said. "No."

Matt stopped at the window, which now reflected the room with its soft gray and clear yellows, the glittering glass walls of the French clock, Laura herself, erect and white, against the green armchair, watching him. He said, over his shoulder, "Since Conrad did not die when he was stabbed, and apparently the murderer thought he was dead and left him for dead—that is, assuming that the murderer was not Maria Brown—then the murderer might get a terrific jolt when he learned that not only you, but Maria Brown, had actually been in the rooming house. Maria Brown must have had some conversation with him. Again assuming that she is not the murderer, the murderer might jump to the conclusion that Conrad Stanislowski had also talked to you before he died. And what would be more likely, if that had happened, than to tell you who stabbed him!"

"He didn't. If he had, I'd tell the police. Whoever murdered him would know that I would tell the police!"

Matt pulled the yellow curtains across the windows and came back to lean one elbow on the mantel. "The point is we can't let it happen again. I'll get Peabody to give you police guard."

"Oh, no! I'll keep the doors bolted after this! '

"Darling," he said in an odd voice, half gentle half stern "you opened the door for Maria Brown "

She could feel the quick flush in her cheeks "I thought it might be Doris. It was stupid—"

Matt took three strides to her and put his hand under her chin, tilting up her face so she met his eyes directly "Don't do it again. I—" He stopped "Well, just don't do it again " He took his hand from her chin, lighted a cigarette and sat down, his eyes suddenly very blue—and altogether enigmatic.

Laura said, still feeling the warm pressure of his hand around her chin, absurdly confused by it and hoping he did not observe her confusion, "I've been warned If anybody really wants to get in, I can stop it. I'll be careful—'

Matt looked at her for a long moment Then he said abruptly, "This woman, Maria Brown, knew your address. Of course she could have looked it up in the phone book She managed to get up here without being seen by the switchboard girl, but then, of course, that wouldn t be hard Certainly she got away in a hurry. She's hiding and she intends to stay hidden. so she's afraid of the police. Her reason for coming here apparently was to find out certainly whether or not Jonny is here So it comes back to the business of Jonny somehow being a—a motive, a focus, for this whole affair. Laura, this time you had a good look at the Brown woman. Describe her, will you?"

Laura did so, in detail. her broad face with a trace of the Slavic in her cheekbones. dark eyes in which scorn had flickered when Laura spoke of the police Her pale firm mouth, the strength of the hand which had clamped down on the telephone, her purposeful movements. her implacable determined manner.

"How about her voice?" Matt said "Are you still sure she telephoned to you?"

"Yes. She has an odd voice, flat, toneless, rather husky."

Matt said, so gravely that it seemed a very important question, "Were you frightened?"

"Yes. I thought she might have a gun—"

"I mean were you—oh, instinctively frightened. with your nerves, not your reasoning process?"

"Oh. You mean because she murdered him—"

"If she did," Matt said shortly.

Laura thought back to that brief interview "Yes. I was fright-ened. Yet I had to talk to her, try to reach the phone I wished you were here. I wished you would come. You'd have known what to do."

The flicker of a grin touched Matt's mouth "Don't rate me too high. I can't think of anything I'd have done that you didn't do.

93

Except I might have managed to hang onto her. Perhaps not. She sounds a little violent."

"No," Laura said slowly, "there was nothing hysterical or emotional about her. It was all cut and dried. As if she had planned every word. As if she knew exactly what she was doing."

"Well, that's not good either," Matt said. "Did she see Jonny?"

"No, she only heard her voice. That's when I caught her by the wrist and she pulled away and left."

"You say she looked young? How young?"

"In her thirties I think."

Matt eyed her for a moment. "I wonder if she was Conrad's wife."

"His wife! But she's dead! Conrad told me."

"Did he say that exactly?"

He hadn't, of course. "I thought that's what he meant. He started to speak of his wife. He said, 'I married—' and then he stopped and said, 'I was left to see to the child'—something like that."

"Perhaps that's literally what he meant."

Again Matt rose and began to pace around the room, circling the sofa and chairs, his dark head bent thoughtfully. "Perhaps that's exactly what he meant. Perhaps his wife did leave him, and she left Jonny, who would have been a baby at the time. Suppose she got to Chicago, heaven knows how. Suppose Conrad knew her address and went to the rooming house because she was there. He as good as told you that there was something he wanted to do, something he had to do, before he could come forward openly and present his credentials, make himself known to all of us and claim Jonny and of course the money. Perhaps the thing that he had to do, or settle, concerned this woman, his wife. And she killed him."

"But she phoned to me for help! She asked me to bring a doctor!"

"And then he died and she ran away. Look at it this way, Laura. If Maria Brown was his wife, if she had left Conrad and deserted her baby, she'd have had to be certainly a ruthless woman. If she had quarreled so desperately with Conrad that she'd leave her baby—yes, she might have the cruelty and ruthlessness to kill him. And she may have had a pretty solid motive."

He was talking now, Laura thought, like a lawyer, concisely, analytically, assembling his case. He stood facing her, hands in his pockets, his face intent. "Suppose he met her and told her of the will! As a matter of fact they must have been in communication, somehow, if he knew her address. So suppose she knew of the will. Suppose she decided to kill Conrad and escape, then later she intended to come forward and establish her claim to Jonny and the money. Certainly if she's Jonny's mother, she would have every reason to expect some of the money to go directly to her after Conrad's death. Certainly she would be the obvious guardian for Jonny."

"Jonny's mother. Oh, *no*, Matt!"

"She left Jonny when she was a baby."

"But she—she did phone to me for help."

"She could have phoned to you after stabbing Conrad, or even before, for that matter, with the intention of trying to establish her own innocence, or to tell some story about someone else killing Conrad, and that she tried to help him and phoned to you. Oh, there could be a dozen twisted reasons for it. Murder is a twisted, stupid affair; a murderer is innately stupid, twisted, unaccountable by reasonable and normal standards. Then after she phoned perhaps she changed her mind. Oh, I realize that all this is only supposition. But there's a kind of logic about it!"

He sat down, with a kind of dissatisfied plunge, in the chair near her. "The fact is, of course, there's no way of knowing exactly why she phoned to you. But we do know that she was in the rooming house with Conrad. We do know she was escaping when you reached the steps. So she could not have expected you to get there so soon, and she was trying to get away before you came."

"But she said, 'Go away.'"

"And she said, 'I shouldn't have done it.' Perhaps she meant exactly that! Perhaps she regretted it." Matt stared at the rug, lost in surmise, and Laura thought of the moment on the steps in Koska Street and, perhaps, a murderer almost literally red-handed, within moments of murder—in the dusk, above a street deserted except for the taxi driver. She thought of Maria Brown's drawn, pallid face in the dim light and the way her dark eyes fixed themselves upon Jonny.

Matt said slowly, as if presenting a case to himself as judge, "She·may seem unemotional and hard now. Certainly she would have to be hard. But she couldn't have simply killed a man and gone coolly away. She must have vacillated a little, changed her mind, got in a flurry, although"—he shook his head—"she doesn't sound like that kind of woman either. Yet all this is only supposition. Nothing much to go on except she is trying to find Jonny. So there's some reason for that."

"Suppose he was murdered for—oh, revenge, something like that."

"You mean a blood feud, extending to Jonny. How did Peabody come out with the interpreter and Jonny?"

"He didn't come out at all," Laura told him wearily. "He was here this morning. You knew that."

Matt nodded. "Peabody told me he intended to question her. I take it Jonny wouldn't talk?"

"No. The man spoke Polish. He was really very gentle. But Jonny wouldn't say a word. They had to give up. But I don't think Lieutenant Peabody feels they can give much weight to a child's testimony anyway."

"It's important all the same. See here, Laura—let's try it ourselves. Where's the Polish dictionary?"

They questioned Jonny, the kitten listening with alert black ears, Matt with a Polish dictionary beside him doggedly looking up words, and Jonny on his knees chuckling at his labored pronunciation—and giving them no information whatever. When Matt contrived a labored sentence *"Ty widzisz ojciec wczoraj"*— "you see father yesterday," she laughed. *"Nie, nie!"* She sought for English words. "You—say—*funny*—"

"It wasn't yesterday," Laura said, "it was the day before."

Matt gave her a disgruntled look. "How am I going to say day before yesterday? Yesterday is good enough so long as I get the word father across."

He studied the bristling consonants and tried again. This time there was undoubtedly a flash of comprehension in Jonny's blue eyes, which then went perfectly blank. *"Nie,"* she said. *"Nie."* And suddenly put her arms around Matt's neck and hugged him and hid her face against his shoulder.

Matt gave Laura the same hopeless look the interpreter had given Peabody over the child's brown head. "She understands all right."

"Why doesn't she answer you?"

"Perhaps she was taught not to," he said slowly. "Conrad must have been out of sympathy with the party in control in Poland for some time. Perhaps there were times when he had to make sure that if anybody questioned her about him, any question at all, she would shut up like a little clam. Refuse to say anything. How can we know, how can we guess the kind of life a man in Conrad Stanislowski's position had to live? Certainly he told you, and I believe it, that he had been making plans to get Jonny out of the country and then escape himself. He must have felt that there was danger every time somebody knocked at the door. Danger with every breath he drew. Yes, Jonny would have been a danger to him unless he taught her not to reply to any question at all, no matter what it was. Even a child can hear and see things. Even a child can be ruthlessly questioned. Well—that's that."

He gave Jonny a hug and put her down. "All right, no more talk."

Jonny waited a moment, looking up at him earnestly. Then she put her hand in an odd, almost apologetic gesture upon his face, leaned forward confidingly and kissed his cheek. It was an infinitely touching little gesture. *"Dobre,"* she said gently. "Good." She gathered up Suki then and ran out of the room.

Matt said, "That ˙settles it. She knows exactly what I was trying to ask her. And she's not going to say a word, not anything at all concerning her father. I think even the Polish language frightens her a little. It puts her on guard. Conrad trained her not to speak, not to answer questions. There's no other explanation for it. He must have been terrified after he made up his mind to escape. Terrified for himself and terrified for Jonny. Yes, he'd fix it so nobody could get anything out of Jonny."

"Matt, if Conrad *was* her father, all that fund goes directly to Jonny. Doesn't it?"

"There's a lot of things to check up on. We'll have to prove he was her father. It'll all take time."

"But whether he arrived here in America, or didn't arrive, we had planned for the fund to go to Jonny."

"That was our idea, yes." His eyes were sharp and intent. "Has anybody objected to that?"

Laura said slowly, "I don't think Doris wants her to have it."

NINETEEN

"Oh." Matt's face closed in upon itself.

Laura said, "But if this man was her father, Jonny would inherit all the fund automatically from him, wouldn't she? I mean—unless Maria Brown is her mother—"

"That would complicate things, certainly. But aside from that, if the man was Conrad Stanislowski and if he died intestate, yes, Jonny would inherit directly. The way things are, of course there'll be some red tape to unwind."

Laura hesitated, aware of his closed-in, uncommunicative face, aware, too, that she was treading on delicate ground. She said carefully, "Has Doris told you how she feels about the money?"

Matt replied promptly. "Not in so many words, no. I can't say she was overjoyed about finding Jonny and bringing her here. But

Doris has got plenty of money, or at least she did have." He caught himself up shortly.

Laura said, "She *did* have! What do you mean?"

"Nothing. Really, nothing, Laura. At least nothing of importance. Don't forget," he said, with a flicker of laughter in his eyes, "she's my client. But I assure you she doesn't need the Stanislowski fund. If you and Charlie, as trustees, agree that the fund should be continued for Jonny and take it to court, I'm with you. And I don't think Doris will object or contest it with her own claim. Not if she follows my advice. Besides, she really feels that the fund ought to go to Jonny. She's a good egg, you know, Laura."

And you're in love with her, Laura thought. She said stubbornly, "I think we should have something settled about that."

"It will have to be settled in January. Now then, I'm going to tell Charlie about this Maria Brown's visit to you and about that affair last night." He went to the telephone.

Charlie was not in his room at the club; he was not in the bar, he was not in the dining room. Matt tried Doris' number.

"Doris? No, I'm at Laura's. Well, I really want to talk to Charlie, is he there? Something rather odd has happened." He covered the mouthpiece with his hand and spoke to Laura. "He's there. Shall I tell them to come here? Right." He said to Doris, "Come over here, Doris, you and Charlie. I'd rather not tell you over the telephone. All right."

He hung up as the little French clock struck seven. Laura started to the kitchen. "I didn't realize how late it is. I'll get out something for them to drink."

Matt went with her and Jonny followed, Suki in her arms, and instantly the bright little kitchen took on a warm and domestic air. Matt got out whiskey and soda, glasses and ice; he found cheese and crackers and put them on a tray and then poured himself a drink and sipped it leaning against the table, while Laura prepared Jonny's supper. He made conversation with Jonny; when the back door bell rang he went to open it, instantly alert and guarded; it was the Christmas tree Laura had ordered.

Matt superintended its journey through the kitchen, and made sure that the kitchen door was bolted before he followed the spreading mass of rustling green, shedding pine needles as it went, into the living room. Matt chose the space for it before the window; Matt coped with the intricacies of the three-legged holder which Laura unearthed from the shelf in the coat closet. Matt tipped the men who brought it, and saw them out the kitchen door again and the door bolted again. And then he got out the boxes of Christmas ornaments. Jonny with difficulty was persuaded to leave the heaps of tinsel, red and green and blue and

98

silver, sparkling and gay, in order to eat her supper. Once convinced, however, she settled down in a polite but businesslike way while Matt talked of Christmas, and then when she'd finished all three of them went to trim the tree. Matt paused at the wood-box and built and lighted a fire in the small fireplace, and stood for a moment watching the flames catch; the golden light touched his tall figure to sharp relief. "Looked nice yesterday," he said to Laura. "Now then—what goes on top of the tree? I'll get the kitchen stepladder."

He was on the ladder, perched precariously to reach the top-most branch with a star whose silver glitter had been rather worn down during the years since it had first been fastened to the top of Laura's Christmas tree by Peter March, nearly twenty years before, when Charlie and Doris arrived.

"Cocktails came in just after you phoned, Matt," Doris said. "We thought we'd have a drink before we came—" She stopped and stared at him, balanced on one long leg and stretching for the top of the tree. "What on earth are you doing!"

Jonny, her hands clasped around a Santa Claus of red and gold, was holding her breath, her whole sturdy little figure tense, watching Matt. Charlie said, "It's a nice tree, Laura. Just the right size. Shall I take your coat, Doris?"

She slid out of the beige-toned coat; a scent of carnations drifted across to Laura. Doris wore no hat and her hair fit her head as neatly and elegantly as a little golden cap. She had changed to a dinner dress, black and filmy, with a lace top and a short skirt; her little feet were clad in sandals which were barely thin straps over the thinnest of stockings. She wore pearls at her throat and diamond and emerald bracelets. She shivered a little and went to the fire and adjusted the lock on one bracelet. Charlie said, "It's getting colder. Looks like it may be a white Christmas." He laid the beige mink coat carefully across a chair as if he had a minute sense of its value.

Doris said impatiently, "It's two weeks till Christmas! Why trim a Christmas tree now! Besides—anything can happen before then. If Peabody decides to make an arrest—"

"There it is!" Matt said loudly and cheerfully as he secured the star, and Jonny clapped her hands and dropped the Santa Claus. Doris tapped her small foot and did not finish her sentence. Jonny fell down on her knees with a little wail but the Santa Claus hadn't broken. "Here," Matt said, "give him to me. I'll put him right below the star."

Charlie strolled over to watch the process. "A little more to the right. It's hidden by a branch. What happened, Matt? Why did you call us?"

"I'll tell you—" Matt secured the Santa Claus and came down from the ladder "Maria Brown was here."

Laura listened. Jonny busied herself with the silver tinsel balls and ovals and gaily colored bulbs, dispersing them earnestly, her little face rigid with concentration, among the lower branches. Suki, his eyes shining red with excitement, crouched at the base of the tree and made sudden forays upon the boxes of Christmas ornaments. Matt poured drinks for all then, coolly, as he talked. Jonny was utterly absorbed in her task; even if she had understood their words, Laura thought, she wouldn't have heard anything they said. It was only when Matt went on to tell them of Suki that her head jerked around, and her blue eyes, startled, fastened upon Matt inquiringly. He observed it, he nodded at her reassuringly. He didn't mention Suki by name again

Both Doris and Charlie were skeptical about Matt's explanation for Suki's sickness.

"Cats are always picking up something!" Doris said, eyeing the kitten distastefully. And Charlie said doubtfully, "It couldn't have been anything very serious." He, too, eyed the kitten, who at that instant lashed his tail, sprang open a tinsel bauble and sent it whirling across the room, Jonny and the kitten after it in hot pursuit. "But this Brown woman—that's very serious. I don't like it. I think I'll have another drink." He leaned over the tray on the long table before the sofa, his discreet face grave.

Doris swung one small foot. "But she didn't threaten Laura! She only asked her about Jonny! She didn't take out a gun or anything like that! I'll take another drink, Charlie." She held out her glass to Charlie; the glass decanter reflected a rosy gleam from the fire; Doris' bracelets shot dazzling little lights. "Of course if this woman, Maria Brown, *was* a witness— I wonder what she knows!"

Charlie handed Doris her glass. "Probably nothing. Except that it was murder. My own opinion is that she had some reason of her own for avoiding the police. She knew they would question her and she's afraid of them."

"She asked about Jonny," Matt reminded him.

Charlie lifted his eyebrows. "She'd read the papers. She had a glimpse of Jonny. My guess is that she scents blackmail. She doesn't know exactly what or how but she hopes there may be some chance of getting some money for herself."

"Maybe," Matt said. "On the other hand, it struck me that she might be Jonny's mother."

Charlie stared at him, his glass at his lips. Doris cried, "Her mother! But she's dead! She's—" Doris caught her breath, lowered her silky eyelashes, and under their cover very swiftly explored the theory, for she said with scarcely a second's pause,

100

"Besides if she was his wife that affects— Exactly how would that affect the Stanislowski fund?"

Laura replied, "If she's his wife, Matt says that presumably she would have a third of the fund. That is, if she comes forward and proves her identity—"

Matt interrupted. "And if she did not murder Conrad," he said dryly, looking down into his glass.

Doris' pretty pink lips set themselves firmly. She turned to Charlie. "Charlie, I think this is too far-fetched. Don't you agree?"

"Well," Charlie said deliberately, "I suppose it is a possibility. But I rather think my own explanation is the more likely one. If she were the mother she'd have come to us, tried to claim the child and the money before now. No, I think she'll prove to be an accidental witness, with a police record probably. I think she'll see to it that the police don't find her. And as to this business about the kitten, really, Laura, I wouldn't take that too seriously. Isn't there some other way the kitten could have got this— sedative, or whatever it was?"

"No," Laura said flatly. "I have nothing of the kind in the house."

"But it seems so—well, purposeless. And certainly it would have been a very dangerous thing for anybody to enter your apartment like that. Suppose you had seen him. I can't help thinking that was an accident."

Doris' cheek had flushed to a delicate pink. She looked at Laura steadily. "The point is, why should anybody try to murder you?"

Matt, leaning on the mantel, looked thoughtfully down into the fire and said nothing. Charlie coughed in a rather apologetic way. "Doris is right," he said. "You say, Laura, that you've told the police everything you know. Why should there be an attempt to murder you? It's true that you are standing in the position of guardian to Jonny, but if Jonny *is* the motive for this murder and you were—removed, it wouldn't make it easier for anybody to— well, to get hold of Jonny, for instance. We would only tighten our guard about Jonny. It would only result in even more care for Jonny's safety. No," he said deliberately, "I don't think that's the answer."

Jonny had turned at the repeated mention of her name. Matt saw it and strolled across the room to select a gay ornament and suggest its position on the tree, and Doris got up with a swish of silk skirts. "Well, for my part I think Laura's imagination is running away with her. The kitten picked up something, cats are always picking things up in odd corners. Nobody is trying to murder Laura. And as to this Maria Brown—I don't say I don't

101

believe you, Laura, but are you sure that all happened just as you told it? I mean—" Doris was suddenly very gentle and friendly. "I mean, you've had a shock, finding that man murdered and all that. Isn't it possible that you exaggerated things? Unintentionally, of course! All of us would understand that."

It flicked a swift, small anger again in Laura. It had always been that way between them. "I assure you, Doris, that I told the truth!"

"You don't like me," Doris said. "You're angry. You—as a matter of fact you've never liked me, Laura! Come now, you may as well admit the truth. You have hated me ever since Conrad married me."

"That's not true!"

Charlie murmured something uneasily, picked up his empty glass and put it down. Matt, having successfully diverted Jonny, strolled back to lean against a tall green chair, a curious, slightly amused but extremely alert look in his eyes.

Doris turned at once to him. "I'm sorry I spoke like that, Matt," she said, all at once gentle again and rather wistful. "I've always liked Laura and tried to be friends with her. Conrad had told me about her. He told me that he had brought up a child, a daughter of a friend of his, a little girl who had no money. I thought it was generous and kind of Conrad, but I—I may as well admit that I was very much surprised when I discovered that the little girl Conrad had taken in and befriended was in fact a young woman nearly as old as I was, and—well a woman senses some things." She went to Matt and put her hand on his arm. She lifted soft brown eyes to him. "I tried to be kind to Laura. But she never liked me. I couldn't help thinking that she had— How can I express it? It sounds cruel to put it in words, but I couldn't help thinking that perhaps Laura herself intended to marry Conrad."

Laura took a stunned, gasping breath. "I never thought of such a thing! Neither did Conrad! He was like a father to me!"

"A very generous father," Doris said. "A very rich father. You *must* have expected to inherit some of Conrad's estate. Perhaps all of it. He had no relatives except for this Conrad Stanislowski in Poland and you didn't know his intention to leave part of his money to him. It *must* have occurred to you that you were closer to Conrad than anyone else. But then he met me and fell in love with me and—I don't blame you, Laura. I understand it. I'm only sorry we can't be friends." She looked at Charlie and smiled, a small and wistful smile. "I think I'd better go now. Dinner will be waiting." She looked up at Matt again. "You are coming, too?"

TWENTY

It was almost a command. Matt smiled down at Doris, patted her hand and said, "I am having dinner here with Laura."

"Oh," Doris said blankly. "Oh, well—" Her glance picked up Charlie, who followed her into the hall.

Matt said, "Is that all right, Laura? I saw some steaks in the refrigerator. I broil a fine steak."

She nodded; she was so shaken with anger she did not trust herself to speak. He gave her a kind of twinkle. "She doesn't mean all that," he said and lounged into the hall. There was a little murmur of talk, Charlie's voice and Matt's, and a soft and musical word or two from Doris.

Matt turned from the doorway. "Doris says good night," he said to Laura, suppressing a grin. Charlie, his hat and gloves in his hand, and his coat on, appeared beside him, looking extremely uncomfortable.

"Good night, Laura. Don't take this too hard. I really think there is some sensible explanation about the kitten. And if this Brown woman comes again, call the police. Call me. Call Matt. Don't let her come in the house. But I doubt very much if she'll come back. Too much risk of the police—"

Doris' voice interrupted him. "Are you coming, Charlie? Good night, Matt darling." She came into view as she spoke, a lovely little figure, furs swirling luxuriously around her. She lifted up her face to Matt, and put her gloved hand on his shoulder. He kissed her briskly. She said, "I'll see you tomorrow." She didn't look at Laura. There was the small bustle of their leaving, then the door closed and Matt came back. He still had an odd, rather twinkling and amused smile in his eyes. He came to the table and poured himself another drink. "Don't pay any attention to Doris."

Jonny, her brown head bent over a heap of glittering ornaments, gravely selected a golden bell, inserted the hook and crawled under a branch to hang the bell. Suki made a dash at the piece of tissue paper in which the bell had been wrapped. Laura said, her voice stiff and constrained, "Matt, not a word of that is true. I never thought of Conrad as anything but—but Conrad! He was everything—friend and father, and everything to me. I never thought of any claim on him! He had already done so much for me!"

He gave her a suddenly serious look. Then he put down his glass, and crossed to her. "Don't defend yourself. There's no need to. Doris gets worked up and flies off on a tangent like that, but it doesn't mean anything. The fact is, Doris is frightened. And as to that, we are all a little frightened. It's not a nice thing. Now then, forget Doris. Forget all of it. I've invited myself to dinner and I really can broil a steak. Come on, Jonny. We'll finish the tree after dinner." He went through to inspect it while Jonny watched him eagerly. Inasmuch as she could reach only the lower branches, the tree was taking on a rather odd effect of plenty below and scarcity above, but he nodded approvingly and lifted Jonny to her feet. "We're going to cook dinner," he told her. "Come and see what a good cook I am."

Again the bright little kitchen assumed a curiously happy atmosphere. Matt busied himself with the steaks, demanding salt, demanding pepper, demanding seasoning salt and charcoal powder, which Laura did not have; delivering a mock serious lecture as to the temperature of a broiling oven, meddling with the French dressing she made for the salad and tasting it—keeping up an energetic conversation which successfully precluded any mention of Maria Brown, of the kitten, of Conrad Stanislowski. It was a gay, a warm and pleasant hour or two, like a normal island in a sea of abnormality.

It was, too, a remarkably good dinner; the steaks, Matt assured with great sobriety, were superb; he hoped she realized that it was an extraordinary gastronomical experience to eat Steak Cosden. He joked with Jonny; he played with the cat. There were French fried potatoes, also from the freezer; there were cheese and apples and grapes for dessert. Through it all Matt talked gaily, and avoided murder and attempted murder. He told of his law practice; he talked of himself, for the first time since Laura had known him. She had known vaguely that he had lived in New York, that his mother and father and a brother still lived there. For some reason he had gone not to an Eastern school but to the University of Chicago where he had taken a law course. "So I settled here," he said. "I like Chicago. And I was young enough then to like being on my own, independent. My brother was older than I, he is a lawyer too, by the way, and so is my father. The idea was that I should join the firm. But I wanted to strike out for myself. I was engaged to Doris then."

He had known Doris in New York, before she married Conrad,

104

and came, too, to live in Chicago. Laura said, "It's past Jonny's bedtime."

"She'll have to stay up tonight. There's the tree to trim." He peeled an apple and offered a slice to Jonny. "I didn't expect Doris to come here to live. I certainly didn't expect her to turn up, married to Conrad. But then, it would have had to be a long engagement. I was barely out of school and trying to get a start." He gave Jonny another slice of apple which she munched solemnly, leaning against his knee. "Doris was my brother's girl when I met her."

"I didn't know that." How much she didn't know, Laura thought, about Matt and Doris.

He nodded cheerfully. "I was home for Easter holidays. Went to dance with Jim and his girl—Doris. By the time the week was over, Doris and I were engaged. Whirlwind courtship."

"Didn't Jim mind?"

Unexpectedly Matt chuckled. "Oh it was all very dramatic. Both of us giving Doris up to the other, very highminded and self-sacrificing. But then Jim met Frances and married her. And Doris jilted me when she met Conrad. She had every right to. You can't expect a girl like that to wait forever. Now then—I can wash dishes, too."

Jonny trotted back and forth with grave importance, helping. And then they took coffee into the living room and finished trimming the tree. When at last, glittering and resplendent it stood reflecting itself a hundred times in the windows, Matt bundled Jonny off to bed.

And it was time for Matt to leave. "You look more like yourself," he said at the door. "I don't think you've had a square meal for a couple of days." All at once there was something different in his eyes, something dancing yet serious, too. "There's something we forgot. We ought to have a big mistletoe bough. Hanging right here—" He took Laura close and swiftly and very hard in his arms and kissed her, and then, slowly this time, kissed her again. Time stood still; time passed; and there was no reckoning of it. Then suddenly, without meaning to, Laura pulled away.

"Why did you do that?" Matt said.

Because of Doris, Laura thought; you're still in love with Doris. You're going to marry Doris.

She said, "Good night, Matt."

He eyed her for a moment; then he opened the door. "All right. I'll let you know if there's any news. But try to put all of it out of your mind. Bolt the door, don't forget. Have a good sleep." He went down the corridor to the elevator. He did not look back. Laura bolted the door. But she didn't sleep—not for a long time.

105

It was strange, she thought once, that she could still feel the pressure of Matt's mouth upon her own. It was as if it had set a seal upon it, indelible and lasting.

Yet he had understood why she had withdrawn herself from the hard, warm circle of his arms; she hadn't said why, but he understood it. He was still in love with Doris. He'd felt sorry for Laura, he'd tried and succeeded in distracting her, extricating her, for a while, from a morass of fear—of murder and attempted murder. That was because he was kind, he liked her, he wanted to help her; that was like Matt. But he was going to marry Doris; after all those years of waiting, he was going to marry the girl he'd fallen in love with long ago at a dance, during holidays, his brother's girl; the girl he'd still loved even after she'd married Conrad.

It was Doris, of course, who had said frankly that she and Matt were to be married; but Doris wouldn't have said it if it hadn't been true. She was too quick-witted, too intelligent, to lie about it; and besides—Matt was still in love with Doris. Laura always came back to that.

She wouldn't think about that moment or two as Matt was leaving. She wouldn't think of Matt—and Doris. She listened to the low, regular moan of the foghorn. And went over and over, irresistibly, every word, every look of Matt's—and of Doris'.

Once, however, she thought for a long time of Maria Brown. Suppose she was Jonny's mother! How had she felt, seeing Jonny? What did she intend to do?

And once, too, as the lonely hours of the night wore on, Laura thought, suppose Peabody is right! Suppose Doris—or Charlie (not Matt, not Laura March) but Doris or Charlie—had known of Conrad Stanislowski's arrival, had known his address, had murdered him!

She turned on the light. She sat up in bed, huddled the eiderdown around her shoulders, and smoked a cigarette. After a while the black phantoms that had seemed to enter the room with the night, surrounding her, disappeared, driven away by the light, the familiar look of the room. She put out her cigarette and read for a while and at last drifted into sleep.

The light was still turned on when the telephone woke Laura. It rang and rang insistently, jabbing through her sleep, so she roused and blinked at the unexpected light from the bedside table and then groped for her robe and slippers and went into the hall to answer it. A man's voice, a strange voice, spoke to her.

"Miss March? This is Sergeant O'Brien. Lieutenant Peabody wishes to speak to you. Will you hold on a minute."

She held on, carrying the telephone to the door where she could see into the living room. The curtains were still drawn. The

Christmas tree winked dimly in the light from the hall. It was still dark. She snapped on the living-room light. The gilt hands of the French clock pointed to six-thirty. What had happened? Why had Peabody called so early? Suddenly she was fully awake. And listening—for all at once, from the street far below, through the heavy silence of early morning there was the wail of a police siren. It seemed remote and far away. It drew closer, and still closer, shrill and eerie, and then abruptly stopped.

Lieutenant Peabody's voice spoke into her ear. "Miss March? I want to see you. I'll be right up."

"What is it? What has happened—" He had hung up.

He'd be right up. That meant, didn't it, that he was in the apartment house? Why?

Fear caught her as if it had hands.

There was no time to dress. She ran to the bathroom and washed her face quickly, ran a comb through the soft, loose curls of her brown hair, seeing her white face in the mirror, listening for the door buzzer. She closed the door into Jonny's room, very quietly, very softly, so the round hump under the blankets that was Jonny did not stir.

She hugged her white bathrobe around her and went into the living room and drew the curtains apart. The Christmas tree looked strangely festive and gay, out of place.

It was a dark and overcast day, with low gray clouds, threatening snow. The door buzzer sounded sharply. She ran, so Jonny would not be awakened; she opened the door and Lieutenant Peabody and a policeman came in.

Peabody's swift glance took in Laura, her bathrobe, her bedroom slippers. He stepped to the doorway of the living room, glanced quickly around, and said shortly, "I'll have to ask you to let us take a look through your apartment. Stay here, please."

"But what is it? What has happened?",

The Lieutenant did not answer, but disappeared back through the hall. She made an instinctive move to follow him and the policeman said, "I wouldn't if I were you, miss. The Lieutenant said stay here." He eyed her with sharp curiosity, and he looked well prepared to keep her there. She said, "But Jonny—there's a little girl here. I don't want him to frighten her."

"You needn't worry, miss," the policeman said. She could hear Peabody in the kitchen and then, which seemed odd, in her bedroom. After a long moment or two he came back.

"You'd better get into some clothes, Miss March. There is something I want you to do."

"What is it, Lieutenant?"

"Hurry, please."

"But Jonny—I can't leave her. What do you want?"

107

"Sergeant O'Brien will stay with the child. You'll not need a coat."

It was barely polite; it was in fact a sharp command.

Laura went back to her room. Her hands were shaking. A zipper stuck and she tugged it, and heard the faint little rip of silk. She pulled on a gray skirt and sweater; got into stockings and pumps. She went out into the hall and Lieutenant Peabody was looking at his watch, and Sergeant O'Brien was standing in the door of the living room gravely surveying the Christmas tree and the little disarrangement of cushions, ash trays, coffee cups, from the previous night.

"All right," Peabody said. "This way. Stay here, O'Brien."

Laura said, "If Jonny wakes up——"

The Sergeant interrupted, "Don't worry, miss. I have children of my own." He stared at her stolidly, yet with a bright, cold curiosity in his eyes.

Lieutenant Peabody opened the door. "We'll go this way." They passed the bank of elevators, turned into an intersecting corridor, turned again and stopped at a service elevator. This, too, was self-operated; there was a panel of buttons; but a man in dungarees stood at the door. He was one of the big, rarely seen yet vitally necessary staff for the apartment house. His face was vaguely familiar, and now pale with excitement. He was obviously waiting for them.

"You want to go right down now, Lieutenant?"

"Right." Peabody motioned Laura into the elevator. They went down and down, in a curious, forbidding silence, so Laura could not say, where are you taking me? Why?

The car stopped. She walked beside Peabody through a wide hall with a concrete floor and glimpses of a vast laundry with tubs and washing machines and drying lines at one side. Somewhere ahead of them and around the corner there was a subdued kind of commotion. There were lights, unshaded and garish, lighting up the gray walls. They turned the corner. A huddle of figures, among them the blue uniforms of policemen, stood in a close circle around something on the floor. A woman, in curlers, a fur coat and bedroom slippers, hovered on the outskirts and sobbed. Two men in plain clothes came in with a businesslike trot from the other end of the corridor.

Peabody touched the nearest policeman on the shoulder, and like a blue wave, the tight nucleus of uniformed figures moved apart.

A woman lay on the floor. She wore a brown coat. A black beret had fallen on the concrete floor. The woman's hair was dark. Laura could not see her face.

TWENTY-ONE

There was, it seemed to her, a long silence. A bright electric bulb glowed directly above her. She felt rather than saw the concerted stare of all those men.

The light above was dazzling, confusing. She put her hands over her eyes.

"Who is she?" Lieutenant Peabody's voice came out of the whirling, queer silence around her.

"I don't know—"

"Look at her."

"No—no—"

A hand touched her elbow. "Who is that woman? Look at her."

I can't, Laura thought; it's like Conrad Stanislowski; I can't look at it again.

But she did look down. And again, with that terrible clarity which she had felt when she looked at Conrad Stanislowski's face, she thought, the woman is dead; she was murdered.

The woman had a swarthy, rather thin face. She had a fringe of short dark hair. A black wool skirt showed where the brown coat had fallen apart; she wore neatly polished black oxfords with rubber heels. Laura forced herself to search that still, rigid-looking face; she had never seen the woman in her life.

Lieutenant Peabody said, "Is it Maria Brown?"

"No," Laura said, and drew back, her knees shaking.

There was another silence. The woman in the curlers and fur coat gave a strangling sob, flung her hands over her face and cried jerkily, "I want out of here. Poor Catherine—I'm going to faint—"

A policeman took her arm. "All right now, ma'am. In a minute you can go—"

Lieutenant Peabody said to Laura, "You are sure it is not Maria Brown?"

"Yes. I'm sure."

"Do you know who she is?"

"No."

"Have you ever seen her before?"

"No. Not to my knowledge."

"All right." Lieutenant Peabody looked at one of the men in plain clothes. "Get out to Koska Street and get the landlady; her name is Radinsky."

He went over to the woman in curlers, who took her hands from her face and stared wildly at him, her fleshy face white and sagging, her mouth trembling. "All right, Mrs. Grelly," he said, "you can go to your apartment."

"Oh, Lieutenant!" she cried with a gulping sob. "This is horrible. She was all right last night—just the same as usual. She cooked dinner and then I went out and—"

Peabody cut her short. "I'll talk to you again later. Thank you." He nodded at the policeman who stood near and seemed to understand an unspoken command.

"I'll take you to your apartment, ma'am," he said politely.

"Oh," Mrs. Grelly gasped. "Oh—" A fleshy, ringed hand came out from the enveloping folds of her coat. She clutched the policeman's arm and went away unsteadily. Lieutenant Peabody came back to Laura.

"Please look at this woman's coat. It's like Maria Brown's coat, isn't it? And she was wearing a black hat—they call it a beret. Is that the same kind of hat Maria Brown wore?"

Again Laura forced herself to look at the tragic figure on the floor. "It's not like Maria Brown's coat. Her coat was full and flowing. This is tailored; it has a belt. It's—oh, it's different, Lieutenant Peabody. But the black beret is about the same. They all look very much alike. Anybody can wear a black beret." She didn't want to ask; she had to know. "She was—murdered. Wasn't she?"

"Yes."

"How—" The word came out in a whisper. She knew that the close circle of figures around her—and the dead woman—was very quiet, listening.

"Strangled," Lieutenant Peabody said shortly. "Has a bruise on her temple. The medical examiner is on his way here."

"Who was she? Why was she here?"

Lieutenant Peabody gave her an odd, speculative look. The little circle seemed to tighten, listening and speculating, too. Peabody replied, "She went by the name of Catherine Miller. She was a cook and general houseworker, employed here, in this apartment house, by the woman who went upstairs just now, Mrs. George Grelly. She was found this morning by the engineer for the building. She'd been dead some hours. You can go now, Miss March. I'll want to talk to you later."

110

Again Lieutenant Peabody must have given a mute command to one of the policemen, for a slim young fellow, who looked as if he hadn't been long out of the Army, stepped forward in an alert and soldierly manner. He said politely, "I'll go up with you, miss."

He walked beside her, back through the wide corridor with the ghostly gleam of washing machines and dryers looming up in the vast, dim stretches of the laundry. They passed the narrow corridor that wound through a huge storage section; Laura had her own storeroom there, a wire cage, full mainly of cartons of Peter March's books. They reached the elevator again.

Another man, vaguely familiar, too, in khaki-colored shirt and trousers, stood there; he was excited. "The superintendent told me to take this elevator. He told me somebody had been murdered. Is that right, officer?"

The young policeman ushered Laura into the elevator. "That's right, buddy," he said. "Just take us up to—" He glanced at Laura. "What floor, miss?"

"The ninth."

Already a rumor had coursed along the grapevine of the great apartment house. Two maids and a handyman were standing by the elevator at the ninth floor, talking furiously. They fell abruptly silent, watching, as the policeman and Laura came out; the silence continued until they turned from the service corridor into the main corridor.

Laura had not brought her key. She tried the door absently and then pushed the little bell. The young policeman stood politely at her elbow. After a moment Sergeant O'Brien came and opened the door. "All right," he said, and the young policeman disappeared as Laura entered the apartment. Sergeant O'Brien eyed her. "The little girl woke up. I'm giving her her breakfast."

Telephone to Matt, Laura thought. Tell him that a woman—wearing a brown coat and a black beret—had been murdered. Tell him she *could* have been mistaken for Maria Brown. Tell him that the police had already questioned her. She started toward the telephone. Sergeant O'Brien's great bulk came between her and the table. "I wouldn't if I were you, miss."

"But I must phone—"

"Orders."

"You don't understand—"

"Lieutenant Peabody said you were to stay here until he came and you were not to telephone to anybody. Don't you want to see how the little girl is doing?"

"Jonny? Yes—" She went to the kitchen and Jonny, in blue pajamas, was contentedly eating oatmeal.

111

The Sergeant noted the surprise Laura felt. "Didn't I tell you, miss, I've got children of my own! Now then, understand, you're not to make a move. Just wait for Lieutenant Peabody."

He took Laura's silence for consent and went back to sit in the chair beside Jonny and apparently resumed a story of Davy Crockett which he was telling her in English heavily laced with an Irish brogue. Perhaps Jonny understood one word in ten; she listened, fascinated; it was obvious she liked Sergeant O'Brien. Once he interrupted himself to glance at Laura who had sunk down in a chair. "Maybe you better have some coffee, miss," he said. "To tell you the truth I needed it myself."

It added a peculiar note of fantasy to the nightmare to watch Sergeant O'Brien's great bulk moving very lightly and dexterously about the kitchen. He made toast, he boiled eggs, he made coffee.

After the first cup of steaming coffee Laura's thoughts began to clear. Yet there was nothing she could do until Lieutenant Peabody came. There was something very solid and immovable about Sergeant O'Brien.

Besides, what could she have done aside from telephoning to Matt and Charlie and Doris and telling them—what? That a woman, a maid employed in the apartment house where Laura lived, had been murdered—and that woman happened to be wearing at the time a brown coat and a black beret.

She had a superficial kind of resemblance to Maria Brown, or, more accurately, to a description of Maria Brown; she was stocky, she had short dark hair, she wore a brown coat and black beret. Only someone who had never seen Maria Brown could possibly have believed that the maid was Maria Brown.

So there must be another explanation for the poor woman's murder.

Lieutenant Peabody was clearly of the opinion that there was a connection with the Stanislowski murder—and with Laura. That was because the woman was murdered in the apartment house. That was because of the superficial resemblance, not to Maria Brown, but to Maria Brown's description.

It was a strange morning, one that seemed suspended in a vacuum. The clouds were heavy, pressing lower upon the city. Oddly enough Laura was grateful for Sergeant O'Brien's presence and the cheerful and normal matter-of-fact way he went about things. He talked to Jonny in his Irish brogue. He played with the kitten. He watched Laura with, she thought, a grudging flicker of approval as she went resolutely about her routine of housekeeping chores, thankful, too, for something to do. Jonny as usual put on a grave little housewifely air and trotted around with a feather duster. She paused for a long time to admire the tree and readjust

112

some of the ornaments; she ran, struck by the thought, to her room and brought the yellow bird Charlie had given her She showed it proudly to Sergeant O'Brien and then with his help fastened it, too, to one of the lower branches of the glittering tree. Sergeant O'Brien and Jonny then stood back to admire the bird, who bowed and bowed, rocking back and forth.

When the door buzzer at last sounded, Sergeant O'Brien and Jonny were intent over a game of checkers in the living room, at the card table, a lighted lamp shining down upon the Sergeant's great red face and bulky blue figure and Jonny's intent blue eyes and neat brown hair The Sergeant said to Jonny, "The next move is yours," and made a gesture with his hand which Jonny seemed to understand and went to the door

Lieutenant Peabody came in. He looked, that gray morning, older than usual and very tired, yet there was also something grim and implacable in his lined face. He saw the interrupted checker game "You might finish the game, Sergeant Keep the child occupied

Sergeant O'Brien nodded. His eyes were very sharp and alert but he turned in a fatherly way to Jonny. "All right, kid," he said, "let's just take this checker board into your little room. We'll finish the game there."

Again Jonny understood; she had clearly taken an instantaneous liking to the big policeman. She gathered up the spare red and white checkers while he took the board carefully in his great hands, so as not to disturb the checkers in play, and led the way out of the living room

Lieutenant Peabody said unexpectedly, "How about some coffee, Miss March? Is there any in the kitchen?"

There was the remainder of the great pot which Sergeant O'Brien had made. Laura brought it to Lieutenant Peabody with cream and sugar and some toast. He sat down at the bridge table and drank the coffee thirstily and munched through the toast without speaking while Laura waited, holding back her questions

But then when he finished he moved to a lounge chair, and it was Lieutenant Peabody who questioned.

He began directly. "Miss March, if you have an alibi for the time between nine-thirty and say eleven-thirty last night, you'd better tell me."

TWENTY-TWO

An alibi. Already! She tried to keep her voice steady. "I have for some of the time, Lieutenant. Matt Cosden was here to dinner. Then we trimmed the Christmas tree. I think he left about eleven—perhaps a little after. He might know exactly what time it was."

"I suppose Jonny was asleep at that time?"

"Yes. Lieutenant, do you think that whoever killed that poor woman thought that she was Maria Brown?"

"Well, I can't say exactly what I think. In fact, I'm not sure what I think. But I don't like coincidence. She answered the description of Maria Brown. She was murdered here in the apartment house where you live. I cannot overlook either of these facts."

"Nobody who had ever seen Maria Brown herself would think that this woman was Maria Brown. She wore a brown coat and black beret. She had dark hair and a rather stocky figure. Otherwise, Lieutenant. there was no resemblance at all."

Lieutenant Peabody eyed Laura for a moment and said unexpectedly, "That's what Mrs. Radinsky said, too. You remember—the landlady at Koska Street. She said flatly that it was not Maria Brown and that nobody who had ever seen Maria Brown herself would have mistaken this Catherine Miller for Maria Brown. It did occur to me that possibly Maria Brown was using another name, Catherine Miller, and perhaps she had gone to the rooming house in order to meet Conrad Stanislowski and murder him; then when she disappeared she could have simply gone back to her real identity as Catherine Miller. But I was wrong. And we have certain identification for Catherine Miller. She has worked for this Mrs. Grelly for three years; Mrs. Grelly has her home address. Catherine Miller lived in a rooming house for women here on the near north side. She was well known there. She had no Polish accent, no Polish connections of any kind. so far as we've been able to discover. No quarrel with anybody. The truth is, Miss March, the only reason for her murder that I see at

114

the moment is the fact that that poor woman happened to work in this apartment house and unfortunately happened to choose to wear a brown coat and a black beret."

It wasn't fair, Laura thought; it was tragically unfair. Catherine Miller, drawn into the dark orbit of murder, dead because she happened to wear a brown coat, because she happened to be at exactly that address, at that time. She said, "Why would anybody murder Maria Brown?"

"Well," Peabody said deliberately, "of course, you realize that we have scarcely begun the investigation into the Catherine Miller murder, but if there's anything to the notion that her murderer believed her to be Maria Brown, then there are two possible reasons for it. One is a very obvious one; her murderer believed that Maria Brown had evidence which would be very dangerous to Conrad Stanislowski's murderer. If that is true, then whoever killed Catherine Miller, killed Stanislowski. As a matter of fact, Miss March, there's another reason for my feeling that the two murders are connected. Lightning may strike twice in the same place, but usually it doesn't. If murder strikes twice in the same place, or I should say in proximity to the same people, then I'm inclined to suspect the same agency. More exactly, the same murderer. Murder is, statistically and factually, in relation to other crimes, an unusual and very desperate crime, springing from desperate and driving motives. Money—fear—are two such motives. It is certainly possible that the murderer believed that she was Maria Brown and that she was coming to see you and might tell you some evidence which would be incriminating."

"But when Maria Brown came to see me yesterday afternoon, she didn't tell me anything. She only asked about Jonny."

"Thus automatically and very definitely tying Maria Brown in with the Stanislowski murder. Is that what you mean?"

Laura paused, and then met the subtle challenge directly. "She did come here, Lieutenant. She did ask about Jonny. There must be a reason for that. And she did say that she knew how to hide and that you'd never find her."

"Well, we haven't found her, that's true enough," Lieutenant Peabody said grimly. "And it looks as if whoever killed Catherine Miller couldn't find the Brown woman either. Now then—" He paused and stared at the rug for a long time. Finally he lifted his eyes to hers; deep in them there was a kind of steely spark. "I'm going to tell you exactly what we know of this. I want you to see exactly what your position is. This woman, Catherine Miller, finished up her work, according to her employer, probably about nine-thirty or ten last night. Mrs. Grelly did not know the exact time because she and her husband went out after dinner, which the maid had prepared, leaving her to clear up the dishes and

115

finish her work. The maid had her own key to the kitchen door; she let herself out. The custom is for the maids in the apartment house to go down by way of the service elevators, as I expect you know. These service elevators during most of the day have elevator men; there are four men whose job it is to turn their hands to any necessary task. However, the elevators are self-service. Sometimes, especially during the late evening hours, the maids themselves use the elevators. So far we have discovered nobody, no other cook, none of the men who saw Catherine Miller leave. So I'm inclined to believe that she left the Grelly apartment, rang for a service elevator, and went down to the basement."

Laura broke in. "But who would know—who would see her?"

Peabody continued. "There is a side entrance, a service entrance, as I'm sure you know. If you'll remember, it was a very foggy night. We have found this bit of evidence which may be important. The doorman at the front was standing on the sidewalk just outside the foyer, at something after eleven. He is not sure of the time. It was not busy, however, at that time of night and he admitted that he had edged around at the side of the entrance, there's a pillar there that makes an angle, in order to smoke a cigarette without being seen. He saw a woman come along the street which runs past the service entrance. He merely happened to notice her because she was alone. He did not see her face and did not happen to know the maid, Catherine Miller; however, he says the woman was dressed as Catherine Miller was dressed; he is sure she is the woman he saw. She crossed the street and waited for a time at the bus stop."

He paused and looked thoughtfully at the window. But before Laura could speak, he went on. "The doorman watched her idly; he could not see her very clearly because of the fog but there's a street lamp there. He says that suddenly she turned, as if she had forgotten something, and went back along the street beside the apartment and disappeared. She had not come into sight again by the time he finished his cigarette and went back inside the foyer; from inside the entrance he can't see the bus stop. I asked him why he thought she had forgotten something and he said she seemed to look in her pocketbook and fumble about for a moment and then I gather made a sort of impatient gesture. In any event, he had the impression that she was one of the maids in the building, and that she came back, passed the corner and went out of sight, he thought, toward the service entrance. Now this service entrance, and this is important, is locked at eleven o'clock. That is, after eleven nobody can enter from the outside. However, the maids, or the engineer, janitors, handy-men—any of the staff for the apartment house—can get out from the inside;

116

it's one of those locks. But there was at that time, so far as we have yet been able to discover, no one about the service entrance, the hall there or the laundry, or any of the various utility rooms. There are dressing rooms and wash rooms, boiler rooms, the various rooms for supplies, storage lockers. The medical examiner says that Catherine Miller was killed several hours before she was found. He cannot specify the exact hour; it is his opinion, before making an autopsy, that she was probably killed before midnight. So as we have it now, the last person who admits seeing her was the doorman. He says that there were a few other people along the street, as usual. Not many. He does not remember noting anyone in particular. He says if anyone followed her, he didn't see it."

"But she was inside the basement—"

"I'm coming to that. The doorman goes off duty at midnight. He heard no sound whatever, that is, no scream or sound of distress, nothing that would have suggested investigation. He goes directly home, without changing clothes. Mrs. Grelly says that Catherine Miller had one of the few keys by which the service entrance can be unlocked from the outside; the maid's hours were irregular. Mr. Grelly travels a great deal and Mrs. Grelly goes with him. They have a dog. Consequently, during their absences it seemed desirable for Catherine Miller to have a key which would permit her to enter the apartment house at any time. So Mrs. Grelly asked for a key and the superintendent gave it to her. So you see, either the murderer followed Catherine closely enough to enter the service entrance at the same time she entered, or was already waiting in the corridor."

"You said she was—strangled. A man—"

"Her murderer was not necessarily a man. There was a blow, a very heavy one, at the side of her head. The medical examiner says that she was struck by some heavy weapon and probably knocked unconscious, he believes, before she was killed. Then she was strangled. An easy murder in a way. A woman could have done it."

The fog outside and the chill had crept into the room. Suddenly Laura shivered. Lieutenant Peabody saw her involuntary movement. "No, it isn't very pleasant, is it? The medical examiner says that there were few abrasions on her throat, that apparently she did not struggle; and he believes the murder weapon itself to have been something like, say"—all at once he was watching her very narrowly—"a scarf, a silk scarf such as a man might wear. Or a woman might wear."

"I—" Laura began and made herself stop; she would not deny until she had been accused. Peabody went on in a strangely dry, matter-of-fact way, which was, Laura then perceived, too dry,

117

too matter-of-fact, as if it were deliberately chosen to mask an implacable hatred of murder—and murderers, "We found an iron bar, a lever which stood, as a rule, near the door. We have taken it to be examined, but I feel fairly confident that the microscope will show that that is the weapon with which the woman was struck. Yes, Catherine Miller could have been killed by a man *or* a woman. The actual murder was done by a scarf. But perhaps the murderer knew that the iron bar stood by the door. Did you know that, Miss March?"

"No!" Laura cried. "No!"

"I wouldn't expect you to say that you did. Probably we will never know why Catherine Miller returned to the apartment house; she may have thought that she had left the gas turned on the stove, there are a dozen explanations; Mrs. Grelly says she was very conscientious in all her work. But if she were followed back from the bus stop, if someone followed her into the basement corridor when she unlocked the door, it was, it seems to me, someone whom she had no reason to fear; that, however, is merely supposition. The corridor is very dimly lighted, although there are lights there all night. It seems clear that the murderer saw the iron bar, seized it and struck Catherine Miller. On such a night as last night almost anybody outdoors would be wearing a scarf." He was speaking almost absently, as if debating and weighing facts. Now he gave a brisk nod. "Yes, it looks to me like what you might call an improvised murder. Done on the spur of the moment. But the murderer must have thought it was an extremely necessary murder. It's an odd picture, isn't it, Miss March?"

It was a terrible picture. Laura said, "Did you find the scarf? Was it still around her neck?"

Lieutenant Peabody shook his head. "The murderer would not be such a fool as that," he said dryly, and all at once Laura knew why, when he had summoned her to the basement to look at Catherine Miller, he had first gone into her bedroom; he was looking for a scarf, hidden away but showing tell-tale wrinkles; he was looking for evidence, his trained mind noting a hundred details. He was asking himself whether or not she, Laura March, had gone out of the apartment, down the service elevator, and waited at the service entrance for Catherine Miller's return.

She said, "I never saw Catherine Miller before. I could not have known, Lieutenant Peabody, that she was returning from the bus stop." She seized the strongest argument in her defense. "And besides—I would have known she was not Maria Brown!"

Lieutenant Peabody rose and went to the window which overlooked Lake Shore Drive. He stood there for a long time, peering down through the fog. Then he came back. "I think you

118

could have seen her, Miss March. There is a street lamp just above the bus stop and from this distance her figure would have been foreshortened, yet it might have looked, yes, it might have looked very much indeed like Maria Brown's."

"You said there were lights in the basement! I'd have seen her. I'd have known she wasn't Maria Brown—"

"It's very hard to say what anybody who has decided upon murder is really conscious of at that last, irrevocable moment," he said gravely. "It seems to me that ordinary perception, a normal sense of reality and self-preservation, must fail to exist for a murderer at the exact moment he strikes. Otherwise there would be no murders. Or course, a theory that you went down to meet her, thinking she was Maria Brown, would presuppose that you had made an engagement with her when she came to see you yesterday afternoon—"

"I didn't," Laura said, "I didn't."

"—and that Maria Brown herself failed to turn up. That—or of course mere chance—that is, that you only happened to see a woman you thought to be Maria Brown."

"Lieutenant Peabody, are you accusing me of murder?"

"No. I'm not accusing anyone. But I've got to get evidence. You were here, in this apartment house; so you had opportunity. According to your own story Maria Brown came to see you yesterday afternoon; you could have made an appointment with her for her to return later; you could have told her to come to the service entrance; you could have been watching from the window. It's nine stories down and it was a foggy night, but still if you saw a woman answering generally to her description, standing there under the street light, yes, you could have thought that was Maria Brown coming to keep her appointment. You could have had a motive; Maria Brown must have some sort of evidence concerning the Stanislowski murder. And you had means —the iron bar—"

"I want a lawyer. I want to talk to Matt Cosden."

"I thought you would ask for him," the Lieutenant said. "That's all right with me. I'll phone to him. I want to talk to Mrs. Stanley, too, and Stedman." He said, with the disarming air of frankness he could on occasion assume, "I'll tell you the truth Miss March, I'd like to keep this murder a secret. I'd like to keep it out of the newspapers. I'd like nobody, not even Cosden or Stedman or Mrs. Stanley, to know anything about it."

"Why?" Laura said, astonished.

"For various reasons. However, it's impossible. There are too many people who know about it. It's all over the apartment house." He shrugged. "Poor Catherine Miller," he said in a somber voice. "Murdered because she happened to wear a brown coat and a black beret. Murdered because she happened to think of some small household chore." His face again looked grim and angry. He said abruptly, "I hate murder. It's my job and I hate it, and I—" He checked himself. He had been about to say, "I hate a murderer, too." He went to the telephone.

He knew Matt's office number without even looking in the little black book which he carried in his pocket. "I am at Miss March's apartment," he told Matt. "I want you to come over here, Cosden, at once. No, Miss March is all right and so is the child. It's something else. Get over here fast." He then phoned to Doris and to Charlie Stedman, saying much the same thing. He went back to the little room where Jonny and Sergeant O'Brien were still playing checkers. Laura heard a low-voiced conversation between the two men. She rose and moved restlessly about the living room, going to the window and peering down at the corner near the bus stop. It was true that, even in the fog, even at that distance, she could have seen the figure of a woman outlined by the street light.

Someone closer could have seen the color of the woman's coat.

Certainly the bus stop was near enough Laura's apartment house for anybody to put two and two together and think, "That is Maria Brown. She is coming from Laura's apartment house." Or—"She is returning to it."

The Lieutenant came back into the room. "You say that you believed a man followed you the other day in the park. You say you did not see his face. Do you think that this man could have been Maria Brown dressed as a man?"

Laura thought back to that shadowy figure.

Lieutenant Peabody did not really believe that there had been such a man; he had been frankly skeptical about it; yet, clearly, he would not dismiss it without investigation. As she hesitated he said, "I realize that it sounds rather unlikely, a woman dressed as a man, but how about it? Could it have been Maria Brown?"

Was he, she thought, testing her, inviting her to throw suspicion upon Maria Brown?

It was probable that he simply wanted to know the truth. She said, "I don't think so. I'm not sure."

"Think, Miss March. Try to remember details. There are a hundred means by which you identify a person subconsciously, infinitely small details, so when you see a person a block away you recognize him without knowing how you do it. Didn't you recognize anything about this person you say followed you? Didn't you have a sort of—impression of say, familiarity, about him?"

"No, I didn't, Lieutenant. I told you I couldn't see him clearly. He never came near us. He never approached us. Yet—he was

120

always there, behind us. He did remind me a little of Conrad Stanislowski, but I think that was something about the way he was dressed. His coat—hat—something foreign about it."

She couldn't tell even now whether Peabody believed her or not. The door buzzer sounded and it was Matt. "*Laura—*" he cried, and then he saw her. He came to her in great strides and put his hand on her shoulder. "You're all right!" He turned to Peabody, "Good God, someone in the foyer said a woman had been murdered! The place is crawling with police. What happened?"

Lieutenant Peabody told him.

Matt put his arm tight around Laura; he did not move or speak until the Lieutenant had finished the short and terrible recital.

Then he said, "So you are going to question all of us, aren't you, Peabody? Naturally. Well, Miss March has an alibi up to eleven, or perhaps a few minutes after. That's when I left last night."

"That gives you an alibi, too," Lieutenant Peabody said neatly, and added, "Up to that time at least; we don't know the exact time when the woman was killed."

"Sit down, Laura. You're trembling." Matt made her sit down in an armchair; he gave her a quick but absent smile. His eyes were cold gray. "That brown coat and black beret—it does look as if the murderer thought she might have been Maria Brown coming to see Laura. But if so, obviously her murderer had never seen Maria Brown herself."

"Perhaps. Perhaps not."

"Miss March had seen Maria Brown—"

"We've gone all over that," Lieutenant Peabody said, but he went all over it again, slowly and deliberately. "So there it is, Cosden. You have to look at facts. And one of the facts is that this woman was murdered in this apartment house. Where Miss March lives. She was murdered within hours after Miss March claims that Maria Brown came here to see her."

"She came here to inquire about Jonny—"

"How do you know she didn't come here to blackmail? How do you know she didn't threaten Miss March?"

Laura and Matt spoke at the same time, their voices mingled. "No, no," Laura cried, and Matt said, "Laura told you the truth!" He paused, and then said more coolly, "Besides, Laura's not a good blackmail victim. She's got no money—"

"She's got the child, Jonny," Lieutenant Peabody said obliquely.

121

TWENTY-THREE

Matt gave him a swift, slatey look. "No, you're wrong, Lieutenant. It's a nice theory: 'I'll keep quiet, if you see to it I get some of the money from Jonny's estate.' But Laura has told you the truth. That's not what Maria Brown said."

Lieutenant Peabody shrugged. "Cosden, you may as well admit the fact that stares us in the face. Up to now there has been a possibility, a rather faint one it seems to me but a possibility, that Stanislowski was, as you suggested, murdered by orders, and his murderer was an instrument of the government he had escaped. That, or his murder was the result of some kind of feud. You suggested that Maria Brown had murdered him, that she may have been the instrument, for instance. But if Maria Brown had been the instrument of a political party, if she had received orders to murder Stanislowski, while it is possible that her later—liquidation had been planned, her murderer would not have killed another woman! Her murderer would have known Maria Brown. There would have been no mistake about it. So that removes that possibility in my mind and I think in yours. We may as well accept that. I think we can check off your suggestion that Stanislowski's murder was in any sense a political murder. At least, failing any further evidence. You suggest that Maria Brown may have been Stanislowski's wife, and that that accounts for his murder, and her interest in the child. Do you still believe Maria Brown murdered him?"

"I think it's possible. Yes."

"Why would she murder Catherine Miller?"

There was a long pause. No reason, Laura thought: no reason. If Catherine Miller's murderer had killed her by mistake, believing her to be Maria Brown, then Maria Brown was automatically cleared. Wasn't she?

Matt said at last, slowly, "Remember the telephone call Maria Brown made to Miss March? If she intended to involve Miss

March in murder, then she is a wily and a subtle woman. Suppose she intended to supply the police with a victim, a scapegoat. Suppose it occurred to her that the best way to remove suspicion from herself would be to supply another murderer. Here was a woman dressed as Maria Brown dressed, a woman here in Miss March's apartment house, so Miss March would be presumed to have opportunity to murder. Suppose Maria Brown reasoned that you would think exactly as you are thinking."

"You're snatching at straws, Cosden. You've forgotten one thing. How could Maria Brown have known anything about the maid? How could Maria Brown have known that Catherine Miller would be wearing a brown coat and a beret? How could she have known that she would leave the apartment house at exactly that time, go out to the bus stop? Return? Your theory would make it necessary indeed that Maria Brown kept a twenty-four-hour watch on this apartment house, and she has not done that. We'd have picked her up," Lieutenant Peabody said simply. "She'd be afraid to hang around that way. No, it's a fetching theory you have evolved, and you haven't had very much time to evolve it either, but it's not one that you or I can seriously entertain." The door buzzer sounded again. Peabody said, "Here is Mrs. Stanley. Or Stedman."

Matt went to the door. It was both Doris and Charlie Stedman. Charlie said, "You are here already! What is going on? There are police all around. Someone said something about murder!"

Doris, her face white, clung to Matt's arm and said nothing.

"A woman was murdered," Lieutenant Peabody began.

There was a long silence after he finished. Then Charlie said, "But—but there's no proof that this woman's murder has any connection at all with the Stanislowski murder!"

"None at all," Peabody said wearily.

Doris lighted a cigarette with hands that shook. She was beautifully dressed; her hair looked as if she had stepped that moment from the hairdresser's, but her face below its make-up was rather drawn and tight. She shot swift glances at Peabody, at Matt, at Charlie, at Laura, and then studied the bracelet on her wrist, turning it over and over again. Doris is frightened, Laura thought, and then thought, but so am I. So are we all.

"Nevertheless," Peabody said suddenly, "I don't like coincidence. I have to ask all of you for an account of what you did last night. Mrs. Stanley, were you at any time last night near this apartment house?"

Doris lifted her eyes, shot him one glance, said, "No," and lowered her eyes again.

"Where were you?"

"I was at home. I was at home all evening." She turned her

123

bracelet, examined one of the jewels on it, and added, "Charlie Stedman was with me. He had dinner with me. He didn't leave until—oh, it must have been midnight. Wasn't it, Charlie?"

It seemed to Laura that there was a flicker of surprise in Charlie's face. He gave Doris an astute, swift look. Then he said dryly, "Well, no, Doris. I left earlier than that."

Doris' lips tightened. "I looked at the clock. It was just on midnight."

Charlie shook his head, half smiling. "You've got nothing to be afraid of, Doris. Nobody thinks you came over here and laid in wait for the very unlikely appearance of Maria Brown."

"That's as may be," Peabody said. "What time exactly did you leave Mrs. Stanley?"

"I think it was about eleven," Charlie said.

Doris turned her bracelet, her lips sulky. "I still think it was midnight, Charlie."

"Then you are mistaken," Charlie said. "When I got down to the entrance and looked around for a taxi, I looked at my watch. I was wondering about how long it would take to get a taxi and whether I should ask the doorman to phone for one. It was eleven and I thought I'd take a chance, and sure enough, I picked one up."

"Soon?" Lieutenant Peabody said.

Charlie gave him a rather disapproving look. "In a moment or two. On the street. I imagine the doorman saw me. You can ask him."

"Oh, I will," Lieutenant Peabody said agreeably. "So you did not come anywhere near this apartment house, Stedman?"

"I passed it in the taxi, of course. Mrs. Stanley's apartment is farther north, as you know. I don't remember noting this place in particular or even looking out from the taxi. I was tired and it was very foggy. I went straight on to my club. You can ask them there when I arrived."

"I'll do that, too," Lieutenant Peabody said. "The fact is, none of you four people has what I would call a real alibi for the time when this woman was killed." He glanced at his watch, "I'll have to get your statements—"

"Statements!" Doris cried sharply. "Do you mean we—any of us—are suspected of murdering this woman?"

"Somebody murdered her," Lieutenant Peabody said. "I can't overlook the possibility of a connection between this murder and Stanislowski's murder."

Charlie said, "Look here, Lieutenant, I see your point of view. But have you explored this Catherine Miller's life? Oh, I realize you haven't had time. But—"

"Oh, we'll cover all that," Lieutenant Peabody said easily and walked out of the room, leaving a kind of wave of surprise and apprehension behind him.

"What's he going to do?" Doris said sharply.

Charlie adjusted his dark, knitted tie. Matt lighted a cigarette. Lieutenant Peabody returned with Sergeant O'Brien trudging along behind him. And unexpectedly, to Laura, the Sergeant proved to be an excellent and speedy shorthand writer. He hauled a fat, ringed pad from some pocket and settled down in a chair which creaked under his weight.

It was an orderly, queerly formal procedure; it took a long time, in spite of the Sergeant's adroit and nonchalant fingers and Peabody's equally adroit and ready questions. Doris, with a glance at Charlie, stuck to her story of the time when he left her apartment the previous night. When it came his turn, Charlie with a quick smile at Doris which was half indulgent, half apologetic, stuck to his story. It was perfectly clear that Doris had snatched at the notion of providing herself, and Charlie, with an alibi; it was clear that Charlie, as well as everyone else, saw through her swift little maneuver and rejected it. A small flush came up into Doris' lovely face.

But then Charlie would have known that it was better to stick to the letter of the truth, even if he had had no regard for the truth as such. When Peabody had finished with Doris and then Charlie and then Matt, he told them they could go.

Doris sprang up; she went hurriedly to get her coat; she couldn't get away fast enough. Charlie accompanied her and Laura heard him speak to Doris. "I'm sorry. But really, Doris—"

Doris twitched herself and her coat, which he was holding, away from him. Matt said to Peabody, "I'd rather stay."

Peabody hesitated and then shrugged. "All right. If Miss March wants you to stay—as her lawyer."

Matt's eyebrows went up; he gave Laura a quick look. She said to the Lieutenant, "I do want him to stay."

The door closed after Charlie and Doris. And Laura made her own statement, slowly, watching Sergeant O'Brien's big red fingers make an irrevocable record in black and white.

It seemed to her that that took a long time, too; there were odd details. What time exactly was it that Cosden had arrived the night before? Was it his idea or hers that he should stay to dinner? How long exactly had it taken them to trim the tree? The tree stood beside the window; were the curtains drawn while they trimmed the tree? Were they drawn at any time? Had she looked down at the street? Was she sure she hadn't? How could she be sure? What time had Cosden left? Well, what time did she think it was? Wasn't there some way to be more exact? Hadn't she looked at the clock? Hadn't she turned on the radio? Well, then, had anybody telephoned to her after he had gone? At any time after he had gone, during the night? Had anybody visited the apartment? Had the doorbell rung at any time?

The Lieutenant went on and on, minutely, repeating the same question in different ways; Matt smoked and watched him, and once or twice started to speak and stopped himself.

"All right." Peabody said at last. "You can sign that after it's typed up."

Sergeant O'Brien folded up his notebook and put it away. They were leaving; Matt went to the door with them. "See here, Peabody," he said abruptly. "if you're going to prefer charges I want to know it—"

"I'm sure you do," Peabody said.

"What's the answer?"

"I don't know," Peabody said, flatly and finally. "I really don't know." Sergeant O'Brien's great bulk loomed up suddenly in the doorway; he gave Laura an odd look, severe, disapproving, yet with a kind of friendliness, too.

"That's a nice little girl, miss," he said. He vanished as if he'd been pulled on an invisible string by Peabody; the door closed with a hard bang. Matt came back.

"He's not got any real evidence against you, Laura," he said directly. "He's not at all certain that this Miller woman's murder has anything to do with any of us."

"What do you think?"

"Well, I—" He hesitated, and then sighed. "Well, I think Peabody's hunch is right. If you can call it a hunch—a better definition is trained observation and experience. Yes, I'm afraid he's right. In any event, we'll have to act on the basis that he's right."

She said slowly, "Matt, I meant it about a lawyer. You—"

"Nonsense!" He gave her a flashing, indescribably comforting grin. "You don't need a lawyer! And—" The smile vanished. He said soberly, "And if I can do what I'm trying to do, you're not going to need a lawyer."

Hopelessness swept her like a wave. "What *can* you do?"

"I don't know really. But for one thing I'd like to find Maria Brown." He looked at his watch. "I'll come in later this afternoon, if that's all right. Early enough to go with you when you take Jonny out. Meantime if you want some legal advice"—again he took the edge from it by speaking lightly, smiling a little, his eyes very blue—"my advice is to do exactly what you've been doing. Just tell them the truth and stick to it."

Just tell them the truth, Laura thought, as she cooked a late lunch for Jonny and herself, and listened to Jonny's chatter, from which once the words Davy Crockett emerged with startling

126

clearness. Observing the depleted supply of food in the refrigerator, Laura set herself to the task of making a list of groceries and ordering; it was a full and comprehensive list; she felt as if she were ordering for supplies for a desert island, to last a long time. That was because there would be, thus, only one delivery; only one boy from the store to identify, carefully, before she opened the door and let him deposit the packages. A desert island, she thought; it was more like a beleaguered post, set in the middle of enemy country. And the enemy, invisible, unidentifiable, had advanced from Koska Street to Lake Shore Drive, to strike with blundering but ruthless aim.

TWENTY-FOUR

Jonny went to take her nap, cheerfully, gaily, chatting with Laura, talking to Suki, going in to take a long admiring look at the Christmas tree before she trotted into her own bedroom and curled herself up under an eiderdown.

But who had murdered Conrad Stanislowski and then—if Peabody was right, because Catherine Miller wore a brown coat, because she had entered the apartment house where Laura lived —murdered Catherine Miller? Thinking she was Maria Brown, because the murderer knew that Maria Brown was dangerous?

Peabody had said that, if that were true, then Stanislowski's murder had no political motive. And he believed that Catherine Miller's death automatically cleared Maria Brown of suspicion of murder. Matt had argued about that, but it was a thin argument, something Matt himself had not, she was sure, accepted.

So if Maria Brown had not murdered Conrad—and had not murdered Catherine Miller, if Conrad's murder was a result of neither a political intrigue nor a blood feud, arising from some long-ago quarrel perhaps, in far-off Poland, then what was the motive for Conrad's murder? Peabody frankly assumed it to be money, the Stanislowski fund. Suppose he was right; that led again to only one conclusion. There were three people, four if Matt were included, who were directly interested in the money, and in Jonny, and thus in Conrad Stanislowski's life or death.

And that in its turn offered an inescapable conclusion. She hadn't murdered Conrad. She loved Matt; she could not have questioned, seriously, in her own mind, whether or not he was a murderer; that was instinctive but it was strong, too. So that left Charlie and Doris, the only other people who had any sort of connection with the Stanley will and the money Conrad would have claimed if he had not been—quickly—murdered.

Doris? Who liked money and was determined to fight for it; who had an alibi for the time of Conrad's murder.

Charlie?

Instinct again rejected it. But that was because there existed an almost impassable barrier to the postulatum that anyone who was a familiar acquaintance, a known friend, could possibly be a murderer. It seemed strange that murder did not leave a mark upon a murderer.

If there were in fact only two suspects, Doris and Charlie, and if she had had to choose between them the more likely suspect, then it was Charlie. So what did she know of Charlie?

She knew everything there was to know about him, she thought wearily. She knew everything anyone knew about Charlie; his life was quite literally an open book.

But that wasn't right either; nobody's life was really an open book; there were always things that even close associates, intimate and old friends might not know. All right; what was there to know about Charles Stedman?

The yellow bird he had brought Jonny had stopped nodding and was leaning now at a jaunty but insecure angle on the tree. She went to the tree and adjusted it and absently straightened one or two bright, tinsel ornaments.

Her first recollections of Charlie were dim; he had gradually entered her small world because he was a friend of Conrad's; occasionally, when she was with Conrad, Charlie was there, too—lunch or dinner or a baseball game; once she remembered an ice show, when Conrad had had to leave unexpectedly and rather than disappoint Laura he had asked Charlie to take her: she was then in her early teens; Charlie had been kind in his remote and impersonal way. Later, of course, she had seen more of Charlie; after Conrad's marriage, Charlie was as frequent a guest in the lavish Stanley apartment as Laura and Matt.

But what really did she know of Charlie?

Well, then, he was a bachelor, younger than Conrad but it was difficult to say how much younger; Charlie was one of those men who perhaps grow a little thinner, a little more exact and precise, acquire merely a more perceptible sprinkling of gray hair, as years go on, but never seem to age. He owned and operated a factory for tools; he manufactured jigs, dies: Conrad had taught her the vocabulary; for years Conrad had done business with Charlie. He was, next to Laura's father, Conrad's closest friend. He had a quick and astute mind; he was innately conventional, he was not a man of a warm or impulsive nature; still he must have friends and associates of whom she knew nothing. After Conrad's death, she and Charlie had worked closely together, in their position of co-trustees. He had not liked the Stanislowski fund and had said so frankly, but he had nevertheless been conscientious, cautious and conservative in his ideas and very helpful to Laura. There was no detail that Charlie overlooked; he was of inestimable value in the tedious legal minutiae connected with Conrad's will, and with the no less onerous chore of the accounts involved. There was a yearly audit by a firm of accountants; Charlie insisted that Laura and Matt and Doris check the audits, as he did himself.

So, Laura thought suddenly, there was no question of any juggling of money. No question of Charlie—or Doris or anyone— having contrived illegally to tamper with the Stanislowski fund. She hadn't thought of that before but probably Peabody had. And besides—even if any one *had* attempted any chicanery about the money (as no one could have done, for it would have been spotted at once)—the estate was to be settled in January. That meant a final, thorough accounting of every penny; any theft, embezzlement would have come to light then, whether or not Conrad Stanislowski were in America or in Poland, alive or dead.

And Charlie did not need money. He was successful; he had always been successful in a very solid way; his contracts with Conrad alone, Laura knew, netted him a very substantial income; he must be, indeed a wealthy man, not in the spectacular way that Conrad was rich, for millions had poured into Conrad's pockets, but Charlie was rich just the same. He lived quietly and unostentatiously, but Charlie would have lived like that in any circumstances; yet he did not stint himself certainly; he had every comfort and every luxury that there was to have. No, Charlie had no need for money.

Unless, of course, he was in fact and secretly consumed with a money greed! It didn't seem likely. Yet that happened sometimes, didn't it? A third of the Stanislowski fund would have been considerable, and very attractive to a man who loved money.

Charlie?

Or Doris.

She was thinking that when the telephone rang. It seemed strangely, apropos, almost as if some telepathic influence had reached out across the dark day and the towering apartment houses between to touch Doris, for she said when Laura answered, "I've been thinking about Maria Brown, Laura. I—I suppose she must have some evidence about Stanislowski's murder. Did she tell you anything yesterday?"

"No. She only asked about Jonny and what the police were doing. That's all."

"And you didn't ask her to come back to see you last night?" Doris asked.

"*No!*"

"Well—I only thought. Laura, if you *do* think of anything about her that you have forgotten or anything about the Stanislowski—or—or—well, tell me, will you, Laura?"

"There is nothing to tell."

"I—" Doris said, "I—" There was a long pause. Then she said flatly, "Good-bye," and hung up.

She's frightened, Laura thought, her flare of anger dying out; and I'm frightened, too.

It roused her from her long and futile train of thought. She looked at the door to make sure that she had locked it and went back to Jonny's room.

Jonny was napping quietly, a round hump under the eiderdown, one brown braid dangling down from the pillow. The kitten lifted his head, jumped down and followed Laura into her room; he leaped up to the window sill to observe the world at large, and gave a hoarse mutter of interest and surprise. It was beginning to snow. Huge white flakes were drifting lazily past the window. Suki crouched and made a dab at them and his dark paw struck the windowpane softly, so he gave an exasperated mutter and lashed his black tail in frustration.

Laura saw herself in the mirror, white and tired, still wearing the skirt and sweater she had snatched up in the darkness of early morning. There were blue shadows under her eyes; she'd forgotten lipstick; her short hair was in loose, disheveled curls; in the sweater and skirt she looked like a forlorn and uncertain child.

But she was not a child; and she had a heavy responsibility toward Jonny.

Suki made another dab and uttered so furious a Siamese curse that Laura laughed, and gathered him up under her chin where he instantly stopped being a jungle animal and snuggled down, purring with abandon.

There were too many questions. She was suddenly, desperately tired. She took a long, hot bath. She wrapped herself in a warm woolen dressing gown. And with Suki a warm, purring bundle on her shoulder, suddenly, as though she had been drugged with weariness, she fell asleep.

It was dusk when she woke. There were no lights in the room.

Gradually she became aware of a distant murmur of voices some-where. Suki was gone, and her blue eiderdown had mysteriously got itself pulled up over her sleeping figure. She roused, drowsy and confused, and fumbled for the bedside lamp. As she did so Matt came to the door.

"*Matt—*"

"You were so sound asleep I didn't want to wake you."

Jonny came to stand beside Matt; her round face looked rather pale in the light from the bedside lamp; her blue eyes were sober.

"Matt, how long have you been here?"

"About an hour or so."

She was still not fully awake, but the full significance of Matt's presence struck her with sudden fright. "*I never thought that Jonny would open the door!*"

"That's all right," he said. "I never thought of it either. Don't say anything more." He pulled Jonny closer to him and twisted her braid around his finger. "I've explained it to her. She un-derstands now."

Jonny might have opened the door for anyone. Anyone could have come in. "*She's never done that before, Matt!*"

"That's all right," he said. "Oh, a boy came with groceries. I put them away. Now then, Jonny, how about making some hot chocolate, while Laura gets dressed?"

"Matt, wait. Is there any news?"

"So far as I know, things are just the way they were this morning. There is an awful lot of investigation, cut and dried routine, they have to get through. It takes time. And of course they have to investigate the possibility that Catherine Miller was murdered for some reason which has nothing to do with the Stanislowski affair."

She pushed the blue eiderdown away and then looked at it. "Matt, did you put that over me?"

He nodded. "You were curled up tight as the kitten. I tiptoed in. It was cold and I pulled it over you."

On some fringe of awareness Laura was conscious of the still-ness in Jonny's figure, pressing against Matt, her blue eyes very sober. It was a fleeting impression. "You looked about as old as Jonny," Matt said, and the telephone rang.

"I'll get it," Matt said promptly and disappeared. Jonny gave Laura a grave look and edged into the room.

In the hall Matt said sharply, into the telephone, "*What's that?*"

There was something in his voice that brought her hurriedly on her feet, pushing away the blue eiderdown, wrapping her dressing gown around her, running into the hall.

"Doris!" Matt said in almost an awestruck way. "For God's

131

sake—*when?*" Laura came so close to him that her white dressing gown touched his elbow. Jonny stood beside her. There was a long, jerky murmur from the telephone; Laura could not understand the words. Matt said suddenly, "We'll be there right away. Sure, we'll bring Jonny. Keep your shirt on, Doris. All right, all right. I know it's not funny. It was in the cards. We'll be there."

He put down the telephone and turned to Laura, his eyes inexplicably blue and dancing. "The sky is raining Stanislowskis. Believe it or not, another one has turned up. Says he's Jonny's father. Has credentials galore! Tells the same story the first one told about his background and all that, I mean. He wants us to bring Jonny."

"There can't be another one—"

"Get some clothes on. Hurry—"

She dressed quickly; she put on red lipstick; she combed her hair. Matt was helping Jonny into her coat and hat and overshoes. She could hear his voice. "It's snowing, Jonny. You can't get your feet wet. Snow. That's that white stuff out the window. See it? Coming from the sky? That's snow."

Jonny said, "Snow—"

But when Laura came out into the hall again and Jonny in her red coat, red hat and white mittens was standing beside Matt, ready to go, Matt was soberly loading a revolver. It glittered dully and coldly in the light.

"Matt!"

"I brought this for you. I'll put it in the drawer of the table, here. It's only because you and Jonny are alone. I just want you to have it." He dropped the revolver in the drawer of the hall table. "All right, let's go."

The lobby was almost deserted but the switchboard girl paused in her work to turn and watch them out the door. The doorman sprang to get a taxi but he, too, gave them a brightly curious look. Somebody entering the apartment house paused, and as they got into the taxi, Laura saw him speak to the doorman, apparently asking him a question. The doorman nodded yes, and the tenant turned to stare at the taxi with unconcealed curiosity. Obviously they had read the papers; as obviously everyone in the busy hive of the great apartment house knew that Laura had been questioned by the police when the woman Catherine Miller had been found murdered.

Snow swirled in from the lake, white in the taxi's headlights. It was a short ride. In a few moments the taxi turned into the curving entrance of one of Chicago's most luxurious and beautiful apartment buildings.

"I always think of a church when I come here," Matt said

suddenly as they went through the enormous, hushed lobby with its dark wood paneling and the neatly uniformed attendants. The elevator man greeted him. "Good evening, Mr. Cosden. It's a bad day out, but then we have to expect snow this time of the year—in time for Christmas." His eyes were curious, too.

Matt said "Yes." Jonny clung to Matt's hand. Usually when she visited Doris' home the magnificence fascinated her; she stared with wide blue eyes. This time she looked at the floor, shrinking a little against Matt. She's tired, Laura thought, with compunction.

Would she recognize this second Conrad?

Her heart quickened. She glanced at Matt and he had noted her questioning glance at Jonny. "That's what I'm thinking, too," he said. "Well—we'll soon find out."

The elevator came to a dignified halt; they entered a hall and Doris came with a rapid swirl of skirts and high heels. She seized Matt's hand.

"Come along. He's in here."

Matt paused, however, to help Jonny out of her galoshes. The butler took Laura's coat. Doris tapped her little foot. It seemed to Laura that Matt took a little longer time than necessary in removing Jonny's galoshes. When that was done, Doris led the way quickly along the enormous hall and into the library.

It was a huge apartment, a duplex, with lofty ceilings and an air of permanence which perhaps had been one of the factors which helped Doris persuade Conrad to buy the apartment, for Conrad always liked permanence and quality. The library door was open.

Charlie sat at one end of the long table in the middle of the room. At the other end, a man sat, a stranger, his dark, bright gaze fixed upon them. He was sturdily built, with a broad mobile face and very white teeth. He jumped up as they entered. He gave Jonny one swift look. Then he came to her quickly, caught her in his arms, drew her up, high against his shoulder—and unexpectedly began to sing.

The words were Polish. Laura knew that without understanding their sense. His voice was gay. And Jonny, instantly, as if released by a spring, joined in the song.

It was an extraordinary scene, the vigorous, thickly built man, Jonny with her brown braids swinging, and her sturdy little legs, with their white socks and black strapped slippers, dangling below her short blue pleated skirt—set against the lofty room, the heavy crimson curtains, the rows of bookshelves filled with books which Conrad had ordered and which looked as if they had never been opened.

All four of them, Charlie and Doris, and Matt and Laura,

watched spellbound while the man before them swung the little figure in his arms and they sang together, Jonny's high treble, gay and light, over the man's deeper bass. And Conrad Stanley's face, in the portrait above the mantel, watched, too.

They sang together only a few bars. They stopped in the same fractional note as if by prearrangement. And then Jonny laughed on a strained, high-pitched note and swiftly, to Laura's thunderstruck amazement, seized the man's ears and swung his dark head lightly from one side to the other in a gay make-believe wrestle.

It was exactly as if he had given her the signal for an established ritual between them, and she had responded. So this had to be the real Conrad Stanislowski.

But then who was the murdered man? Who was Maria Brown?

TWENTY-FIVE

Conrad Stanislowski hugged the child, kissed her cheek and put her down. He took a handkerchief out and touched his eyes.

There was no doubt about recognition this time, no doubt at all. Jonny gave one startled glance around her. Her eyes were brilliant, almost black. There were pink flames in her cheeks. She became aware of the strained observation of all those people. She gulped and ran to Matt, thumping across the rug. She clutched for his hand. He put his arm around her, pulling her close.

Charlie said, "Well—that seems to settle it."

Doris sat down. Her bracelets glittered as she lifted one small hand and gestured toward a rather worn-looking heap of papers on the table. "Of course, all that will have to be confirmed," she said sharply.

Stanislowski dabbed at his eyes. Laura tried to find in his face some traceable resemblance to Jonny. There was none, really. He had dark eyes, a rather prominent and square chin and jaw, a broad face so his eyes looked deep sunken. He had thick, vigorous dark hair and a ruddy complexion. Aside from that suggestion of the Slav about his features which showed in Jonny's small face

134

too, there was no resemblance at all to Jonny. But, then, Laura realized rather dismally, there had been no traceable resemblance between Jonny and the murdered man either. Except the first Conrad's eyes were blue, even if rather bleak and faded, while Jonny's were a vivid, clear and sparkling blue. However, there was not likely to exist a very marked resemblance between a little girl going on eight and a mature man.

Charlie followed Doris' gesture. He rose precisely, took up the heap of papers and handed them to Matt. "There's the letter you left at the orphanage, Matt. Various cards of identity, you'll see those, and his passport."

Doris said suddenly, "Do sit down, Laura. Matt, we've got to thresh this thing out." She rose herself, however, and went to the door where she touched the little mother-of-pearl bell, set in the casing, with an imperious forefinger. Matt sat down and Jonny huddled in the curve of his arm, excited color still high on her cheeks. But she was perplexed, too; she shot a swift glance at Stanislowski, and then fixed her eyes on the round toe of one black slipper. Laura sank down in a big, red lounge chair. She was directly opposite the enormous fireplace, its mantel carved of dark oak, with Conrad Stanley's portrait above it. The portrait had been painted shortly after his marriage to Doris, and it was excellent. Laura looked up at the broad face, the wise, wary yet humorous and tolerant eyes and for a moment it seemed to her that Conrad himself was in the room bidding them be cautious, ask questions, listen, weigh every answer and, Laura thought with a pang of remembered grief in her heart, asking them not to take their responsibility in the life of this little great-niece too lightly, too swiftly or carelessly. The door opened and the butler entered. Doris said, "Tea—something to drink."

"Yes, madam."

The door closed. Matt was glancing through the thin bundle of papers Charlie had given him. Conrad Stanislowski had apparently conquered his tears although he still had a large white handkerchief in his hand. He sat down in a composed way and watched Matt.

Matt said, "Here's my letter, all right."

Laura was seated so near him that she could see the letter as he unfolded it and a few words leaped out in clear black and white. Matt glanced rapidly at it, as if merely to identify it; then he returned it to an envelope which was addressed simply "Mr. Conrad Stanislowski." There was no postmark on the letter, of course, and no stamp, but Laura thought suddenly, there was a postmark. Murder was the postmark.

It was as if it were stamped in invisible ink, with no trace, no clue to the lethal hand that had made that stamp for a letter

135

which outlined the contents of Conrad Stanley's will. A letter which had brought this second Conrad Stanislowski to Chicago—and almost certainly had brought the first Conrad to Chicago and to his death. He had known of the letter; he had known every one of the words in Matt's handwriting.

Postmark murder, Laura thought again, and remembered, too, the tragic, huddled figure of Catherine Miller in the fatal brown coat and black beret.

Postmark murder. Laura stirred restively. It was very quiet in the room. When Doris reached impatiently for a cigarette, the sputter of the match was sharp and clear.

Matt said, "And here's the passport." He opened it and very deliberately examined it. When he reached the photograph he looked at it for a long time and looked at the man seated at the other end of the table, comparing the two with frank care. Conrad Stanislowski bore the scrutiny with composure, and there was no doubt about it, Laura could see the photograph, too. It was that of the man sitting there waiting, one sturdy leg crossed over the other. So he was Conrad Stanislowski.

Matt fumbled through the other papers.

Charlie said, "I've looked at them, Matt. They seem to be in order."

"Oh, yes," Matt said in an absent way. "I expect they are all in order."

"There's the letter you left at the orphanage. His passport is not visaed for the United States. We'll have to do something about that but I don't think there's much doubt he's Stanislowski. I for one." Charlie said. "am convinced."

Doris gave Charlie a long look, and lowered her eyelids. Matt put the heap of papers neatly together and returned them to Charlie who put them on the table. It was almost like a board meeting, somehow, with the long table before the fireplace, Stanislowski at one end of it and Charlie at the other, and the papers upon it, the immediate and urgent agenda. Stanislowski touched his eyes again with his handkerchief, then put it in his pocket.

Matt said to him directly, "How did you get into the United States?"

Stanislowski glanced at Charlie. "I take it that this is the man who left that letter for me."

"Oh, I'm sorry! I didn't introduce you. This is Matt Cosden, you know who he is. And of course. Miss March—"

Stanislowski bounced at once to his feet. bowed and sat down again.

Charlie said. "You know that Cosden is Mrs. Stanley's lawyer. It was he who found Jonny. You know all about that." He said to

Matt, "We've informed him of the situation—all of it—while we were waiting for you." He turned to Stanislowski again. "I expect you'd better tell Cosden the whole story of your arrival, as you told Mrs. Stanley and me."

"Certainly," Stanislowski said politely, and paused a second or two as if to collect his words. His clothes, too, like the murdered man's, had a kind of difference about them which Laura could only classify as foreign, except they did not have that ineffable air of shabbiness and wear that the first Conrad's had had but instead looked new and spruce except for a rather worn, bright silk tie. His glistening oxfords were startlingly new and American-made. He leaned back in a composed way and addressed Matt. "It's quite a short story really. I'm a language—they call it an expert. I studied English in London, indeed I intended to teach, but then of course—" He shrugged. "The war. After the war I was more or less obliged to go along with the party in control in the government. I had a child to support. There was nothing else to do. Don't think too harshly of me for that. Nobody can say what a man would do until he finds himself in exactly identical circumstances. However, with me it was only a matter of survival until I could find a way to escape. I did find a way to send Jonny out about two years ago."

Matt interrupted. "How did you do that?"

Stanislowski shrugged again. "Escapes are made, Mr. Cosden. More than you dream of, more than ever reach the newspapers. This, however, was quite simple. A friend of mine from student days shared my real sympathies. We had to keep our intentions a secret, naturally, but he found a way to get out to Vienna and he thought he could make his escape from Vienna, then, later. I was at that time, I thought, being watched rather closely. It seemed to me it would be easier for me to get away if I could send Jonny out first. And of course I wanted to be sure my child was safe. It happened that this man, his name was Schmidt, felt that he would have a better chance to get away if he had the child with him—a matter of some slight disguise, you understand. We knew of this orphanage in Vienna. He took Jonny with him. I took care to fasten her birth certificate inside her clothing so there would be no question of identification or my claim to her when I eventually made my own escape to Vienna. He sent me word, we had arranged a kind of code, that Jonny was safely in the institution. However, it was two years before I managed to get myself on a commission for the Polish government as a language expert and eventually thus to Vienna. Eventually I made my arrangements to leave Vienna. I went to the orphanage for Jonny. They told me that you, Mr. Cosden, had taken her to America and they gave me"—he nodded at the papers on the table—"your letter. My intention in the beginning had been to escape either to England or to the United States with Jonny. There I intended to seek asylum. When I learned that Jonny was in Chicago, naturally I decided to come here."

The door opened and the butler came in with a tray of decanters and glasses and ice. He went to the end of the long oak table and set them down; a maid, trim in black and white, brought in a tea tray; the butler pulled up a small table in front of Doris. It was a perfectly executed little ritual.

The silver gleamed in the light. Doris poured tea for Laura and the butler brought it to her; the maid followed with a delicate porcelain plate full of tiny watercress sandwiches. It was all perfectly done. Doris' rings sparkled, her little white hands seemed as delicate as the porcelain. Charlie poured drinks for Stanislowski and Matt. There was a glass of milk for Jonny, who took it politely from the tray the maid offered her but held it in both hands until Matt gently relieved her of it and put it on the table beside him. Jonny accepted a cookie, too, politely again, but did not so much as nibble on it. It's been too much excitement for her, Laura thought, troubled.

Conrad Stanley's portrait surveyed the little scene. The windows were darkening, and the butler went to close the curtains with a decorous swish which reminded Laura suddenly of the night when she had pulled the curtains in her own small living-room—and then known that someone was in the apartment.

Who?

Who had murdered the first Conrad?

Suddenly and strangely it struck her that there was now another person who was interested in the Stanley will. Logically, another person had entered that too small circle of people. That was the man who sat composedly at the long table, and called himself Conrad Stanislowski. And had a passport with his photograph.

And whom Jonny had recognized.

The maid had retired, quietly. The butler gave a glance around the room, murmured something to Doris and Doris dismissed him with a nod. The door closed. Matt said to Stanislowski, "How did you manage to get into the country?"

Stanislowski took rather a generous drink, then smiled at Matt, showing very white teeth. "I came as fast as I could. I thought my child was in safe hands, but as I indicated to you her arrival in Chicago gave me a focus, governed my decision to come to the United States. I got to Genoa and managed to get a berth on a little cargo boat. She was short-handed so they didn't ask too many questions. We reached New Orleans and there I simply jumped ship. It was easy to do. I came to Chicago by train and arrived here today. I only stopped to buy some shoes"—he glanced at one new and shiny oxford and smiled in a rather deprecating way—"then I came straight to Mrs. Stanley."

Doris glanced up at Matt over her teacup; there was a perceptible edge in her voice. "He simply rang the bell, the doorman announced him and my butler came to me and gave me his name. It was a great surprise. I thought I should see him. I telephoned to Charlie and tried to reach you at the office but by that time Mr."—the edge in her voice sharpened but she said it— "Mr. Stanislowski had arrived at the door. He showed me his passport and your letter, and as we were talking Charlie came. I tried to telephone to you at your office again and you weren't there. Then it struck me that you might have gone"—her brown eyes went to Laura in an odd look, then she lowered her eyelashes, surveyed the cup of tea in her hands and said—"to see Jonny." She lifted the teacup and sipped from it.

Matt said mildly, "I can see how it would be a surprise. I might even say we are amazed, Stanislowski."

Stanislowski eyed him calmly. Charlie said suddenly, "We must make some sort of arrangements for you, Stanislowski. I take it you've not had time to go to a hotel or anything of the kind."

Stanislowski shrugged. "I checked my baggage at the railway station. As you know, Chicago is a strange city to me."

"I'll get a room for you at the club," Charlie said politely. "That ought to suit you nicely until you can make some permanent arrangements."

But Stanislowski shook his head. "No. Thank you very much. I think it better for me to take an apartment at some hotel. It may be some time before I decide just where I'll live or what I'm going to do."

Perhaps the same thought flashed across all their minds, through the room like a little chain linking them together. Doris put it in words, swiftly. "But you'll have to live in America, Mr. Stanislowski. That is if you wish to inherit from my husband's will."

She didn't like Stanislowski; or rather, Laura thought, she didn't like his arrival, his claims, and the authenticity of those claims. The reason was clear; she could not, now, fight Jonny's claim to the Stanislowski fund. It would go, all of it, to the man sitting there before them, composed and certain of himself, armed with proof of his identity. No; Doris didn't like that. And at the moment she saw no way out of it, so her voice had a sharp edge; her eyes, her lovely face were cold and angry.

Charlie said dryly, "Well, yes. That is the provision, Stanislowski. You do understand it?"

Stanislowski nodded. "Oh, yes. And I'm quite prepared to abide by it. But you see all this is very new to me, America and all that. It is a dream I have held for so long a time that it doesn't seem quite real. I'd like to look about me a little and decide just what to do, where exactly to live—in America of course, but where. I must tell you that the provision of my uncle's will touches me deeply. It makes me feel very humble."

Inexplicably and suddenly Matt's eyes were dancing. He said soberly, however, "I expect Stedman or Mrs. Stanley told you, Stanislowski, about this other man who claimed your name and was—murdered."

Stanislowski's ruddy face assumed lines of grave concern. "Yes. It is dreadful, shocking. I cannot imagine who he was nor how he knew of my child, or about the Stanley will or, in fact, any of the circumstances. You will see at once that it was necessary, indeed it was vital to me, to tell no one anything of my intentions. As a matter of fact, I did not know anything about the will until I reached Vienna and the orphanage. Certainly I told no one there what I intended to do, and on the boat I made no confidential acquaintances. You must believe me when I tell you that anyone escaping from behind the Iron Curtain finds it advisable to keep his own counsel. I have talked of this to no one."

Charlie tapped his fingers on the table. "We quite understand that, Stanislowski. At the same time this first man did know all these things. And he told very much the same story that you have told us."

Laura said shortly, "It was precisely the same story."

Charlie nodded. "So he must have learned it from somewhere. We'd like to know how he knew it. The police would like to know."

Stanislowski shook his head. "I cannot answer that."

"There's a woman in the affair," Matt said. "They told you that, too?"

Stanislowski nodded. "Maria Brown. It seems extraordinary that your police have not found her."

Matt said mildly, "Oh, I think they'll probably find her some-time."

Doris put down her teacup with a sharp clatter. Perhaps again the same thought had flashed between them. Doris said, "That woman who was murdered this morning—if somebody thought she was Maria Brown—"

Stanislowski lifted his thick shoulders. "Very tragic."

The dancing gleam had left Matt's eyes; they were as cold and gray as steel. He said softly, "It was tragic. Do you know of any woman who might have taken the name of Maria Brown? Have you been in communication with anybody at all in this country?"

Stanislowski leaned his sturdy body forward in his chair. "You

140

mean, I take it, was there some woman in Poland in whom I might have confided and who might have gone to America at some time ahead of me? You mean, did I stop when I reached Chicago, or in fact at any time since I entered your country and communicate with this woman, telling her all these details? That's what you mean, isn't it?"

"That's exactly what I mean. You're quite sure there's nobody like that who could have taken the name of Maria Brown?"

Doris interrupted. "Do you mean, Matt, that she could have put this first man up to it? I mean a—a conspiracy! Trying to get Jonny's money!"

"It's a possibility," Matt said shortly, watching Stanislowski.

But Stanislowski leaned back in his chair and smiled. "You're quite wrong, Cosden. There's nobody like that, I assure you. You'll have to believe me when I tell you that I have told no one anything at all of my plans, of Jonny, of this Stanley will or of what I intended to do."

There was a silence. Matt took the cookie from Jonny's hand and put it on the table. Charlie eyed the papers on the dark oak table. Doris' bracelets clattered as she put out one cigarette and lighted another.

Conrad Stanley looked down at them from the portrait—warning them, Laura thought; saying, be careful.

Conrad Stanislowski said at last, coolly, "Have you any question of my bona fide, my identity?"

Matt did not reply. Charlie waited a moment, considering it deliberately. Doris started to speak, and stopped with a quick, angry yet frustrated gesture. Charlie said precisely, "There is no question of your identification, Stanislowski, none that I can see. You have the right papers and, of course, Jonny recognized you. There are certain requirements which concern us—Miss March and me as trustees, and Mrs. Stanley and of course Cosden. You understand why we will have to check certain points of your story. Now let me see, you said the cargo boat you took was a—" He ruffled through the papers and Stanislowski said, with a curious, half-amused gleam in his dark eyes, "It was the *Mirador*. Portuguese registry."

Matt said, "Where is the ship now?"

"She was to leave at dawn the day after I jumped ship. I suppose she left according to plan. I don't know her next port. The port authorities at New Orleans can probably tell you. I do realize that this makes it difficult for you to check my story, or for me to satisfy you in this regard, but that's the way it is."

There was another little silence. Then Matt said very quietly, "Is your wife still in Poland, Stanislowski?"

141

TWENTY-SIX

Laura looked at him quickly. There was nothing at all but polite inquiry in his face—but was Matt, too, thinking, who then is Maria Brown?

Stanislowski's reply was prompt. "I believe that she is. I don't know. I'm sorry to say that my wife and I were separated when Jonny was a baby. We have different views of politics and also"—he shrugged—"we were what is called out of sympathy with each other. I believe the word is incompatible. I have no idea what happened to her. I think she left Cracow but that's all I know. Her name was Marya—Marya Gradžicka." He looked thoughtfully at Jonny. "I doubt very much whether Jonny would remember her."

Marya, Laura thought; Maria.

Matt's face had no expression at all. Doris looked up with a quick, angry impatience. "Charlie! Matt! What should we do?"

Stanislowski rose and stood before them, short and thick and stocky, and dominating the room all at once, much as an actor dominates the middle of the stage in a well-rehearsed role. "That is simple, Mrs. Stanley. I intend to take my child. That is why I want a hotel apartment. I intend to take her with me now, immediately. Mr. Stedman, will you be so kind as to recommend a hotel?"

"Why—why, certainly. There's the Ambassador, very fine, not far from here. And the Drake; that's nearby, too. Laura—" He hesitated, tapping his fingers on the table; then he said pleasantly, "It would seem sensible for Laura and the child to be near each other—at least for a few days. I realize that the child recognizes you but you have been separated for a time. It might, let us say, ease the change for the child if Laura may spend considerable time with her."

Stanislowski's white teeth flashed; he made another bow in Laura's direction. "If you will be so kind, Miss March. And of course she'll need her clothes—that kind of thing. Thank you, Mr. Stedman. Now I think Jonny and I will go at once to the

142

hotel. I'll send a porter for my baggage." He fumbled in one pocket. "I have some claim checks for it."

Charlie said, "Well—well, it seems rather sudden. Still I'm sure we understand the way you feel."

Doris looked at Jonny and at Stanislowski and said nothing. Matt did not move, except his arm must have tightened around Jonny; the little girl's head lifted and she gave him a questioning look. Stanislowski took a step forward, his hand out to Jonny. And something inside Laura pushed her to her feet. *"No,"* she said.

She said it too loudly, too firmly; it sounded like a challenge. She knew that heads jerked, startled, toward her. Stanislowski's flashing white teeth took on a thin line. For a second or two he seemed to measure this unexpected resistance. Then he said, politely enough, "What do you mean?"

What did she mean, Laura thought rather wildly; she didn't know what she meant. But she said firmly, "I'm one of the trustees. You can't take the child until I give my consent."

There was a startled silence. Matt's expression was unreadable; he held Jonny close. Charlie rose, sat down again, adjusted the crease in one trouser leg and finally said, reasonably, "But look here, Laura. There are his papers. Everything is in order."

An odd defiance spurred Laura. "You haven't checked anything yet."

"Well, that's true, that's true, of course," Charlie said, and sighed. "But Jonny recognized him."

There was no answer to that. Laura took a long steadying breath. She went to Jonny and detached the child's hand from Matt's. Matt gave her an odd glance as he rose, a kind of encouraging gleam which Laura scarcely noted. Her heart was thudding. She turned to face Stanislowski. "Nothing has been checked yet. Nothing is proved. I am going to keep Jonny until then. Come with me, Jonny."

Stanislowski hesitated; for the first time he seemed indecisive and surprised; he shot a baffled glance at Charlie who had supported him. Then he straightened himself belligerently; he started for the door as if to stop her by force. "She's my child. You have no right to take her from me. She's my child—"

But Laura and Jonny had reached the door. Laura opened it. Stanislowski, again with a baffled, odd air of uncertainty, stopped and stared at her. Charlie was watching, frowning, uncertain and surprised, too. Doris' brown eyes were curiously intent. There was a faint smile on Matt's lips. Laura said, "It will be easy to prove, then. But until it's been proved I'm going to keep Jonny."

She led Johnny into the hall, leaving a kind of thunderstruck silence behind them. From the back of the enormous foyer, the

143

butler appeared, his pale face and the V of his white shirt looking rather ghostly above his dark coat. She snatched up Jonny's coat and galoshes and hat with trembling hands, hurrying, sure that one of them would come to the door and stop her.

In fact, it was Doris who came into the hall. "It's all right, Hopkins," she said to the butler, "I'll ring for the elevator." She leaned over in the first gesture of motherliness which Laura had ever seen her show toward Jonny and fastened one of Jonny's galoshes, and said in a whisper to Laura, "Why don't you believe him?"

Laura fastened the top button on Jonny's coat. "I don't know. But I'm going to take Jonny home."

Matt came from the library. He picked up Laura's coat and held it for her. "Be sure the doorman gets you a taxi. Don't hang around outside. I'll talk to you later."

Doris' pretty mouth set rather firmly as Matt went to the elevator. It came at once. Doris moved to link her arm in Matt's. They made a picture standing there together, Doris' pretty head almost touching Matt's shoulder as the elevator door closed and Jonny and Laura were swooped steadily downward.

But she remembered Matt's words; she had the doorman get her a taxi.

Jonny nestled against her during the short ride, with the lights of the great apartment houses on their right looming up into the black sky far above them, and the shining street lamps outlining the Drive, and the swish of tires constantly passing them.

Why, Laura thought, had she done just that?

This new man had credentials; he told a story that squared with the facts as they knew them; he knew that they would check every detail of his story.

And Jonny had instantly recognized him. Obviously, the gay little song, the formula for a romp which he had initiated and in which Jonny had joined, was one of the innumerable, tender little games between a father and his child. Jonny had recognized him.

She had made no move to go to him after that; she had made no resistance when Laura took her away. But she was accustomed to the mysterious and arbitrary acts of the adults who had made up her world. She was, lately, accustomed to Laura, and Matt, as authority. Besides, two years in the life of a little girl is a long time.

He was her father. So why could not Laura accept him as Conrad Stanislowski? What had there been in the first man, the murdered man, when he appealed to her, that there was not in this second man, and which made her accept the first Conrad's claim without question?

The second Conrad had convinced the others—at least, he had

144

convinced Charlie, who was not easy to convince, who examined every fact with scrupulous and cautious care; he had convinced Doris, who didn't want to be convinced, didn't want to accept a claimant to the Stanislowski fund, frankly did not intend to give up her share of the fund unless she was forced by law—and this new claimant's arrival—to do so. Laura was not sure that he had convinced Matt. But what was the stubborn block deep within her which stood against her own conviction? She had no reason for not believing him, or if she had one, it was intangible, it could not be analyzed or pinned down; yet it was rooted somewhere, somehow in her short interview with the first man, who had died then so soon. She could summon no sound argument to support her action in taking Jonny home, or her defiance.

When they reached her apartment, the phone was already ringing. Charlie, she thought, or Doris. And then she thought suddenly, is it another of those curiously frightening telephone calls when nobody answers?

But those had ceased, it struck her suddenly. Hadn't they? Why?

She didn't want to answer the telephone. She helped Jonny off with her galoshes. She removed her own coat. The telephone still rang with long, demanding jabs. She finally took up the receiver. Matt said, "Laura? You got there all right. I only wanted to be sure." He lowered his voice. "I am still at Doris'. I'm using the pantry phone. Looks as if I may be here awhile. I suggested talking to Peabody. I don't think Stanislowski liked it; he got a little indignant and agitated. But Charlie calmed him down. Anyway—Peabody's coming here; says he wants to talk to Stanislowski."

"Matt, I don't believe him. I don't know why. But I simply don't believe he's Stanislowski."

There was the faintest, smallest suggestion of a laugh. "Stick to your guns," he said and hung up.

At nine o'clock, with Jonny and the kitten asleep, and Laura roaming uneasily through an apartment which was locked and bolted as if it were besieged, Lieutenant Peabody himself arrived. He settled himself in a chair, sighed, rubbed his eyes, then eyed her thoughtfully. "I've just seen Stanislowski. You want to keep the child, don't you?"

Laura braced herself for opposition. "I intend to keep her until this man's identity is established."

"I've seen him. I've talked to him. I've looked at his papers of identification. I understand the child recognized him."

There was no answer to that. Laura said slowly, "I realize that. But I—I don't believe him."

Lieutenant Peabody leaned back and gave her a long, weary

145

look. His pale eyes were red-rimmed with fatigue. He said, however, crisply enough, "Why not?"

"I can't say—I don't know—but I—I don't believe him."

He said nothing for a moment, yet it was as if invisible tentacles caught at her with questioning fingers, and at last nudged her into further speech. "I can't tell you why. I don't know why. Lieutenant Peabody, what do you think of Maria Brown? Who is she?"

He shrugged. "I don't know."

"But—what are you doing to find her?"

"Many things. It's all routine."

"What about Catherine Miller?"

He rubbed his eyes again. "It's been a long day, Miss March. I'll probably not get much sleep tonight. We're trying every lead we can find. So far there's nothing we've uncovered to account for Catherine Miller's murder except the fact that she was wearing a brown coat and a black beret—and was murdered here."

"Could there be—" she said hesitantly. "Could there be any possible link between Maria Brown and this Catherine Miller?"

"Not so far as we've discovered; I doubt it very much. Robbery was not the reason for her murder; her pocketbook was in the pocket of her coat; a few bills and bus fare, nothing else. There's nothing Mrs. Grelly could tell us, nothing anybody who knew her has so far been able to tell us which would suggest a motive for murder. She lived in a rooming house, a kind of club for working women. I told you that. She had no family, and no relatives in Chicago. She came from Springfield eight years ago; I've talked to the chief of police there; she had a brother in Los Angeles; I've talked to him. Believe me when I tell you that so far we've drawn a complete blank—except for—" He sighed and said flatly, "A brown coat, a black beret, her presence in an apartment house where you live. I told you, I don't like coincidence. In the absence of any other discoverable motive we have to go on the theory that Catherine Miller was murdered because someone thought she was Maria Brown. So therefore, provided of course no contrary evidence comes out, it does seem to me very unlikely that Maria Brown killed her. However, that is by no means a conclusive statement. Circumstances can alter it. Miss March, are you sure that when you went out to the rooming house on Koska Street, when you went to the drug store, at any other time that evening, you didn't see anybody you know?"

Somebody else had asked her that question. Oh, yes—Doris. Laura said, "No. Nobody."

"This business of Catherine Miller's murder has one odd likeness to that of the man who was murdered, whoever he was. There is a troublesome lack of sound alibis, among the people

146

concerned with the Stanley money, for the time when both murders occurred. You," he said specifically, "Stedman, Mrs. Stanley. Cosden."

"But Matt was here—"

"He left at an hour which neither you nor he was certain of except it was between eleven and twelve. Stedman was at Mrs. Stanley's to dinner; he left at about the same time, and came directly past this apartment. The elevator man and the doormen at Mrs. Stanley's apartment house say she did not leave her apartment that night. But there are service elevators there, self-operated, and a service entrance which is locked by the engineer at one o'clock when he leaves. The fact is, all four of you were in the vicinity when Catherine Miller was murdered. When this first man was murdered you were admittedly at the rooming house; Cosden has no alibi for that time; he says he was Christmas shopping but there's no way to prove it. Stedman has no alibi; he says he was at his club, resting, and then took his car and drove out to his factory. The factory is on the west side not too far from Koska Street." He gave a tired, half-stifled yawn. "Mrs. Stanley, of course, was at the dentist's; I've talked to him and his office girl. But you and Stedman—and possibly Cosden— could have been at Koska Street at the time of the murder. The same thing was true last night. You were all in this vicinity. It's an odd likeness. Isn't it?"

The list of suspects was too small, she thought again, with a queer kind of horror as if, for the moment, she accepted it without reservation. Charlie? Doris? Not Matt; not herself.

But there was Maria Brown. And there was the new man claiming to be Conrad Stanislowski.

As if he sensed her argument, he said, "Maria Brown was at Koska Street at the time the first man was murdered; we don't know where she was last night. Stanislowski, he says, was on the train—a day coach, crowded; he threw away the stub of his ticket. Let's get back to him, Miss March. Naturally your intention as trustee, and Stedman's intention, and for that matter Mrs. Stanley's and Cosden's, is to check on his story. That will take considerable time. Things being as they are, with the difficulty of communicating with anybody in Poland, and a very definite difficulty in checking his story about shipping as a hand on the *Mirador*, that's going to take a very long time. In fact, you may never be able to confirm every detail of it. There was a cargo ship called the *Mirador*; I've talked to the New Orleans port authority. But whether or not the skipper will willingly admit taking on a man without proper papers, is another thing. However, I understand that you intend to try to confirm his story."

147

"Yes."

"The details of it may be impossible to confirm. Have you considered that?"

She hadn't really. She said, "I only know how I feel, Lieutenant Peabody."

"In other words you feel that the first man was really Conrad Stanislowski."

"I can't explain it to you. I only know that I want to—to wait."

"But you believe that the first man was Stanislowski. You admit that."

"I don't know what you mean by admit. But—yes, I did feel he was Stanislowski."

"You believed he was Stanislowski. Therefore, you believed his claim to the Stanislowski fund. You knew also that if he died the money would go to you, to Stedman and to Mrs. Stanley."

"No, to Jonny."

"Maybe and maybe not. You can't always tell what the courts will do. In any event this first man turned up. As the situation stood before his appearance the child's inheritance was unsettled; there was a question about it; it must be taken to court. What is rather important, too, all four of you would be obliged to agree to continue the trust fund for the child. However, at this point the first man turns up; the situation changes very abruptly. He is to get all the money. But he is murdered very soon, you might even say immediately, upon presenting himself to you. He told you his address, he talked to you, he told you to tell no one of his appearance. That in itself is rather a curious circumstance, didn't you think so?"

"Yes. But I—believed him."

"Exactly, you believed him. And you were the only person who knew anything about him."

TWENTY-SEVEN

"But I didn't kill him, Lieutenant Peabody. You can't believe that I killed him—"

"Please hear me out. The father, or the man who convinces you he is the father, actually appears and then dies." Lieutenant Peabody's wiry figure leaned forward. "I suppose it didn't strike you that his death would make the child's position much more secure? That consequently there would be no problem of the trust fund? She is her father's heir—"

"But there's Maria Brown. If she *was* his wife—"

"Yes, yes. Cosden and I had a long talk about that. It's a very convenient notion. But there's not a vestige of a fact to support it. We have to go on facts, and the fact is that the death of this first claimant might be considered a short cut to the child's eventual possession of the trust fund. If the murdered man had been really Stanislowski, as you believed him to be, there would be no question of a court's decision. Jonny would almost automatically be considered her father's heir. She would inherit from her father. And she would have to have a guardian, wouldn't she?"

He waited for Laura's assent. "Yes," she said. "Until she is of age."

"Exactly. And you would have been the logical choice to continue to see to her."

"But I—"

"Please wait. In all probability it would have been in a sense a lifetime relation. The child would have been grateful to you. Your influence over her would have continued."

"Stop! That's not true. I never thought of that."

He leaned back in his chair and ran his finger around his wrinkled shirt collar. "This is murder," he said wearily. "A policeman must follow any leads he finds to follow. We've cleared the Pittsburgh angle; Conrad Stanley's brother Paul died unmarried; no heirs. So far you must grant the fact that there are only four people whom we know to have had an interest in this first claimant's life or death."

"Maria Brown—" she began.

He said shortly, "She's important. She may have evidence. Obviously, she's very important to somebody; Catherine Miller was killed. Now then, Mrs. Stanley would have had a third of the money if Conrad hadn't turned up or at least a man who claimed to be Conrad. Mrs. Stanley is already a rich woman. She didn't need that extra third."

But she wants it, thought Laura swiftly. She likes money, she spends money. That's why she's against the plan to keep the trust fund intact for Jonny. Lieutenant Peabody went on. "I've investigated all these people, believe me. It's a very easy thing for a policeman to do. Stedman has a good solid business, tools and dies. He lives quietly but luxuriously. He has no family, no personal claims which might provide an urgent need for money. He

149

is willing to accept this second claimant; he does not oppose his proofs of identity; therefore I cannot believe that he would have opposed the first claimant, if he had had sufficient proof of his claims. Certainly not to the extent of murder."

That had not occurred to her. She said, "Do you mean that clears him of suspicion?"

"None of you is cleared until we get at the truth," Peabody said grimly. "Don't forget Cosden has a motive, too."

"Matt! He's not a suspect!"

"Oh, isn't he? Consider this: Cosden and Mrs. Stanley were to have been married when she met Stanley; she jilted Cosden. As soon as Stanley died she went back to Cosden. She gave him her legal business. She saw him constantly. Mrs. Stanley's interests are Cosden's interests. She says, or implies, that he's going to marry her. Money is a very real and compelling motive for murder."

"Matt didn't even know that Conrad—I mean the murdered man—had come! I didn't tell him! He didn't hear anything about him until I told him! He didn't know his address! He didn't know—"

"But you did know," the Lieutenant said quietly, bringing her around a full circle again. He added after a moment, with again a flash of that curiously disarming frankness, as if he were putting all his cards on the table, "You were very young to be made a trustee for this fund Stanley set up."

"He knew me. He trusted me."

"I know all the circumstances. I know what Stanley did for you and why. I also know that of all the people who would supposedly profit by that man's death, you were the only one who needs money."

Anger brought her to her feet. "I can support myself!"

"But a windfall in the way of cash would help you. Wouldn't it?"

He must be made to see the truth. She said, "Lieutenant Peabody, I didn't kill that man. Doris didn't kill him; she has an alibi. Charlie didn't; he does accept the second man; he doesn't oppose him or the settling of the estate. Matt couldn't have killed anybody. I *know* these people. I know—"

"Nobody knows what anybody's like really when it comes to a very strong wish for money. Or when it comes to murder," he said in a strangely somber voice. "I know what you want me to believe. You want me to believe that Maria Brown lured that man to the address on Koska Street, killed him, phoned to you for help, then ran away. Later you say she came here and asked about the child and ran away again. You want me to believe that someone tried to murder you, got into your apartment, put some

150

sort of sedative in that hot milk. It would be a very dangerous thing to do. Suppose you had seen this remarkably invisible person."

"It happened," Laura said, her lips dry and stiff. "Matt saw the kitten."

"But you had already washed the thermos, hadn't you?"

"Yes. And the saucer. But it did happen like that, Lieutenant. And somebody did follow us in the park that day."

"Somebody you didn't see closely enough to identify or describe." There was an edge of dry skepticism in his voice.

But she must make him see the truth, she thought again desperately. "But Maria Brown did come here. She—"

"And the girl at the switchboard downstairs didn't see her. Nobody saw her apparently except you."

"But the girl at the switchboard doesn't see everybody. She's busy. It's a big apartment house. People coming and going all the time."

He said thoughtfully, "We're trying to find Maria Brown. We're doing everything we can to find her. Either she knows something or she merely went to a dying man's aid and then got scared. We're combing the city, inquiring at every rooming house, at every small hotel. Eventually we'll find her unless of course"— he shrugged—"she's got a friend somewhere who has taken her in. I feel now that that is the answer. There's someone to whom she could go, someone who would hide her. But there we are. The landlady out at the rooming house knows nothing of any friend. We've inquired at the store where she worked. She worked there for a very short time. She'd been very uncommunicative. So far we've unearthed nobody who knew anything about her. Now, it's not easy in a city of this size to find a woman dressed as she was dressed, nothing much to identify, nothing much in the way of description, no photograph. Her description as we have it would fit a thousand women. We did find the yellow-taxi driver. He says he took you and a child to the rooming house. He says a woman came out and spoke to you for a moment and then got into the taxi. He took her to the Union Station and there she disappeared. It's the end of that trail so far. I'm telling you all this because I want you to see how the situation stands."

He paused, thought for a moment as if marshaling facts, leaned forward with his elbows on his knees, and his hands linked, and went on. "As to the day of the Koska Street murder, the situation was this: the landlady says that she, the landlady, was shopping during the afternoon. She says the murdered man arrived about noon and rented a room; then the landlady went out. He did not ask for Maria Brown. I asked the landlady if he had given any references; she said, no. I asked her if anybody had sent him to the rooming house; she said not to her knowledge. She had the room vacant, he looked respectable, he paid the rent she asked. The point is he did not ask for Maria Brown and we haven't been able to find her or find any trail of her since she disappeared from the Union Station. I needn't tell you that there are thousands of people coming and going there, all the time. It would be almost impossible to trace her from there."

"She came here! She must have read the newspapers. She knew where to find me."

"She already knew your name and telephone number. It wouldn't be hard to find your address. But you are the only person who saw her here. Now, mind you, I don't say that she didn't come here to see you, but you do realize that we have only your word for it. Only your word about the kitten. Only your word about some mysterious stranger following you in the park."

"It's true, Lieutenant."

"I don't say it isn't true. I don't say these things didn't happen. Also, I think it perfectly possible that anybody who was intent upon killing you—and that is the theory that you expect me to accept—killing you with a lethal dose of sedative *would* select the thermos that had coffee and milk in it, rather than the one with chocolate. It would be an obvious conclusion that the thermos of chocolate was meant for Jonny and the other one for you. But if that's true, if someone is trying to kill you, why? Can you tell me that?"

Oddly she could not really accept that premise herself. Murder was for the newspapers; it happened to other people; it couldn't happen to her. Perhaps everyone felt that deep instinctive conviction. Yet in another way, a curious, physical way, she did acknowledge her own jeopardy, for a kind of chill lethargy seemed to envelop her. That was fear. Matt had said it; fear is a paralysis. She said, "I don't know."

He watched her thoughtfully for a moment. Then he said, "Of course, there are not very many people who would know of your custom about the thermos bottle. Mrs. Stanley might know it, did she?"

"Perhaps, perhaps, but Doris—"

"Stedman, would he know about it? Cosden?"

Again she said, "Perhaps. Yes."

"All right," he said, "who else would know it?"

Who else, indeed? She said slowly, "You said that anybody might have guessed."

"Well, that's true. But how would anyone have known that there would be any place, say, for him to deposit a lethal dose of sedative? Wouldn't anybody be running rather a risk, in the first

152

place, to enter this apartment and then just hope to find some means by which he could induce you to take a sedative?"

"Yes," she said slowly. Doris, Charlie, Matt. By no stretch of the imagination could she vision one of them working the latch on the door, creeping into the kitchen, trying to murder her. Lieutenant Peabody was watching her as if he could read her thoughts. He said, "*Why*, Miss March? *Why* would anybody try to murder you? Don't talk of the Brown woman. I realize that you saw her and could identify her, but the landlady could identify her, too, and there have been no attempts to murder the landlady. And there's another thing. These mysterious calls you say you had. Telephone calls where nobody answered. Have you had more such telephone calls?"

"No."

"You're sure that no man's voice spoke to you in Polish, like the voice which spoke to Stedman?"

"Nobody said anything. Lieutenant Peabody, could the man who phoned to Charlie that morning when I was at Koska Street with you, could that have been Stanislowski? I mean—"

"The man you don't believe is Stanislowski? I considered that. I asked Stedman. In his opinion it was not the same voice. Stanislowski said he arrived in this city only this afternoon. I asked him if he had made a long distance call from New Orleans. He said, no. We can check that—" The door buzzer sounded sharply. Laura rose mechanically. "Wait, Miss March. What did that murdered man tell you? Why did you believe that he was Stanislowski? If there's anything you know you'd be well advised to tell me—"

"There isn't anything!" she cried. "There isn't anything I can tell you!" She went into the hall and opened the door, and it was Charlie Stedman. He put down his coat and his hat neatly on top of it. "I thought we better have a little talk about Stanislowski," he said, and then saw Lieutenant Peabody. "Oh, Lieutenant Peabody. Any news?"

"Not since I saw you," Lieutenant Peabody said flatly. "It's been only a few minutes."

Charlie sat down. "Of course but—look here, Peabody, Stanislowski's arrival simplifies the thing, doesn't it? The murdered man must have been an impostor. Surely, somehow, you can identify him."

"We haven't yet. Stedman, I've been talking to Miss March about alibis. We can't get around the fact that all four people who are directly concerned with the Stanislowski fund were admittedly in the vicinity last night when this poor woman was murdered."

"That doesn't prove any of us murdered her, does it, Lieutenant?"

"Almost the same situation is true of the afternoon when the first claimant to the Stanislowski fortune was found murdered."

Charlie shrugged. "Unfortunately, yes. Except, of course, for Mrs. Stanley."

"What about you, Stedman? Have you thought of anybody at all who saw you the afternoon that man was killed?"

Charlie's face tightened wryly, as if he had tasted something unexpectedly sour. "No," he said. "I went to my club—the doorman in the elevator saw me. I took a nap and read awhile, then I went down again and I'm sure they saw me then, too, got out my car and went to the factory. I got there late, after everybody had gone. I've told you all this, Lieutenant. I made a statement and signed it to that effect."

"There's a side entrance to your club and a back stairway. No doorman there."

"Peabody, believe me, if I had been intending to murder anybody I'd have fixed myself an alibi."

"That's a little harder to do than you seem to think. Do you have any doubts at all about this second man's identity?"

"Stanislowski?" Charlie considered it deliberately. "No," he said finally. "I can't say that I do. You saw his papers just now. You heard his story. You weren't there when the child recognized him, but she did recognize him. There's no doubt about that. We'll have to check on him, and that's going to take some time. As a matter of fact it may prove to be impossible. I don't see how we can do it from the Polish end; he's admittedly escaped from Poland. This cargo ship's a problem, too; I doubt if the ship's officers will admit that they took on a man without proper papers—particularly if they think there may be trouble, inquiry, that sort of thing. It's going to be a very awkward affair all around. I never approved of this will."

"Why not?"

"Well, for one thing it was not fair to Mrs. Stanley. Conrad Stanley had never so much as seen this nephew. I could understand his motive but I really didn't think it was fair to Mrs. Stanley. In a way I didn't think it was fair to Laura, either. She had been like a daughter to Stanley for many years. I really felt that he ought to have provided for her."

"He did provide for me," Laura said. "He couldn't have been more generous. He *was* like a father to me! He educated me. He gave me something nobody can take away from me, a way to earn my own living."

Lieutenant Peabody gave her a curious glance, as if he doubted her sincerity; she thought, how noble that sounds, how pretentious; yet it's all true.

Charlie said dryly, "Nevertheless I thought that Conrad ought to have left you a sum of money outright. Of course, he knew that there was a very strong chance that his nephew would never turn up and that, therefore, you would have a sizable sum of money. Doris would have her third of it. I would have a third, too. You'd have had to know Conrad Stanley to understand him, Peabody. All this, his will, and what we assume to be his motives, are comprehensible to anyone who knew Conrad."

"I don't doubt it," Lieutenant Peabody said shortly. "You said you disapproved of the will."

"I did disapprove of it. I didn't think it quite fair to his wife or to Laura and I didn't think it was a sensible thing to do. I thought it was going to be a tiresome business. It seemed to me the kind of thing that any good legal adviser would have strongly advised Conrad Stanley against. I thought it invited trouble—and I was right. However, this is the way things have worked out. Jonny is here and she is undoubtedly Conrad Stanislowski's child. So therefore it is our duty to carry out the provision of the will."

"And you agree, Stedman, that this fund should be turned over to Jonny to be continued until she is of age? Or rather did you agree to it before this man arrived this afternoon?"

Again Charlie paused to consider the question and all its angles. Then he said, "I'll be frank with you, Lieutenant. I did agree and I didn't. Mrs. Stanley is a little against it; you can see her point of view. She still feels that it was unfair to her. I can sum up my own opinion this way: if Mrs. Stanley and Miss March agreed to continue the fund, then I would have agreed to it. I rather think —" He paused for a moment and looked at Laura. "You're not going to like this, Laura. But I rather think if Doris had held out strongly against it, I would have been a little inclined to be on her side. She was Conrad's wife. However, no matter what the decision was I would be in favor of taking care of Jonny. I'm sure that's what Conrad would have wanted us to do. I'm not sure that I would be in favor of giving Jonny this very large sum. You, Laura, are determined to have it continued for Jonny."

"Yes," Laura said, "Conrad would have wanted it."

Charlie nodded. "Perhaps you are right," he said equably. "In any event this discussion is beside the point now. Conrad Stanislowski is here. We'll have to do everything we can to confirm his claims. But in my opinion, there's really no question of his identity. And in the meantime—I know how you feel about this, Laura, too, but I feel that we'll have to let him have the child. It's the only humane and sensible thing to do. They've been separated for two years. He loves her, she's his child."

155

"No! Charlie, please. Not yet. Let's wait."

Peabody said abruptly, "Where were you, Stedman, the afternoon following the Koska Street murder?"

"Where—" Charlie looked startled. Then he gave a short laugh. "Another alibi? I think—yes, I'm sure I was at my club again. It's getting to be a habit with my approaching age; I usually go to my room after lunch and rest. The doorman in the elevator must have seen me but, of course," Charlie said with an edge to his voice, "as you have pointed out, there's a side entrance. However, I assure you I didn't follow Laura and Jonny, if that's what you're getting at. If I wanted to see them all I had to do is come up here and ring the bell!"

"Was it Stedman, Miss March?" Peabody asked imperturbably. "Was it Cosden?"

"No! That is—I told you—I couldn't see his face but—"

"Was it by any chance Stanislowski?"

TWENTY-EIGHT

Stanislowski, Laura thought. If he had arrived in Chicago before he said he had arrived, he could have found her address and then attached himself to her and Jonny as they left the apartment. She said slowly, "I'm not sure. It might have been, but—" She tried to dredge up some salient and distinguishing feature from her memory of that ubiquitous figure. It remained only the shadowy, distant shape of a man. "I don't know."

Lieutenant Peabody turned to Stedman. "I asked you if you thought it could have been Stanislowski who talked to you on the phone the morning when Miss March went out with us to the rooming house."

"And I answered you, Lieutenant Peabody," Charlie said. "I don't think it was the same man. You heard him. He flatly denies it."

Lieutenant Peabody turned back to Laura, "That's all that happened? He didn't approach you, didn't speak to you. You just saw a man who took the same route you took around the park."

156

"Yes," Laura said, "but he—he was always there, wherever we went. And then I thought he was in a taxi that followed us."

"Did you see him clearly?"

"No, no—there was just a figure in the back seat."

"So you aren't at all sure that anybody followed you?"

"Yes," Laura said defiantly.

But it sounded weak even to her own ears. There was a short but skeptical silence. Then abruptly Peabody rose and started for the hall, picking up his coat and hat as he went. At the door, however, he paused. "Miss March, when you make up your mind to tell me exactly why you are so sure that the first man was Stanislowski—let me know," he said almost solemnly and went away.

Charlie had followed him to the door. He said, "Good night," closed the door and came back. Laura could almost see his astute mind leaping like quicksilver to the exact meaning of the Lieutenant's words. He sat down, however, in a leisurely way. He settled his neat tie; he took a cigarette from the little silver dish on the table beside him and lighted it. Finally he said, "Peabody believes that murdered man was still alive when you got there. What *did* he say to you before he died?"

"He was dead. I told the police that."

The Lieutenant had not believed her. Neither, she realized suddenly, did Charlie. He said quietly, "Laura, you were obstinate about Stanislowski this afternoon. You took the child away. You refuse to let him have her. That's not like you. He has not had an easy time, that's clear. Reunion with his child must have been his goal, his dream, his hope. I am cautious; I'm not easy to convince; I'm aware of my responsibility to Jonny and to Conrad Stanley. I think he should have the child now. We can straighten out all the details later."

"No—"

"You must have some reason for refusing."

She had none, nothing that would convince him or anybody. She said desperately, "Charlie, if I knew anything—anything at all, I'd tell the police."

Charlie considered that, too, deliberately, and again he didn't believe her. "Maybe," he said, "maybe not. You are usually a very reasonable young woman, Laura. Remember, I've known you since you were a little girl. I've known you better since we've shared this rather onerous chore. I've always thought you were a very level-headed young woman. I don't think you'd do anything without a reason. It's possible that you may have some notion of trying to solve this thing yourself. I don't really believe that, I think you are too smart. But there is something that you're not telling anybody."

"No."

"Then why are you so determined not to give up the child? You must believe that this first man was Stanislowski in spite of everything. And your whole attitude is—different, Laura. I don't understand it. Of course, you may realize that an accusation of murder is a very serious thing. So you may have some notion of trying to prove something, yourself, before you tell the police."

A kind of weary anger flicked her. She said with sharp impatience, "Charlie, you want me to give up Jonny. I won't. Not now. I have to think, I have to decide what to do. I'm not going to talk about it!"

She rose. Charlie eyed her for a moment, then he put out his cigarette and rose, too. "All right," he said, "I'll not try to persuade you."

She followed him into the little hall where the mirror reflected her own figure and Charlie as if there were four in the room instead of two. He took up his hat and overcoat and opened the door. Down the corridor the elevator stopped and two women, furred and gloved, emerged, chatting of a moving picture they had seen. They saw Charlie and Laura standing in the open door and instantly silence fell between them, their eyes sharpened. They walked on and around the corner toward another apartment.

The evening papers lay in the hall outside the door. They had now enormous headlines. The Stanislowski murder. Charlie bent, picked them up, and glanced at the headlines.

"The whole story's here at last. They're making a big thing of it. It's the Stanley name." He handed the papers to Laura. "I ought to tell you, Laura, that murder is something dangerous. Be very careful."

Fear again touched her as if it had cold fingers. She said, defying it, "I'm not afraid. Besides Matt's left me his gun." She put the papers with their great black and red headlines on the hall table. She opened the drawer; Matt's revolver gleamed coldly within it. Charlie lifted his eyebrows. "Good," he said. "Well, good night, Laura."

After he'd gone she bolted the door; she made one of her many reassuring trips back to the kitchen to be sure that that door was bolted and the chain was securely fastened across it. Jonny was sound asleep. She came back to the living room. The talk with Peabody and Charlie plucked at her nerves.

Perhaps all of them, Matt and Doris, too, believed that she must have some sound, some convincing reason, something other than weak and unreasonable instinct, for believing that the murdered man had been in fact Conrad Stanislowski.

And Peabody had said frankly that her belief in the first

Conrad's claims constituted a possible motive for murder. Surely Peabody would need more convincing evidence than that for a murder charge.

She took what comfort she could from the fact that Peabody had questioned Charlie about his lack of an alibi for the time of Conrad Stanislowski's murder. He had questioned Doris, of course, and Matt. And he had questioned all of them concerning the murder of Catherine Miller. So that meant that Peabody did not have a strong case against her, Laura, didn't it? He didn't have a case which left no loopholes; he did not have what was called jury evidence. So that must mean that the investigation was not at an end. And that Peabody was not going to arrest her, not now.

Arrest *her*, she thought again, with incredulity. It was not possible. Murder wasn't possible either, not in the orderly circumference of her life. Yet it had touched her twice.

The black headlines of the newspapers leaped at her. The story had blown up into full prominence. That was, as Charlie said, because of the Stanley will. She read her own name with again a feeling of disbelief, yet again the black and white of the newsprint seemed to set a kind of authenticity upon it, too. Miss Laura March had discovered the body. The murdered man had claimed to be a nephew of Conrad Stanley. Miss March had been his ward, according to the newspaper story, and the daughter of an old friend. She had been caring for Conrad Stanley's great-niece, Jonny Stanislowski, the daughter of, presumably, the murdered man. His identity, however, was still not established. A date for the inquest would be announced, shortly.

There followed a résumé of the Stanley will: Doris' name, Charlie Stedman's name, her own. Matthew Cosden, Mrs. Stanley's lawyer, had discovered the child, in Vienna, and brought her to Chicago. It was all at once an important, a sensational news story.

She thought of the glances the two women who had come out of the elevator had given her as she stood talking to Charlie; avid glances, sharp with curiosity.

There was, of course, no mention of the new Conrad Stanislowski. These were the early evening papers. That would probably be in the morning edition.

If the first man really had been Conrad, then of course the second man, the man who arrived that day, had to be an impostor.

Suppose he had murdered the first Conrad! Suppose he had taken the real Conrad's papers to support his claim, a false claim, to Jonny and the money! But how would he have known about the Stanley will? How would he have known all the circumstances

159

of the first Conrad's life? How would he have known the background, which dovetailed exactly with the story the first Conrad had told, and with what they knew of him?

And besides, the second Conrad had a passport showing his own photograph. There was no question of that.

But more convincing than anything, Jonny had recognized him. I'm wrong, Laura thought; I've got to be wrong. But I'm not going to let him have Jonny. Not yet.

The little French clock had struck ten, its tinkling chime sounding hurried and breathless, as if fright were contagious, when Matt came. He brought with him a middle-aged woman, dark and heavy with a faint black mustache, who, he explained, spoke Polish. He introduced her; she was Miss Nowak. And she was to question Jonny. There was all at once a subtle difference about Matt.

It was nothing Laura could analyze; nothing she could describe, only a kind of tensely restrained energy, like latent electricity before a storm begins. He brought Jonny in, drowsy and pink-cheeked. And Miss Nowak questioned Jonny for over an hour.

Clearly Matt had coached the Polish woman in the questions she was to ask; they were in all probability much the same questions which Peabody had already asked Jonny through the interpreter he had brought. Again none of the questions produced any clear results.

The sturdy little figure in blue pajamas, red bathrobe and white bunny slippers began to droop against Matt's arm. But Jonny still at certain questions lowered her head and replied, *"Nie—nie."*

At last Miss Nowak turned to Matt with a hopeless shrug of her massive shoulders. "She only says, no. She refuses to speak of her father. She refuses to speak in Polish at all, Mr. Cosden. That's all she'll say, no, no. Yet I'm sure she understands me." She hesitated, looking at the child, and then said, "I think that you are right, Mr. Cosden. I think that she has been taught to answer no questions which have, shall I say, an official character. Perhaps it would be truer to say, no questions a stranger asks her. There's really no more I can do. Whenever I mention her father—" She shrugged again.

There was a moment of silence. Jonny scuffed her white slipper along the rug. Her round little face, with the flush of sleep on her cheeks, was a guarded, complete blank, but as the silence lengthened, suddenly she gave a long, weary sigh.

Matt sighed, too, as if he was about to force himself to do something he did not wish to do. He gave a quick nod at Miss Nowak, rose, lifted Jonny in his arms and swung her up high. At the same time Miss Nowak burst unexpectedly into song. She had a deep, tuneless voice but the song was recognizable. *"Krakowiaczek cija w Krakowiem sie rodzit—"*

It was the song the man calling himself Stanislowski had sung that afternoon. But this time Jonny only gave Miss Nowak a bewildered, troubled look and buried her face in Matt's shoulder.

He glanced at Laura over the child's brown head. "It means 'I'm a little Cracovian. I was born in Cracow.'"

Miss Nowak said in a pedantic way, "It is a Cracovian song, an old one, very well known. It sprang up during the division of Poland. Most people of my country know that song—"

Jonny buried her head still deeper in Matt's shoulder, both arms tight around his neck. He gave her a reassuring hug and put her down. She stood, both chubby hands on the arm of the chair, looking down.

Matt turned to Laura. "What would you think of asking Miss Nowak to come here and stay for a few days? Perhaps, as Jonny grows accustomed to her, she'll talk." He hesitated. "It may not work. But it's a chance."

They had talked of an interpreter when Jonny came to live with Laura, thinking it might cushion the child's first weeks in a strange country. Laura had been against it; it would have been a little difficult to find such a person; and, in fact, after a few days had passed, Laura had found that instead of language being a barrier between her and Jonny, it had become a game, a point of mutual interest, something new and engrossing for Jonny to learn. A pleasant little pattern of conversation had developed at once; Laura had made it a custom to talk while she and Jonny were together, speak of what she was doing, call things by their names and point; Jonny would repeat after her, soap, sugar, dish, cat, drink, milk. Until the arrival of the first Conrad, language had not constituted a barrier between them.

But now it was very important that there should be no barrier at all. And Matt's plan might work. Laura turned to Miss Nowak. "Will you do that, Miss Nowak? Can you come tomorrow?"

There was a gleam of interest in Miss Nowak's eyes. Almost certainly Miss Nowak had read the newspapers. But she had lessons to give the next day, she said; they would understand that she was obliged to keep her appointments. "Perhaps the day after tomorrow? Would that help you?"

"That would help," Matt said. He went with her to the door and gave her a bill which she tucked into a brown handbag. She turned back to say politely to Laura, "Good night, Miss March," and she smiled at Jonny. *"Dobra noc,* Jonny." Jonny's eyes lifted, startlingly blue, between black eyelashes. She did not reply.

The door closed and Matt came back. "Jonny's tired," he said and carried Jonny back into her little bedroom.

So I was wrong, Laura thought, again; the second man is the real Conrad. Only Jonny's father could have known the gay, tender little game with the song, and Jonny had instantly responded. When Matt attempted to imitate it, she had been only troubled and silent.

It was true that the child was by then puzzled, tired, perhaps frightened by all those questions; she was also clearly on guard. Matt's theory that she had been trained to answer no questions that in any remote way could concern her father was almost certainly the right one. But that afternoon, when the second Conrad had caught Jonny up and begun to sing, there had been no hesitation, no reluctance.

There were sounds of a romp going on in Jonny's room. Jonny was shouting with glee. All her silence of the previous hour had gone; she was bubbling with her own special mixture of Polish and English conversation. Matt was apparently speaking for Suki —who was, as a matter of fact, quite capable of speaking for himself and usually did with great vehemence, but not in the English language. It was a long conversation which ended when Matt said in his natural voice and very firmly, "Now go to sleep. Good night, Jonny."

Jonny's high treble answered. "*Dobra noc,* Matt.".

After a few moments Matt came back. "She's asleep."

"That song—he *is* her father, Matt."

"If he isn't, somebody's taken a lot of pains to coach him."

"Somebody—what do you mean?"

"I don't know, except if he's an impostor somebody's had to tell him about the real Conrad's background, the circumstances of the Stanley will, even that little song."

There was again a subtle flicker of excitement in Matt's face. She said, "Matt, you know something. What?"

He looked at her for a long moment; then he came to her, put his hand under her chin and looked down into her eyes. "I've only got a sort of idea that this second Conrad is the impostor, the first Conrad was the real one, and so—" His face sobered. He straightened, shoved his hands in his pockets and said, "If I'm right, then of course the second Conrad's appearance is significant, and very important."

Something he had said to Doris over the telephone floated out of her memory. "It was in the cards, you told Doris that. You mean you expected another Conrad?"

"I thought it was a possibility. There must be some plan. Some focus—"

"But he knows that song, Matt. Charlie believes him. Doris believes him. Lieutenant Peabody believes him—"

He jerked around to look at her. "Peabody! He was at Doris'!

162

He talked to Stanislowski. Do you mean he's been here again? What did he have to say?"

She told of the long talk with Peabody and the short one with Charlie. Matt listened, sitting opposite her in one of the lounge chairs, folding and refolding an empty book of matches.

He grinned rather wryly when she told him of Peabody's reason for including Matt himself as a suspect. "He says that—that since you are going to marry Doris, her interests are your interests."

Matt tossed the crumpled book of matches into an ash tray. "Peabody questioned me, of course. He has made no secret of the fact that he feels that anybody concerned in any way with the Stanley will is a suspect. But I didn't know he suspected me of killing the man in order to marry money. I don't have an alibi. I went Christmas shopping after I left here that afternoon. I didn't go back to the office at all. Since I didn't find anything that struck me as just what I wanted, I don't even have a purchase or a charge account item to back me up. And of course it's true that none of us really has alibis for the time of Catherine Miller's murder."

"He suggested," Laura said in a small cold voice, "that someone already inside the apartment house might have been waiting for her when she returned."

TWENTY-NINE

Matt shot her a quick glance. "It is far more likely that somebody followed Catherine Miller when she came back to the service entrance, close enough behind her to catch the door before it latched. Or for that matter whoever killed her could have spoken to her, made some excuse for coming in the service entrance. If she *was* murdered by mistake then she would not have known or suspected anyone."

"Matt—who murdered her? Peabody seems to suspect you or me or Doris or Charlie, nobody else."

"You've been sitting here thinking that, haven't you?" He

163

glanced at the heap of newspapers. "Reading the newspapers and thinking who killed Conrad? Who killed Catherine Miller? Don't forget that there's also Maria Brown and now this new man, this second Conrad. They are suspects, too."

"Why should Maria Brown murder Catherine Miller? Whoever murdered her must have believed that she was Maria Brown. And there's another thing, Matt; if this second Conrad *is* the real one, who is Maria Brown? She can't be *his* wife."

"Why not?" Matt said shortly. "She could be anybody." He rose with a restless motion and began to pace the room up and down, his hands in his pockets, his dark head bent. "Six suspects if we include Maria Brown and Conrad the second. Four if we include only the people who would have benefited by the will if no claimant had turned up, and that, of course, is you and Doris and Charlie. Me, too, according to Peabody! I know you didn't do it; I know I didn't do it, so that leaves Doris and Charlie. Doris has never liked the provision of the will; that's comprehensible. But I can't see her going out there and sticking a knife into a man. Besides, she says she knew nothing about him and she has an alibi. Now Charlie would have got a third of the trust fund if no claimant turned up. But if he married Doris, he'd have married money, so Peabody's motive for me would hold for Charlie—"

"Charlie marry Doris!"

Matt turned to give her a look which suddenly held a gleam of laughter. "Didn't you know that?"

"No! Charlie's a confirmed bachelor—"

"I thought you might have guessed," he said, an amused laughing note in his voice. "In any event it's true. Doris told me."

So Charlie, too, had yielded, after years of comfortable and secure independence, to Doris' beauty and her gentle feminine charm. Laura said slowly, "Somehow I never thought of Charlie marrying anybody."

"Why not?" Matt said. "As a matter of fact, I'll confess that a base suspicion as to his affections crossed my mind. It did occur to me that just possibly he was fond of the Stanley business, too, and would not have been averse to taking that over and running it."

"But that was sold. Right away. Charlie didn't object to that!"

"No—no," Matt said. "He did point out its value to Doris. Remember?"

Laura thought back to the many conferences between the four of them following Conrad Stanley's death. "So did you," she said after a moment.

Matt laughed. "Certainly, I did. It seemed a pity to get rid of a business like that, even for the price Doris got."

Laura said suddenly, "But Doris isn't going to marry Charlie. She"—the words came out in a rush—"she told me she's going to marry you."

An odd look came into Matt's face; he picked up an ash tray, examined it closely and said, "Did she?"

Laura swallowed hard—and had to go on. "Of course, I know that you've been in love with Doris for a long time."

Again Matt gave her an odd, straight look. Then he said, "The point is Doris said she refused Charlie. So no matter how much money Doris might get from the Stanley fund, it wouldn't do Charlie any good. I can see Charlie neatly dispatching anybody, regretfully perhaps, but quite coolly and impersonally and very, very efficiently if he thought it was the thing to do. But I think he'd have been efficient, too, about covering his tracks. I think he'd have arranged a very solid sort of defense first. And I certainly don't think he'd take such a risk on the chance of Doris changing her mind eventually and deciding to marry him. Besides, Doris isn't the kind of girl to turn over her bank account to anybody, not if I know Doris and I think I do."

And you're in love with her, Laura thought. She said, "Charlie is willing to accept the second Conrad. His papers, passport, everything, have convinced Charlie. He doesn't oppose him. So why should he have murdered the first man? I mean—"

"You mean he has not murdered the second one?" Matt laughed shortly. "There's still time for that! No—I don't mean that, Laura. It was a bad joke. I see your point. The only thing we are certain of is that Jonny's the pivot. Jonny's the motive. Jonny and the money. And I rather think that Maria Brown may have the key to the whole affair." He hesitated. "You asked me why I felt that the second Conrad is the impostor. I'll tell you one small thing but don't give it too much weight."

He gave her a rather serious and anxious look, as if he didn't want to run the risk of disappointing her. "It is trivial: there are a hundred possible explanations for it. All of them reasonable. But this new Stanislowski was wearing an American-made tie. Naturally I was on the lookout for any inconsistencies about him. His clothes looked right somehow, foreign, all that. It seemed to me he was rather at pains to explain his new American-made oxfords. But his tie was a Solvina, American-made and it had been worn. It wasn't new. He could have got it in England before the war. He could have picked it up in Vienna—oh, there are all sorts of ways. On the other hand it was a small inconsistency."

She thought it over for a moment. It seemed too small, too easily explained. "He knew about that song."

Matt picked up a cigarette from the little silver dish beside him and rolled it over in his fingers. "Suppose somebody told him all

165

about that, coached him. Miss Nowak said it's a well-known song; anybody of Polish blood might know it. Suppose Jonny was taken by surprise and she reacted automatically. She didn't do anything when Miss Nowak tried the song except clutch me around the neck. But she was tired and puzzled. It was all different. She was on guard. She wasn't going to give anything away. She was going to do what she had been taught to do."

After a moment Laura said, "Who coached him?"

"Well, of course that's the question. The obvious answer is that Conrad himself told him. Maybe this new guy knew the first Conrad in Poland. Maybe he knew all the circumstances. For that matter he could be Schmidt."

"Schmidt?"

"The man who took Jonny to the orphanage. Obviously a friend of the first Conrad, or at least he had some connection with him. That's a possibility. Maybe the first Conrad told the second exactly what he was going to do. Maybe the second Conrad—" He checked himself. "Too many possibilities! I'm going off on tangents. But maybe Maria Brown can answer some of the questions."

Laura fumbled for his meaning and then understood. "Do you mean that Maria Brown is in a conspiracy with this second Conrad to—"

"To get Jonny and the money? It's possible. She could be in cahoots with the new Conrad. She could have known the whole story."

"But if—if she was the first Conrad's wife, I mean the murdered man, if she coached the second Conrad, if she's behind all this—" Laura caught her breath. "But if she's Jonny's mother —*how could she?*"

"She left Jonny when she was a baby," Matt said coolly. "She was in the rooming house when Conrad the first was killed. She got away from the police. She came here to see you, and to make sure that Jonny was here. She knows that you can identify her and somebody, Laura"—suddenly his face was white and stern— "somebody tried to kill you with that sedative." He came over to the hassock beside her and sat down; he took her hands. "Laura, is there anything, no matter how small or trivial, that you haven't told me?"

There wasn't anything she thought. And then remembered a drifting smell of fragrance of perfume, Doris' perfume in a little booth on the west side. But Doris had been at the dentist's. She said, "Those phone calls, Matt. When nobody answered. They've stopped."

"Oh, yes. Those phone calls." He rose abruptly, "Well, it's late. I'm going to have a talk with Peabody in the morning. I'll tell him about that Solvina tie. I want Peabody to question this new Stanislowski again, give him a real workout. Put the fear of God into him. Of course Peabody may laugh at me but I don't think he will and maybe—just maybe this Brown woman will turn up."

"Matt! What do you mean—"

"Don't get your hopes up," Matt said, but he was suddenly cheerful. "I only said maybe."

He went back to the kitchen where he made sure that the chain was fastened. He went to the door of Jonny's bedroom and looked in at the sleeping child. He came back and gathered up his coat. "Don't let anybody in, Laura. Remember. I don't think Jonny will open the door for anybody again, as she did for me this afternoon. I am sure I got that across to her." He opened the drawer of the table and glanced at the gun. "Remember, it's murder," he said, and closed the drawer. "Good night, Laura."

He swung off down the corridor. As he stepped into the elevator, he turned and gave her a kind of salute. But after she had bolted the door the apartment again seemed very empty and exposed, high above the sleeping city, and lonely. She, too, opened Jonny's door. In the stream of light from the hall she could see Jonny, her face buried in the pillow. Suki lay curled tightly against Jonny's shoulder; he opened one eye, twitched a whisker and went back to sleep.

Again when she filled the two thermos bottles, she put them immediately in her room. She went into the living room, emptied the ash trays and turned out the lights in the Christmas tree. Jonny must have removed the yellow nodding bird Charlie had given her from its perch on the tree, for it was gone. She turned out the lights in the living room and went to bed. It was a long time before she could sleep.

If they could have induced Jonny to talk, the important question of Conrad Stanislowski's identity would have been answered. Laura had not really expected Jonny to reply to the interpreter's questions, not after she had witnessed Jonny's refusal to reply to the interpreter Peabody brought. But surely there must be some other way of extracting that all-important information from the child. Surely there ought to have been some slight indication, for instance, of the child's reaction to the second Conrad.

There was none. She had taken refuge in cautious silence. She had seemed neither reluctant to leave the second Conrad, nor afraid of him; she had laughed and joined in the song—and that was all.

After the first Conrad had gone, Jonny had sobbed, wildly and heartbrokenly. Perhaps, Laura decided, that was one reason why she felt so strongly that the first Conrad was Jonny's father.

But that night, while Miss Nowak questioned her, Jonny had

seemed tired and a little frightened—hadn't she? That was natural; that was to be expected. It had been a long and to the child a perplexing and tiring day.

Thinking of Jonny's behavior, scrutinizing it for any clue to the child's feelings, it struck Laura suddenly that in fact Jonny had seemed different, troubled, that afternoon. She had stood at the door of Laura's room, when Laura awoke to find Matt there, pressing close to Matt as if for protection, her eyes unusually grave—as if she were frightened.

But that was before Doris had called to say that another Conrad had arrived.

The barrier of language was a barrier now; Laura wished she could talk to the child, carefully but freely. But she must be mistaken in thinking that the child had, somehow, been frightened during the long sleep Laura had had that afternoon. There was nothing that could have frightened or troubled her.

After a long time, still debating, she went to sleep.

The next morning, however, Jonny was still thoughtful and silent; her face was pale, her eyes looked heavy and tired and very sober. She followed Laura like a sturdy little shadow. Suki, too, was pensive and refused to play; he sat on top a bookshelf, his tail curled tightly around him, his eyes lambent, as if he felt danger somewhere near. When Laura sought to distract Jonny from her brooding—frightened?—silence with toys and looked for the yellow bird in Jonny's room, it was not there.

The newspapers that morning again had sensational headlines. Once a reporter telephoned from the lobby asking for an interview. Laura, taken by surprise, temporized; she couldn't see him that morning, she said. Later, then? "Yes," Laura promised. "Yes. But there's nothing I know that is not already in the papers."

"We'd like a picture, Miss March."

Matt would tell her to see reporters if necessary; she forced herself to reply. "Yes—certainly. Later," and hung up before she was obliged to say exactly when. Her hands were shaking when she put down the telephone; it gave her a small preview of what a murder trial would be.

Charlie and Doris came an hour or so later, together. They had met in the lobby, Charlie explained quickly, and turned to Doris. "Now then, what's wrong?"

"I couldn't tell you there. And there was that woman in the elevator—" Doris' face was white; her pink lipstick was smeared. She caught a gasping breath ."The police know I was there!"

"What do you mean, Doris? *Where*—"

"I wasn't at the rooming house! But I was at Koska Street that afternoon. I was in the telephone booth in that drug store." She shot a furious look at Laura. "You told them! You saw me there! You told me you didn't see anybody! But you told the police I was there!"

"Wait a minute—" Charlie began. "What—"

"I didn't see you!" Laura cried. "I didn't tell the police I saw you. You were at the dentist's!"

"What are you talking about, Doris? Tell me," Charlie said tersely.

Doris cried in an angry wail, "I *was* at the dentist's! But I went to Koska Street. I was going to go to the rooming house. But then I didn't. I went to the telephone booth. I was going to phone to you, Charlie. I was going to phone to Matt. But then I didn't do that either. Laura saw me and she told the police!" She whirled toward Charlie; she flung herself into his arms. "Charlie, Laura hates me! She's always hated me! She—"

"Now, now," Charlie said, holding Doris. "Take it easy. Let's have the story straight. Just what happened?"

"The police came to my apartment this morning. They said they found my fingerprints in the telephone booth. Goodness knows how!" She put her head against Charlie's shoulder. Her hair was disheveled, her words came out in gulps against Charlie's immaculate white shirt. "They must have got the fingerprints right away—that night. Somehow they finally weeded out one of mine. There must have been hundreds of persons using that little telephone booth! He said—Peabody said—they'd just this morning identified one of mine!" She twisted her head around to look at Laura. "*You* told them, Laura! That's why they hunted for my fingerprints! You hate me. You're jealous of me. You hated me when I married Conrad. You knew I was going to take your place. And you've always been in love with Matt! You hate me—"

"Now, now, Doris!" Charlie took off her coat; he put it over a chair. "Now, my dear, take it easy. Why did you go to Koska Street?"

"Because that man—the first one, the one that was murdered—he telephoned to me. That's why." She caught her breath, smoothed back her hair, gave herself a little shake to settle her dress into smooth lines, and eyed them both with suddenly calm but defiant brown eyes.

THIRTY

Charlie took out a handkerchief and dabbed absently at some pink lipstick on one shirt cuff.

Laura said blankly, "I don't understand—"

"Neither do I," Charlie said. "Doris, do you mean to say that this first man—the murdered man—talked to you?"

"Of course he did, Charlie." All at once Doris was sweet, gentle, completely self-possessed. "He telephoned to me. He asked me about Jonny. He asked me where she was."

"And—what did you tell him?"

"I told him that she was with Laura. What else could I say?"

"And he told you that he was Conrad Stanislowski?"

"Yes. He said he was Conrad Stanislowski and he had just got here and he wanted to know where his child was, and I told him."

Laura found her voice. "What did you do?"

Doris didn't look at her; she spoke to Charlie. "Well, I didn't do anything—not right away. I—I was upset about it. I didn't know what to do. I had the appointment at the dentist's, so I went. And I had a bad filling. The dentist gave me a light anesthetic, and after he put the filling in, the nurse put me in a little room with a couch so I could rest until I got over the anesthetic. And I got over it right away and I simply walked out. Nobody saw me leave. He had told me where he was staying, I asked him. I decided that I would go over to that rooming house, and—and talk to him. I got a taxi and started out to the west side. But then on the way I decided to phone to you and to Matt, and tell you about it before I saw him. I, really, Charlie"—her little white hands went out to Charlie's arm—"I didn't know what to do. It was all so strange and unexpected and—anyway I changed my mind. I stopped in a drug store there on a corner. I started to dial your number and Matt's, and then I thought that I—well, I thought I wouldn't. I came home. I didn't go near the rooming house and nobody can say I did!"

"But you told the police—" Laura began.

"Of course I said that! If nobody claimed that trust fund,

170

some of it was to go to me. The police might suspect me! I *had* to lie! Didn't I, Charlie?" She said in a sweetly reasonable way which utterly disclaimed responsibility.

Charlie ran an uneasy finger around his collar. "But, Doris— the police— You should have told me. Did you tell *anyone* that this man telephoned you?"

"No, I didn't, Charlie." Doris' voice was gentle and pleading. "I know it was wrong of me but I thought I'd better wait and see what happened."

"Did he ask you to tell nobody about his arrival?"

Doris was suddenly very busy. Her small white fingers were folding the corner of Charlie's lapel. "Yes, he did," she said. "And that made me think there was something—there was something very odd about it. But I didn't tell Matt, or you Charlie, or anybody because I— I decided to think it over first."

She meant, Laura thought, with clear and cold understanding, that she intended to think of ways and means to fight Conrad's claim. A wary note in Doris' voice all but admitted it.

Doris lifted her soft brown eyes to Charlie. "You do understand, don't you? I couldn't just act without thinking it over. I had to think about all the implications—everything. And besides I knew that this man—if he were really Stanislowski— would come forward at some time. And then you could deal with it. You and Matt."

"Of course," Charlie said. "Of course." And Laura thought suddenly, that's why Doris has been frightened. That's why she tried to claim an alibi for herself for the time when Catherine Miller was murdered. That was why she had asked Laura if she had seen anybody she knew at Koska Street.

"Your perfume," Laura said slowly, "there was your perfume in the telephone booth."

Doris flashed around. "So that's what you told them!"

"No, I didn't."

"My perfume! I thought you'd seen me. You see"—she whirled around to Charlie—"I told you, she hates me. She'd do anything."

"I didn't tell anybody about the perfume," Laura said. "I thought you were at the dentist's. I thought anybody might have used that perfume."

"I didn't murder him!" Doris cried. "You can't say I did! Nobody can say I did! I didn't go near the rooming house. Nobody saw me. I didn't go there." She turned back to Charlie. "Charlie—they can't arrest me because I was there at that drug store. Can they?"

"No, Doris. No. That's not evidence. What did Peabody say?"

"He just questioned me," Doris said coolly again, mistress of the situation. "When he said they'd found my fingerprints, I told them the truth."

"I am sorry that you didn't tell me and Matt, the instant that man phoned to you—"

"Oh, I was wrong! But—after all," Doris said with a child-like note of frankness, "there was all that money! He said he was Conrad Stanislowski, but—but then he said to keep his presence a secret. He said he didn't want to come forward openly yet so—well, for all I knew, he would never come forward. So I thought I'd wait!"

She wanted to think of ways around it, Laura thought again; she was as cautious and wary as a cat—and as gentle and confiding as a kitten when she chose to be. She brushed her head in a coaxing way against Charlie's shoulder. "Come with me, Charlie. Take me out to lunch somewhere. Let's pretend nothing has happened. I'm upset."

"All right," Charlie said. "I only came to ask Laura if she'd changed her mind about Stanislowski."

"No," Laura said.

He didn't attempt this time to argue with her.

She watched them leave, Doris hanging on Charlie's arm, smiling and talking to him. There was an air of triumph about Doris' small face as she turned back from the elevator and gave Laura a complacent glance. The elevator door closed.

Clearly Doris felt herself out of danger from the police. Clearly, her visit to the drug store in no sense was proof that she had also visited the rooming house. It was not evidence.

Yet Doris had been near Koska Street at about the time the first Conrad was murdered. She had known that there was a man who claimed to be Conrad. She had always intended to oppose the plan to keep the trust fund intact for Jonny. This first Conrad's arrival had threatened Doris' third of that trust fund, and she had known there was such a claimant.

Charlie, too, admittedly had been in the vicinity of the rooming house. And the little scene with Doris proved that he was wax in Doris' soft white hands.

But she, Laura March, had found the murdered man.

Jonny was in her room looking, or pretending to look, at a book of pictures. She had not come out to greet Charlie; that was probably because she had heard Doris' voice, too. Laura studied the quiet little figure bent over the picture book, absorbed in it— too deeply absorbed, it struck her. When exactly had Jonny seemed to change? Why?

Or was there, really, a change? She could not question her. With a feeling of helplessness Laura turned away.

A few moments later Peabody came again; this time a police-

172

man, not Sergeant O'Brien, but also a stenographer, came with him. He sat down in a straight chair behind Lieutenant Peabody on the sofa, and whipped out a pad and pencil and without preamble the Lieutenant brought forth his evidence. He pulled it as a matter of fact from his pocket and put it in Laura's lap. "Does that belong to you?"

It was a scarf, a white silk scarf, with her initials "L. M." embroidered on it in red. It was the scarf Matt had given her.

She looked at it incredulously. It was no longer white. It was stained with dark grimy marks. One corner was torn.

"So it does belong to you," Lieutenant Peabody said.

"Yes."

There was the whisper of the stenographer's pencil scribbling.

Catherine Miller had been killed by a scarf, drawn and knotted tightly about her throat.

"That's all I wanted to know," the Lieutenant said.

Laura caught her breath. "Where did you find this?"

"It was found in a trash basket, a large trash basket,' over at the corner of State Street. We had sent out a blanket order for anything like this to be handed over to the police. It was found last night and brought to me."

"I didn't—I don't know anything about it! I didn't kill Catherine Miller! I didn't throw this in a trash basket—"

"Do you mean that somebody else put it there?"

"I don't know—I—yes! Somebody—"

"In that event somebody has gone to considerable pains to arrange evidence against you. Who?"

Keep your head, Laura told herself; don't be frightened. "I don't know any other explanation for it. The scarf was in a drawer in my room—"

"When?"

For a moment she couldn't remember. "I wore another one—yesterday. Yes. A red one. I don't remember seeing this one, then. The day before—" She had gone to the moving picture; she could see herself adjusting the white scarf. "Yes," she said. "I wore it then."

"So you say that sometime in the last forty-eight hours somebody took that scarf?"

"Yes. I didn't lose it, I'm sure. I'd have known."

"Who took it? Who had a chance to take it?"

Who? Nobody, to her knowledge. Except Matt.

She wouldn't tell Peabody that. He waited a moment; then he glanced at the stenographer, who rose. "That's all," the Lieutenant said, and started toward the door. The stenographer followed him. Laura thought, I can't move; I can't speak. But she did move. She ran across the room, and put her hand on Peabody's thin arm. "I didn't do it," she cried. "You must believe me. Somebody—"

"Oh, yes," he said wearily. "Somebody took the scarf. Somebody came in here at great risk to themselves and put a sedative in the thermos bottle. Somebody followed you in the park. But it's never anybody you can identify."

He went away without a backward look, an edge of her once-white scarf dangling from his pocket. The policeman marched behind him. Laura bolted the door automatically.

So, now, he had evidence.

Who could have taken the scarf?

Who could hate her to the extent of planting evidence against her? Evidence of murder.

The Lieutenant had not arrested her. He had not made a murder charge. Nevertheless he now had tangible evidence.

A long time later, she thought, I've got to tell Matt. As she went to the telephone, it rang. "Hello," she said. "Hello."

Matt replied. "Laura, I want you to come over here, to my apartment. Hurry."

She said like a sleepwalker, dazedly, "Matt, something—something's happened. My scarf—"

"Your *what?*"

"The scarf you gave me. The scarf with my initials on it. Lieutenant Peabody was here. The scarf was found in a trash basket, at the corner of State Street. Matt, it's evidence."

There was a short silence. Then Matt said, "Has Peabody got the scarf now?"

"Yes. He took it away with him."

"Are you alone now?"

"Yes, except for Jonny. Earlier, Doris and Charlie were here."

"What did they want?"

She didn't seem to know. Nothing mattered. She could only see that scarf—the gift from Matt, once so white and lovely, now stained and knotted as if it had been twisted hard. "They came together. Doris was at the drug store near Koska Street—"

Matt interrupted. "Yes, I know all that. Peabody told me. But —there's something else now, Laura. I want you to come over here. Bring Jonny. When you get to the hotel, phone from the desk to me. I'll come down."

"All right," Laura said.

Jonny was quiet, too quiet, as she got obediently into her coat and hat. All her former cautious docility had returned, the dreadful docility of a child who has been too well trained in unquestioning obedience. It touched Laura's heart with pain and compunction. Perhaps she ought to have sent Jonny away, at once. Where?

They got a taxi. It was threatening snow again. Christmas weather.

It was only a few short blocks to the towering apartment hotel where Matt lived. As they entered the lobby, Matt himself emerged from an elevator, and came quickly to them. "It's Maria Brown," he said in a low voice. "She's upstairs in my apartment. I want you to hear her story."

He took them quickly into the elevator. With a glance at the elevator man, he said to Jonny, "How are you, Jonny, this morning? I think it is going to snow. You know, snow."

"Snow," Jonny said obediently, but with no answering sparkle in her blue eyes.

Laura said, "When did she come? How did you find her?"

The elevator stopped. Matt led them out into the wide corridor. "I put an advertisement in the Personal Column last night. I said in the advertisement, 'Jonny needs mother. Protection promised,' and gave my phone number. And she answered it. Just came here to the hotel. When I got back from talking to Peabody, there she was sitting in the lobby waiting for me."

"What did she say? *Is* she Jonny's—"

"I don't know. I put the advertisement in, on the basis that she is Jonny's mother and that there might be some legitimate, some comprehensible reason for the fact that she left her husband and baby. If that's true, some of her behavior can be explained. That is—maybe. In any event, it seemed worth taking a gamble. Nothing lost if she didn't answer it. I rather thought Peabody or some of the police would turn up this morning and question me about it, but apparently they missed it."

"And she's here—now!"

"Unless she got out the back way, while I went to meet you! But I don't think she did. Because you see, if she is the mother, there are two alternatives. Either she is on the level about things, and simply wants her child, or she wants her child all right, but she is either in cahoots with the second Stanislowski or she murdered the first one in order to get hold of Jonny, herself. I want you to listen to her. I don't know whether she is telling the truth or not."

He led the way on down the hall and opened the door of his apartment.

But he didn't take Jonny to meet Maria Brown; instead he shunted her instantly into a tiny study at one end of the short hall. There was a jig-saw puzzle on the table. "Here, Jonny. Here's a picture puzzle. Take your coat off first—"

In a moment he came back and nodded at Laura. "All right, she's in here."

175

He led the way into the living room. Maria Brown sat stiffly erect in a straight chair.

Her brown coat lay over the arm of the sofa. She wore a rather shabby black dress with a touch of white at the throat. Her black beret was pulled low over her short fringe of hair. Again her face seemed to have a greater pallor than was accounted for even by the lack of cosmetics; her mouth was a kind of ashy blue. She held her handbag in both hands, eyed Laura and said nothing.

Matt offered cigarettes and Maria Brown took one with a curious, almost greedy quickness, as if, Laura thought, cigarettes were a luxury to her. Matt held the light for her and the tiny flame touched her sallow face to a warmer tint. He lighted Laura's cigarette, too. He pulled up a chair. He said in an easy, conversational way, "Now then, I'd like to go over your story again. I want Miss March to hear it."

"Not the police," Maria Brown said flatly.

"No, not the police until you are willing to talk to them. I promised you that."

Maria Brown took a long puff of smoke. She looked at the wall, past Laura and past Matt. "Very well," she said, her words flat and toneless, heavily accented, yet fluent, too. "Very well. Shall I start at the beginning?"

"Start at the beginning. When you left Poland."

"Yes," Maria Brown said. "Yes, when I left Poland—"

Matt said, prompting her, "The night when Conrad came home and told you that you were to be arrested the next morning."

"Yes. I was to be arrested. I was part of what you would call a resistance movement, a movement against the government. I was outspoken. Conrad in his heart was in sympathy with me, but he was more careful, more discreet. I had written some pamphlets. I had helped distribute them. I was caught." She took another long sucking breath of cigarette smoke. Then she went on as flatly and tonelessly as if she were reading some impersonal account from a book, which had nothing to do with her. "Conrad"—she glanced at Laura and said heavily but without any trace of feeling in her voice—"he was my husband, you see. The man you found murdered."

Matt said softly, "The night you left Poland—"

"Yes. Conrad had discovered that I was to be arrested the next day. He said I must leave. He said that was the only thing to do. He said he would follow, and would bring Jonny with him, but I had to get out then. He said they wouldn't do anything to him. They might suspect him; they might watch him, but that he and Jonny would be safe. He said that as soon as he could he would leave the country, too, but there was a way to get me out. He knew it. He said I had to go that night. I didn't want to go."

176

She paused. She didn't want to go, yet her voice in speaking of it, was as devoid of feeling as if it had not happened to her. Or, Laura thought suddenly, as if she had learned that speech; as if she knew word for word what she was to say.

THIRTY-ONE

"But you did go—" Matt said.

"Oh, yes. I could see there was nothing else to do. It seemed the only way to protect Conrad, my husband, and my baby. There was no time to delay. I had to go. So I did. Eventually I got to England."

"And you communicated with Conrad?" Matt said.

Her eyes flickered. She made an oddly baffled gesture with the cigarette. "I am sorry. I know the English language. I studied it. I have spoken English for years now but sometimes a word—"

Matt said, "Communicate. I mean, you wrote to Conrad."

She gave Matt a queer, cold look. Her cheeks looked sunken below her broad cheekbones; there were brownish patches around her eyes. She nodded briefly. "Oh, yes! I wrote to him, very seldom, you understand, only general letters such as anybody might have written. I signed another name. The only important thing in the letters was that he would know I was well. Then I would put a return address on the letter so he would know where I was. He wrote to me the same way, very cautiously. Letters which anybody might read. You see, there is a sort of spot censorship and, of course, Conrad was by then an official. He was watched because I had escaped. They doubted his loyalty. But then gradually he grew to feel safer."

She paused and suddenly seemed very far away, lost in some distant, shadowy world where they could not follow her. Matt said, "I know this is tiring. But as you know Miss March is a trustee—"

Maria Brown flicked a somber glance at Laura. "I understand. But that's all, really. Conrad got the child to Vienna. He sent her with a friend."

177

Matt said, "Did you know the friend? Could it have been the man who now claims himself to be Conrad Stanislowski?"

Maria shook her head. "I don't know. I don't even know his name. I think though that this man who came to you yesterday is someone from Poland. I think he is trying to get my child and the money and take them both back to Poland."

Matt said nothing to that. After a moment he asked, "So then your husband came to Chicago?"

"Yes. I was in England for a long time, you understand." She looked at Laura briefly and looked away again, staring at nothing as if she were reading from a book which was invisible to Matt and Laura. "Then I got my status regularized. I had a passport. I came to New York. I was there when I heard from Conrad. It was just a note but in it he mentioned Chicago. He said, as I remember it, Chicago would be an interesting place for anyone to visit; I knew of course that he was about to escape, that he had his plans made and that he wanted me to go to Chicago. I came to Chicago. I went to the rooming house there. It's in the Polish section. I looked at several. This seemed clean and neat. I wrote a very short note to Conrad. I said nothing that could possibly give me away, or Conrad or my child. I merely put a return address, 3936 Koska Street, on the letter. So when Conrad reached Chicago he came there." She stopped.

Matt waited; then he spoke to Laura. "They had a very short time together. Mrs. Brown worked mornings. She came home at noon. She says her husband was already there and he told her that Jonny was in Chicago."

Maria Brown said suddenly, "I made a mistake! I wanted to be sure my child was in Chicago. Conrad only had the letter from the orphanage."

"You saw the letter?"

She gave Matt a level look and shook her head. "No, no. We had so little time. I wanted him to find out about Jonny. I wanted him to see her. The letter—there might have been some mistake, some change. I felt I would be content if he saw Jonny with his own eyes and came back and told me he had seen her. Do you understand?"

She didn't look at either of them. She stubbed out her cigarette with the strong hand which had clamped down on the telephone in Laura's apartment. There was not a flicker of emotion in her face.

Do I believe her, Laura thought. She leaned forward. "When I talked to your husband, he started to speak of you and then he stopped and then said that he had taken care of the child. I assumed—"

Maria Brown gave her a long look. "You assumed I was dead.

178

Conrad promised me to tell nobody that I was here in Chicago. You see—I am still frightened."

"What are you afraid of?" Matt said gently.

Maria Brown looked at him as if he were a child asking foolish questions, and did not reply.

"But the government of Poland would not pursue you, here in America. You are perfectly safe. Conrad was safe."

Maria Brown brushed it aside again as if it were the suggestion of a child. "I am afraid. I am afraid for Jonny, too. I made Conrad promise not to claim Jonny, not to do anything about it until he found a safe place for us. That's all we wanted. He was going to find some place outside the city, where we could take another name, where we could live in peace. Then he would come back and show you all his credentials and take Jonny and bring her to me. That was our plan."

Matt said quietly, "I don't think either you or Conrad and certainly not Jonny could be in any way valuable to the Communists. There's nothing you know that could endanger them—is there?"

Again the woman didn't answer.

Matt went on. "I understand that it's hard to accept security. If the habit of fear is engrained into you—yes, I understand it. But I wish I could make you see that now you're perfectly safe. You can seek asylum."

"Yes, that's what Conrad said. That's what he intended to do. But you see there's something you don't understand. This will of my husband's uncle which would give him so much money—that money would make him valuable, don't you see? And that money makes my child valuable."

"But she can't have the money, your husband couldn't have had the money, unless he remained here and lived his life in America."

"So you say," Maria Brown said in a phlegmatic, flat voice which utterly denied Matt's statement.

"It's true. Now I want you to go on, if you please. I know this is hard but it is important. Wait a moment—" He went to a table at the other end of the room where a tray with decanters stood. There was a coffee service there, too, a thermos and cups from the hotel. He poured hot coffee, splashed in a liberal amount from one of the decanters, and brought the cup to Maria Brown. "I put some brandy in it. Drink it—"

Again there was a pathetic suggestion of greediness in the gesture with which she took the cup and gulped the hot coffee. It suggested a long period of doing without any of the small luxuries of life. She put down the cup. "What happened, happened. I can't undo any of it. Conrad went to find Jonny. I waited in the room-

179

ing house. He was gone a long time. I was impatient. And someone came into the house. Nobody had been there while Conrad and I talked. All the lodgers are working people; they're gone all day. The landlady had gone out to market; I saw her go; it was only after that that Conrad came to me. While he was still gone someone came; it was not Conrad; he'd have come to my room. But this person came very quietly up the stairs. I thought he went into Conrad's room. That was two rooms down from mine but the walls are thin. I was terrified. The moment we had reached each other after all those years—pursuit began."

"Pursuit—" Laura said, and heard the doubt in her own voice.

"I was sure that it was some member of the government party who had either followed Conrad or received orders from Poland. I waited. I didn't want him to see me. Then Conrad came home. He went to his room and the visitor there spoke to him. I listened. They had a drink. The visitor had brought it. Conrad got glasses. They both drank. Conrad never had a head for drinking and he was exuberant, he was gay, he was happy, he had found his wife again, he had found his child. Conrad talked. But he didn't mention me. He said not a word of me. I could hear Conrad's voice easily. He talked of Jonny. I think he answered questions about her."

Laura said in a stifled voice, "Who was it?"

Maria Brown did not so much as glance at her. "I don't know," she said flatly. "I don't even know whether it was a man or a woman."

That, certainly, did not sound true. Laura glanced at Matt, who lifted an eyebrow. He said to Maria Brown, "Surely if you could hear the visitor's voice—"

"I could not," she said promptly. "The visitor's voice was very low. I could hear only a sort of murmur. It was Conrad's voice that was high and clear, especially when he drank. But I knew he was answering questions." Maria Brown paused and seemed to consider her own words. "I was terrified. My head was not clear. I was only afraid. I knew that Conrad was deceived. I thought that his visitor was somebody he must have known, because he talked so freely. But I thought that he believed that person to be well disposed, harmless. The visitor asked questions, I was sure of that. The subject must have been Jonny because Conrad's replies were about Jonny. He didn't say that he had just seen Jonny. But he talked of her, little things—about her childhood."

Her curiously monotonous voice stopped. Matt looked at Laura. "Among the incidents he told his visitor was a game he played with Jonny. When he came home, when he greeted her, he would swing her up in his arms and sing—"

"Oh, yes," Marie Brown said, "that song, 'I am a Cracovian—

He told about that, laughing, proudly—fondly." She reached for another cigarette and said flatly, "And there were other things they talked of. Conrad's passport. It was not visaed for the United States. I think the visitor—" Maria Brown paused to light her cigarette. She continued in as monotonous a tone as if she were talking of the weather "—I think the murderer threatened Conrad about the passport, for I heard Conrad say very clearly, 'Oh, yes, yes, I understand. You will see to my passport. Very good of you, very good indeed. You will see to my passport. I'll stay quiet. I'll stay out of sight. I won't talk to any of them until you see about my passport.' " She nodded firmly. "Conrad said that. Then the visitor said something and Conrad said, 'Oh, no, I don't like officialdom. We in Poland do not like officialdom.' "

For the first time Maria Brown's face and voice showed a touch of animation. She lifted her shoulders and a queer smile touched the corners of her pale lips. "Conrad was lying. The fact was he intended to seek asylum. He was not afraid about his passport! He knew that that could be arranged if he went to the proper authorities. He only pretended to be afraid because he, too, had a reason for wishing to keep his arrival secret. That reason, I've told you. He intended to take me to some safe place. Then he would come back for Jonny. That's why he pretended to be afraid about the passport. But his murderer used it to keep Conrad from seeing you"—she looked at Laura—"or you"—her dark eyes went to Matt—"or his uncle's wife or the other trustee or anybody."

Matt said, "Drink your coffee. Is it still hot?"

"Thank you. Yes." She drank with long hard gulps, then she lifted her head. "There was then a sound. Just a—sound. Something fell hard on the floor. There was a momont or two. And then someone came out, very light, very soft, and down the stairs. I was afraid to look. I knew—I knew— The door downstairs closed. I ran to Conrad's room. He had been stabbed. I did not know what to do. Conrad opened his eyes. I tried to help him. I took my handkerchief. I asked him questions. He said your name, Miss March. There was a telephone booth in the hall below. I ran down there. I telephoned to you. When I got back upstairs Conrad was dead."

She lifted the cup, drank and put it down. "There was nothing more I could do. I had telephoned to you. You would bring doctors. But the police would come. The police, the newspapers. If the police asked me questions, if it was in the newspapers, then our enemies would find me. They would find my baby. I ran to my room. I hurried. I cleared out the drawers, everything. I left nothing, I was sure. But then as I left you arrived. I told you to go away—" She leveled her gaze at Laura. "You had my child

181

with you. I told you to go away. I told you I should not have telephoned to you. Why didn't you go away? We are targets, Jonny and I. They will never stop."

Matt said, "I promised you protection."

"All we wanted to do," Maria Brown said, "was to go away to some safe place, take new names, then get our child and live quietly. Safely."

Laura's throat felt tight.

Matt said, "This new claimant, this man who came yesterday, has a passport. His photograph is on it."

Scorn flickered over Maria Brown's face. "Passports have been faked. He is not my husband."

"Who is he then?"

"I told you. He is an enemy. He is from Poland. He wishes to take Jonny and the money back. That would be a coup, that would be a triumph. Yes."

"But he can't have the money unless he lives here."

Again it made no impression upon Maria Brown. Her face was perfectly still.

Matt waited for a moment. Maria Brown waited, too. Finally Matt said, "How long was Conrad away from the house on Koska Street?"

There was a suggestion of surprise in the way Maria Brown's eyelids lifted. "I am not sure. Perhaps two hours. Perhaps longer."

"He was in Miss March's apartment about—ten minutes?" Matt gave Laura a questioning look and she nodded. Matt said, "Allow thirty minutes each way for bus or taxi. Some extra time for finding the way in a strange city. A few minutes for making a phone call—"

"A phone call! He made no phone call."

"Mrs. Stanley says he called her just before she went to the dentist's. Her appointment was at four. She says he asked where Jonny was."

Maria Brown considered it, and gave an abrupt nod. "Yes. Yes, he might have done that. I never thought of it. He must have inquired. He had to know that Jonny was in Miss March's care. Before he died he only said—your name." Her dark gaze went to Laura. "Your name—and the word, doctor. That was all. At first I thought he meant to tell me who had stabbed him," she said simply. "Then I knew he meant that you must bring a doctor."

Matt said swiftly and very quietly, "I am sure that you would be willing to swear to that—"

"Swear! I will not talk to the police. You promised me—"

"Yes. Yes, but—" Matt paused, thinking rapidly.

It could be construed as an accusation. Laura March, the dying

182

man had said. Chill fingers tightened around Laura's heart. Matt said calmly, "I only meant that you have no doubt whatever as to his meaning— Get Miss March. Have her bring a doctor." He went on quickly, as if his legal mind warned him not to stress that dangerous point too heavily. "I'd like to know exactly what your husband did during that time. Two hours or longer. You see it looks as if he must have talked to the murderer *before* the murderer came to Koska Street, doesn't it?"

Maria Brown considered that, too, and abruptly agreed. "The murderer knew the address. He knew about my husband's passport. He knew there was a child."

"So he must have talked to the visitor, the murderer, either in Poland, after he knew your Chicago address, on the boat coming here—or in Chicago. The interview at Koska Street, with the drinks and the questions about the child, must have been, at least, a second interview. The murderer clearly came, prepared to ask Conrad questions about his child. That little business of the song is a very convincing detail. What ship did you say your husband took here?"

"I did not say," Maria Brown said flatly. "I do not know. He said he left from Genoa. He said when the ship reached port he jumped ship."

"Did he say what port?"

"No," Maria Brown said flatly. She looked at Matt and added, "I do not think Conrad would have told anybody about his plans except somebody he trusted. Whoever came to see him in his room, whoever murdered him, he trusted that person."

Matt said thoughtfully, "His murderer knew about his passport. He seized it as an excuse to keep Conrad quiet until he could arrange a murder. That had to happen before the interview at the rooming house. Conrad told you, Laura, where he was staying and he told Doris. He could have told his murderer where he was staying. The murderer came to Koska Street prepared to murder. He could have taken the letter from the orphanage—"

"The man saying he is my husband did that! He is an impostor. He is a murderer. Why do you not believe me?" Maria Brown said heavily. "I tell you he intends to get my child and the money and take them to Poland." She looked at Laura and said again, "Why do you not believe me?"

Laura had no answer. It was a story which might answer many questions. On the other hand, did that very fact, in a certain way, weaken it? Was it *too* apt a story? Matt said, "I wish you would talk to the police."

THIRTY-TWO

A blank, cold light came into Maria Brown's eyes. She lifted one hand and brought it down on the table beside her with a hard blow. "I told you I will not do that. You promised me—"

"All right. But think about it. Now—you said you have a passport?"

Again a kind of somber lightning flashed in Maria Brown's face. "I will not show you my passport. I have it in a safe place. It is very important to me. I will give it to nobody."

"All right." Matt appeared to accept it easily again. "Will you tell me where you have been staying?"

"No," Maria Brown said flatly. "I will not see the police. I will not tell anybody where I stay. I will tell you nothing. You don't believe that the government party in my home have long, terrible memories. You don't believe me, either of you."

"But don't you understand how easy it would be to make us believe? You could show us your passport. You could show us any papers of identification you have. You can tell us where you are staying. Are you staying with friends?"

Again Maria Brown simply and conclusively did not reply.

Matt said, "Well, then, how about money? Are you supplied with money?"

"Enough," Maria Brown said.

Matt's face was hard. "One more question. Are you sure when Conrad spoke to you he did not tell you who killed him?"

"He said only Laura March, that name. Laura March—doctor, that is all he said."

Matt met Laura's eyes. He answered the terrified question in her mind. "She had no doubt as to his meaning. And in any event —I've got to keep my promise not to turn her over to the police."

Maria Brown gave Laura an oblique, sliding glance and said nothing. Matt said to Maria Brown, "Later, then—did you telephone to Miss March? I mean before you went to her apartment?"

184

"Yes, I did," the woman said flatly. "Once I got myself into a safe place I thought about my child. I was thinking of her all the time, you understand. I had to be sure she was safe. I telephoned to Miss March and she answered but——but then I was afraid to talk. I thought from her voice, it sounded all right, you understand, that no harm had come to Jonny. But I was afraid to talk. I was afraid it would be traced. I was afraid somebody would hear me. I was at one of those pay telephone booths. It was in a public place. I was afraid. I hung up and ran out and I went back to——" she stopped.

"And then you telephoned again?"

"Yes, I did. I told myself this time I would talk to her but again——no, I could not."

Matt said carefully, "Did you ever speak into the telephone? Did you ever speak Polish, say, into it? Did you ever mention Jonny's name?"

"No," Maria Brown said flatly. "No." She thought for a moment, watching Matt. Then she said, "Somebody did that, is that right? Who was it? Was it the murderer? Was it a man? Was it a woman? Women are trained to this kind of assassination as well as men. Who did that?"

Matt replied, "I don't know. Somebody telephoned and spoke in Polish. Somebody mentioned Jonny's name. We don't know who it was."

"That should be clear! It is this second man. It is this man calling himself Conrad Stanislowski. He is an impostor. He is a murderer. You've got to give me my child."

Oh, no, Laura thought; not yet! Matt sensed her panic. He came across the room and put one hand on Laura's shoulder. He said to Maria Brown, "If I assure you that Jonny is safe, will you wait for a few days to see her? She is here, you heard her voice. She is safe."

"You are trying to trick me."

"No, I'm not. I'm going to leave you here in my apartment. You are perfectly safe. You can lock the door. Don't answer any telephone calls. If anybody knocks, don't open the door. Please think of our position about Jonny. We have to ask you to identify yourself in a way that will satisfy Miss March, the other trustee and Mrs. Stanley. It is our obligation. You understand that. Now —I'm going to leave you here. I want you to think, too, about talking to the police and telling them just what you have told me. But if you wish to leave, if you wish to hide yourself again, you can."

He looked at Laura. "We'll get Jonny. I'll go home with you."

Laura rose. But at the door Matt turned abruptly back. "There

185

is another question. Did you know a woman by the name of Catherine Miller?"

"No." Maria Brown said.

"Did you—" Matt hesitated. Then he said, "Did you go to Miss March's apartment more than once?"

"No," she said in a flat tone of unequivocal finality. She did not look up. Laura's last glimpse of Maria Brown showed simply a stolid, silent figure staring at nothing. Matt closed the door of the living room.

"Oh, Matt," Laura cried, but softly so Maria Brown did not hear. "We should tell the police!"

"I'm doing what I think is right. I'll get Jonny."

Laura stood transfixed, listening. There was no sound beyond the closed door to the living room. She heard only Matt in the study speaking to Jonny. "We'll take the puzzle with us. I'll put it so the picture you've already made won't break. See, I'll put it in this box. There—" There was a soft little clatter of the jig-saw puzzle. Presently Matt came out again, Jonny beside him in her red coat, a box clasped under her arm. The door to the living room did not open.

They went down in the elevator. In the taxi Matt talked to Jonny steadily, inventing a story to go with the jig-saw puzzle.

Suppose Maria Brown's story was true, Laura thought. It explained so much. But it failed to explain so much, too.

When they reached Laura's apartment Matt first established Jonny in her room, with the jig-saw puzzle. He came back into the living room and stood for a moment, staring absently at the Christmas tree.

"Matt—do you believe her?"

"I don't know." He went to the Christmas tree and plugged in the lights. They sprang up, red and green and white, all over the tree, lighting the room with a poignant glow of promise. "Did you believe her?" Matt asked.

"I don't know. It could have happened like that. And if she is Jonny's mother—"

"I know. If you believe her, it's a tragic and terrible story. After all those years of separation and anxiety, she and Conrad had so little time together. No, it's not nice. On the other hand, is it true? Her manner is so—well, you know, Laura—that flat, toneless voice, that stolid manner, that phlegmatic way of replying. It's hard to tell whether she's a tragic and brokenhearted woman, beaten down with tragedy and anxiety—or whether she's a ruthless and very clever liar. And a murderer. *I* can't tell."

"What about the police?"

"I ought to tell them. I'm a lawyer. It's evidence. And I think Peabody would believe her statement as to Conrad's intention in

186

speaking only your name and the word doctor. It's not news to him; you told him why you went to Koska Street; her statement squares with your own. If he'd heard Maria's statement first, he might have questioned whether Conrad meant it as—an accusation, the name of his murderer, or as he did mean it. But as it stands I think her evidence as to that would be an advantage in the end. I really do think that, Laura. And I think that she'll decide to see the police. I don't think I'm taking much of a chance. If she's really Jonny's mother, she's going to stay there in my apartment and after a while she'll consent to see the police. An alternative is that she is Jonny's mother but her story is not true; she simply wants to get hold of Jonny and the money, and she murdered Conrad. In that event I think she'll disappear but turn up again in a few days, because if she's going to claim Jonny she's got to come forward with her identification and credentials. I think I made that clear enough to her. The third alternative, of course, is that she's in a conspiracy with this second Conrad."

"Why, then, would she answer your personal notice?"

"To establish herself as Jonny's mother, perhaps," Matt said rather doubtfully. "I talked to Peabody this morning. He went to see Conrad the second. She says he's the murderer, so that doesn't look like a conspiracy between them. On the other hand, thieves do fall out. Much of her story sounds true; that is that the first Conrad knew her address, went to Koska Street, the landlady was gone, nobody was there; she sent him at once to confirm Jonny's presence— Yes, that sounds human—true. It does seem to me that she ought to know at least whether the mysterious visitor was a man or a woman. Yet certainly anybody planning murder would not shout out to the world the questions he asked Conrad about Jonny. He wouldn't have known perhaps that the rooming house was entirely deserted except for Maria. Obviously he didn't know Maria was there; obviously Conrad purposely didn't tell him. Always provided her story is true," Matt said with a rather dejected note to his voice. "There are details that were right—the two glasses the police found, and you saw. There was no bottle of any sort of liquor there. The murderer could have taken that away, wiped the glasses so there would not be fingerprints on them. She told me she left her handkerchief—that was the handkerchief that Peabody found. That detail has not been, so far as I know, in the newspapers. And her story makes her telephone call to you and then her escape completely logical. All that sounds true."

"She won't show you her passport. She won't tell you where she's staying."

"She's still frightened. I mean—she's either frightened or she's giving a very good performance of being frightened."

"She says she knows nothing of Catherine Miller. She denied that."

"Yes," Matt said. "Laura, that scarf. Tell me exactly what Peabody said."

She told him quietly, her voice seeming to take on something of Maria Brown's flat and toneless recital.

Matt's face was like a hard, white mask. "When did you last see the scarf?"

"I think it was the day we went to the movies. I remember wearing a red one yesterday when we went to Doris', but I don't remember seeing the white one then."

Matt rose. "I'm going to talk to Jonny."

She followed him. Jonny looked up gravely. Suki, sitting on the table and watching, took advantage of Jonny's distraction, pushed a piece off the table, and sprang to retrieve it. Matt said, "Jonny, yesterday afternoon you opened the door, you let me in, remember? Was anybody else here yesterday? Did you open the door another time?"

Jonny shook her head in a troubled way. "Please?"

"She doesn't understand," Laura said.

"I'll show her." Matt led the child out into the hall. He opened the door, he closed it. He got out the Polish dictionary. "*Nie*," Jonny said, her eyes sad and anxious, "*nie*." But then she went to the door, opened it, shook her head, said, "*Nie, nie!*" closed it, and stood with her hands at her sides.

"All right, Jonny. It's all right," Matt said. "Go back to your puzzle."

The child sighed. Then she trudged along the hall. Matt sighed, too. "It's no use getting an interpreter."

"Do you mean she let somebody in—yesterday—when I was asleep?"

"I don't know. I came in then. Jonny opened the door. You were sound asleep. You didn't hear me."

"She would have opened the door for Charlie," Laura said slowly. "For Doris perhaps. Nobody else, Matt."

"I'm not so sure. If Stanislowski, I mean Conrad the second, came and spoke to her in Polish— Look here, Laura, has anything at all been moved or—or searched, or is anything missing besides the scarf?"

"No. Not that I—" A small memory struck her. "There was a bird, a toy, a yellow bird Charlie gave her. She fastened it on the tree. It's gone. I thought Jonny had taken it to play with. But when I looked I couldn't find it."

188

Matt stared at her for a moment. Then he took the Polish dictionary and went to Jonny's room. Laura followed. A long fifteen minutes later they knew only that the absurd yellow bird was not to be found anywhere.

Jonny was by then biting her lips to hold back tears. Matt took her in his arms. "It's all right, Jonny. You don't understand—it's all right." But he took her with him to the telephone, and dialed a number.

He asked for Miss Nowak. "Miss Nowak? This is Matt Cosden again. I wonder if you would ask the little girl a question or two right now, over the telephone? Will you ask her who came to see her yesterday afternoon?"

He then gave the telephone to Jonny. "Talk to her, Jonny. To please me—"

Jonny pressed the receiver against her ear. But at the first words Miss Nowak spoke, her little face turned a stony, rigid blank. She shook her head, she stared at the floor, then suddenly she turned and pushed the telephone receiver back at Matt and ran away into the back of the apartment.

Matt said, "Thanks, Miss Nowak. It's no good," and hung up. "Well, that's that. Of course the fact is anybody could have got in here, I suppose, while you were gone, and taken that scarf. But that yellow bird—why? It suggests Charlie because he gave it to her. But why should anybody want to point to Charlie in just that way? It's fantastic. It makes no sense. Besides, who would know that Charlie had brought it. Laura, you're sure it didn't—oh, fall off, get thrown out? Something like that?"

"I'd have seen it."

"I suppose so. Still—oh, it probably means nothing. Laura, I'm going to see Peabody."

"What about Maria Brown?"

"I'll give her an hour or so to think it over, then I'll go back and talk to her. Unless," he said wryly, "she's disappeared again. I wish I knew whether she's telling the truth or not. She says that she heard Conrad's voice, it was very loud and clear, especially after he had had a drink or two. But I think she must have heard the murderer's voice. No matter how much of the rest of her story is true, I think that part is a lie. I think that she is afraid to put herself in a position to identify the murderer. She's afraid of revenge on the part of the Polish government party or one of their emissaries. And oddly enough, if she's lying about that, the lie would make the rest of her story more credible. Are you going out this afternoon with Jonny?"

"Yes. She knows something's wrong, Matt. She's frightened. I've got to try to distract her."

189

"I know," he said dubiously. "As a matter of fact you ought to get out yourself. But it you do, go where there are crowds. Stay with other people. Take her Christmas shopping."

But at the door he paused for a moment and went back to Maria Brown. "There's another important angle to that Brown woman's story. She said that Conrad did not tell the murderer that he had seen you and Jonny. He talked about Jonny, she says, you heard her. He went on and on, telling incidents of her childhood, that little song, but he *didn't* say he had seen her and he didn't say he had seen you. It must have given the murderer a terrific jolt to discover, after he had obviously left Conrad for dead, that Conrad not only wasn't dead, but he had talked to Maria Brown and that you had actually gone to the rooming house. Well—my guess is eventually Maria will talk to Peabody. In any event, it's the only way I see to play it."

It's the only way to play it, Laura thought, after he'd gone. Wait like a chess player for the next move. What exactly would the next move be?

The important thing was Jonny—and the troubled, sad look in her face. She went to Jonny, she helped with the puzzle, she cooked Jonny's favorite lunch, she talked, gaily and constantly, she exerted every effort; by the time Jonny took her nap, Laura had succeeded in coaxing a spontaneous smile and some answering chatter from the child.

About two-thirty she and Jonny took a taxi to the Loop. Christmas shopping, Matt had said.

The day was still heavily overcast. Lights were already on in the shop windows. The traffic was thunderous and heavy. Again the Michigan Avenue bridge was up and they waited, with the throb of motors all around them, the occasional shrill hoot of the taxicabs and the lower yet piercing and eerie moan of a cargo boat making its way between the massive abutments of the bridge, which reared up into the foggy sky, and out to the gray, mysterious reaches of the lake. They had reached a door of the great department store, when Laura discovered again that someone was following them.

THIRTY-THREE

She wasn't sure of it at first. She only noted that a taxi stopped behind her taxi as she and Jonny got out. Then she saw that the dimly outlined man's figure in the second taxi was vaguely familiar. She couldn't see his face.

She hurried Jonny across the sidewalk, through the revolving door into the lights, the familiar, the crowded and busy atmosphere of the great store.

The dimly seen figure in the taxi had had a bulky dark shape about his shoulders; a widely brimmed hat shielded his face. She had glimpsed that much. Clusters of shoppers intervened now between her and the door.

Murder is dangerous. Be careful.

Murder or attempted murder couldn't happen then and there, with crowds of shoppers milling about, busy salesgirls, glittering lights. Nothing could happen there. All the same it was pursuit.

Her heart was thudding. She led Jonny to the nearest escalator, through the swirling, package-laden crowd. They would lose themselves, she and Jonny. They would go to the toy department.

Jonny loved the escalator. She stepped on it promptly; she clutched the moving rail and looked out over the brilliant scene below, with its festive Christmas decorations, huge loops of tinsel and red and green going from pillar to pillar. At the very top Laura risked a look downward. She did not see any dark-coated, foreign-looking figure. She hurried Jonny on around a corner and into the toy department.

The huge toy department was gayly decorated, too, with great festoons of red and gold and green, with Santa Clauses and tinseled Christmas trees. It was packed with shoppers, mothers, fathers, children and more children. Jonny's eyes widened with excitement.

If there were somebody following them, then it was, it had to be, the second Conrad Stanislowski. What could he do?

He could try to take Jonny from her.

191

But she could ask for help. She could approach a salesclerk, ask for a manager. What could she say? A man who claims to be this child's father is following us? Who would believe her? Besides, by that time the shadowy figure would have unobtrusively but completely vanished.

Perhaps she was mistaken.

She ought not to have come to the toy department! It was an obvious place for anybody to search for them.

She had made herself stare fixedly at the dolls on the counter before them; her neck muscles were stiff and rigid with her effort not to look back—and suddenly she could bear it no longer and gave a swift glance back toward the corner near the escalator. A shoulder in a bulky dark overcoat moved swiftly out of sight, away down at the end of the crowded aisle, and behind a huge pillar.

Laura caught Jonny's hand.

"Come, Jonny. Come—"

Jonny gave her a startled glance and instantly obeyed. They ducked and dodged around other shoppers toward another flight of escalators that wound upward and downward through the great store. They'd go back down to the first floor, Laura thought, in full and panic retreat. They'd take another exit, opposite the door by which they had arrived, on another street entirely, a full block across. There were always taxis on that crowded street. Hurry, she thought. Whoever it was and whatever the motive, it was a surreptitious pursuit; therefore it was dangerous.

They went down the escalator. Jonny's face was serious, now. Laura said, "It's all right, Jonny. It's all right—" Her voice was unsteady. They reached the first floor and started for the revolving doors ahead. The counters were stored now with jewelry. Diamonds and rubies and emeralds glittered against white velvet. They were almost at the door when Laura looked back and he was following them.

He was far back in the packed aisle. She couldn't see his face, but through a sudden shift in the crowds of shoppers, she saw a movement like a shadow, sliding furtively again out of sight. The ranks of shoppers closed in. But he was there. And he knew that they were hurrying to the door. She looked around swiftly and saw the small, almost hidden elevator which went directly to the Fashion Shop.

She swerved and led Jonny into the tiny elevator. The Fashion Shop was a luxurious, small department where exclusive models, with famous labels, were sold. Doris bought most of her clothes there. Laura had rarely entered it. The elevator, like the Fashion Shop, was known mainly to the women who could afford to pay the prices famous couturiers demand. Once in the elevator, Laura sank into one of the little, gray French armchairs which made a tiny drawing-room of the elevator. Her heart slowed down a little. She managed to smile reassuringly at Jonny and Jonny returned her smile although her eyes were still serious and troubled. He wouldn't know about the elevator. He wouldn't know about the Fashion Shop, not Conrad Stanislowski. It was a refuge.

They emerged from the little elevator into the wide and luxurious room with its showcases, its gay "Boutique," a counter or two laden with luxurious frivolities of dress. They were ushered into an enormous fitting room, with deep chairs upholstered in gray velvet. A neatly uniformed maid brought coffee. A pleasant, friendly saleswoman brought dresses for Laura to see. They were for the moment safe.

But she asked for a telephone and when it was brought and plugged in, she telephoned to Matt's apartment; no one answered; if Maria Brown were still there she wouldn't answer, of course. She tried Matt's office; his secretary said that he was not in. She debated calling Lieutenant Peabody and after a time decided against it. He was already skeptical as to the reality of that furtive, shadowy figure, and it would disappear as if it had in fact no reality at the arrival of police.

She looked at dresses and dresses. Time passed and the windows beyond the thin silk curtains grew steadily darker. Presently it began to snow, great white flakes drifting down against the background of gray sky and the lighted tiers of windows, set like jewels in the massive buildings across the street. Laura looked at herself in a flame-colored dinner dress, thin and molded around her waist, leaving her shoulders white and bare, and swirling around her feet. The girl in the mirror was suddenly slender and lovely. Her gray eyes glowed. Her slender face took on a mysterious something which was almost beauty. It was as if she saw herself, Laura March, poised for a strange and lovely gift. A different girl, another woman.

Jonny touched the dress. She had been deeply interested in all the dresses, sitting there with her little red coat over a chair, her sturdy little legs dangling, her small face lighted. She had apparently forgotten the uneasiness which had touched her when Laura hurried her down the escalators, through the store, up another elevator. All at once going on eight she was intensely, completely feminine. She said softly, *"Ladna sukienka,"* and smiled up at Laura. "Pret—ty." And all at once, not intending to, Laura said, "I'll take it."

Why? It was a holiday dress, a gay and luxurious dress meant for parties and dancing. Dancing, she thought unexpectedly, with Matt.

That was silly. But she stood watching herself again in the

193

mirror, turning as the fitter knelt to adjust the hem. Another girl, another woman, not Laura March, not even a woman Laura March could ever be. She had never paid so much for a dress in her life; it was a silly extravagance; it would hang in a closet; it would give her usually very moderate charge account a shock, she thought wryly. Nevertheless she would take the dress.

The snow outside the window was increasing; it was by then almost dusk, with the early fall of December twilight. They would have to leave sometime. Surely it was safe to do so then. But again she tried Matt's apartment. Again no one answered.

She put on her gray dress and her gray coat with its long flowing lines and its warmth, so it was like a very soft, very warm fur coat. She adjusted her little hat. Jonny with her usual sturdy self-reliance got herself into her red coat. She thanked the saleswoman who beamed. "Happy Christmas, Miss March. You look lovely in the dress."

Laura thanked her. She led Jonny at last out of the safe and secure little refuge and a man at the outer desk stopped her. "Miss March?" he said pleasantly. "A gentleman was inquiring for you. I told him," he smiled with an air of indulgent conspiracy, "I told him you were looking at dresses. I told him it would be some time before you were ready to go. I hope that was right?"

Laura's heart caught in her throat. "Yes. Yes, that was right. How long ago was that?"

"Oh, at least an hour. He went away."

"Thank you," Laura said. An hour ago. He went away. She turned away from the desk, and behind her suddenly the man's cordial and polite voice became warmer. "Why," he said, "Mrs. Stanley!"

Laura whirled around. Doris was standing at the little Boutique counter. The manager advanced to greet her with cordiality. "It's nice to see you, Mrs. Stanley. What can we do for you?"

Doris said shortly, "Oh, nothing. I'm just looking," and then saw Laura and Jonny. She came across to them.

She wore her long mink coat; a little black hat was poised on her shining hair. She wore loose luxurious-looking suede gloves, and carried a big black handbag. But as she neared them, even in the soft and flattering light, her face below its careful make-up was drawn and rather white. Her eyes flickered uneasily. "Laura! Matt said you were going Christmas shopping. What are you doing here?"

"Looking for a dress," Laura said shortly. Jonny as always in Doris' presence seemed to press a little closer to Laura.

"Oh," Doris said. She bit her lip, eyed Laura and added suddenly, "I phoned to Matt. I was—lonely. Fidgety. He said you

194

planned to go shopping with Jonny. I—I phoned to you about two-thirty. I thought I'd go with you. But nobody answered."

"Did you—look for us?"

"Well—yes. I thought you'd go to the toy department. But I didn't see you. The place was packed. I didn't expect to find you here."

It was coincidence, nothing else. Rather, it was not so much coincidence as a perfectly natural act on Doris' part; if she were lonely and nervous—frightened—with time on her hands, she would drift to the Fashion Shop. Besides, by no stretch of the imagination could Laura envision the smart, fashionable figure before her done up in a man's overcoat and hat, making her way through the store, following them.

Laura said suddenly, "Have you seen anyone else you know?"

Doris did not perceive the oddity of the question. "No." She moistened her lips. She glanced at Jonny. "I'm going home. My car is waiting. I'll take you home."

It was only Doris. She was not afraid of Doris. Yet Laura did not want to trust Jonny to Doris, to anyone. Not then. She said, "We're just going to look for some other things, Doris. We're not finished yet. Thanks just the same."

"But you—" Doris began and stopped. Her eyes flickered. Then she said with a kind of rush, "Come with me, Laura! It's not really safe, is it, for you and Jonny to go around like this. It's almost dark outside and after—after all these things have happened." Her brown eyes shot sideways toward the manager of the store, who, however, had politely stepped back and gone to the desk again. No one was within earshot. Doris said in a low voice, "It isn't safe. It's dreadful, all of it. Come with me. I can't get any of it out of my mind. I'm not frightened but I don't like to be alone—"

It was the first time that Doris had made what sounded like a genuinely friendly advance. In an odd way, however, the appeal only stiffened Laura's resolution. "I know. But you'll be all right. Come, Jonny."

Jonny, mindful of her manners, said politely, "Good afternoon, Doris," enunciating the syllables separately and carefully.

"All right," Doris said abruptly. "If you must go, go ahead. Good afternoon, Jonny."

She turned, with an impatient swirl of coat and gloves and perfume. Instantly the manager was aware of her movement and sprang to meet her. Laura led Jonny out of the Fashion Shop.

But a man in a clumsy, dark coat might be waiting, watching somewhere. Laura wanted to hurry back to the fitting room—where she'd bought a dress which made her into another woman. Another woman!

195

There were other clothing departments on the same floor: clothing for women, clothing for children, less expensive than the Fashion Shop, more widely patronized.

Perhaps thirty minutes later a young woman dressed in a brightly plaided red topcoat and a brimmed red hat, with a child in a green coat and hood, her braids tucked up under the hood, went quietly down the escalators and out into State Street and instantly got a taxi.

THIRTY-FOUR

It was almost dark. The brilliantly lighted windows spread great areas of light across the shoppers, across crowds of people now leaving the offices and hurrying for bus or sreetcar or elevated or train. Nowhere among them Laura saw a surveillant figure hovering near like a bird of prey.

Simple, she thought, merely a change of clothes. Was it too simple?

Snow was falling steadily. The streets were wet and glistening. The traffic was so heavy that the taxi had to nudge its way along, checked at every corner for the red lights. The traffic policemen wore dark mackintoshes which glittered with wet snow. Their long two-noted whistles sounded eerie amid the rush and thud and clatter of the traffic. The taxi turned onto Michigan Boulevard, and lights in the great buildings on either side seemed to lift up into the sky, dimly veiled by the falling snow.

They went on and on, across the river and between the great bulk of the Tribune Tower, lighted to the very top, and the white façade of the Wrigley Building, lifting up into the sky on the left. When they approached her own apartment house, Laura tensed watchfully, and thus she saw a taxicab drawn up and waiting, its lights dimmed, in the side street—the side street from which opened the service entrance to the apartment house, the side street which Catherine Miller had walked along at night, through the fog, to murder. It was too dark to see anyone in the taxi but it was parked in such a way as to command a view of the apartment house entrance.

Laura's heart began to thud. She waited until she had paid the driver, then she hurried herself and Jonny out of her own taxi, into the lighted doorway, across the lobby and into the elevator. She didn't stop to pick up mail or telephone messages. The elevator door closed; there was no one else in it; she pressed the button for the ninth floor with a feeling of escape.

But if anyone sat in that taxi waiting for their return, he had only a flashing glimpse of a woman in a red plaid coat, a child in green, altogether different from the clothes of the figures he would be expecting.

She unlocked the door of her apartment. There was a light in the hall, she had left it burning. The Christmas tree was still lighted, too, and spread a warm, mysterious radiance through the living room. They were safe. She bolted the door.

Suki did not come to meet them as usual, uttering hoarse cries of mingled delight at their return and indignation because they had left him alone. Jonny was hungry.

"Choc," she began tentatively, and couldn't say the English word and said instead, "*Czokolada.*"

Chocolate was almost the same in any language.

"I'll make some chocolate," Laura said.

She put down her handbag, tossed the new red plaid coat and hat across a chair and started back toward the kitchen. Jonny, in the living room, called "Suki—Suki—"

The kitchen door was open; it was brilliantly lighted. Jonny was still calling, "Suki—Suki," when Laura saw the grotesque huddle on the floor. The face was turned upward, the light full upon it. It was Conrad Stanislowski, the second Conrad Stanislowski, and he had died as the first Conrad Stanislowski had died.

This time the weapon had not disappeared, it lay on the floor, catching the light. It was a switch-blade knife, open, tough and sharp and deadly. A dark overcoat was flung half across a chair, falling down on the floor like a black and sinister stain.

For a dreadful instant Laura felt as if she were seeing a moving picture run twice, so she knew exactly what was to happen next. Jonny was coming along the hall.

Laura ran to meet her. She snatched her hand. "Come with me, Jonny. Come to your room." Put her there, Laura thought. Close the door. Tell her to stay—then telephone for the police.

The scurry of their feet was the only sound in the silent apartment. The door to Jonny's bedroom was closed. They had almost reached it when it opened.

It opened soundlessly and stood there, still and ajar.

The room beyond was dark. The black, faceless aperture seemed to speak. "I've got the gun."

197

Laura's lips moved. Only a whisper came out. *"No—no—"*

"Wouldn't it be easier to die quickly like this than to go through a trial? They'll never let you off. Both men killed. You found the first one. This one murdered in your apartment. It's circumstantial evidence. You had a motive. Besides, there's that scarf. Catherine Miller was killed with a scarf. Not that one; mine. But the police will say it's suicide, a confession. *Don't move.*"

Don't move—so the gun could be accurately fired, so shots would not go wild and betray the fact of murder, so the first one would reach its mark. Laura whirled around. Jonny ran with her into the front hall, to the front door. Laura snatched at the door; she had bolted it. Her hands were shaking, fumbling; she could not shift the bolt.

Footsteps ran after them. "Jonny, get out of the way!"

Jonny flung both arms tight and hard around Laura, her brown head almost upon Laura's heart.

"Go into the living room, Jonny." There was coaxing now, a horrible, smooth coaxing. "Go on, child. In there."

Laura's throat unlocked itself. "You can't! Jonny will tell them."

"Who'd believe her? She'll be in my care. I'll see to that. Stop that screaming. If I miss I may get the child."

Laura hadn't known she was screaming. Her hands flew to her throat, and then, frantically, to Jonny's little hands, trying to disengage Jonny's hold, but it was sheer instinct, not reasoning or heroic motive. Jonny wouldn't let go. She clung with all her sturdy strength.

"Jonny, please—" Laura cried wildly.

The child hugged harder. Laura was only dimly aware of muffled distant sounds, a voice shouting something, footsteps somewhere, but when the door buzzer sounded sharply beside her, this time Jonny screamed.

Again Laura's hand moved without volition on her part, and groped behind her for the bolt and it turned as a shoulder thudded hard against the door. The door flung inward, pushing Jonny and Laura behind it. Matt plunged down on his knees on the rug. Lieutenant Peabody shot nimbly over him; his lean gray figure disappeared toward the kitchen. Matt scrambled up and ran after Peabody.

Sounds thudded on beyond the kitchen and echoed hollowly in the service corridor.

The sounds diminished.

After a long time there was a short series of loud, reverberating crashes. Gun shots. Nothing else could sound quite like that.

Presently she moved. Jonny moved. Laura snapped on lights in

198

the living room. She sat down as if her knees had collapsed. Jonny stood for a moment, still listening, her face very quiet but her blue eyes wide and alert. Then she cried, "Suki," and ran to the fireplace.

Suki was standing on the mantel, his back arched, his eyes blazing garnet-red. As Jonny reached up for him he came down thankfully to her shoulder. Jonny came back to Laura, and settled down, cross-legged, at her feet. Suki crawled cautiously from Jonny's shoulder and settled himself on Laura's lap, facing the door.

They were sitting like that when Matt came back. He gave one look at Laura and Jonny and then his eyes went to the bright, red plaid coat. "Where in hell did you get that?"

She told him, rapidly, almost incoherently.

"You fooled me," he said. "We were in that taxi on the side street, Peabody and I. We had tried to phone to you and nobody answered. I knew you'd planned to go shopping. We saw Blick come into the apartment house. We were going to wait for you, and stop you. That was the important thing. I saw a woman and a child run across from a taxi and into the door, but I'd never seen that." He nodded toward the coat. "I had never seen Jonny in green. It was minutes before all at once I had to make sure."

"Who is Blick?"

"Stanislowski. Conrad the second. I mean Conrad the second is Blick— Wait—" She then heard sirens wailing along the Drive far below. Matt went back to the kitchen, closing the door behind him. Presently Laura heard a muffled commotion of voices and the heavy footsteps of men. It lasted a long time. At last Matt returned. "Peabody wants to talk to you later, not now. Look at this—and this."

He gave her a piece of paper. It was a telephone message, written on a long slip of paper, and pushed under the door when she was out. It read. "Mr. Stanislowski phoned. He will come to see you about five."

Laura looked up at Matt. "What—"

"Our murderer got here ahead of you and found that message under the door. Are those keys yours?"

She looked at the other object which Matt showed her, two keys on a little chain. "Why, I don't—Yes!"

"Where were they? When did you lose them?"

"It's a duplicate set. They gave them to me when I rented the apartment. I'd forgotten all about them. I put them somewhere— I think in the drawer of the hall table. I never thought of them again."

Matt went into the hall and jerked open the drawer. "They're not here now. It was easy enough for anybody to take them at

any time during the past few weeks. The deal has been cookin
since I brought Jonny back. Possibly even before that. As soon a
we discovered that Jonny was in Vienna."

Laura said huskily, "What deal?"

"A very simple deal." Matt picked up the kitten and stroke
his chin. The kitten lifted blue eyes and purred. "Jonny was th
motive, Jonny and the money. The first Conrad was the real on
the second was the impostor."

"You said—Blick."

"His name was John Blick. This morning Peabody questione
him. He stuck to his story all right, insisted he was Stanislowski
but Peabody thought he was scared. Peabody decided to explor
the possibilities. He said that obviously any impostor would hav
to know something about the real Conrad and about the money
or somebody would have to tell him all the details, like that son
and Jonny. He said that if somebody told him about it, then tha
somebody was a sort of master mind—cooking up the deal in th
first place, making all the plans and then employing an imposto
to do the job. Therefore the impostor would have to be somebod
who was available, somebody who could be found pretty readil
He would have to be somebody, too, who spoke Polish and migh
already know that song, and somebody without scruples. The firs
line of inquiry for such a man was Charlie's factory; Peabod
drew a blank there. Then he got in touch with a former superin
tendent for Conrad Stanley; he's still working at the Stanle
factory, under the new owners. Right away the superintenden
told Peabody that shortly before Conrad Stanley's death, he ha
fired a man by the name of John Blick who had worked there as
bookkeeper. He had been fired for stealing petty cash; Conra
had not preferred any charges; he had just fired Blick. Blic
spoke Polish and he answered to the description of the secon
Conrad. There wasn't time to get the photograph of the secon
Conrad and show it to the superintendent, or to take him to se
and identify the second Conrad, not just then. But the descrip
tion was right; John Blick filled the qualifications, and since th
thefts had not been reported to the police, it was safe to assum
that Conrad had told somebody, and that somebody consequentl
had a hold on John Blick. It was also safe to assume that Blic
wasn't a man of many scruples and that he'd leap at a chance t
make money by posing as Stanislowski."

"Jonny," Laura said. "And the money."

"That was it. Blick was to pose as Conrad with a fake
passport as identification. He was to get possession of Jonny. An
I think it just might have worked," Matt said slowly. "Jonn
can't speak much English, she understands only a few words. I
they had worked it right and fast enough, she might have bee

induced to at least show a friendliness with Blick, who spoke Polish, and who knew all the background that he had been given. Jonny is accustomed to being shunted around from one person to another. She is accustomed to obedience. Accustomed to the mysterious ways of a world she doesn't understand. If she had objected to being turned over to Blick, we'd have only thought that after two years' separation she felt strange with her father and confused. Yes, I think it could have worked. Then after Blick got control of Jonny, Peabody thinks that he would have taken her probably to some distant place, New York, San Francisco, New Orleans, some place in America, then turned over Jonny and the money, been paid off and quietly disappeared. There'd have been some story to cover the thing, but our murderer would have got the money."

Laura said in a cold, small voice, "What was to happen to Jonny then?"

"Nothing, probably. I don't think murder was a part of the original plan. I think she'd have been sent to school somewhere, in France perhaps or Switzerland, so none of us would be likely to see her often. I think she'd have been cared for all right but she wouldn't have had her money, ever. In any event, it's a long time until Jonny's of age; that was all in the future. Peabody says the plan was made probably when we first heard about Jonny. It would take time to arrange. He thinks the deal was all set and was about to be put in operation when the real Conrad turned up. Oh, Maria Brown talked to Peabody."

"She told us the truth."

"Except for one lie. She heard the murderer's voice, all right; she knew whether it was a man's voice or a woman's. She wouldn't admit it because she had resolved not to be obliged to identify the murderer; she was afraid of revenge. Her story squares with the things Conrad must have done that afternoon. Conrad had told her about my letter only in a general way—remember, their time together was very short. He didn't go into detail about our names, but of course he knew them; Maria didn't. When he left her, he made his telephone calls; he found where Jonny was. He came to see you. Then he went back home. By this time our master mind, our murderer, had decided that murder was the only way out. You see, the murderer believed that nobody knew that Conrad was here. If he were killed at once, he'd go down on the police record as an unidentified man; the original plan still could be put into operation and there was now a chance to add very convincing details. The murderer came to Koska Street, prepared to get all the information possible out of Conrad—and Conrad, exuberant, excited, made a little drunk, was more than willing to talk of his child. He told of that song

201

among other things. When he was stabbed, his passport, my letter, papers of identification were taken away. The passport was probably destroyed but the other things were given to Blick to bolster up his claim. It must have seemed a foolproof opportunity to build up a rather shaky scheme which, in all likelihood, there was still some hesitation about launching. Blick did as he was told. But murder hadn't been a part of the deal. Peabody thinks Blick was scared all along, and after the questioning this morning, Peabody thinks Blick decided to get out fast. Peabody thinks he was scared and defiant and said flatly he'd had enough. Peabody says obviously Blick had decided to tell you the truth—probably because he was afraid to talk to a man, or to the police directly, and hoped you'd intercede for him. In any event he'd get away fast. But he must have made the mistake of saying that that was what he intended to do."

Jonny put her hand on the kitten and Matt said, "Jonny gave us a clue. But I didn't see it. Jonny—where's the yellow bird?"

THIRTY-FIVE

"Bird," Jonny said questioningly, having trouble with the "r."

Matt laughed and went to get the dictionary. Jonny peered over his shoulder—and suddenly her little face set in implacable anger. She ran to the woodbox, groped under the logs and drew out the yellow bird. "Bad," she said, "bad!" She dropped it as if it burned her fingers and ran to stand before Laura in an oddly protective way, as if she were the adult.

"You see—" Matt began and the door buzzer sounded sharply. Matt, holding the kitten curled against his shoulder, went to answer it.

Doris' high voice cried, "Matt! The police phoned to me! They told me it was Charlie!"

Doris' coat was flung anyhow across her shoulders. Her face was white. Her eyes darted around the room. Matt said, "Oh, yes, it was Charlie. He killed the first Conrad; he was the real one. He killed Catherine Miller. Peabody thinks, as he was leaving your place that night, he saw Catherine Miller waiting under the light above the bus stop. He thought she was Maria Brown, stopped the taxi and got out. She turned back to the apartment house; he followed her and got in the door before it could close and killed her with whatever weapon he could find, the iron bar and his own scarf. Yesterday afternoon, Laura was asleep and Jonny opened the door for me. Peabody thinks that Charlie came earlier; he had the key. He probably rang the doorbell but Laura didn't hear; perhaps Jonny let him in but"—he eyed the woodbox—"I think that he had let himself in, thinking Laura and Jonny were gone, and Jonny saw him. Perhaps we'll never know exactly what happened; probably he went very quietly to Laura's room, took her scarf, debated perhaps as to killing Laura then and there when he had a chance, decided against it because he hoped the scarf would clinch Peabody's case against Laura and left. But, Jonny—there are things you can't deceive a child about. Jonny knew there was something threatening, ugly, wrong, in the way he crept into the place and took the scarf and went away—"

"That's when she changed," Laura said slowly. "She didn't come to speak to Charlie the next time he came. I remember that—"

"She hid the yellow bird Charlie had given her. She wouldn't have it on the Christmas tree. And somehow she knew that he was a threat to Laura."

Doris let her coat slide from her shoulders onto the floor. "I don't believe it. Charlie—but Charlie wanted to marry me! Charlie said he was in love with me!"

Matt said gently, "He had to have money, Doris. Perhaps that was a short cut; you see, if you'd married him he'd get your money—at least, you wouldn't go bankrupt."

"Bankrupt! Charlie would never go bankrupt."

"Yes," Matt said grimly, "he would and he was going to. Peabody got a search warrant this afternoon. Charlie was away. He was out of the office. As a matter of fact he was trailing Laura and Jonny. He had done that before. He had to get rid of Laura."

"Wait," Doris said, "wait. I don't understand. A search warrant."

"Yes. That was a clue Peabody turned up this morning. When he went to Charlie's factory hunting for a man who would answer the impostor's qualifications, he discovered that a lot of men had been fired during the last three years, too many men. The fact seems to be that Conrad Stanley's contracts with Charlie had kept his business going for years; Conrad was always loyal to his friends; he'd kept on with Charlie and even influenced some of his other business friends to give Charlie contracts. All that dropped away when Conrad died and Conrad's business was sold.

The new owners didn't renew contracts. Charlie borrowed to the hilt; he was in a tough spot. He obligated himself, counting on a third of the Stanislowski fund. About then we discovered Jonny. And Charlie saw a way to get the whole fund. He'd worked that out—and the real Conrad turned up. So it was murder or bankruptcy. And once he undertook murder he had to go on. Peabody got a search warrant, he went to Charlie's office in the Loop. Charlie wasn't there. Peabody went over the place, books, records, everything. Charlie was desperate. He cooked up a deal with Blick—the second Conrad, the impostor." Matt explained it.

"But how did Charlie know about the first Conrad, the murdered man?" Doris asked.

"Conrad must have telephoned to Charlie before he telephoned to you and before he telephoned to Laura. Charlie already had this deal in progress; it must have rocked him when Conrad Stanislowski telephoned. Perhaps he met him somewhere, went out the side door, perhaps he talked only over the telephone. In any event, he found out where Conrad was staying and he found out that Conrad's passport wasn't in order. He told him it was a serious matter and he'd see to it; certainly he told him not to see the child until Charlie had fixed up the passport question. Conrad pretended to accept it because he intended to get his wife to a place of safety before he claimed Jonny. That's why he asked Laura and you and certainly Charlie to keep his presence a secret. He hoped you wouldn't get together about it until he'd got his wife out of the city—"

"His wife!" Doris said blankly.

"Maria Brown," Matt said and explained that, too. "It looks as if Conrad didn't want to go back to her until he had actually seen the child, so since Charlie had evaded him, he phoned to you. Then he came here. We're not sure of all this, but it must have happened because in the intervening time Charlie had a chance to plan murder—"

Doris said suddenly, "Don't tell me any more!" But then she looked at Laura and looked at Matt and had to ask a question. "Did Charlie try to kill Laura?"

"Oh, yes," Matt said. Suddenly he looked rather grim and white. "He tried to kill Laura. He had to. You see he had left Conrad for dead. But then the police said that Conrad had lived for a few moments, long enough so a woman tried to help him and phoned to Laura: Maria Brown." Matt turned to Laura, "You told the police that Conrad was dead when you got there but Charlie must have thought, *was* he dead? A guilty man is hagridden by fear. You might have told the police the truth, but also you *might* know something else just the same, which would in some way implicate Charlie. It might have been even something

204

you didn't recognize as evidence but something that the police would track down and establish as evidence. Yes, he was terrified. Everything had gone wrong. He had to—get rid of you. He had your keys; he must have taken them in case he needed them when his scheme began to develop. He knew about your custom of hot milk and chocolate in the two thermos bottles. That was dangerous, but if you saw him in your apartment he could invent some excuse and postpone an attempt to murder you. He followed you that first day in the park, hoping for an opportunity. You didn't give it to him. But when John Blick made his claim, you confirmed Charlie's fear by refusing point-blank to accept Blick as Conrad. That settled it with Charlie. He didn't know exactly why you weren't telling the police whatever it was you knew or your reason for refusing to accept Blick as Conrad. He couldn't guess; he tried to get it out of you; but he was convinced that you had some very sound reason. You insisted that you wouldn't give up Jonny; you blocked his whole scheme. This morning Blick ran out on him and, we think, told Charlie that he was through, and was going to talk to you or somebody. Charlie was in very deep. He had to get rid of Blick. If he could get rid of you at the same time so it would look like a murder and a suicide—a confession, in short—he'd be safe. He got my gun. It was in the drawer of the table—"

"Has he confessed to all this?" Doris cried.

"He will confess. He'll have to. Some of all this is merely surmise but Peabody's got the main facts. Charlie was shot through the shoulder. He was trying to escape. He'll stand trial. Don't forget he was caught in the act of attempted murder."

Doris gave Matt a long look. Then unexpectedly she turned to Laura. "Laura, come home with me. Stay with me for a few days, you and Jonny. I sant to know Jonny better. Perhaps—we could know each other better, Laura, than we have up to now."

She meant it. There was something wistful and appealing in her eyes.

Laura said, "Thank you. We'll come."

"All right." Doris turned to Matt, put one hand on his shoulder and with a curious air of finality, said, "Good-bye, Matt."

Matt looked down at her for a moment, then he leaned over and kissed her cheek lightly. "I'll see you later," he said. He held Doris' coat for her.

"Yes," she said, "yes," and went away.

Matt said briskly, "It's surmise—some of it, but it's logical, too. Peabody says Charlie followed you this afternoon, only to make sure where you were going and what you were doing, because Blick had defied him this morning and threatened to see you. When Charlie followed you up to the Fashion Shop, the guy there convinced him that you were really shopping and would be there for some time. So he hurried back here to do something about Blick. He used your key, and found this message, saying that Stanislowski, that is, Blick, would be here. So he waited—and that was it."

"But he was dressed both times—not like Charlie, I never thought it was Charlie."

"It was an excellent disguise in its way, not odd enough to attract anybody's attention, and it looked as you said vaguely foreign, so it suggested somebody else, an outsider. You can get clothes like that in a hundred little places—second-hand shops. And of course he took care not to come near enough for you to see his face."

And Charlie had told her almost in so many words why he had tried to murder her. He had even warned her: murder is dangerous, be careful. In other words, think well, be careful. Don't tell the police you suspect anybody.

Matt said, "There is another small thing—funny, but it set me thinking about Charlie. I didn't really suspect him, yet in a way it pointed to him, and that was that telephone call the morning after the murder, when you had gone out to Koska Street. You see, I telephoned you that morning, I told my secretary to get you and you were gone."

"Oh!" Laura was struck by a small memory. "When I called you she said, 'Oh, you've got back.'"

"There was the telephone call from Maria Brown, only one that morning. There was my telephone call. I got thinking about it and yesterday I was curious enough to stop and ask the switchboard girl downstairs if she had a record of any other telephone calls that morning. By that time she was paying close attention to any calls that came to your apartment. She said that as far as she could remember there had been only two telephone calls. One rang and rang. As she was about to plug in and take the message, it stopped; that must have been Maria. Then there was another one that rang and rang. Just as she started to take it, it rang off. So you see, the first telephone call must have suggested a little scheme to Charlie; he told us all that he had answered it and that a man's voice, speaking in Polish, talked of Jonny. It was a little red herring—and it did in a queer way begin to point to Charlie."

Maria Brown, Laura thought. Jonny's mother. "Is Maria still in your apartment, Matt?"

"Yes. Actually she has no friends here. She simply inquired, looked in Classified Ads and went to another rooming house. Where apparently they never connected her with the Maria Brown the police were looking for."

"Jonny's mother," Laura said and heard a note of horror in her voice. Matt understood it.

"Yes. I wonder what Charlie planned to do about her. Clearly he thought he had silenced her when he killed Catherine Miller, but then it wasn't Maria, and how could he find her? In any event, he had to silence you first. He couldn't stop. He had entered a long road which had only one end. Sometime, somewhere, he must try to find Maria Brown, but that had to wait."

Both of them looked at Jonny and Jonny looked at them gravely and went to take the kitten from Matt. Laura said, "We must take Jonny to her mother now. She is waiting."

"Right. We'll take her to Doris' place, too. Look here, Laura, there's something I want to get straight. I couldn't until Doris saw it, too. I was in love with her; you know that. After Conrad's death she needed me. She was alone. I'm very fond of her. I was the only person she could turn to. And she was bewildered about money; she's been spending wildly; I had to help her to get things straight. I owed her loyalty. But I'm not in love with her. And—she knows it."

"She's—in love with you."

"No, she isn't. Not really. She only needed me. She doesn't really want to marry me. And—" Unexpectedly, Matt laughed. His eyes danced. "I've got other ideas about the girl I am going to marry."

Jonny gave Laura a suddenly mischievous and feminine twinkle, cuddled the kitten on her shoulder and walked across the apartment to stand at the window, her back turned sedately upon them. A small song drifted across the room. "I am a little Cracovian."

Matt laughed again. "You are a little American, Jonny. I'll teach you "The Star-Spangled Banner." But not right now. I've got something to say to Laura." His eyes now were very blue and intent, his face sober. There was a moment of stillness between them. Then he came to Laura.

After a long time, Laura saw Jonny beyond the close, hard curve of Matt's arm. She was holding the kitten curled snugly under her chin, watching them, her blue eyes dancing in the lights from the Christmas tree. "*Dobre*," Jonny said, and added unexpectedly and rather impatiently, "Say—it—Matt."

DON'T MISS THESE OTHER GREAT BOOKS BY P.D. JAMES!

__ **THE BLACK TOWER**   *(B31-001, \$2.9*

__ **COVER HER FACE**   *(B31-002, \$2.9*

__ **DEATH OF AN EXPERT WITNESS**   *(B31-003, \$2.9*

__ **INNOCENT BLOOD**   *(B31-004, \$3.5*

__ **A MIND TO MURDER**   *(B31-005, \$2.9*

__ **A SHROUD FOR A NIGHTINGALE**   *(B31-006, \$2.9*

__ **UNNATURAL CAUSES**   *(B31-007, \$2.9*

__ **AN UNSUITABLE JOB FOR A WOMAN**

(B31-008, \$2.9

To order, use the coupon below. If you prefer to use you own stationery, please include complete title as well as book number and price. Allow 4 weeks for delivery.

WARNER BOOKS
P.O. Box 690
New York, N.Y. 10019

Please send me the books I have checked. I enclose a check or money order (not cash), plus 50¢ per order and 50¢ per copy to cover postage and handling.*

_____ Please send me your free mail order catalog. (If ordering only the catalog, include a large self-addressed, stamped envelope.)

Name _____

Address _____

City _____

State _____ Zip _____

*N.Y. State and California residents add applicable sales tax.